"*Suffer the Children* takes the reader through some of the darkest possible territories. Craig DiLouie weaves a...

"Terrifying. . . . A stark, brutal, and chilling vision of the end of days."
—David Moody, author of *Autumn* and *Hater*

"The most disturbing book I've ever read. *Suffer the Children* unnerves you more and more as you come to realize how much of it is true."

—Peter Clines, author of *Ex-Purgatory*

"I don't believe I have ever been so freaked out by a story. *Suffer the Children* truly demonstrates in a wicked and frightening way how far a parent will really go for their child. It is honest and hits a chord with anyone who is a parent."

—Jackie Druga, author of *The Flu* and *Then Came War*

"A relentless burn of a novel, a compelling tale of hunger and desperation, recalling P. D. James's *The Children of Men* but injecting that tragic apocalypse with a mad thirst for blood."

—Jason Bovberg, author of *Under the Skin* and *The Naked Dame*

"*Suffer the Children* grabs you by the gut early in the book and doesn't let go until the final page."

—Scott M. Baker, author of *Rotter World*

"Every parent's worst fear is just the first round of terror in *Suffer the Children*, a book that grabs you by the throat and won't let you go. Craig DiLouie weaves a remarkable tapestry of raw emotion, loss, and guilt, then soaks it with terror. *Suffer the Children* is one horrifying ride."

—Stephen Knight, author of *The Gathering Dead* and *Earthfall*

SUFFER
the
CHILDREN

a novel of terror

CRAIG DiLOUIE

GALLERY BOOKS
New York   London   Toronto   Sydney   New Delhi

G

Gallery Books
A Division of Simon & Schuster, Inc.
1230 Avenue of the Americas
New York, NY 10020

Scripture quotations are taken from the Holy Bible, New Living Translation, copyright ©1996, 2004, 2007 by Tyndale House Foundation. Used by permission of Tyndale House Publishers, Inc., Carol Stream, Illinois 60188. All rights reserved.

First Gallery Books trade paperback edition May 2014

GALLERY BOOKS and colophon are registered trademarks of Simon & Schuster, Inc.

For information about special discounts for bulk purchases, please contact Simon & Schuster Special Sales at 1-866-506-1949 or business@simonandschuster.com.

The Simon & Schuster Speakers Bureau can bring authors to your live event. For more information or to book an event contact the Simon & Schuster Speakers Bureau at 1-866-248-3049 or visit our website at www.simonspeakers.com.

Interior design by Aline Pace

Manufactured in the United States of America

10 9 8 7 6 5 4 3 2 1

Library of Congress Cataloging-in-Publication Data

DiLouie, Craig, 1967—
Suffer the Children : a novel / Craig DiLouie. First Gallery Books trade paperback edition.
pages cm
1. Vampires—Fiction. I. Title
PS3604.I463S84 2014
813'.6—dc23
2014000930

ISBN 978-1-4767-3963-2
ISBN 978-1-4767-3964-9 (ebook)

The good mother knows what her children will eat.

—AKAN PROVERB

I

We All Fall Down

ONE

Joan

23 hours before Herod Event

The children were driving Joan Cooper bananas.

One meltdown, two spills, three time-outs, and counting.

Ninety-seven minutes until her home-based day care closed for the weekend and she'd have just her own kids to manage.

Megan assumed a commanding pose. "You have to share!"

"But this one is *mine*," whined Josh.

Joan had just set a box filled with reject plastic-lens eyeglasses, a donation from a local LensCrafters, on the floor for the kids to play with. Dillon and Danielle put on oversized black frames and made faces at each other. The room filled with hysterical laughter.

Then Josh snatched the green pair. Megan wanted them.

"Be nice to people!" the girl shouted, hands on hips. Joan thought the gesture seemed familiar. Her four-year-old daughter, she realized, was imitating her own style of scolding.

Josh was close to tears from her nagging. "*I* want to wear it."

"Megan, wait your turn," Joan said, using the warning voice.

"But I had it *first*."

Joan picked the funniest pair out of the box—big and red and

3

round—and put them on. "So how do I look?" She held out her hand to shake. "Hi. Nice to meet you. I'm Mommy."

Megan laughed. Then Josh ruined it.

"*My* glasses," he said, walking away in a huff.

Megan stared at her mother in a mute appeal for justice. Her chin wobbled. In a moment, she would wail full throttle, and Joan would scoop her up and let her cry it out into her shoulder. Half the time, Joan walked around with dried snot on her shirt.

"Here, Megan, you can play with these until Josh is done," she said. She took off the red glasses and waved them. "Play nice for the next half hour, and I'll give everybody a piece of gum."

"Gum!" Megan crowed.

The other children eyed Joan. They wanted in on the action.

She repeated her offer, and the kids all cheered. "Half an hour, though," she repeated. "Playing *nice*."

"Me too, right, Joanie?" said Josh, who had dietary restrictions.

"That's right, buddy."

"I love Dubble Bubble," Megan announced. "It's my favorite!"

Joan smiled. Where discipline and distraction failed, bribery won out every time. It was her last resort, the Alamo of parenting.

She'd launched her day care three months ago, inspired by an article that said stay-at-home moms didn't count in the gross national product because they didn't get paid. Sell some cigarettes and pesticides, that counted. Chop down a rain forest, bully for you too. Raise two kids in a loving home 24/7 and watch them grow up one day at a time, though? It didn't count one bit.

It pissed her off. Joan had never thought of doing anything else but what she did. It wasn't about finances or lack of child-care options. She had always wanted to be a mom and housewife. She'd grown up with a mother who'd poured all she had into parenting. She'd wanted the same fulfillment, the same sense of satisfaction. It sure as hell had *value*.

Her eight-year-old, Nate, attended school all day, leaving her with Megan. She'd figured, why not watch over a few more kids and get paid to do it?

Only it had turned out to be a hell of a lot more work than she'd anticipated. After three months, Joan was still learning the ropes.

And her dreams of how they were going to spend the money were turning out to be just that—dreams. No sooner did she get paid than the money bled away on all the little things—hockey equipment for Nate, a new outfit for Megan, dinners out at Denny's.

Her friends asked her how she could handle four children every day. The simple answer was she had no choice; she'd signed up for it and wasn't about to back out now. She also loved it, though she often was too busy to realize this fact.

The front door flew open. Joan felt a gust of cold air. Nate trudged into the house, stomping snow off his boots.

"Home again, home again, jiggety-jig," he said, and roared, *"Mom!"*

"I'm right *heee-re*," Joan sang.

He shrugged his jacket onto the floor. "I'm hungry, Mom."

"We'll be eating supper as soon as your father gets home."

Nate sat on the floor and pulled off his boots. "But I'm really hungry *now*."

"Mommy said I could have Dubble Bubble if I'm good," Megan bragged.

Nate stopped and looked at his mom hopefully. "Can I have some gum?"

"You can have a peanut butter sandwich," Joan told him.

"Awww."

She eyed the playing kids like an engineer looking for cracks in a dam and judged it safe to leave them alone for a few minutes. Dillon was playing near the Christmas tree, but not near enough for worry. Megan and Josh were sharing the green glasses. They were laughing. For the moment, all was right with the world.

Outside the big picture windows, her small suburban corner of Lansdowne, Michigan, white with snow, was already dimming to gray. Soon, the windows would be black with night and she'd feel closed in. Damn, another day gone in a blur. *One thing at a time*, she reminded herself. She made a mental note to plug in the tree.

5

"Come *on*, Mom," Nate called as he headed into the kitchen. He'd taken off his winter hat and put on his favorite, a Little League cap emblazoned with its Giants team logo.

Joan sighed as she followed. The drawings the kids made that morning still cluttered the kitchen table. It was easy to spot Josh's. He was into monsters now. A giant black thing devoured a burning city skyline one building at a time. The Wiggles played in the background on the CD player, a song she'd heard countless times and knew by heart. She spread some peanut butter on a slice of bread and poured a glass of milk.

Nate crammed the sandwich into his mouth and said, "No school tomorrow."

"Yeah, thank God it's Friday," Joan said. She glanced at his hat, considering another battle to get him to take it off inside the house. He caught her looking and pulled it lower over his eyes.

"Are we still going skating tomorrow?" he asked.

"We're going to Sandy's birthday party at the park." She noticed the unread newspaper on the counter as she put the bread away. The thrilling world of *Spy Master* called to her from the movie listings. It was coming out this weekend. She needed a break. If she could talk Doug into taking over with the kids for the party, she'd sneak away for a matinee showing with her friend Coral.

"Yeah, but it's a *skating* party, Mom."

"I stand corrected."

Her daughter's voice: *"Mommy! Mommy, come quick!"*

Joan raced into the living room. "What? *What?*"

The kids looked at her with wide, watery eyes and pointed at the Christmas tree. She'd been ready to give up this year and get a fake, but Doug had insisted on a real one with all the trimmings. He'd had it rough growing up and always wanted his kids to have everything. It looked majestic and prosperous, heavy with ornaments and garland. All it needed were presents. Once plugged in, the house would feel warm and cheerful, like the holidays.

Josh lay on the floor under its branches, writhing and clutching his stomach.

Ramona

23 hours before Herod Event

Ramona Fox was terrified.

The man she intended to terminate this afternoon had just entered her office. Tall, handsome, and dressed in a well-tailored gray suit, Ross Kelley looked like a CEO, though all he really did was handle employee insurance.

As an HR manager, Ramona knew how to handle a termination. One small problem: She'd never actually fired anybody.

She'd sat in on enough terminations to learn firsthand it was a confrontation, and she hated confrontation at work. The superstore chain's employees generally bought into the perception that she was on their side, which allowed her to mediate their conflicts with the company.

This time was different. Ross worked directly for her, and today would be his last day with the company.

"You wanted to see me?" he asked.

"Yes," Ramona said, her mouth dry. "Close the door and have a seat, please."

She considered her inability to bring him around a failure on her part, but he'd simply given up. Ross was a great guy, but most days, he just stared at his computer and did the bare minimum. It was typical behavior among people who knew they were facing termination—they drew a check for as long as they could while doing as little as possible.

The only reason he lasted as long as he did is because you have a little crush on him, she thought, then scolded herself. That wasn't fair. Nothing about this was personal.

For the entire week, Ramona had mentally prepared for this meeting. She'd spent a lot of time this morning fussing over how she looked and put on her blue suit for the occasion. More nervous than if it were a date, she wanted everything to be perfect.

Ross sat in the chair across from her wearing a curious smile. Ramona's heart pounded so hard she wondered if he could hear it.

Get right to it, she told herself. *You know the saying: Hire slow, fire fast.*

"I'm sorry, Ross, but this isn't working out. The company is letting you go."

He blinked in surprise. "Really? Why?"

She paused, pleased with the way she'd broken the ice. Her tone sounded strong but neutral. She felt poised and confident. The meeting was off to the right start.

"The company values—"

Her cell phone rang.

Only a few people had this number, including Joan Cooper, and Joan wouldn't call unless it was an emergency. *Oh God. Josh.*

"I'm so sorry," Ramona said, her face reddening. "I, um, have to take this."

"Are you serious?"

Ramona politely raised a hand to Ross and turned her chair away from him for privacy.

"Ramona Fox," she said.

"Ramona, it's Joan Cooper. I wanted to let you know Josh is pretty sick right now."

"His stomach?"

"Yes, it's as if—"

"Is he in pain?"

"Yes, but it's—"

"I'll be right there," Ramona said, and terminated the call.

Minutes later, she hurried across the frozen parking lot to her car. She barely remembered what she'd said before grabbing her bag and rushing out the door.

Sorry, you're fired, gotta run.

Very sensitive. You're a model HR professional.

"Lay off me," she said aloud to clear her head.

Ramona raced her Toyota to Joan's house and parked out front.

The sidewalk and driveway were neatly shoveled. Joan kept a clean and orderly home. It was one of the things that had convinced Ramona she could trust Josh to Joan's care. He'd had acid reflux as a baby—he'd refused to eat, and this spiraled into a series of allergies, digestive issues, and food aversions. One of his biggest problems was gluten intolerance. When he ate anything made with wheat, his immune system reacted violently, damaging his small intestine and preventing it from absorbing nutrition from food. It also gave him the runs and one hell of a gut ache.

Josh had eaten something today he shouldn't have, Ramona was sure of it. Something she'd explicitly told Joan he shouldn't eat. She practically ran to the front door, seeing red.

When it came to her son, Ramona had no problem with confrontation.

A worried Joan opened the door. Ramona was struck again by the contrast between them. While she herself was tall and thin and pale with long red hair, Joan was big and curvy, dressed in jeans and a blue and gray Lions sweatshirt. Her cheeks were flushed from chasing kids around all day.

"He's doing fine now," Joan said.

"Where is he?"

Josh approached meekly, gazing at his feet. Ramona's heart went out to her pale, scrawny boy with his beautiful, sensitive face. Behind him, the other kids clutched each other and watched, excited and a little scared by his getting sick.

"Ramona, I'm so sorry," Joan said.

"Sorry, Mommy," Josh echoed.

Ramona knelt and felt his forehead to see if he had a fever. "How are you feeling?"

"My tummy doesn't hurt anymore."

"Did you go to the bathroom?"

"Uh-huh, yeah."

"Was it hard or runny?"

"Runny."

"Was there any red in it?"

Josh shook his head. "No."

He seemed fine now, but his tongue was bright red. Ramona had never seen that before. It was alarming. What did it mean?

"Do you want to come in?" Joan asked. "I can make some coffee."

"I'm taking him home," said Ramona. "Please get anything in the house that belongs to him and bring it to me. Now, please."

Joan blinked with surprise, reminding Ramona of how Ross had reacted to the news of his termination. "Can I ask if he's coming back to us on Monday?"

Ramona put on Josh's coat. "I don't know yet." Joan had broken the first commandment of Josh's care; on the other hand, Ramona didn't have a lot of options or much time to explore them. "He has celiac disease. I *told* you that. It's not some New Age yuppie thing. It's real. He's gluten intolerant. He can't eat any wheat or he gets sick. What did he have?"

Joan bowed her head in thought. "Sliced apples for a morning snack. Bologna sandwich on gluten-free bread for lunch. Later on, we had strawberry smoothie pops for the afternoon snack."

"He ate *something*, Joan. This doesn't just happen."

"I don't see how—"

"I trusted you."

Joan flinched. The kids behind her looked scared now, sensing the additional tension between the grown-ups.

Ramona added, "I can't take time off like this. When I do, it's noticed." She hesitated; this definitely wasn't coming out the way she wanted. "There's a cost."

Now Ramona made it sound like all she cared about was her career, but it was more than that. She was on her own. There was nobody else providing for Josh. Just her. What she failed to add was that the better she did at her job, the better the life that Josh would have. He'd have better care, more fun, greater opportunities. As with everything, it all came down to money.

And the money came from the job.

"Okay, I'll get his things," Joan said quietly.

"Thank you." Ramona finished dressing Josh to go home. He wouldn't look at her. He was scared too, but it was more than that. He was hiding something.

Joan returned with Josh's drawings. "He likes to draw monsters," she said with a shrug.

"Can I give Joanie a hug good-bye?" Josh said.

"No," said Ramona. "Mommy's taking you home now."

"I *am* sorry, Ramona," Joan said. "Please call me whenever you can." She crouched in front of Josh and smiled. "Bye, Josh. Hope you feel better."

Ramona took his hand and pulled him to the car. She buckled him into his car seat in the back while he wept and clutched his drawings.

"Josh, please stop crying."

"I don't want Mommy to be mad at Joanie," he wailed.

"Okay, Josh. But first, tell me, what did you eat? I promise I won't get mad."

Josh let out another sob. "I ate the play dough."

"What?"

"We made it out of salt and flour and some other stuff. Joanie said it was safe. We put stuff in it to make different colors. Then we played with it."

"And it looked so yummy you ate some."

"Yeah. I'm sorry, Mommy."

Food coloring. That's why his tongue was red.

He said, "Joanie said it was extra safe to play with but we shouldn't try to eat it because it tasted bad. She was right. It tasted really bad. It was really *salty*."

An innocent mistake. Ramona sighed and looked back at the house. The front door with its plastic wreath was closed. The family Christmas tree sparkled in the window. She figured she owed Joan an apology.

Something else to feel guilty about. Add it to the fucking list.

She'd call Joan over the weekend. Maybe call Ross while she was at it. Apologize to everybody for everything. When she had time.

"It's okay, little man. Don't cry. Mommy's not mad. I just hope you learned your lesson."

"But I want to come *back*. Don't be mad at Joanie!"

"I'll bring you back on Monday. I promise. But first we have to see Santa tomorrow, don't we?"

Josh perked up a little. "Santa at the mall?"

"That's right." She got into the driver's seat and eyed him in the rearview. "I love you, little man." She couldn't hide the exasperation in her voice. "I really do. Are those your new drawings? Can Mommy see them?"

She took the sheets of construction paper and rested them on the wheel. As Josh approached the age of five, his drawings had gone from crude stick figures to highly detailed renderings. He insisted his mother tape every drawing to the refrigerator door and, when that space ran out, the walls of his room. Praising his artwork always cheered him up.

But these new ones were disturbing. She leafed through them quickly with a frown. Black shapes chased fleeing people in every one.

Her son, who normally drew knights and animals, was now drawing monsters.

David

22 hours before Herod Event

David Harris listened to Shannon Donegal's life story, scribbling notes into her file while ignoring the dull ache in his leg.

She was eighteen, beautiful, and glowing with robust health. In three months, she would bring another life into the world, a baby boy she was calling Liam.

David held a license as a pediatrician, not an obstetrician. He treated children, not pregnant women. When he'd returned to work after the accident, however, he'd started offering free one-hour prenatal consultations to rebuild his patient base.

He considered it an investment. He was beginning to feel hopeful about the future for the first time in a year. Not a lot, but enough to make an extra effort to restore his practice to what it once had been.

Shannon had her own problems, it seemed.

Valedictorian of her class, she'd earned a scholarship to attend George Washington University in the fall, where she would have studied international relations. Instead, at a graduation party, she'd had sex with her boyfriend Phil, who, despite being the football team's star running back, had no scholarship or real plans. He'd seemed destined to remain stuck here in Lansdowne while Shannon went off to bigger and better things. Two missed menstrual periods later, however, she discovered she was having a baby she wanted but Phil didn't. Now it was Shannon who seemed destined to remain in Lansdowne, while Phil had left town as fast as his feet could take him.

Little of this story proved relevant in any medical sense, but David listened with polite interest, reminding himself to take his time and make a good impression. He steered the conversation back to her and the baby's health. Did she smoke? Who was her obstetrician? Were there any health issues she was concerned about?

No health issues, it turned out. Just questions.

"Should I breast-feed or go with formula?"

"I recommend breast-feeding for at least six months. A year is even better. Breast-feeding can prevent allergies and protect the baby from a number of infections and chronic conditions."

"So Liam and I would pretty much be breast-feeding all day and night, right? What's the term? 'Glued at the boob'? I mean, isn't that the trade-off?"

"To an extent, but not all the time. My wife used a breast pump to store milk, which I fed to our boy in a bottle once per night. That gave her some uninterrupted sleep."

I'd hug little Paul as he cried against my chest in the boy's warm, dark room, swaying side to side on my feet and shushing him to get him to return to sleep.

A file drawer slammed shut in the reception area outside his office. Nadine, going about her work and likely eavesdropping. He cleared his throat, forgetting where he was for a moment.

"Oh yeah, I will definitely be exploring that," Shannon said. "Phil's gone, but I will have help." She wrote it down in her notebook. "What about circumcision?"

"There are health arguments on both sides of that question, although the percentages are low for any risks. It's really a personal decision."

Shannon winced. "Doesn't it hurt?"

"A topical cream or some other anesthetic is used."

"What did you and your wife do?"

David suppressed a frown. He didn't like to talk about his personal life with his patients, although he'd brought it up. "I'm circumcised, and I wanted Paul to look like me. When I realized that was the only reason we were going to do it, we decided against it."

"What about shots?" Shannon said. "Did you immunize him?"

"Of course we did."

"Some people say it can cause autism."

"Studies have found no link. As a doctor, I rely on empirical evidence. What I can say is if your child is not immunized, he risks contracting a deadly disease."

"What about the disease itself? You can get measles from the vaccine, right?"

"Not really. The odds of something like that happening are very small. Your baby would already have to have a severely compromised immune system for such a thing to be likely. Again, such a thing is very rare."

Shannon sighed. "Okay."

"I like your questions. You came well prepared."

"I am really, really scared."

He smiled. She was utterly adorable and far too innocent. "You should be. It's a very serious thing to bring a life into the world."

"Then please give me some advice as a father, not as a doctor. What's the most important thing you've learned?"

"You don't need personal advice from me. Did you have any other medical questions?"

"Come on, doctor. Please? Just one thing. Consider it a question of supreme importance to my mental health." She held up her notebook and showed him a page filled with her neat handwriting. "Look, I'm keeping a diary of good advice from everybody I know."

"All right. Well, not to be flippant about it, but my advice is to be careful about soliciting too much advice. No matter how much advice you get about things like keeping your child happy, no one will know your child better than you will. Trust yourself."

"Wow, I like that," she said. She wrote it down in her notebook. "Thanks, doctor. There are just so many things to deal with."

He remembered holding Paul and thinking, *Don't grow up, baby boy. Stay just like this forever.* "Millions of women have done it before you—most of them under very primitive conditions. Take it one day at a time, and you'll be fine."

"One day at a time, huh?" She smiled. "That's going to be my mantra every time I think about all those diapers I'm going to have to change."

"When it's your child, you don't care about those things. The fluids, smells, crying at all hours of the night." His eyes stung, and he turned to stare out the window. Snow fluttered onto the parking lot. "None of it matters because you love this tiny thing with every atom in your body. The biggest problem every parent has is it goes by too fast. Cherish every minute you have with your child."

Shannon's eyes welled up with tears. "Oh my God."

He tried to smile. "Sorry about that."

"No, it's really beautiful." She sniffed and fanned herself with her hand. "Do you have a photo of Paul?"

David picked up a framed picture of his son from his desk and handed it to her. In it, Paul grinned and held a Tonka truck over his head like a trophy.

"What a cutie. What do you do for day care? Does your wife stay home? If you don't mind me asking."

"I, uh . . . Paul passed away, Shannon."

The girl slapped her hand over her mouth. "Oh. My. God."

"Almost a year ago. There was an accident."

She stared at the photo. Tears welled in her eyes. "I am so sorry."

"No, I'm the one who should apologize. You came here for medical advice, not to become upset." He cursed his stupidity. The idea of death was infectious; it wouldn't take long for Shannon, her body raging with hormones, to imagine her own child dying. After taking the photo back, he picked up the phone, punched Nadine's extension, and asked her to bring a package of public health literature. "I'll get you some brochures to take home."

"I was judging you in my head, wondering why you don't smile," she said. "You looked so grim. I had no idea this happened. I am *such* an idiot."

"Not at all." He opened a drawer and produced a box of tissues.

"Can I ask what happened?"

Blinding light filled the car and winked into dark just before the BOOM.

"It was . . ."

The world spun and glass shards splashed up the windshield.

"Dr. Harris," a familiar voice said.

He woke to a hissing sound, his wife still holding the wheel, looking dazed, his leg pierced by a barbed tongue of metal.

"Paul?"

He tried to twist in his seat to look behind him, but his leg exploded in agony.

He gritted his teeth and tried again—

"Paul!"

"David."

He looked up in surprise. Nadine stood in the doorway of his office. She entered and slapped a handful of brochures onto the desk, glaring at him before turning to Shannon.

"What happened to the doctor is none of your concern," Nadine said. "It's a private matter."

She turned on her heel and stormed out of the office.

"I'm really sorry," David said, reddening. "She shouldn't have said that to you."

"What did I do?" Shannon wondered. "What was that all about?"

"That," David answered, "is Nadine Harris."

"Harris? You mean she's—"

"My wife. Paul's mother."

Might as well put it all on the table at this point, he thought.

He doubted, after this visit, that Shannon Donegal's son was going to become a patient of the grim Dr. David Harris.

Doug

20 hours before Herod Event

Doug Cooper liked that it wasn't as cold as yesterday. He liked that the trash he picked up today didn't contain any broken glass or disposable needles. He liked that the bags didn't rip open and spill rotten meat, asbestos, or shit-filled diapers all over his boots. He liked that no homeowners yelled at him, no cars came close to hitting him, no dogs tried to bite him.

And still it was a shit day, just like all the rest.

When Otis called him into his office after he'd changed out of his work clothes at the end of his ten-hour shift, Doug had a feeling it was about to get a whole lot worse.

He scowled under the grimy brim of his red LOVIN' LANSDOWNE

baseball cap, which the Plymouth County Department of Solid Waste Management handed out last year to all its employees who worked in the city. Broad-shouldered, standing at an imposing six feet two inches, he towered over his supervisor. His stubbled jaw and handlebar mustache made him look comical when he laughed and meaner than a dog when he got angry. Right now, he wore his mean face.

"Grab a seat," Otis told him, and took a seat himself, leaning back in the creaking chair with his hands folded on his massive belly.

Doug sat and dipped his head to light a Winston. They weren't supposed to smoke in here but did so anyway when the long, hard day was done. The old office smelled like an ashtray. Doug recognized stacks of yellowing paper on Otis's desk he'd seen months ago. Nothing ever changed in here except the months and years on the calendar hanging on the wall.

Whatever was on the man's mind, Doug hoped the conversation would be quick. He had no time for small talk or pictures of Otis's grandchildren. Joan was putting supper on, and he wanted to get home and see his kids.

"So how are you, Doug?"

"Peachy," Doug answered.

"Good to hear. I got some news from the County. Some pretty major news, actually."

"Oh boy, here it comes."

"Why do you always think the worst? I'm trying to tell you they approved the contract for the Whitley rigs."

Doug felt a surge of heat in his chest, like heartburn. "I thought that was dead."

Otis lit his own cigarette and waved the match. "It's alive, and it's here." His face turned an alarming shade of red as he coughed long and hard into his fist. "Better get used to it, Doug. They'll be delivered in the early part of the year. We should be seeing the first vehicles on the road by springtime."

Every day, Doug worked his ass off as part of a two-man sanitation crew—one man driving the truck, the other dumping trash into the rear of the rig, where it was compacted. The new Whitley trucks that the County wanted side-loaded waste using automatic lifts. The rig had a mechanical claw that grabbed the garbage can and dumped its contents right into the hopper.

It sounded great—unless you were a sanitation worker hoping to keep your job during a time of shrinking budgets. The automatic rigs needed only one man to operate them.

When Joan had gotten pregnant with Nate, Doug had sworn he'd do anything to provide for his family. He became a waste collector. At the time, he'd thought it was one of the safest professions on the planet. Sure, it was a tough and dirty job, but everybody needed it done, a good union protected it, and it couldn't be offshored.

He'd never anticipated that a new type of garbage truck might make him obsolete.

Spring was only four months away.

He stood, suddenly filled with nervous energy that he didn't know what to do with. "Shit, Otis. What about my job?"

"Sit down, Doug. Nobody's going to lose his job. The County will reduce head count through normal attrition. Guys move, others retire, and they won't be replaced. That's it."

Doug expressed his skepticism for that news with a snort. Whatever the politicians had told his boss, when it came to budget cuts, they had a way of changing their minds once they smelled blood.

Otis planted his elbows on his desk. "Look, that's what they're saying, okay? Don't go telling people otherwise, Doug. I don't need a goddamn panic."

"I don't gossip like some schoolgirl, Otis. But I will be checking with the union to see what kind of guarantees the County is offering in writing. I got mouths to feed at home."

"You're not seeing the big picture here. Why is there always a conspiracy theory with you? You got to look on the bright side."

"Yeah?" Doug asked, mean face in full effect. "And what's that?"

"Sanitation is being revolutionized," said Otis, as if it were a fast-moving, glamorous field. "Faster, cheaper, better. Trash pickup at a thousand homes a day, and the driver never leaves the cab. If the garbage isn't in the bin, it stays where it is. No rain, no rats, no stink."

Otis looked almost wistful about it. Doug guessed the man wished he had these rigs during the thirty-five years he'd spent hauling garbage in the rain and snow.

It was sad to witness. Otis had been a hairy son of a bitch back in the day, a hard drinker and a bar fighter, but now he just looked worn out, ready to retire himself. Doug always thought he'd end up just like him, marking time on a calendar in some crappy office and managing the next generation of hairy SOBs. He wondered now if he'd even get that privilege, thanks to the Whitley trucks.

What was he going to do if he lost his job? How would he face Joan and the kids, who depended on him? The very thought made him grind his teeth. What good was a man who couldn't provide for his own?

Doug had grown up in hard times. He'd known hunger as a child—not the I-wish-I-had-more-treats bullshit but real, gut-gnawing hunger. His biggest wish was to give Nate and Megan the childhood he didn't have and, he hoped, a chance at a decent future.

His kids came first. They would always come first.

"See?" Otis asked. "Change isn't all bad. There's a huge upside to this."

"Yeah, it's a bold new era in picking up other people's shit," Doug said with mock enthusiasm. He stabbed his cigarette into the ashtray on the desk. "Good night, Otis."

Minutes later, Doug drove his truck out of the lot and onto the long road home. Snow swirled in his headlights; it was already shaping up to be a crappy winter. The roads were thick with snow, but he drove nice and slow and trusted his four-wheel drive, one hand gripping the steering wheel and the other rooting for his lighter in the breast pocket of his flannel shirt. The orange glow of the sodium streetlights marked the way home. Leo Boon, his favorite country and bluegrass singer, crowed on the truck's CD player: *The buck stops here.* Yes, sir.

Otis had accused him of always thinking the world was out to get him, but it really did seem that way sometimes. Nobody was looking out for Doug, that was for damn certain, and he sure as hell was the only guy looking out for his family.

The truck rattled as he picked up speed. He glanced at his speedometer; sure enough, it read a little over forty-five. His pickup needed an alignment, another hundred twenty bucks he didn't have. He tapped the brake with his foot until things stabilized. An old rage burned in Doug's chest. Every time he got paid, something needed fixing or replacing. His life seemed like one big race to earn as much money as he could as fast as possible to replace everything that was always breaking.

"Goddamn it," he said quietly, still thinking about the new rigs. *Damn everything.* He wanted to punch something. He wanted a drink. He lit another Winston instead and counted to ten. No way he was bringing this shit home with him, not again.

The cab filled with dry heat and cigarette smoke, oddly comforting smells. He soon recognized the houses flanking the street, each drenched in Christmas lights and decorations. Lansdowne was a mid-sized city comprised of sprawling cookie-cutter housing communities surrounding an old industrial core. After the latest revitalization effort had failed, housing became its major industry for a while, which had struck Doug as a starving man eating his own foot to sustain himself a little longer. When that failed, the city suffered waves of foreclosures and discovered it had an even bigger homeless problem. Most people here worked low-end jobs at gas stations, supermarkets, big box stores, fast food joints, and the like. They still believed in America, even though they'd been betrayed by its failure to live up to its promises.

Like Doug, all they wanted was to give their kids a chance at a good life.

He pulled into his driveway and parked in the garage. Major, the Cooper family dog, sensed Doug's arrival and launched into his welcome-home barking ritual in the backyard.

Shucking his jacket in the entry, Doug felt warm for the first time all day. Hank Williams was belting out an old song from the kitchen.

He heard zany cartoon voices on the TV in the living room. The smells of Joan's homemade spaghetti sauce made him feel human again.

After washing up, he found her in the kitchen wearing an apron with her hair done up in a ponytail. He watched her dance as she stirred a pan of frying meat on the stove. Doug remembered the night they first met at Cody's Bar. AC/DC had roared from the speakers while Joan stood in front of the jukebox picking the next song, slim and curvy, her hips swaying to the beat and driving every man in the place crazy. Including, of course, Doug.

He blinked, and the memory passed.

He wrapped his arms around her and hugged her. She melted into him with a smile.

"What's for dinner?" he said.

"Spaghetti and meatballs. How was your day?"

"You don't want to know."

"Join the club."

"I'm going to shower and change. All right?"

"Try to make it a quick one. Supper's ready in fifteen."

Doug entered the living room, which looked perfect. Joan constantly fussed after the kids, snatching up books, toys, and cups. Keeping things nice and neat. Nate hung off the edge of the easy chair with his head resting on the carpet, watching the TV upside down. Megan sat cross-legged about two feet from the screen.

"Anything good on?" he said.

"Hey, Dad," Nate said vacantly, his eyes glued to the TV.

Megan jumped to her feet and ran at him, screaming, "*Daddy!*"

He caught her and twirled her laughing through the air.

"Hey, princess."

"I missed you today, Daddy."

His heart warmed to hear that. It always did.

It was always good to come home after a long day. He swallowed his anger and his worries. Swallowed them hard. Everything he did in his life, this was the reason.

Sometimes it was too easy to lose sight of that.

Joan

11 hours before Herod Event

Joan awoke during the night. Her heart pounded. She stared into the dark.

The clock read 3:02.

She'd been here before. A random creak, and she'd wake up glaring fiercely at the hazy outline of the bedroom door, ready for battle.

Next to her, Doug snored softly on his stomach. Joan took comfort in his presence. The man could sleep through the Rapture, but if she managed to wake him up, he'd get the baseball bat he kept under the bed and lumber downstairs to check things out.

There was never anybody there, but Doug always went anyway. Sometimes she thought he wanted to find a burglar on his property, just so he'd have the legal justification to beat somebody to a pulp. Whatever his motives, she was glad for it.

Joan considered herself a practical woman with her head screwed on straight. Doug periodically obsessed about things like avian flu and global warming, but she had no use for such worries. Nonetheless, she sometimes wondered if she'd left the stove on while out shopping, worried over whether the doors were securely locked, and thought she heard her children crying for her when she was in the shower or drying her hair. And once she heard something go bump in the night, she couldn't return to sleep until Doug pronounced the house secure.

Was it a bad dream that had woken her? Maybe she was still worked up about Ramona and Josh, and she'd had a nightmare. If she had, she couldn't remember it now. The other night, Joan dreamed she held Nate's head in her hands. It was absurd—his body was at the shop being fixed, but the technician had lost it—yet it had seemed so real to her, holding his lifeless head in her hands and wondering if they'd ever find his missing clockwork body. As the horror mounted with the realization that Nate was gone forever, she'd woken covered in sweat.

Joan lay back and closed her eyes. She was home. Nothing could harm her here. Her family slept around her in the dark. She sensed the children breathing in their beds down the hall. She felt herself lulled back toward sleep. The morning and its routines would dispel her night fears.

The world was a dangerous place, but not here. Children were suffering in other parts of the world—everywhere there was poverty and famine and war—but not in this house. She returned to sleep with the knowledge her children were safe and sound, and nothing would ever harm them.

TWO

Ramona

2 hours before Herod Event

The food court was bustling.

After fighting crowds of Christmas shoppers and carrying Josh halfway across the mall, Ramona was already worn out, but she perked up when she saw her friend.

Bethany looked perfect as usual. She had a boyfriend and a profitable career in real estate sales. Her five-year-old, Trent, was thriving in private school. She made it all look so easy.

Nothing was easy for Ramona. It was unfair.

They hugged, and each told the other how great she looked. They bought their lunches and found a table next to the indoor playground, which swarmed with screaming children. Trent wolfed down his food, grabbed Josh's hand, and pulled him toward the jungle gyms.

Stabbing at her salad with a plastic fork, Bethany complained about the number of people she had to shop for this Christmas. It was a drawback of dating Brian; he had a large family to impress.

I wish I had your problems, Ramona thought, but forced a sympathetic expression.

She didn't actually want what Bethany had. It wasn't that kind of

25

envy. She held no illusions that Bethany's life was as effortlessly perfect as portrayed. But she wanted that perfection anyway, romanticizing a life in which her career wasn't so demanding, Josh wasn't sickly, she dated a man who was worth it, and there were enough hours in the day.

Ramona's inner clock told her it was time to check on Josh. She scanned the playground and spotted Trent laboring up the plastic rock-climbing wall. Her eyes darted across the faces, searching for her son.

Where is he?

"Josh!" she called.

"I'm right *here*, Mommy," said Josh, trotting over. "I was drawing on the floor."

Ramona still felt rattled. It had never happened before. Just like that, he'd disappeared.

Like losing your car keys. Way to go. You're mom of the year.

"Josh, why aren't you playing with Trent?"

He showed her his pad. "I still can't make a straight line!"

"Go play with the other kids, Van Gogh," she commanded.

"I'm *not* Van Gogh. I'm *Josh*."

She made him surrender the pad. "Go. Fun. *Now*."

Josh sighed, stood, and ran toward the playground.

"Everything okay with him?" said Bethany. "How's his health?"

"He doesn't eat enough. He picks at his food. He's been drawing monsters."

"Monsters," Bethany echoed with concern.

"Monsters eating people. That kind of thing."

Ramona didn't add that she thought she recognized herself in one of the drawings, a tall stick figure with long red hair.

And you still don't know if you were being depicted as a victim or monster.

She'd been afraid to ask.

"It sounds to me like he's processing something," Bethany said. "Has he had any big changes or traumatic experiences lately?"

"For the past few weeks, he's been in a new day care."

"Right. You told me about the woman who runs it. Her name is Joan?"

"Yes. She's good people. Although I just chewed her out for something stupid." She recounted the story of her rushed firing of Ross, Josh's getting sick, and his confession he'd eaten the homemade play dough.

"No, you were right to be angry," said Bethany. "She shouldn't have made anything with flour in it that he might eat, even if it was meant to be a toy."

"It's understandable, though." Ramona glanced at the playground and located Josh. "She has four kids in her home every day. She can't watch Josh every second."

"Even more reason not to have made the play dough. She should have connected the dots and understood the risks."

"You're smarter than her. Tougher than me."

"Nonsense," Bethany said, though she smiled at the compliment. "Our kids have no one but us. No one is going to fight for them but us."

"I like to think of Josh's caregiver as a second parent. I think Joan would fight for him. God, I don't want to be the working mom who goes psycho on her nanny for loving her kids a little too much. The whole thing was an innocent mistake."

"Ramona. Listen. I don't want to upset you, but you have to at least consider the possibility this Joan is abusing Josh in some way, which might explain the changes in his behavior."

"What? Oh, Bethany, come *on*. That's insane. No, I honestly don't see it."

Joan shined with children and loved them in a selfless way that was genuine, if a bit intimidating to other moms. Ramona often wondered if Joan was what nature intended. Yet the woman seemed to exist only for her kids. Didn't she want anything for herself?

Meanwhile, Ramona was stuck feeling guilty because she worked. But what choice was there as a single mom?

Either way, she'd learned, no matter what choices you made as a mother, somebody always looked down on you, or at least you imagined they did.

"A four-year-old doesn't just go from drawing angels to monsters without a reason."

"He probably saw a video or had a nightmare— *Oh. My. God.*"

Bethany watched Ramona duck in her seat. "What? *What?*"

"I can't believe it. It's Ross. The guy I fired yesterday."

Ross stood near the Chinese food place with a tray in his hands, scanning for an empty table.

"'Oh my God' is right," Bethany said. "He's cute."

Ramona shielded her face with her hand. "It was kind of hard for me to see him that way, to be honest," she lied.

"But now you don't work together. I can see why you fired the guy. Now there's nothing to stop you from sleeping with him."

Ramona burst out laughing. She shook her head. "Look at you. Drooling over the vicarious thrill."

"I'm a normal woman with normal urges."

"Normal, huh? To quote Inigo Montoya, I do not think that word means what you think it means."

Ross spotted an empty table and headed toward it. He disappeared from view.

"And there he goes."

"Show's over."

"So why *did* you fire him?"

"Because I couldn't trust myself to keep my hands off him."

The women laughed at their silliness. An elderly couple at a nearby table turned and glared at them, which made them laugh even harder. This was one of the reasons Ramona looked forward to these lunches. She could let her hair down with another grown-up.

"So you're sure it's not the day care lady," Bethany prompted, renewing their previous conversation.

Ramona barely heard her. Her eyes scanned the playground. The children swarmed over the monkey bars and slides and rock-climbing wall.

Josh was gone.

She stood. "I'll be right back."

"He's right there," Bethany told her, pointing him out.

Ramona took a deep breath. Her heart pounded. "Oh. Right."

Bethany eyed her with obvious concern. "Are you okay?"

That's a big question, Ramona thought.

"I'm fine," she said, wearing a crooked smile. She remained standing. For her, lunch was over.

Joan

2 hours before Herod Event

Saturday morning.

Nate played outside with his friends, and Doug was sleeping late. Joan enjoyed the opportunity to have some special Mommy and Megan time before her movie date with Coral.

They'd mixed more play dough out of salt, flour, water, cream of tartar, and food coloring, and shaped it into Megan's favorite animals. After that, Joan helped her with a craft project while they listened to a kids' disco CD. Megan enjoyed working with scissors. The hair on the left side of her head was still ragged from an attempt to give herself a haircut last week.

Now she sat on the floor wearing a ragged purple princess costume and plastic tiara, cutting out heart shapes from a piece of paper.

"I can't wait, I can't wait, I can't *wait*." Megan grinned at Joan. "Santa's coming."

Joan laughed. "That's right, sweetie."

She tried to remember what it was like to be so young and waiting for Christmas to come. The sheer glee and wonder. The nearest adult equivalent was winning the lottery. Still smiling, she started an early lunch for the kids: bologna, cheese, and mustard on toast.

The front door opened. Joan poked her head out of the kitchen in time to see Nate huff into the house. He shucked his coat and kicked off his boots.

"Home again, home again, jiggety-jig," he said. "The projectile son returns."

"Prodigal son," Joan said, correcting him. Nate often came home with mannerisms and phrases he picked up from Keith, his best friend.

"Yup, that's me. Can I watch some TV?"

"Not right now, okay? We're having lunch in a few minutes; then we're going to the park."

"Oh. Excellent. I'm *starving*."

Joan turned on the radio and set the dial to Woodradio 1300 AM so she could check the weather as she finished making the sandwiches. Nate sat at the kitchen table, gazing at an open textbook while wearing his Giants hat.

She glanced at the color pages displaying the world's flags.

"That's an interesting one right there," she said.

"That's Brazil," Nate told her. "It's a really big country in South America. The stars represent states, just like on our flag. They speak Portuguese."

"You're very smart."

Joan wondered at Nate's passion for some subjects in school and apparent rejection of others. Last winter, amid his ongoing enthusiasm for hockey, he'd announced he wanted to be a doctor. He hadn't said it since, but Joan had engraved it in mental stone. She squinted at her apple-cheeked boy and tried to see the man he someday would be.

Eight years old and steadily pulling away from her. While Joan readily empathized with Megan, Nate's mind seemed alien. She knew he idolized Keith, whom she considered a bad influence, as he was a bigger risk taker than her son. Nate often came home with cuts and bruises from their escapades. She worried one day she'd get a call saying he'd broken a bone or worse.

She set the sandwiches on the table with glasses of milk. Nate crammed his into his mouth while Megan climbed into her chair and took her first dainty bite.

Joan heard creaking upstairs, signs Doug was awake and starting his day. *About time, sleepyhead.* She was already planning their exit. Boots, hats, gloves, scarves, jackets, snacks. She put the kettle on for hot chocolate and pulled the thermos down from the cupboard.

"Mommy, are monsters real?" Megan asked.

Joan wiped crumbs from the counter into her cupped hand and dropped them into the sink. "Of course not, sweetie."

"Josh was drawing them. Sometimes I worry a little bit they're going to get me while I'm sleeping."

"They're probably not going to get you, Megan," Nate said, his cheeks bulging as he chewed.

Megan gulped. "Probably?"

"Mom, they're not going to get her, are they?"

"No," said Joan.

"But are you sure?" Nate pressed.

"Positive."

"Keith saw a monster once."

"Nate," she warned him.

"It was a *thunderbird*. It lives in the woods behind his house and eats raccoons."

Megan stared at him and whispered, "Is it going to eat *me*?"

"Probably not," Nate said. "Mom, it won't eat Megan, will it?"

"What?" Joan had been listening to the radio, which predicted cold with a high of thirty-four degrees for the day. "No!"

He shrugged. "I was just wondering if thunderbirds eat people. Thought you knew."

"There's no such thing," Joan said with a sigh. "Monsters are just make-believe."

"Don't worry, Megan," Nate said. "Nothing's going to happen."

"My fairy wand will protect me."

"Yeah, and Dad watches over us. Right, Mom?"

Joan poured hot water into the thermos and screwed the cap on. "That's right. Both of us do."

"But Dad keeps a baseball bat under the bed," Nate enthused.

She smiled. *I don't need a baseball bat. If anybody ever touched you, I'd rip him apart with my bare hands.* "Finish up there, Nate. We're not going anywhere until you feed Major."

"Okay, okay, okay," he grumbled.

"Mommy, is Josh going to be okay?" Megan asked.

"I'm sure he'll be fine, sweetie."

Joan, on the other hand, still felt a little shaken by how Ramona had treated her. Pissed off, actually, but also a little guilty. The truth was, she was going to miss Josh if Ramona pulled him out of her day care. She'd grown quite fond of the weird little kid. She even liked Ramona. Sure, the woman was a little full of herself, but she was so beautiful, always perfectly groomed and dressed, and lived an exciting life filled with choices. It wasn't the life Joan had chosen for herself, but she could still admire it for what it was.

Doug plodded into the kitchen and accepted a hot mug of coffee from Joan with a nod of thanks. He sat at the kitchen table and yawned. Joan started an omelette on the stove.

"Hey, Dad," said Nate.

"Daddy!" cried Megan.

"Kids," Doug said with a nod. He sipped his coffee. "When is this skating party again, Joanie?"

"We should leave in forty-five minutes," Joan told him. "Once we get there, I'm off to see my movie. We might do a little shopping at the mall after. I'll be back home before five."

Doug said nothing further but didn't look too happy to be baby-sitting at a kids' party today. It had taken every ounce of persuasion she possessed to get him to agree to it. By the end of the week, he was exhausted and wanted nothing better than to putter around the house doing projects or maybe take the dog into the woods for some hunting. But she was tired too. Sometimes he seemed to forget she had a full-time job just as he did, twenty-four hours a day, every damn day.

I shouldn't have to beg, she thought as she put his omelette in front of him and smothered it in salsa. Doug stared at it for a moment with bleary eyes and dug in.

"So who's this Josh?" he said.

"One of my kids. Ramona's boy. I might be losing him."

"She's got money, though, right?"

"It's not that. He got sick yesterday. Ramona thinks he ate something here."

"She's crazy," Doug said. "Kids get sick all the time."

Joan smiled. Her irritation faded. The man had his faults, but she could always count on him for certain things, one being that he always took her side.

She glanced at the clock and hurried her preparations.

There was always so much to do and not enough time to do everything.

David

Hour of Herod Event

David hated Nadine's silences. The angrier she got, the quieter she became.

Right now, she was downright furious.

He drove slowly, both hands on the wheel, eyes on the road. Somebody passed him, horn blaring, and he cringed. He'd only started driving again within the past two months and was being extra careful. The rehabilitation had been hard on him—David no longer used a cane but still walked with a limp.

Nadine had been driving the Mercedes last New Year's Eve. Normally, it would have been David, but he'd had one too many. They'd picked up Paul at the babysitter's and carried him sleeping to the warm car, wrapped in David's coat. On the way home, a pickup truck slammed into them on an icy bridge. Paul died in the impact.

Nadine blamed herself.

If only, if only.

The big question was: Why?

Nadine was still searching for meaning. David, meanwhile, had embraced the horrible, simple truth of the accident. Often, there was no reason why bad things happened to good people, just a cause. Shit happened, and sometimes, it happened to you.

Now, as they drove in silence, he decided to try again to get her to talk.

"We haven't seen them in six months," he said. "It'll be fun."

David's friend Ben Glass was the county medical examiner. His primary function was to cut into corpses and determine the cause of death, analyze blood and DNA in a lab, and testify in court. Ben had chosen this path in medical school because he didn't like treating living people. Dead people were easy, he believed. They didn't scream; they didn't die under your care and haunt your conscience for the rest of your days.

David and Nadine had been friends with Ben and his wife, Gloria, for years. Ben always had an interesting story to tell about helping the police solve a crime using forensic pathology, just like on TV. *Dead men tell tales*, he liked to say. *The dead are real blabbermouths, if you know how to listen.*

Since the accident, though, they'd hidden from everybody they knew. And in Ben's case, they didn't need another reminder of death. The night of the accident, death had stopped being an abstraction, the end of a long, satisfying journey. It was evil incarnate that had stolen their child.

Nevertheless, after a chance meeting at the grocery store, David had lobbied Nadine hard for this lunch, part of his resolution to try to move forward. She went along with it, but he could tell it was only to please him.

Still Nadine said nothing. David glanced at her, sighed, and turned the radio on.

Seeing Shannon Donegal and the other happy, pregnant women in his office over the past few weeks had helped him stop dreading the up-coming anniversary of Paul's death and think about the future.

Every day, David brushed his teeth and tied his shoelaces, even though every atom in his body told him to lie down and never get back up. He'd learned to accept the days when it didn't hurt as much and the days when it hurt even more. He wanted to be finished with death being the center of his world. He was tired of grieving and living in an endless haze.

He wanted to see his own life again. He wanted to share that life with Nadine.

So this morning, over breakfast, he'd told her he hoped they would eventually try to have another child. Not right now, but at least they could think about it. Maybe even talk about it.

The very idea seemed to offend her, however.

Now she turned the radio off.

"I dreamed of him again last night," she said. "He was playing on the shore of Lake Michigan. That place we went to two summers ago? I stood behind him, looking at the water, big and deep and black. I wanted to protect him."

"Nadine. Don't."

"He didn't care about anything. He just laughed and played. He held up his little fist and let the sand trickle out of it. So real, when I woke up, I thought it'd actually happened. For just a moment, I thought he was still alive."

"Okay." David understood she couldn't move on, at least not yet. Maybe ever. She'd experienced something she believed one did not sim-ply *get over*. And that meant she might never feel ready to have another child. David knew that, in her mind, he wouldn't even ask for such a thing if he loved Paul as much as she did.

But he *did* love him as much. Paul's loss had left a gaping wound in David's heart that would never go away regardless of how much therapy he got or how many support groups he joined. He loved his son differently, that's all.

And he still loved life enough to want to live it.

Nadine said, "He's still here, with me." She pressed her fist against her chest. "I feel him. Right here. Alive. I can't just let him go. Do you understand?"

He's a dream, a memory, David wanted to say. *The real Paul is gone, Nadine.* But he understood. He parked, and they sat together while snowflakes fluttered onto the windshield and the heat drained out of the car. LED icicles, strung across the busy retail street, sparkled and drizzled drops of light. People crowded the sidewalks. They looked happy.

"Listen. We don't have to do this. Have lunch with them, I mean."

She reached and covered his hand, still gripping the steering wheel, with her own. "No, I want to."

This much she could do for him. He wanted more, but it would suffice.

"Are you sure?"

She forced a smile. "Come on. They're waiting for us."

"I love you, Nadine."

She'd already opened her door. David watched her step onto the sidewalk. He sighed, exited the car, and limped to join her. As always, they presented a visually interesting couple—David tall and aristo-cratic, Nadine petite and a bit ethereal.

She extended her elbow and allowed her husband to escort her into the restaurant. Ben and Gloria welcomed them with smiles, hugs, and concern in their eyes. The couple couldn't produce children themselves and had doted on Paul as if he were their own. During the awkward conversation that started their meal, David felt their need to unburden their own pain as well as comfort him and Nadine.

When the subject they were actively ignoring finally came up over salads, they all cried except for Nadine, who stared at them vacantly, as if watching a movie unfolding in a foreign language. It was a painful but essential ritual. They talked about Paul as long as they dared, and by the time the main courses arrived, the conversation had moved on to safer ground. David slowly felt himself unwind as they settled back into the easy rhythm of their relationship.

He realized he was smiling and thought, *That's why I'm here. To smile a little. To feel good.*

His family used to have so much fun together when Paul was alive.

His smile faded. As always, pleasure had its sad echo.

They finished their meals surrounded by the sounds of cutlery and idle conversation. David ordered a cappuccino for himself and an espresso for Nadine.

"They have good food here," Gloria said to Nadine. "The tuna was *fantastic*. I have to say I'm proud of Ben. Not once did I catch him checking out the football game on the TV in the bar."

"Furtive glances," Ben confessed. "Dallas is playing Detroit. David, you've always been a Cowboys fan, haven't you? Want to know the score? It's rather grim, I'm afraid."

"I haven't followed them this year, unfortunately," David said.

"So how's your new business idea working out? Giving free pre-natal consultations to women in the hopes their kids will become patients?"

"I won't know until the children are born," David answered. "But I had sessions with three mothers in the past week. I think two of the children will become patients."

"My God. You've discovered the pediatric version of ambulance chasing. Ingenious."

"It's actually fairly common," David said, smiling again. "But here's something that will interest you. About a month ago, Nadine and I treated a child with a very special disability and found a way to dramatically improve her life."

The waiter brought a tray of cups. David accepted his cappuccino and sipped it. The hot drink made him feel warm and mellow. He glanced at Nadine. She stared blankly at her espresso.

"Go on, David," Gloria said. "I'd like to hear it."

"Well, we were treating a young girl—who must remain nameless, but let's call her Kathy—with two afflictions. She's visually impaired. She's also allergic to dogs. Of course, this ruled out guide dogs."

"Oh, the poor thing," said Gloria.

"Why don't you tell them the solution, Nadine?" David said. "After all, you did most of the research."

Nadine said, "We recommended she use a guide horse."

"You're joking," Ben said.

"Oh no, it's no joke," David responded. "She means a miniature horse, of course."

"*Now* you're joking," Gloria said.

"Miniature horses—horses with dwarfism—are quite real," said David. "The smallest miniature horse was just over a foot tall. You can look it up in *Guinness World Records*."

"No, we can't get one," Ben said, casting a warning glance at Gloria.

She ignored her husband. "Can you pick them up and hold them?"

When Nadine didn't answer, David stepped in again. "They can be great guide animals. They're calm, they have a wide field of vision, they remember things, and they're always on the lookout for danger. Some of them live up to fifty years or longer."

"What about the smell?" said Ben, looking skeptical.

"Not a problem if you give them regular baths. Guide horses can even be housebroken. They don't get fleas. And the child loves the horse. Treats it like a person. And yes, Gloria, she picks him up and holds him, though horses don't need affection like dogs do."

"What did she name him?"

David turned to Nadine and waited for her to answer this time.

"Tiny Tim," she said.

Gloria laughed. "Oh God, I love it. If I had a miniature horse, I would name him something brave and bold, like Champion or Hulk." She nudged Ben, who stared at the TV wearing a tense expression. "Aw, come on. Can we get one, honey?"

"Wait a second," Ben said.

"Dallas making a comeback?" said David.

"No. Something's going on."

His tone made them all turn toward the television.

The game was gone. In its place, ambulances and flashing lights filled the screen. In the upper-right corner: Live.

38

"What is it?" Gloria asked.

"I don't know," Ben answered.

Whatever it is, it's something big, David thought. *They don't just interrupt a major football game unless the world is ending.*

The image on the screen cut to a group of people kneeling around something. David glimpsed what looked like a child's arm. Parts of the restaurant fell silent.

They gasped as a caption appeared: HUNDREDS DEAD IN CALIFORNIA.

The camera zoomed out and tracked a man rushing across the street with a small boy in his arms. Behind him, the sidewalks as far as the eye could see were jammed with crowds of people huddled around figures lying on the ground.

"Jesus Christ," somebody muttered.

"We need sound," somebody else called out. "Turn it up! Please!"

The rest of the restaurant quieted with baffled looks. Men crowded around the TV.

"David," Nadine whispered, her voice edged with panic.

David reached for her hand and held it tight.

The bartender found the remote and changed the channel to CNN, which showed a worried-looking Lyle Stanley behind a desk. He turned up the volume.

"The death toll already appears to be much larger than we first reported," Stanley declared. He blinked. "Wait. I'm not going to say that."

Is this one of those moments? David thought. *One of those moments that changes everything?*

The anchor glared at somebody off camera. "That can't be right." He held up the sheet of paper. "The report about the—I'm not going to say that on the air until somebody verifies it."

Nadine gripped David's hand even harder.

On air, Lyle Stanley stood up. "I need to call my wife."

There was an abrupt cut to a commercial for a new Chrysler minivan.

The diners filled the ensuing silence with shouting.

"Where was that? What city?"

"San Francisco, I think. Union Square."

The bartender switched to Fox, which showed the same video of people huddled around bodies on a sidewalk. The reporter was babbling, not making any sense.

"What do you think happened?" Ben asked David. "Some type of terrorist attack?"

David shook his head. He had no idea. "We should get home."

"Why? Whatever it is, it's not here in Michigan, right?"

Nadine squeezed David's hand.

"What's wrong?" he asked.

She said nothing, staring over his shoulder. He followed her gaze toward the front door of the restaurant, where a dazed woman stood alone.

David watched her ball her fists and scream, silencing them all.

Doug

Hour of Herod Event

Doug wished he had a shotgun in his hands.

He pictured himself deep in the woods, doing some hunting.

The skaters flowed clockwise around the outdoor ice rink. While some parents skated with their kids, most sipped coffee and smiled from the sidelines.

He stood apart from the crowd in the hope nobody would approach him to engage in banal small talk. None of these people were his friends. He couldn't say he really had any. Acquaintances, sure. He had lots of those. Guys he worked with and husbands of Joan's friends with whom he was occasionally forced to socialize.

He didn't mind; he wasn't much of a social guy anyway. He considered himself related to the cave bear. His family was everything to him. If you weren't in his tribe, he didn't care much about you and had a hard time faking it.

Doug checked out the moms, but even that got boring. This babysitting was for the birds. He didn't understand these "breaks" Joanie needed every once in a while. She'd wanted kids; he'd given her kids. Taking care of them was her job. His job was to work ten hours a day, plus overtime, doing hard, dirty work to keep a roof over their heads. His job was to fix what needed fixing around the house. Hell, he needed breaks too. A little *me* time.

Like hunting. Sitting in a tree enjoying nature, with a thermos of hot coffee to keep him warm. The deep silences. Last year, he'd shot a doe and put a lot of meat in the freezer. Venison was good eating if you cooked it right. Roasts, stews, burgers.

Nate skated to a halt at the edge of the ice. "Is that hot chocolate, Dad?"

"Yup." Doug handed it over.

His son poured a cup, gulped it down, and gasped for air. "Jeez, that's really hot."

"Warm you up good, kid."

"I got invited to a game of shinny later. Can I play, Dad?"

"Sure. Just keep an eye out for Keith."

"I will," Nate grumbled.

Nate loved playing pickup games of hockey, but Keith McDonald always got carried away and reefed the puck, sending it flying above the ice among kids without protective gear. Normally, Doug wouldn't say a word; he wanted Nate to learn how to handle these things for himself. But he was in charge today, like it or not, and intended for both his kids to give their mom a glowing report card for Daddy.

"And get home before dark, understand?"

"Okay, Dad."

"Daddy!" Megan yelled. She trudged along the ice in her bulky snowsuit and helmet, pushing her bright orange training aid. "Look at me!"

41

"See you, Dad," Nate said as he sped away.

"You're doing great, princess," Doug told Megan.

"I want you to come with me as I go around, Daddy."

"I will in a minute."

She ground to a halt in front of him and promptly fell on her butt. He laughed.

"No, *not* in a minute," she groused. "Right *now*." She grabbed two handfuls of snow at his feet with her pink mittens and flung them over her head. "Dad-deeeee!"

"I will in a minute. Promise."

"You have to chip in, you know," Megan added in a perfect imitation of her mother.

Definitely the same blood there. The apple doesn't fall far and all that.

Nate tested boundaries like any other kid but otherwise didn't give his old man lip. Doug had never hit his kids and never would, but his size was naturally intimidating. Megan, on the other hand, was turning into the mother-in-law he'd never had. A real nag, but he was totally fine with it. Little Meggie could do no wrong in his book.

"I'll see what I can do," he told her. "Daddy's trying real hard."

"Okay." Megan returned to skating along her slow circuit. "Bye, Daddy!"

He watched her go, noting with pride how she got right back up after falling.

And he thought: *My life is pretty fucking good.*

As always happened, once he gave up thinking about what *he* wanted to do and resigned himself to focusing on the kids, he loosened up and began to enjoy himself. Sometimes playing along. Other times, like now, just watching.

One of the children took a nose dive onto the ice, producing gasps and a little laughter among the other kids.

Doug winced. *That had to hurt.* Several of the older kids and adults gathered around and gawked. Doug's eyes flickered to Nate and Megan to make sure they were still trucking.

"Hey, partner." Coral's husband, Earl, sidled up to him, hands buried in the pockets of his jacket. He wore an absurd plaid winter hat with floppy earflaps. "I thought I'd find you here. Girls' day out, eh? How you been?"

"Peachy," said Doug. He cupped his hands to light a Winston.

"What's in the thermos?"

"Hot chocolate. For the kids."

"Nothing stronger, huh?"

"Nope. Don't drink." He watched the crowd grow around the fallen kid. It looked like somebody was going home with a sprained wrist or worse.

The parents buzzed along the edge of the rink. *Concussion*, Doug heard.

"Eh, too bad. I could really use a boost right about now." Earl wiped his nose with the back of his glove. "Man, I wish I was off on my own today."

"Yeah, tell me about it."

"I'll tell you what I'd rather be doing. You got yourself a snowmobile?"

Doug resisted the urge to laugh in the man's face. "No, Earl, I don't have any snowmobile."

"Me and Coral just bought one. It's a cross-country model. It'll take you *anywhere*. Fuel-injected four-cylinder engine, easy steering, adjustable rear suspension. You know where Route Twenty-Three wraps around the lake?"

"Yeah," said Doug. "Hey, what's going on over there, you think? That kid's hurt bad, from the looks of it."

"There's a little road about a mile before the evergreen farm," Earl kept on, wrapped up in his petty boasting. "Takes you right into some fantastic open country where you can cut loose with some off-trail sledding. I'm taking Peter out there next weekend."

Doug grunted his irritation. Earl worked in heating and cooling and took home about as much money as Doug did, but he and Coral spent everything they earned, and then some, on themselves and their kids.

Not Doug, though. He remembered the red-faced old regulars he'd seen huddled around the bar at Cody's Bar so many years ago, slowly drinking their pension checks. They'd always talk about how things were better back in the day. Those old farts had worked factory jobs with union wages. All gone now. Times were tough all over. These days, a lot of folks in Lansdowne had to work two, even three jobs to put food on the table.

Maybe Earl and Coral had the right idea, though. If you were screwed, why not borrow as much as you could, blow it having fun, and declare bankruptcy? Ten years later, you could be back on your feet. Doug pictured himself riding a snowmobile next weekend with Nate. He had a credit card; it was really that simple. They could have it all, at least for a while.

But that wouldn't be fair to the kids. Doug had a deep drive to see them do better in life than he had. Maybe Nate and Megan wouldn't necessarily have a better future, but at least Doug could say he'd given them a fighting chance. And that meant putting every extra dollar they had away for college.

Another kid, this one a little girl, fell face-first on the ice. She didn't get up. Earl didn't notice, blathering on about his snowmobile.

"Something's not right," Doug murmured.

"What's that?" said Earl.

A small boy's knees buckled. He went down hard. Doug saw blood squirt from his nose on impact. Somebody screamed.

There's something wrong with the ice.

"Megan!" he called. "Nate, come on over here now."

Parents crowded the edge of the rink, shouting out names. Three more kids fell all at once. The parents swarmed onto the rink. A flurry of panicked shrieks rent the air. Doug stepped onto the ice, almost lost his footing, and pushed through the crowd shouting for his kids.

He slipped and fell hard. Pain flared in his hip. He hauled himself to his feet.

"Megan! Nate!"

He found his little girl sitting on the ice, crying into her mittens. The training aid lay on its side. Nate knelt behind her, arms locked around her body in a protective hug.

Doug fell hard again. The thermos rolled away. A boot slammed into his head. He rose to his hands and knees with a groan and crawled.

"Dad!" cried Nate.

Doug enclosed his children in his arms. Was this enough to protect them? He glared at the people swirling around, ready to knock anybody flat if they so much as even looked at his boy and girl. His heart leaped in fear at the sight of bodies on the ice. Everybody was screaming. He couldn't think. His head ached.

"What's going on, Dad?" said Nate. "Dad!"

The ice is bad! Get them off the ice!

He scooped the kids under his arms and glided across the ice until he reached the edge. He kept on going toward the parking lot, leaving the path and cutting through a snowy field.

Halfway across, he set them down to check on them.

"You all right?"

Megan uncovered her face and yelled at the crowd behind: "*Stop.*"

Doug sighed with relief. His kids were fine.

He'd saved them from something, but he didn't know what.

Nate sniffed the air. "Somebody's toast is burning."

Doug looked at him. "What?"

Nate fell backward. His body thudded into the snow.

Doug stared in disbelief. "Nate? *Nate!*"

He crouched over his son and shook him. "Wake up. Come on, stop kidding around."

Nate didn't move. His eyes were open. Glassy and staring at nothing.

"Daddy, what's wrong with him?"

Doug spared a glance at Megan. "Nothing, princess."

He's dead.

"He's *fine.*" He shook the boy again. "Come on, wake up. Wake up!"

"Daddy, my head really hurts!"

"Hang on, princess. Daddy has to—" His body tingled from his heart to his fingertips. He wheeled. "No, *no, wait, wait, WAIT GOD-DAMN IT—*"

Megan fell onto her side. Her foot jerked several times. Then stopped.

"Kids," said Doug.

He picked up Megan and hugged her. He felt numb. He couldn't breathe. His vision swirled with dots of light.

"I've got you," he said. "Come on. We got to get you to a doctor. We're going to fix this."

Megan's head flopped against his shoulder. She felt much heavier than when he'd carried her this morning. He'd tossed her laughing in the air like she was nothing. He picked up Nate's limp form with his other arm. Dead weight.

He stumbled toward his truck in a daze. He didn't make it. He fell to his knees with a long, primal cry of anguish. Behind him, panic had given way to shock and grief, the park quiet now except for intense sobbing and the odd scream.

Across the entire park, not a single child was still alive.

Ramona

Hour of Herod Event

Ramona had reached the end of her rope.

The mall was hot, dry, and overcrowded. Josh wasn't feeling well and had to be carried. He pestered her with a revolving list of demands: *Let me walk by myself, take me to the LEGO store, I want a piece of gum.* The promise of meeting Santa couldn't compete with these needs that took on massive importance as soon as he thought of them. Every time she said no, he flew into a fresh rage.

Screaming: "I don't like Mommy anymore!"

"Josh, stop this right now."

"I want to go to Joanie's!"

Good idea! thought Ramona. Monday, the start of another dull, grinding workweek spent in a fluorescent office, sounded perfect right about now.

She tried once more to draw him out. "I love you even though you're mad at me."

He wailed against her shoulder, leaving a smear of snot. The shoppers milled around her. She caught fragmentary glimpses of people's faces, expressions of amusement and pity.

"Josh." Her voice hardened. "If you don't stop right now, I'm taking you home."

He continued to cry and kick his legs.

"All right." She clenched her teeth. "That's it. We're not going to see Santa. We're going home."

"No! No! I'll stop crying."

He trembled in her arms. Ramona sensed his struggle to put a lid on his emotions. It reminded her he was four and this was what four-year-olds sometimes did. They threw tantrums. They lost control.

"Hey, little man. It's Santa's castle. We made it!"

He looked for himself and grinned at what he saw.

Ramona wiped his face. "Do you want to see Santa?"

"Okay."

"Then no more yelling at Mommy. That is *not* acceptable. Okay?"

Josh looked down. "Okay."

The display was massive. Santa sat enthroned on a stage in front of a backdrop representing his workshop on the North Pole. Brilliant Christmas trees, giant bow-covered boxes, and piles of cotton snow completed the scene. A cute teenage girl dressed in an elf costume ushered a little boy onto Santa's lap, where Santa spoke the magic words in his booming voice:

"What's YOUR name? Robbie? Well, Robbie, what do YOU want for Christmas?"

Ramona thought the mall's management had picked the perfect Santa—naturally rotund, and even the beard looked authentic. He had a kind, jolly face. The line of parents and their children snaked down the ramp onto the floor of the mall, where another elf greeted them.

She tried to judge if Josh would be able to hold it together without another meltdown.

"Santa," he said in a reverent tone. He still rested his head, grinning, against her shoulder.

That settled it. They'd come this far. She would have to try. The goal remained to create a happy memory for her boy.

"Josh, do you have to pee or anything before we get in line?"

"No, I'm okay, Mommy."

"Do you remember what you want to ask Santa to bring you on Christmas Day?"

"I want a Bob the Builder tool set. And some trucks!"

"Ho, ho, ho," said Santa.

Her arms and back ached from carrying his weight for so long. His body blazed with youthful heat. She was sweating in her coat. She wanted to put him down for a few minutes but was afraid of disturbing his equilibrium. He seemed better now. She wanted to keep him that way as long as she could.

The line crawled along. Ramona rocked Josh in her arms. He began to fidget.

"Do you want me to put you down?"

"No." He held on tighter.

"Okay, let's see . . . Did I ever tell you the story about the friendly monster?"

"Tell me the story, Mommy."

If he liked monsters now, so be it. She'd indulge it. But she'd convince him the monsters weren't scary. They were actually nice, if only you tried to make friends with them.

"There was a monster who was tired of living all alone. He wanted to live in town with people, but the townspeople were scared and told the monster to stay away."

Josh, concerned: "He didn't have any friends to play with?"

She planted a kiss on his forehead. "Not a single friend. He was very sad. Then one day, the monster saw a little boy lost in the woods. The boy was afraid of him but was even more afraid of being lost. The monster took the boy's hand in his big paw and took him home to his mommy. After that, everybody loved the monster and wanted to be friends with him. The end."

Josh looked up at her and smiled. "I like that story."

"I'm glad, little man."

"Can you tell me another one?"

"Ramona?"

She turned and yelped. *Oh. My. God.* "Oh, hey! Ross! What are you doing here?"

He held up a bag. "Just some Christmas shopping."

"Right," she said. "Um . . ."

"I'm pretty much done, which is good, seeing as I'm completely shopped out. Thank God it's only once a year, right?"

"Yeah. You know, Ross . . ."

"Don't." He laughed. "Honestly, we're cool."

"No. No, I have to."

"Listen, I'm really not upset."

"Ross, no." Her voice cracked. "That was the *worst* thing I've ever done to *anyone* in my entire career. I'm so sorry."

"Your kid had a medical emergency. If you'd stayed, what would that have said?"

"Wow. You're very nice. But it shouldn't have happened. Not like that."

"You want the truth? I already had another job lined up, but I don't start until January."

"Oh," she said, processing this. No wonder he'd been slacking off.

He shifted his gaze to Josh. "So who's this little guy?"

"This little guy is Josh," she said with relief at the change of topic. "Say hi to Ross, Josh."

"How are you today?" said Ross. He smiled at Josh, who slowly smiled back.

"He's tired," Ramona answered for him.

"Mommy, I have to go pee-pee," Josh said.

"Josh, I asked you—" She stopped. Reminding him that she'd asked him less than ten minutes ago if he had to go would be a pointless exercise. "Can you hold it until after we see Santa?"

"No, I have to go right now."

"We're going to lose our place in line."

"Hey, listen," said Ross. "I don't have anything planned for the rest of the day. If you want to take him, I'll hold your spot for you."

"You don't have to do that."

"I honestly don't mind."

"I really don't want to hold you up or anything."

He gave her a shrewd look. "How about you buy me an Orange Julius on the way back, and we'll call it even? Do we have a deal?"

Ramona laughed. "Well, okay then. Yeah, it's a deal."

They stood smiling at each other for a moment.

Is he flirting with me?

She again felt a little flutter of attraction, which she'd resisted more than once during the time they'd worked together.

Except now you don't work together anymore.

Yeah, because she'd just fired him. *Awkward* didn't begin to cover it.

Don't go crazy. It's just flirting. You could use a little flirting.

Which was true. She hadn't been on a real date in months, unless she counted those Friday nights lying on the couch in her pajamas watching a romantic comedy and spending a little time with her vibrator afterward. She'd given up on dating for a while. Men pursued her but later ran scared from the responsibility of playing dad to a sickly boy. It was too complicated, and after a while, they gave up.

She wanted something more. She wanted the happiness Bethany had found with Brian. It was possible. It had to be.

"Be right back then," she said.

A woman screamed.

Ramona cringed at the bloodcurdling sound. On the stage, Santa held a limp child on his lap. The little girl's limbs flopped loose as the old man stood and offered her to her dazed mother, who took the child in her arms.

Dozens of shoppers froze where they stood and watched the scene.

Ramona heard gasps as a second figure collapsed near the Gap. She saw people in their dark coats kneel around a small boy.

In the distance, a scream. Then another. Ramona wheeled toward the sound.

"What the hell is going on?" Ross said.

The screams multiplied across the mall like a hellish choir.

Josh buried his face against her chest and whimpered.

"It's okay, Josh," she said. "It's going to be all right."

"The kids," Ross said.

"What?"

"Jesus, Ramona, *it's all the kids*!"

Ramona hugged Josh closer, her eyes wild, as the scene erupted in chaos.

People sprinted in all directions, knocked each other down, stumbled over bodies. She caught a glimpse of children lying on the floor as if asleep. *They're dead*, she realized with a sudden shock. Ross was right; something was happening to the kids. Her heart thumped against her ribs. Her vision shrank to a small circle.

Only seconds ago, people had been milling about doing their Christmas shopping.

"What's happening?" she asked weakly.

"I think we should get Josh out of here," Ross said.

Ramona turned toward the nearest exit as a woman smashed into her. Shopping bags crashed to the floor, where they were kicked and trampled to shreds. Ramona staggered but kept a tight hold on Josh, who howled into her coat. Ross grabbed her elbow.

"Ramona, listen to me. Okay? We have to get out of here!"

She saw everything clearly now, from a distance, the sound muted. People ran past in slow motion. Wrapping paper swirled around the runners' feet. Tiny bodies sprawled on the ground amid clothes and toys. Ross stood with his arms spread, trying to protect her, his mouth moving. A man ran by holding a little girl in his arms. Blood poured from the girl's nose and sprayed across the floor.

Run.

The world roared in her ears as events around her speeded up and left her behind.

Don't stand there like an idiot! Get Josh out!

"Ramona!" Ross shouted.

She glared at him. He seemed to fill the horizon, blocking her escape no matter which way she turned.

"Get out of the way!" she shrieked, and he did.

"Mommy!" Josh cried.

She hugged him tighter. "No. *No.* Not him."

There must be someplace that's safe.

The concourse emptied as people swarmed against the exits. She ran past stores filled with screaming people. A warm sensation spread across her stomach as Josh wet himself.

Don't stop. Keep moving. Find somewhere safe. You can do this.

Ramona cut a wide berth around the toy store. Children lay among the scattered toys. Two men were beating each other with their fists in blind panic next to a board game display.

She glimpsed Bethany kneeling over the body of her son. Ripping out her beautiful blond hair by the handful.

The massive Christmas tree loomed ahead. Covered in ornaments and lit up in brilliant colors, it beckoned from its place near the central fountain.

Behind her, another flurry of bloodcurdling screams.

The shining star at the top called to her. It promised safety. Nobody could die near that star. It was Christmas. *A king is born.* Her ears filled with the roar of rushing water as she zigzagged past people clumped around the bodies of their children.

Josh stiffened in her arms.

"We're almost there," she gasped. "Hang on."

Her legs gave out. She sank to her knees in front of the tree and sobbed.

"I love you, Josh," she said. She kissed his flushed cheeks and forehead. "Mommy loves you. Don't go. Please don't go."

His eyes glazed. "It's eating me."

"What is? What's eating you, baby?"

"Tool set," he said dreamily, just before his face twisted into a final grimace.

Joan

Hour of Herod Event

Joan loved a good thriller. *Spy Master* was everything she'd hoped it would be.

The moment she and Coral had left the park, Joan began to miss her kids, but she resolved not to think about them for two hours. They were in good hands with Doug, even if he didn't particularly want the job. Thirty minutes into the movie, she was making good on the promise she'd made herself. She'd already eaten half a tub of popcorn and had become totally immersed in the movie.

The Iranians had planted a bomb in Washington, DC, and Hunter Talbot and his elite spy team had to find out where it was. The clock was ticking. Every time Talbot found a new lead, some shadowy figure got there just ahead of him, killed key witnesses, and destroyed essential files. All while his shortsighted superiors kept yelling at him for operating a CIA team on U.S. soil.

Joan suspected the Vice President had some sort of deal going with the Iranians. He was an old friend of Talbot's from the CIA, a helpful and kindly old gentleman, but she just didn't trust him.

"I don't understand," a female voice shouted from somewhere near the front row.

Joan and Coral laughed together at one of Talbot's one-liners.

"How can that be?" the voice cried again.

Joan blanched as the spell broke. One moment, she was in the action, the next, sitting in a dark, half-empty movie theater.

The woman cried out once more while Talbot and his team scaled the facade of a high-rise building. Nobody shushed her. Either she was crazy, or something horrible had just happened.

"What's going on?" Coral hissed.

Joan gritted her teeth. "I don't know. I'm *watching*."

When Megan woke up too early, Joan would send her back to bed and then lie there with her eyes clenched, willing herself to return to sleep, even though she knew it was useless: She was awake, and she was getting up. Likewise, now that the woman had broken the illusion of the movie, Joan was having a hard time getting back into it.

She watched Talbot drop onto the roof and pull up his ski mask, exposing his brilliant blue eyes and chiseled jaw. In the distance, the Capitol shined brightly against the night sky, so strong and yet so helpless.

This is supposed to be where the Iranian cell is based, she reminded herself. *Unless it's another trap—*

"Please," the woman wailed. "*Please.* Just tell me what happened."

"Oh, come on," Joan said. The movie was officially ruined.

Coral whispered, much too loud, "Should we go help her?"

A man hurried down the aisle with a flashlight. Joan and Coral watched him pass.

"That must be the manager," said Coral.

"He'll take care of it."

A cell phone rang in the dark. Then another. Joan chuckled as the distractions piled up. "Somebody does *not* want me to see this movie."

The manager stood in front of the projection screen and waved his arms. "Excuse me!" he shouted. "There's an emergency. You all need to exit the theater in a very calm and orderly fashion!"

On the screen, Talbot leaped as the wall behind him exploded in a hail of gunfire.

"They're kicking us out," Coral said.

"It's probably nothing. It's always a false—"

She blinked as the lights came up. Moments later, the film stopped.

A woman shrieked into her cell phone. *Nobody's dead! Nobody!*

"What the hell is going on?" Joan wondered.

"I'm going to call Earl," Coral said.

A couple hurried past, rattled. There were several women crying in different parts of the theater now.

"I, uh, think I'll call Doug," said Joan. She fished her phone out of her purse, activated it, and waited for a signal. Her heart pounded.

"Damn it," said Coral.

"Earl's not answering?"

"The lines are jammed. All circuits busy. Oh God, this is not good."

"Let's take this one thing at a time." Joan called Doug's cell. "I got a ring!"

"Oh good. Doug's there with Earl. Ask him about Peter and Joey."

"I will, I promise."

Doug's voice: "*Joanie?*"

"Doug? I'm so glad I got you. They're telling us to leave the theater. Some kind of big emergency. Do you know anything?"

She sucked in her breath. Doug was *crying.* She forced herself to breathe. "I'm coming straight there. Just tell me the kids are okay."

"*Joanie . . .*"

"Listen to me. I said I'm coming there." Her voice was shaking. "I just need to hear the kids are okay before we leave."

Coral watched her with large, watery eyes, her hand over her mouth.

"*They're gone, babe.*"

Rage burned in her chest. "What do you mean they're 'gone'? What does that mean?"

"Oh my *God*." Coral began to cry. "Ask him about Peter and Joey, please! I need to know they're all right!"

"Wait, Doug." Joan covered her exposed ear with her finger. "I still don't understand. Tell me what happened and that they're okay."

"They're not okay! They're gone!"

"What happened? What did you do?"

"They're dead, babe. They're gone. I tried. I really did."

Her vision blurred with tears. "What are you saying? I went to a *movie*."

"We all tried, but we couldn't save them. We couldn't—"

Joan screamed. Coral was shouting at her and trying to hold her shoulders. Joan lashed out, scratching her friend's hands and drawing blood.

She made it halfway up the aisle before she blacked out.

II

Herod's Syndrome

THREE

Ramona

41 hours after Herod Event

Ramona wandered her home like a ghost.

Josh was in his bedroom, tucked into bed. His presents still sat under the Christmas tree. His shirts, socks, and underpants went uncollected in the dryer. The remains of his breakfast rotted on a plate on the kitchen table.

At last, tired of wandering her house searching for something that wasn't there, she returned to her bed and curled into a ball under the blankets.

From the day Josh was born, Ramona feared the worst would happen. She'd imagine him dying of accidental suffocation or violent collision, and blind terror would rip through her.

Now that the worst had come, she was surprised by how little she truly felt. She'd expected a giant outpouring of grief, not this mindless implosion.

Sometimes she sensed a dull ache in her heart and other times, nothing. Just a general numbness. She felt she could chop her finger off and not even notice.

Maybe this is what they meant when they said a part of you died with the person you loved.

She remembered driving for hours after leaving the mall. The hospitals were surrounded by cars and thousands of screaming people carrying dead and dying children in their arms. She called 911 repeatedly but got nothing but a busy signal. The air filled with the wail of sirens.

Whatever had happened, it'd happened everywhere, to everybody.

The frantic voices on the radio confirmed it. After a while, she turned it off. Then she pulled over and screamed until she had nothing left.

With nowhere else to go, Ramona took him home.

Dead weight, his arms and legs dangling like a puppet's.

By the time she washed him, dressed him in his pajamas, and tucked him into bed, his face had gone rigid. The rest of his body soon followed. Stiffened like a block of wood.

His flesh had turned pale, but he was still a little warm. When she kissed him after tucking him in, she tried to pretend he was still alive.

"Good night, Josh," she said. A part of her still hoped he might wake up. He didn't.

The next day, he began to smell. She closed his door, but it didn't help. Soon, the entire house smelled like him. She turned the heat down in the hope of slowing the decomposition process.

Time blurred after that. Now the clock read 7:03. Monday morning, or at least she thought it was. She tried once again to sleep. Every time she closed her eyes, she saw Santa giving the dead girl to her crying mother.

"No," she moaned. *Not again.*

She didn't want to relive it yet again.

Tool set, Josh had said dreamily, just before his face twisted into a grimace.

The truth of this world is people love you, and then they leave. Ramona never knew her mother, who'd died giving birth to her. Her father had died of a heart attack when she was nine, and Pam, her stepmother, emotionally abandoned her after that. She thought she'd found happiness with Josh's father, a young attorney named Shawn, but he'd left her to raise Josh on her own.

Now even Josh was gone.

Hunger drove her out of bed. She entered the kitchen in a daze and found Josh's cereal in the cupboard. She sat at the table staring at the bowl and wondering what came next. The phone rang, reminding her she'd been doing something important. Slowly, her hand reached out, picked up the box, and poured some cereal into the bowl. The phone stopped ringing. Minutes later, she opened the carton of milk. It smelled iffy, but she poured it onto the cereal.

The chair next to her, the one in front of the plate with its rotting breakfast, sat empty. She stared at it for what felt like hours, filled with longing.

We're going to see Santa today, right? he'd said.

"That's right, little man," she said aloud.

She couldn't pretend, but she could remember. She remembered everything.

I'm going to tell him I want a Bob the Builder tool set. Do you think he'll bring me one?

"If you're good, I'm sure he will."

I'll be good.

The doorbell chimed.

The memory dissipated. She recalled what she'd been doing. She spooned cereal into her mouth and spit it out. The milk was fine. She just hated soggy cereal.

The doorbell chimed again. Insistent knocking followed, making her flinch. Ramona shuffled to the garbage can on bare feet and dumped the entire bowl, spoon and all. She went to the cupboard, pulled out a fresh bowl, and sat and tried again.

The knocking wouldn't stop.

She found herself standing in front of the door.

"Who is it?" she called.

"It's Ross. Ross Kelley."

She opened it. Ross filled the doorway, holding bags of groceries.

His handsome face lit up at seeing her. She dully stared back at him, seeing him through a fog.

"Hi, Ramona. I'm so sorry for your loss. I am really, really sorry."

She continued to stare at him.

"I thought you might need some groceries. Can I come in?"

He gave her a long hug at the door. He was warm, but otherwise, she didn't feel a thing. Her arms stayed at her sides. When he let go, Ramona turned and shuffled back to the kitchen to sit at the table. She dipped her spoon and let the soggy cereal drop back into the bowl with a plop.

"Shit," she said.

"I brought milk, coffee, bread, eggs, some lunch meat," he said as he emptied the bags' contents onto the counter. "A bunch of different things. And this." He held up a white rose. "I'll put it in water. You have no idea how hard it is to get flowers right now, but I got the best of the bunch."

He winced at the smell. Ramona watched, helpless, as he cleared Josh's plate into the trash. He sniffed again, puzzled that the smell was still present.

"Wow, it's cold in here. Aren't you cold? You could make Popsicles." He turned up the heat.

Ross was destroying her museum. *Stop it. Leave.*

"Why are you here?" she asked him.

"I was with you when it happened. I still can't believe it did happen. It's like being in a nightmare. The world will never be the same."

She said nothing.

"Anyway," he said, "I wish I could have done something. I was thinking maybe I could help you now."

"You're sweet, Ross," she said. "Really. But your help is the last thing I need right now."

"I've been worrying about you. It's not healthy being alone at a time like this. Don't you have anyone?"

Ramona glanced at the phone, which had rung unanswered on and off for the past few days.

"Just go," she said.

"Ramona. Let me help you. Please."

He really wants to help, she thought from far away. It was an attractive idea.

She thought of her best friend ripping her hair out at the toy store. Bethany had Brian to console her, but Brian couldn't bring Trent back any more than Ross could resurrect Josh.

Attractive, but pointless.

"This is not about what you want," she said. "It's about what I want. And I don't want you here."

Ross hesitated, his expression filled with self-doubt.

"You need help, Ramona."

"Get. Out. Of. My. House."

"Oh. Wait. I'm just trying to—"

She clenched her fists. *"GET OUT!"*

He held up his hands in surrender. "All right, okay. I'll leave. I'm sorry."

She followed him to the door. "What did you think you were going to do? Boss me around and ask me if I was all cried out yet, and then I'll snap out of it and won't be sad anymore?!"

Ross paused at the door to put on his coat, his face reddening with confusion and anger. "All right, Ramona. I was trying to help and screwed up somehow. I'm an idiot, okay? I'll leave you alone now."

"Really? Are you sure I can handle that?"

He opened the door with a loud sigh and stepped onto the porch. Ramona noticed the walk had filled with snow since Saturday morning. She wanted to yell at him some more; it felt so good to be angry. It was good to feel *something*.

It didn't last. The anger dissipated as rapidly as it had come, leaving her hollow again.

Ramona thought of the endless, empty day ahead of her.

"Wait," she called after him.

Ross stopped at the sidewalk. "What?"

"Don't go," she told him. "Please don't go."

Doug

42 hours after Herod Event

Otis called Doug on Monday morning to offer his condolences.

"This is the worst tragedy, Doug. We're all in shock."

"Sorry about your grandkids," Doug said. "How are you holding up?"

"One day at a time. My daughter's a mess. The whole thing is too horrible for words."

"Yeah, it is." Doug didn't want to talk about it anymore. "Well, I appreciate you calling." After a long silence, he added, "Something else on your mind, Otis?"

"Actually, there is. It's kind of hard to say."

"Why don't you just say it."

"Well, I hate to make things worse for you, but I need to ask you to come to work today."

"Go to hell," Doug said, and hung up.

Moments later, the phone rang again. He answered it and said, "Otis, don't make me come down there and beat the living shit out of you."

"Just hear me out for a second."

"I'm not picking up any trash today, you son of a bitch."

"It's not—"

"I'm grieving for my kids!"

"It's the bodies, Doug."

"What?"

"The bodies. Somebody has to pick up all the bodies."

Doug blinked. Then he set his jaw. "No way. It's a job for the mortuaries."

Otis snorted over the line. "Brother, there ain't enough mortuaries in the world to handle this."

"The hospitals then."

"There's *ninety thousand* kids in our county alone who have to be picked up."

64

Doug said nothing. The number rang in his brain like a bell.

He glanced at the door to the garage, where Joan had laid out their kids and wrapped them in plastic. A dead body could be stored for up to five days, he knew. After just a few days, it started to rot, even at very cold temperatures.

Joan had lain in bed trembling in a state of deep shock before emerging to care for their children yesterday afternoon. She'd washed them and dressed them in their church clothes, muttering to herself the whole time. She practically hissed at Doug whenever he came near.

Ninety thousand. This was everybody's tragedy, not just his.

And putting them in the ground with some dignity was the top priority.

He said quietly, "Where are they all going to go?"

"Public land outside of town. They've got digging equipment out there already. More on the way. Temporary internment. Until things get back to normal."

Mass graves. Otis was talking about mass graves. Doug's kids were going to be put into a big hole, and a bulldozer would fill it up. That's how it was done.

Not the millionaires, though. They'd get cemeteries and flowers and all the trimmings.

His kids wouldn't even get a coffin.

"It's a mess," Otis added. "Nobody knows who's in charge. The State, the Feds, the County. Different departments fighting over every little thing. I can't keep track of all the acronyms. Last night, the governor issued an emergency order. We got to bury them."

"And now that's my job. While I'm grieving."

"The governor called out the National Guard to handle most of the lifting. But he issued a call for volunteers and a draft of all essential workers. He wants everybody, Doug. And I mean everybody."

"A draft, huh?" The governor could stick that up his ass.

"We need to do our part to help lay them to rest," Otis pleaded. "This is a national emergency. You see what's going on around you."

"What does the union say about this?"

"We negotiated a special-project labor agreement. You'll get a premium wage."

"Fine, I'll be there in a half hour," Doug told him.

It wasn't about the threat of coercion or the promise of extra money.

He wanted to get out of the house before he slammed his fist through a wall.

The presence of his children haunted this place. Every time he entered a room, he half expected Megan to come flying at him. He kept checking the clock, irritated Nate hadn't returned home yet. Then he'd remember them falling in the snow. Maybe if he returned to work, he could empty his mind, if only for a short while.

He also wanted to see what would likely be the final resting place of his kids. He wanted to put them in the ground himself.

Joan nodded when he told her, watching him pull on a hooded sweatshirt and his old work boots and Lovin' Lansdowne cap. Not in agreement but resignation, as if she'd expected this final indignity. She looked more haggard with each passing minute.

"I called the mortuary and got a recorded message," she said. "They're not taking any more kids. They're all full up."

"There's too many. They can't handle it. We'd have to be rich to afford a mortuary now."

"So you're going to bury our children with all the rest in some mass grave."

"They'll be tagged and mapped, Joanie. We'll know where they are. We can have them taken out at any time and given a proper burial once things get back to normal." Which was a lie, he knew; things would likely never get back to normal. "I'll bring them myself."

"What time?" What she meant was: *How much time do I have to say good-bye?*

He couldn't believe how strong she was.

"I'll put it off as long as I can. As long as you need. Okay?"

"No," Joan said, her voice cracking. "Nothing is okay anymore."

He tried to hug her. She avoided his arms and told him to go.

He'd parked his truck in the driveway. He opened the front door and stepped into the cold. He paused to take a deep breath and get his bearings. Art Foley, his neighbor, stood on his porch smoking his pipe and staring at him. Accusing him with his eyes.

His wife's voice in his head, shouting: *What did you do?*

Doug winced, his face burning. *It wasn't my fault!*

But Foley wasn't actually being accusatory about anything. He was looking at Doug with more like mute pity. The man had no kids himself. He clearly wanted to offer his condolences but was afraid of crossing some line of decorum with his neighbor. There were no rules of etiquette for this; they were all pioneering new territory in grief. Doug acknowledged him with a nod and got into his truck, where he lit a cigarette, feeling like he could chew through metal.

Pity yourself, Foley. We're all victims today. The whole damn human race.

Doug arrived at the Department of Solid Waste Management with little memory of how he'd gotten there. He found the compound crowded with government workers, volunteers, and Army National Guard piling into and out of olive-green trucks. He recognized a few coworkers who'd retired, suddenly called back into service because of the crisis. A local vendor had set up a stand to hand out free coffee, and Doug got a tall one, cream, no sugar.

"Doug!"

He turned and saw Otis huffing toward him waving a handful of papers. Release forms for Doug to sign, it turned out.

"The training session's just starting," Otis told him. "If you hustle, you can get in. Sign these as soon as you can."

He took the forms. "Lots of soldiers here with guns. All to make sure I do what I'm told."

"They're here to help." Otis gripped his shoulder. "You're a tough son of a bitch, brother. You're going to be okay. We're all going to get through this together."

Doug scowled, but he was touched. "Thanks."

The men running the session worked for FEMA. They gave him a bright yellow hazmat suit and told him to put it on. He tried the respirator mask just to see what it was like. It smelled like rubber and ass. They told him he wouldn't need it. He'd be wearing a simple hospital mask in the field.

He sat on a chair in the crowded room. Some of the men were smoking, so he lit a Winston. He drank his coffee and listened.

"Contrary to popular belief, the dead pose little health risk to the living," said the instructor, a nerdy government type. "The bacteria that cause decay in dead tissue aren't dangerous. But you still have to be careful if the child had an infectious disease like HIV or tuberculosis. That's a risk. It's also obviously rare, though."

A man in the back raised his hand. "How do we know when there's a risk?"

"The next of kin was supposed to report any infectious diseases when they registered their child for burial. It's all in your information packets." He checked his watch and turned to another man behind him. "Mike, can we get those passed out?"

Mike distributed the packets to the men, big manila envelopes stuffed with paper. Doug opened his and inspected the contents. Pickup lists and forms. Grief counseling contact lists. Flash cards telling him what he should and should not say. Everything looked hastily photocopied. It was a thrown-together operation.

It had been nearly two full days since the children died, and the clock was ticking. Every day that went by without burial, the bodies of the children continued to fall apart.

Like Otis said, somebody had to pick them up.

An hour later, Doug drove a twenty-four-foot U-Haul truck down Shanks Road. The vehicle had been freshly painted white with a red cross to cover up the company's logos. On the passenger side, Tom Rafferty, a beefy man with an earnest face, leafed through the pickup list. Tom was a volunteer.

"So many," the man said. "All in one day? Are they serious?"

"We'll do them one at a time and see what happens," Doug told him.

He took a swig of coffee while Tom played with the dial of the radio.

The radio murmured: *"If there are any living children in your area, please call the toll-free number at the CDC—"*

"Turn that off," Doug growled.

"We need to stay informed."

"There's nothing to inform," Doug told him. "Nobody knows shit."

Or rather, they already knew everything. Everything worth caring about, anyway. And nothing could change what they knew.

They passed a school, ignoring the playground speed limit. Doug remembered waving as Nate entered his school on his first day of second grade.

Funny how Nate's so strong in some subjects, like math and geography, and weak in others, like English. Joanie thinks a parent-teacher conference would help. She wants to blame the teacher. Nate knows who's to blame. I'd like to lean on him, and Joanie's always at me, telling me to help her out with disciplining the kids, but every time I do it, out comes Mama Bear protecting her cubs. Nate will get the message from me loud and clear one way or another. It can't be all on me. I'll give him a shot, but he's got to step up and take it. He's got to do his part.

"Doug? Doug!"

"What? Was I talking?"

"Man, you were shouting."

"I haven't really slept in days."

"Are you okay now? You freaked me out."

"Peachy." Doug ground his teeth. "Everything's just peachy."

He wished he could have a drink. One little drink. Something to dull the pain.

"You ever do anything like this?" he asked to change the subject.

Tom, startled: "No."

"I mean waste collection. Biological waste in particular."

"No. I'm a volunteer. I just want to help."

"Well, I have experience with this stuff, so I'll take the lead, all right?"

"No problem. Whatever you say."

"Did you lose anybody yesterday?"

"No, sir. I don't have any kids. I didn't even see it. I was out cross-country skiing with my girlfriend when, uh, everything happened. You?"

Doug ignored the question. "You ever seen a dead body before?"

"My uncle died a few years back. There was a wake. My granny, when I was a kid."

"I mean a *real* dead body. One that's been decomposing for two full days."

Tom swallowed hard. "Not really. I mean, we saw a few when we drove back into town, but at a distance."

"What I'm saying is, if you're doing this for the excitement, I can let you off here and find somebody else. No harm, no foul."

"I really want to help."

"What you see today is going to stay with you a long, long time."

Saying this decided an important issue for him. He parked the truck on the street in front of a strip mall and killed the engine.

Doug said, "I have to pick something up. I'll be back in a few minutes."

All the storefronts stood dark and empty except for one. A line of about a hundred people snaked out of it across the parking lot. They hugged themselves to keep warm. A big man with a baseball bat guarded the entrance. When a customer left, he let somebody else in.

Doug didn't have time to stand around. He cut in line at the door. The guy with the bat took one look at his hazmat suit and stepped out of his way.

The door jingled as it closed behind him.

In every aisle of the store, people slammed liquor bottles and six-packs into shopping carts. It was ten in the morning, and half the shelves had already been emptied. They stopped to stare at his suit. They knew what it meant. He ignored them.

He found a bottle of Jim Beam and studied the label. In the old days, he'd been a real hell-raiser. He and Joan started dating just after high school and partied hard almost every night of the week. After they got married, he expected the party to go on forever, but Joan got pregnant with Nate and quit her wild ways. The party was over. The wildcat he'd courted and married turned into a responsible parent and upright citizen. Doug would still go to the bar after work to unwind and shoot the bull with the other san-men. The only problem was he could never have just one. Next thing he knew, he'd wake up in his truck and have to drive straight to work.

Joan made him quit. *Nate needs a real father*, was all the reason she gave him. For him, it was enough. He'd heard once that to quit anything that got ahold of you, you had to give yourself up to a higher power. His kids were it.

Now they were gone. With trembling hands, Doug unscrewed the cap and sniffed. It smelled like old times.

He took a quick sip and gasped. The bourbon was like fire in his throat. Another sip.

Take it slow. Make it last.

Then another. Another. *Just need to get a little numb here.*

It took everything he had not to chug it.

Doug got in line at the register. The proprietor, a man with a beard that sprawled across his big stomach, dropped the bottle into a paper bag and pushed it back across the counter. Doug added a steel hip flask to his purchase while he was at it. He couldn't walk around in broad daylight with a bottle in a bag like some wino.

"No charge for you, friend," the man said.

Doug mumbled his thanks and walked back outside. He couldn't help but feel guilty. He hadn't had a drink in eight years. Not only had he given in to an old vice he'd sworn to Joan he'd never do again, but here he was doing it at ten in the morning. This part wasn't like old times. Drinking used to be for fun. Now it was medicinal.

Head down, he trudged across the parking lot and got back into his truck. He set the bag next to him and took another nip from the bottle before filling the flask. He lit a cigarette and sat there blinking, already feeling a buzz that threatened to morph into a splitting headache.

They're never coming back.

Tom watched him with alarm.

Doug offered the flask. "Snort?"

"Uh, no thanks." The man rolled down his window to let the smoke out.

Doug took a long pull on the bottle, capped it, and put it under his seat. He slipped the flask into the breast pocket of his jacket inside the hazmat suit. He felt flushed and boozy.

"You all right?" said Tom.

Doug started the engine. "Yup."

"You know, you never told me if you lost someone yesterday."

He guided the rig back onto the road. "You're right. I didn't."

They drove in silence. The roads were virtually empty. The whole country had come to a halt, still reeling from the shock of what had happened.

Tom pointed to a blue house up ahead on the right. "This is twelve twenty-four. The Emersons. Two kids, aged six and eight. No infectious diseases."

Doug pulled over and parked. He and Tom left the truck and tied hospital masks over their mouths and noses. They pulled on their gloves. Doug grabbed the clipboard with its forms. Tom went to the back, unfolded the stretcher, and followed him to the front door. Somebody had taped a piece of paper onto it, on which was scrawled: *Take whatever you need.*

Doug knocked and waited. Knocked again. Nobody home. He glanced to his left and saw a young couple staring at him through the window of the house next door. He turned and noticed others gazing at him from their porches.

Tom waved. Nobody waved back.

"Friendly," he said with obvious sarcasm.

"We have a bunch of stops here," Doug said. "These people all have kids."

"Oh. Right."

"To them, we're the Grim Reaper."

72

He tried the door. Unlocked. He opened it, entered the house. And stopped.

The smell of death smacked him with an almost physical force.

Tom joined him and said, "Oh, man."

A boy and girl lay in the middle of the living room floor. Their parents lay on either side of them. The Emersons hugged their kids even in death. Their faces had turned blue.

The mother's eyes were open. She stared at her son's profile.

Tom took a step back. "Do you think Herod's syndrome might be spreading to adults?"

Doug shook his head. "No. They did this to themselves." He pointed to the empty pill bottles on the carpet next to the father's head.

"Holy shit," Tom said again. "That's nuts."

"It might be the sanest thing I've ever seen somebody do," Doug said.

Tom glanced at him but said nothing.

Doug couldn't shake the feeling these people had known something he didn't, had a higher level of courage he lacked. *They won't be needing any grief counseling here*, he thought. The Emersons had dealt with their grief head-on.

He sighed. "Rest in peace." To Tom, he added, "Let's go in the kitchen and get the paperwork done. Then we'll move the bodies."

They had a lot more houses to visit before they finished.

David

47 hours after Herod Event

David watched CNN in his living room with the volume turned down while talking to Ben Glass on his cell phone, getting bad news from both.

Children were dying in Asia. By yesterday morning, the phenomenon the news channels were calling Herod's syndrome had jumped the Atlantic and continued its eastward creep. One by one, cities exploded in panic and violence. Millions migrated east in anything that moved, trying to stay ahead of its advance.

Everywhere the disease spread, the children died. The story was always the same. The children complained of headaches, strange burning smells, parts of their bodies going numb. Many became confused and uttered cryptic statements that later would haunt parents searching for meaning in the deaths.

The math was simple. If you hadn't yet reached puberty, you died. In Michigan alone, the disease had claimed the lives of one and a half million children, including the twelve young patients in David's recovering practice. Fifty million in all of America, or one out of six people.

A talking head on CNN said that, at its current rate of spread, Herod's syndrome would circle the globe in about thirty-six hours. The last children would die tomorrow night after it swept across the Pacific.

At the bottom of the screen, the caption read, HEROD'S NEARS DELHI.

Two billion, or about one out of four people, throughout the world.

A world that soon would no longer need pediatricians like David.

The constant speed of transmission suggested it wasn't an ordinary disease. It was like an invisible wall that spanned the globe from pole to pole, rapidly moving east. The children appeared to already have been infected; for some reason, whatever was inside them was now becoming activated. Even children isolated in atmospheric chambers died.

There was no escape, no cure. Just the certainty of death. It wasn't only the world's single greatest tragedy but its biggest medical mystery.

"It's a madhouse here," Ben was saying. "They're trucking in bodies faster than we can process them. The freezers are overflowing. I've got sixty people performing autopsies. Coroners, retirees, students, anyone I can get to show up. We've got twenty data-entry operators printing death certificates around the clock."

David tuned the television out of his consciousness and focused on his friend's words. Forget the mourning, the mass vigils, the endless praying to God to spare the remaining children. What Ben was doing, he believed, was the most important thing being done.

Right now, medical examiners across the country were autopsying thousands of bodies, collecting tissues and fluids, and shipping them to the Centers for Disease Control in Atlanta for analysis. In Michigan, the medical examiner didn't need permission from next of kin. It was unlikely their efforts could save any of the children still alive in the Far East. But they could save the next generation.

David itched to get in on the action. He wanted to help. He'd called the parents of his patients to offer whatever comfort he could, but they no longer needed his services. He was tired of sitting around with nothing to do but watch the news.

"Do you know what you're looking for yet?" he asked Ben.

"Everything is on the table. Bacterium, virus, parasite, environmental toxins, even nanotechnology. Whatever it is, it's affecting the blood. Changing it into something else."

"Something like a runaway strain of staph A?" *Staphylococcus aureus* bacteria lived in the nasal cavity of one-third of all people and had an appetite for human blood—hemoglobin, specifically. It was the origin of the MRSA superbug.

"We don't know. Figuring this out is going to take a long time. All we can do now is keep feeding everything we have up to CDC. Things are frantic over there. They're handing down new guidelines and protocols on the hour."

"Does this thing even have a name?"

"Everyone's still unofficially calling it Herod's syndrome, like on the news," said Ben. Herod being the Israelite monarch who slaughtered the firstborn of Bethlehem after the wise men, following a star, rather unwisely told him a king had been born there. "You have to admit, it's catchy."

David grunted. CNN was now showing footage of massive crowds filling the streets outside a hospital in Delhi. Most of the people were holding crying children. Buildings smoked in the background, the result of fires set during the chaos. Herod's hadn't yet struck there, but it was coming fast.

A wild-eyed young man waved his arms at the camera. Behind him, a crying woman held a little girl.

"Hamari jaan chor do! Dafa ho jao!"

David didn't need a translation. The man wanted help, dignity. Anything but the camera's passive yet invasive eye.

"David, are you there? Hello?"

A massive roar of grief and rage washed over the crowd. One after another, the children went limp in their parents' arms. The father who'd shouted at the camera howled and tore at his clothes while his wife screamed.

David had no choice but to watch. No matter how many times he'd seen scenes like this in how many cities over the past few hours, the horror transfixed him.

The father pulled a handgun from his pants and fired it at the camera. David cringed at the flash. The camera's eye lurched, offering a final glimpse of the distraught man turning the gun on himself before it ripped to black.

David gasped. "God, I can't take this anymore."

"You all right?"

David turned off the TV. "Yes." He took a deep breath. "Yes, I'm fine. You were saying?"

"All right, let me get to the point. I'm losing my mind, David. I need you here."

"To do what?"

"Anything. Everything."

"I'm not licensed for your line of work." Worse, David wondered if he could handle seeing all the bodies. It'd been horrible enough watching the children die. It might be even worse to see them stacked like wood in some hospital.

"You think that's an issue right now? We're handing out licenses to *students*, for crying out loud. But if you don't want to do any wet work, I can use you on the admin side helping me run this three-ring circus. I'm barely keeping the office functioning. Just attending all the meetings is a full-time job. I need someone I can trust at my side. Just name your price."

"Well . . ."

"Well what? Will you help me?"

"All right," David said. "I will."

"Thank God. When are you coming down?"

"Hang on." David cupped his hand over the phone and shouted for Nadine. She'd left early this morning to visit Caroline, an old friend whose daughter Kimberly had fallen to Herod's.

No answer. The house was still empty.

Over breakfast, he'd shared his idea that the most patriotic thing people could do was get started producing the next generation and thereby ensure humanity had a future. Who could argue with this? Nadine, apparently. She told him the future didn't matter; the human race wasn't ready to have a future until it mourned, and that could take years. The world had become a living nightmare. How could David be so rational about it?

We need to pick up the pieces, he replied.

There are no pieces, she threw back at him.

The argument had exposed the break in their relationship that had been there, right in front of them, unseen but felt, for months.

They'd become strangers. She'd left the house soon afterward and hadn't yet returned.

"I'll be there soon," he told Ben.

After he hung up, the phone rang again almost immediately. He snatched it up, hoping it was Nadine.

Shannon Donegal, crying.

"The baby," she said. "He stopped moving. I'm having cramps. I'm really scared."

She couldn't reach her obstetrician, who'd lost two children himself to Herod's. Everything was closed. She needed help. The hospital was a madhouse. She had no idea where else to turn.

David told her to meet him at his office in thirty minutes.

He realized something else: *No births are being reported on the news.*

Every minute, two hundred fifty babies were born. More than half a million around the world since Herod's struck, he estimated. Surely, showing new births would be a great story, providing hope for the future in the midst of so much tragedy.

Nothing.

Could they all be stillbirths? Are they all dying as soon as they leave the womb?

The implications were horrifying.

When he arrived at his office, he found Shannon and a middle-aged man waiting for him in the parking lot.

He got out of his car. "How are you, Shannon?"

"Can we go inside?"

She looked like a different person. The last time he'd seen her, she'd glowed with robust health. Now her eyes appeared vacant and sunken, her hair and clothes unkempt.

She's not just worried. She knows.

The man introduced himself as Charlie, Shannon's dad. They shook hands. David led them inside and turned on the lights.

"We appreciate you seeing us on such short notice, doc," Charlie told him.

"Check the baby," Shannon said. "Please. Forget everything else. Just check the baby."

David and Charlie helped her onto the examination table. David exposed her belly and prepared a handheld Doppler.

"Somebody told me, if I tweak my nipples, they're supposed to hurt," she told him. "I also read online, if you drink some Sprite and lie down for a bit, the baby should kick a little. I'm not feeling anything. Just these cramps."

"Try to relax for me, okay, Shannon?"

"Okay," she said in a helpless voice that broke his heart.

"Good. Now let's find that heartbeat."

David placed the microphone against her belly and listened. The Doppler whooshed rapidly, confusing him. It took him several moments to realize he was hearing only Shannon's heart, beating so fast he'd mistook it for the baby's.

"What's happening?" she asked, her voice shrill.

"Please don't talk."

Nothing. *Damn it.* He gave up.

"I'm sorry, Shannon, I can't find a heartbeat."

"Oh God," she said, crying freely now. "I knew it."

Charlie gripped his daughter's hand. "Are you sure about this, doc?"

"Not a hundred percent," David told him. "I'm not an obstetrician. Obstetricians have fetal stethoscopes and a trained ear. They have ultrasound imaging equipment. I just don't have the equipment you need here. The Doppler I'm using might very well be unreliable."

Shannon pressed her palms against her leaking eyes. "How? How did this happen?"

"*If* it happened—"

"Just tell me."

"Possible causes include placental abruption, bacterial infection, birth defect—"

"And Herod's, right?" Charlie said.

David winced. "And Herod's. That's correct."

If Herod's syndrome is killing all the babies in their wombs, then all of us are infected. The children die, but we're all carriers.

What about the next generation? Will death occur shortly after conception, resulting in spontaneous abortion?

If so, this is truly the end.

Unless we find a cure, the human race just went extinct.

"See, it's not your fault, honey," Charlie told Shannon, and turned to David. "Doc? What's the next step here? What do we do?"

"Shannon should get further testing."

"Understood. But what if . . . ?"

79

"What if he's dead?" asked Shannon.

David considered his words. "If—and I can't stress that word enough, Shannon, *if*—the pregnancy has terminated, you would have several options for delivery."

He hesitated. She appeared stricken by what he'd said.

"Tell me," she breathed.

"Maybe now is not the time—"

"Tell me, doctor."

"Commonly, labor will begin on its own within the next one or two weeks. If that doesn't happen, it could be induced."

"Will I get to see and hold him?"

"Yes, if that's what you want."

In fact, as heartbreaking as it sounded, studies showed it reduced the risk of depression.

How's this for depressing? In a hundred years, there won't be any people left.

"The sooner the better," he muttered.

"Why's that?" Charlie asked. "Is Shannon in some sort of danger?"

"Nothing," said David. "It's not important."

"You meant she should deliver as soon as possible. Wasn't that what you meant?"

"Yes."

"Why?"

David knew he shouldn't have said anything. What could he tell the man? The sooner the medical examiner autopsied the fetus, the more information the CDC would have in its fight against Herod's? Would this mean anything to these people, who were absorbed in their own grief?

"Mr. Donegal, if Herod's did in fact take your grandson's life, it's very possible that the same thing is happening everywhere. We don't know whether what caused Herod's is permanent or not. That might mean no more births. Ever."

Charlie paled. "Goddamn, doc."

"The more the CDC has to work with, the more of a chance we

have to prevent the same thing from happening to future children. Understand?"

Shannon sat up and closed her coat around her belly. "So you want me to push Liam out and hand him over so you can chop him up?"

Charlie looked from David to Shannon with an anxious expression.

"No, Shannon," said David. "It's about what you want. That's the most important thing."

"But *you* want to chop him up."

"The autopsy would be minimally invasive. A few tissue samples. But again, it's your choice. I didn't mean to make you uncomfortable. Please forget I said anything."

"I just found out Liam is gone," she told him. "I thought he was safe." Her voice rose to a high-pitched scream. "*I thought it'd happened to everybody but me!*"

Shannon Donegal was facing one of the most horrific things that could happen to a human being, yet David found that he just couldn't focus on it properly. All he could think about was the big picture.

All the babies are gone, and it's the end.

David closed his eyes. He felt dizzy. "I'll make some calls to help get you an appointment with an obstetrician."

"Fuck you. And you don't talk to me about my son anymore, you fucking *vampire*."

Joan

49 hours after Herod Event

Joan wanted the wake to be perfect.

The mortuaries wouldn't take her children. The only choice you had, when you registered the deaths online, was mass burial or cremation. The website had crashed three times before she was able to register both her kids. She chose burial.

The government was going to put them in a mass grave. There was one other alternative, of course, and that was to bury them herself in her backyard. The penalties for doing this didn't scare her. It just didn't seem right somehow. Nate would want to be with other kids. And Doug had said they would be told where their children were buried, so she could visit and lay flowers whenever she wanted.

That didn't mean they would depart their home without dignity. She intended to say good-bye with love and respect. Tomorrow, she and Doug would host a wake.

The preparations kept her busy. There was a lot to do and not a lot of time. That was good. If she stopped, if she had nothing to do, she might have to deal with her grief directly. Grief that could eat her alive. She wasn't sure she was strong enough to handle that yet.

All morning, she'd rolled up her sleeves and given the house a thorough cleaning. She didn't touch the kids' rooms. She just closed the doors and left them alone. In every other living space, though, she'd erased all evidence of their existence. She couldn't cope with what she was feeling if she had to wash her face every night before bed while staring at Megan's little pink Dora the Explorer toothbrush.

By midafternoon, she finished getting the house into shape. She'd called her guests, found appropriate music from her CD collection to play during the service, and dug up some candles. Now she needed to buy some refreshments to serve everybody. She hoped she could get Pastor Gary to visit and say a few words.

First stop was Major's kennel to fill his bowls. Joan knelt next to the dog while he ate and stroked the fur on his back. Major glanced at the back door of the house.

"Are you looking for Nate?"

The dog looked up at her with hope.

"Nate's not coming today." She rested her cheek against his warm back and listened to his steady heartbeat. "When I get home, would you like to come inside for a bit and see how you like it? Do you want to be an inside dog? Would you like that, Major?"

The dog nudged the bowl along the wood floor with his sloppy eating. Joan closed her eyes and smiled for the first time in days. It didn't last.

She walked out in front of the house, where she found her Dodge Durango. She'd parked it on the street to avoid disturbing the children in the garage. She scraped the ice off the windshield, got in, and started her errands. The streets were eerily deserted. The playgrounds empty. Everywhere she went, nobody had their Christmas lights on. It struck her that in most of the world, there wasn't a single human being who believed in Santa Claus.

Her local supermarket was open. Joan bought as many items on her list as she could find. Many shelves had been emptied. The pharmacy had run out of sleeping pills. Even the allergy and cold medicines had been cleaned out. Teenagers and old men ran the cash registers. The cheerful Muzak made her want to scream.

She packed her groceries into her car and drove off.

The next stop was the church. Her heart fluttered as St. Andrew's came into view and she heard its bell calling the faithful. She felt both drawn and repulsed by the prospect of going inside to find Pastor Gary. She was a churchgoing woman, and the familiar comforts of her religion sounded good right about now. But she couldn't reconcile the idea of a loving God with what had happened. It was one thing to strike down a family member before his or her time and leave it to the survivors to find meaning in it. It was another to completely cull the world's children.

The Lord worked in mysterious ways, but this time it looked like plain old genocide.

Maybe she would find some meaning to all this inside. *Why did this happen?* she wondered. *Who should we blame? Ourselves? Terrorists? Global warming, pollution?*

God?

And if it was God, why? What are we supposed to learn? If God is teaching a lesson, what could it possibly be?

Saint Andrew's appeared to be packed. The church parking lot had filled to capacity and then some, and Joan was forced to park several blocks away. She left the car and followed other people streaming toward the church. Most wore black; the entire world was in mourning. The bell tolled again.

Joan hesitated at the entrance. She'd never seen it so crowded. The pews had filled. A long procession of mourners waited their turn in the aisle to place candles, flowers, toys, and photos at the altar. The organist played a neutral tune, something to fill the air so you couldn't hear the sobbing. Otherwise, there was no structure to the ceremony, no clergy providing comfort to the afflicted. The atmosphere was thick with tension, grief, and anger. Hysteria and madness channeled into the rituals of coping with death. She pictured somebody pushing somebody else, and that would be the only thing necessary to turn the room into a violent bloodbath.

She recognized members of the congregation, some neighbors, a few friends. The simple act of breathing seemed to demand every bit of energy they had. She saw Coral and resisted an impulse to offer some comfort, maybe even get some herself. She didn't have the energy. Moments later, her friend blurred into the background with the rest.

We're all alone now. Look at us. Packed in here like sardines, but we might as well be miles away from each other.

One of the mourners sent up a keening wail. Then others joined in, the urge to scream washing over the congregation like a wave, filling the enormous space with the heartrending sound of their grief—

Get out of here NOW.

Joan rushed out the doors and stopped on the church steps, taking deep breaths. She'd left just in time. She'd been about to join in. It would feel so good to lose control, but once she started, she wasn't sure she'd be able to stop.

In any case, she'd learned something valuable. There were no answers to be found in there. Just unyielding horror. Emptiness.

A bearded man in a long black coat stood smoking near the chain-link fence at the edge of the congested parking lot. She passed him on the way back to her car.

"Pastor Gary?"

The man stared at her. "Hello, Joan."

"I didn't know you were a smoker."

"I quit when Jane was born," he said. He took another drag.

"I'm very sorry for your loss."

"We lost them all. All three."

"Nate and Megan are gone as well."

"I'm sorry too."

"I was at a movie when it happened," Joan confessed.

"And you feel guilty about that?"

She bit her lip and nodded.

"Let me tell you something. It might give you some perspective."

"Please do." She listened closely.

"My youngest died on the stairs. He was always getting himself hurt, and I found him lying there in this little"—his voice cracked—"this little tangle of arms and legs. The first thing I felt was irritation. The first thing I actually thought was, *What did you do to yourself now?*" He glared at Joan, his eyes wet and fierce. "What kind of father am I to think that? To feel that?"

She recoiled. "That's awful."

"*That's* guilt. What you feel is something else."

"I am so sorry."

"We're all sorry, I guess. Did you come for a service? We're not doing anything formal today, as you probably saw. People are free to use the church for whatever they need."

"No, I came to see you." Joan thought her request seemed petty now. The man had the loss of his own children to cope with. "We're taking Nate and Megan to the burial ground tomorrow night, and Doug and I will be hosting a wake at our home. I was wondering if you might come over and say a few words. I hope you don't mind me asking."

Pastor Gary dropped his cigarette and stepped on it. "I don't think I can do that."

"It's all right. I figured you'd be too busy."

"I'm not busy at all. I just don't want to do it. I really don't want to do anything, to be honest."

"Oh," said Joan, surprised.

He lit another cigarette and coughed. "Please don't take it the wrong way. I always liked you. I mean, you came to church every Sunday to listen to my sermons. What a different world it was only a few days ago, right? There was so much to believe in. We had no idea. No idea at all."

Joan nodded. The truth was she didn't know which was more like a dream, the past or present.

"When you get home, you should look up the Kübler-Ross stages of grief," he told her. "That's what I was trained to use as a pastor to provide comfort. I could tell you a little about it if you want."

"Please. I'd like to hear it."

"When you're ready to process what actually happened, you will likely try to deny your own suffering. Understand? You might decide to get mad about it and blame yourself or others. You may try to bargain with God, offer blood sacrifices and burnt offerings or whatever. But God created death as well as life and will deny your request. You may become depressed, which is of course the active process of grieving, and that's good, but grieving isn't the goal. Accepting your loss is. That's the final stage. All the other responses are normal as long as they lead you to acceptance." He shrugged. "That's what I used to say to people in the congregation when they lost a loved one, Joan. I hope it will help you and Doug."

It was like getting a swimming lesson from a drowning man. The loss of a child was bad enough for any single person to bear, Joan knew. But to know it had happened to everybody was even worse. There was nobody who could comfort you. Everywhere you looked, you saw your own pain reflected in somebody else's face.

"I think what I really want to know is *why* this happened."

"You mean why God allowed this to happen. And you think I might know. Honestly, I was hoping maybe you could tell me. It's all I'm thinking about. Any ideas?"

"No, not really," said Joan.

"We all just want to understand. As human beings, we need to come to terms with it. The thing we have to acknowledge is not all miracles are good. Some miracles are evil. God allowed His own son to die, but it was for a reason. It was a sacrifice. Why did He allow our children to die? Maybe we were wicked and God wanted to punish us. But what did we do that was so bad? Seriously, why did God feel He had to come down and do just about the worst thing He could do?"

Joan felt compelled to answer, as the man was now glaring at her. "I don't know, Pastor."

"Remember how the Egyptians wouldn't give up the Jews?"

"You mean, in the Book of Exodus?"

"Exactly. God inflicted nine plagues on the Egyptians. He turned their water into blood, and still they wouldn't release the Hebrews. He threw hail and darkness and wild animals at them, and still they said no. Then God did a simple thing. He killed their firstborn children. The next day, they let the Jews go." He snapped his fingers. "Just like that."

"So if we did something wrong—if this is some form of punishment—how do we get right with God again?"

Pastor Gary burst out laughing so hard that Joan took a step back. "I don't know. I really don't. Maybe next time, God will come down here and tell us what He wants instead of expecting us to guess, and murdering our kids when we've guessed wrong."

Joan touched her face as if he'd slapped her.

"An even bigger question has been bugging me, Joan. The question is: Why did I bother? I thought, because we worshipped Him, that He liked us. But now, after witnessing all this? Call it blasphemy, but I'm starting to think He never really liked us. So I wonder why we wasted our time. I wonder why I bothered. My whole life is a waste."

"I don't know what to tell you," she told him, close to tears.

"Of course you don't know. Neither do I. We'll just have to keep on guessing." He dropped his cigarette into the slush at his feet and lit another. "Or stop trying altogether."

Doug

50 hours after Herod Event

Doug drove the big U-Haul truck off the highway and onto the dirt road that led to the children's burial ground.

The soldiers at the checkpoint waved him through. The truck rumbled over the rough ground. Inside, sixteen bodies lay cocooned in black bags.

Nine stops today. Nine homes with screaming mothers and angry fathers looking for somebody to blame. They'd decided to give up for the day after somebody took a potshot at them with a rifle from a bedroom window.

Doug nipped at his flask and shook it. Almost time for a refill. "We're just about done here. You coming back tomorrow?"

"I don't know," said Tom. "Jesus, I really don't."

Doug nodded. Nothing more needed to be said.

He continued driving at high speed, careless of the risk. The truck topped a rise and the fields beyond spilled into view. Big yellow construction machines performed an awkward ballet across the scarred landscape, followed by drifting clouds of dust.

"It's huge," said Tom, moved at the sight.

"They've been at it since last night."

"Oh, Christ. Look, Doug."

The government had run out of body bags. Hundreds of bodies lay in neat rows on the frozen ground, covered with a dusting of quicklime.

Tom wiped his eyes. "It's horrible. It's like the end of the world."

The end of the world. Doug remembered how he used to worry about that. Electromagnetic pulse, peak oil, asteroids, superflu, you name it. He kept emergency stocks of food and water in his basement just in case his family had to live off the grid for a while.

They drove into the works. Construction signs flashed in the distance. Bulldozers fitted with single-shank rippers tore into the frozen, compacted soil. Excavators lurched in their wake and dug trenches five feet deep and three hundred feet long. Army five-tons, U-Hauls, refrigerated trucks, and pickups rolled along with little puffs of exhaust, stopping to allow men in hazmat suits to jump off and unload body bags into the trenches. At each finished trench, bulldozers pushed hills of earth to cover the dead.

He drove toward a bustling village of trailers and vehicles. Doug pulled up next to several men in orange vests and hard hats warming their hands over a fire burning in a metal drum and rolled down his window.

"Who's in charge here?" he called.

The men looked at each other and shrugged.

"I've got a full load," he said. "Where do you want them?"

"Over there's fine," one of the men said, pointing vaguely. "You've got to register the load first."

Doug turned to Tom. "Back in a minute."

He used to worry about taxes and making ends meet.

He got out and waited in line at the door of a trailer. Inside, the bald giant behind the desk checked the ZIP codes in his pickup area and told him he was in the wrong place. In the next trailer, a teenage girl typed the information on his forms into a computer set up next to an overflowing ashtray. Doug lit a cigarette but quickly put it out; it felt hot and stuffy in the overheated space. The girl cursed as her computer froze. Behind him, the line of impatient drivers continued to stack up.

The general lack of competence in this massive, thrown-together operation didn't inspire confidence that the children were being properly mapped for later retrieval. He'd have to remember himself where he'd put Nate and Megan.

Cold air filled his lungs as he left. He stumbled on the steps.

I'm wasted, he thought.

Which was strange, because he didn't feel drunk at all.

He used to worry about somebody breaking into his house when he wasn't home.

He found Tom sleeping when he got back, curled into a ball against the door, practically sucking his thumb. Doug honked the horn to wake him up.

"Shit," said Tom, wiping drool from his cheek. "I'm still here."

Doug drove into the works. A man waved at him with a pair of glow sticks and pointed at another man in the distance, who directed him toward a freshly dug trench. Cold wind blasted him when he opened the door.

Two workers were waiting for them there, looking dirty and cold to the bone. Jack, a fiftysomething with leathery skin and a slim, athletic build, and Mitch, an overgrown teenager with a mean face.

Doug used to worry the government was going to take his guns.

"We'll unload the truck and hand off the bags to you guys on the ground," said Jack. He squinted at Tom. "You're looking a little pale, brother. You all right?"

"I just hadn't expected so many."

"We're getting forty thousand at this site alone. You'll get used to it."

"No, he won't," Doug growled.

Jack shrugged. Doug handed him his flask, and he and Mitch each took a long pull.

"Wish I'd thought to bring something," said Mitch.

"When you're old enough to drink, you can," Jack told him.

"I'm not a kid. Or didn't you hear? All the kids are dead."

The men laid out the bodies in a neat row along the lip of the trench. Jack announced a break while they waited for the clergy to come and read over the dead. He produced a tin of Red Man, and he and Mitch each put a plug in their cheeks. They stomped their feet to keep warm. Doug lit a cigarette and stared at the bodies in the bags.

Tomorrow night, he would bring his own children here. After the wake that Joan was putting together. He would lay them in a trench just like this one, and the bulldozer would come and blanket them with cold earth.

Despite the warmth of the bourbon in his blood, he shivered.

He used to worry about losing his job because of side-loaders.

"What do you do for a living, Tom?" he asked to pass the time.

Tom started. "What?"

"I asked what you do for a living."

"I work in the Office of Economic Development. We help corporations come and do business in the county—site selection, permitting, tax incentives, and so on."

"Economist, huh?" Jack asked him. "What do you think is going to happen with the economy? With the children being taken and all that?"

"Well, I'm not a real economist, but I did study economics and political science in college."

Mitch smirked and spat tobacco juice onto the ground. "College, huh?"

Tom ignored him. "We've got serious problems ahead. Think about all the industries serving kids. Toys, books, TV networks. Movies, breakfast cereal, clothes, car seats. Schools, teachers, pediatricians— jeez, the list goes on and on. They're all basically out of business. We're talking hundreds of billions of dollars, a big chunk of the GDP right there. There's going to be a massive recession."

Jack looked humbled. "I guess we're in for a bit more trouble then."

The clergymen arrived in their orange safety jackets and respirator masks. Covered in dirt, they stood in a row over the line of body bags and muttered the words that consecrated the burial according to their different faiths. Trying to make this terrible place holy.

Tom went on as he warmed to his subject. "That's not even the half of it. There's going to be at least a twelve-year gap in student enrollment in all schools and colleges, in workers contributing to Social Security, in new people entering the workforce. Think about how many geniuses we lost when Herod's struck. Kids who would have grown up to cure cancer or make a better lightbulb."

The clergymen left. Doug nudged him with his elbow, and they hopped into the trench.

Doug used to worry about the economy.

"Shit," said Jack, shaking his head. "Any advice?"

Tom shrugged. "Buy stock in liquor companies."

"Very inspiring," Mitch said as he and Jack picked up and lowered the first body. "They should have you speak at the vigil tomorrow night."

Nobody laughed.

"What do you think, partner?" Jack asked Doug.

"It don't matter what I think," he answered. He laid the first body onto the frozen ground. "The world's gone to shit. It can't get any worse in my book."

Tom snorted. "It can get *a lot* worse—"

"Yeah?"

"Well, yeah, I mean—"

"Look at where I am, Tom. Look what I'm doing. I lost both my kids. How much worse could it possibly get for me? What else can be done to me that hasn't already been done?"

Tom shut up, looking paler than ever. Doug accepted the next body and laid it to rest.

He used to worry about whether his kids would go to college.

A gunshot rang out across the frozen field. Doug peered over the top and saw men running toward the next trench over.

"What happened?" said Tom.

"My guess is somebody wanted to be buried with his kids," Doug told him.

He used to worry about whether his children were safe.

"Holy shit," said Mitch.

"Damn," said Jack. "I guess this sort of proves your point, Doug. Don't it?"

He didn't answer. He wasn't listening. He took off his gloves, unscrewed the cap of his flask, and tilted his head back to take a long burning swallow.

For the first time in days, he smiled. "Here's to you, guy."

Doug didn't have anything to worry about anymore.

FOUR

Joan

76 hours after Herod Event

The wake began at six o'clock.

Nate and Megan lay on a table in the living room in their Sunday best. Their slack faces glowed pale in the light from the fireplace. Major paced and whined under the table until Doug put him back in his kennel.

Joan had arranged a series of photos at their feet. Megan prancing in a princess costume. Nate after a game of shinny, grinning and flushed. Megan as a baby, giving Doug a toothless smile. Nate asleep in his crib. A smiling Joan holding both kids on her lap on Christmas morning. So much had already happened in their short lives, so much had been captured in memory and in pictures, and Joan wanted to share as much of it as possible.

She'd worked hard and now took pleasure in how everything looked. The only thing out of place was the Christmas tree, which stood near the front window with its lights off. She hadn't had the heart to take it down.

Her parents had come, as had her brother, Jake, and his wife, Sylvie. Aunts and uncles and cousins. Joan offered sandwiches and made sure everybody's drinks stayed filled. She felt her nerves bleeding out. This was it.

Tonight, she would mark her children's passing and later join the rest of Lansdowne at the vigil while Doug did his part and put them in the ground. Tomorrow, she'd have to begin to really process what had happened. The prospect terrified her.

She poured herself a gin and tonic and sipped it. She found it comforting to have her own flesh and blood in the room. Dad had Doug pinned by the fireplace. Doug hadn't shaved, but he'd put on a black suit and tie with a clean white collared shirt. He slouched and swayed on his feet. He'd been drinking. She should have been furious but found she didn't really care.

She approached just in time to prevent a scene.

"They're in a better place now," Dad was saying.

Doug bristled. "Oh, you think so?"

She linked her arm in her husband's and guided him toward the other side of the room. She knew he didn't like the house being so crowded. He wanted everybody to get the hell out as soon as possible.

He said, "Your asshole dad thinks Nate and Megan are happier not being here."

"Let it go," she whispered. She glanced at him and saw a man in deep emotional pain. In the coming days, she was going to have to decide whether or not she still loved him.

"Old Bob thinks they're better off dead."

"Stop it."

"He never thought I was good enough for you and the kids anyway, and you know it."

"He wasn't talking about you. He was trying to be supportive."

"You call that supportive? Running me down like that?"

"This is why you shouldn't drink. Always getting into fights."

"Don't you start on me too," he growled.

Joan stepped away from him and called for everybody's attention.

"Thank you for coming tonight to pay your respects to Nate and Megan. I want you to know that Doug and I are taking great comfort from you being here. Now we're going to have Sylvie start things off with a reading."

Maybe Pastor Gary was right. Maybe God was a son of a bitch. Vindictive enough to kill the children, or callous enough to let them die. Joan wanted a Bible reading anyway. If there was a supreme being and an afterlife, she wanted her children to arrive right with God. They were not always good, but they were always pure. They were innocent.

"This is from the Book of Mark, chapter ten, verses thirteen and fourteen," said Sylvie, reading: "'One day some parents brought their children to Jesus so he could touch and bless them. But the disciples scolded the parents for bothering him. When Jesus saw what was happening, he was angry with his disciples. He said to them, "Let the children come to me. Don't stop them! For the Kingdom of God belongs to those who are like these children."'"

Joan remembered reading the same verses in the King James Bible and had admired the archaic language. *Suffer the little children*, it had read. Don't stop them. Let them go to Jesus.

She tried to picture Megan sitting on Jesus' lap right now up in Heaven. Knowing her little girl, she was telling him what she wanted for Christmas. She smiled at the image.

Here they are, God. Meet Nate, age eight, who loves hockey and NASCAR. Meet Megan, age four and a half, who loves to play dress-up in princess costumes and lick the mixing bowl after baking with her mommy. You gave them life, and then you let them die for no good reason.

"Amen," said Sylvie, closing the book.

"Amen," the crowd muttered.

"Lord, we give you our littlest angels. Too sweet for this earth. Too soon to leave it."

Joan gave Sylvie a long hug. She then told a story about Nate; after his first day of first grade, she'd asked him what he'd learned. *Not enough, I guess*, he'd answered, just like the old joke: *They said we all have to come back tomorrow.* The stories were about small things, and none very funny, but everybody listened, and laughed, and told their own. For just a short while, Joan felt like her kids were still alive.

Yet she knew she wasn't doing them justice. The right words failed her. Her family knew Nate and Megan from visits. Nobody knew her kids as well as she did, not even Doug.

She wanted to tell them all about the real Nate, how he was always on the go, rushing breathless from one thing to the next, inquisitive and always up for anything. Nate wanted to be a doctor and loved geography. The world fascinated him. He never seemed to feel fear.

She wanted to reveal the real Megan, the girl who lived in a fantasy world where magic and fairies were real, who slept hugging a stuffed animal under each arm and dreamed of hearts and kisses. Megan had always surprised her with how well she could articulate her feelings. She already knew the words to her favorite songs and liked to invent new lyrics. She had empathy for every living thing and mourned the passing of birds and ants. She wore all her feelings, too big for such a small girl, on her sleeves.

They lived in Joan's head now, but she didn't trust herself to keep them alive that way. She wanted to share the burden.

"What about you, Doug?" Jake called out.

Doug stared at the liquor in his glass for a moment. "I'm just listening."

"I was hoping you would say a few words."

He meant it. While Joan's father and Doug had little love for each other, Jake always looked up to Doug as a hardworking family man.

The room quieted as Doug considered his words. Joan watched him.

She said, "Doug feels—"

"They were good kids," he said.

Everybody waited, expecting more.

"They know how I feel about them. It's time to say our final good-byes, Joanie."

The room stayed quiet. Whatever joy they had accomplished through memory, Doug had drained it with a simple reminder of reality.

"Not yet," she whispered.

Doug stood over Nate and Megan. Joan joined him. They stared at their children for a long time.

He scooped Megan into his arms. "Come on, princess."

Joan lightly kissed the top of her head.

"Good night, Meggie."

He took her little girl outside to the truck, where he put her in a body bag.

Joan clutched Nate's hand and kissed it.

"Send me a sign you're okay," she whispered. "I just want to know you're safe."

She didn't want to say good-bye.

Doug returned. The mourners parted for him.

"Come on, sport."

Joan watched in horror as he picked up their son. Doug stared at her hand, still holding on to Nate's smaller hand. She let go.

"Good night, sweet boy," she said, kissing the top of his head.

"I'll take good care of them," Doug told her.

"Don't drop him."

He scowled. "What did you say?"

She took a step back. She saw cold rage in his eyes. He'd never hit her once during nine years of marriage, but she'd seen what he could do to a man with his fists. She knew that right now, she was well within that violent territory that was her husband's emotional state.

"Nothing," she said quietly, appalled that she'd blurted out something so cruel. She had no idea why she'd said it.

"I'll see you at the park."

Tonight, the entire nation would hold a vigil as Herod's syndrome completed its projected sweep of the globe. They would bring candles to public places and mourn. Lansdowne's was being held at Union Park. The skating rink was there, where her kids had died while she'd been seeing a movie. Where they'd died while Doug could only watch.

She'd had them for three days, but now they were leaving for good.

All she had left were her family and Doug, and she felt a sudden burning desire to see them all go away. Any comfort she'd gained tonight was leaving the house with her children.

Doug paused in front of her father. "Time to get my boy to that better place."

Bob looked back at him wearing a stricken expression. Somebody gasped. Joan didn't care. As Doug walked out the door with her son, she fell to her knees and watched, keeping all her screams deep inside. She knew she'd never see Nate again.

The horror of having her children here was ending. She was already missing it.

Without the horror, she had nothing.

Doug

78 hours after Herod Event

Cody's Bar hadn't changed in years.

It was still a honky-tonk beer joint with loud music belting out of a jukebox, broken peanut shells coating the floor, and plenty of red neon. And there was Cody himself, wiping the countertop in a sleeveless black Rolling Stones T-shirt, arms knotted with muscle, now in his early fifties with flecks of gray in his flaring sideburns and a growing beer gut.

Men ringed the bar nursing beers and smoking. They stared at nothing with haunted faces. Doug knew right away they were fathers in mourning. A bunch of rowdy teenagers sat at the wood tables around the empty stage. He stared at them and wondered just what the hell there was to laugh about.

"Hey, look what the cat dragged in," said Cody, extending his hand.

They shook. Cody's hand was dry and rough, like his own.

"Been a while," Doug said.

"Sure has, motherfucker. Sure has. Been a *long*, long time." He drew a mug of draft and dropped it on the counter, where it stood foaming. "What do you say? Shall I make it a doubleheader?"

"You read my mind."

Cody tapped his forehead. "Bourbon, if I'm not mistaken."

"You have the memory of an elephant." Doug put his pack of Winstons and Zippo on the bar top.

Cody slammed down a glass and poured a quick shot of Wild Turkey. "I don't believe I've ever seen you wear a suit before, though. You look like a G-man."

Doug looked down at his black jacket sleeves. He'd forgotten he was wearing it. "We had a bit of a funeral tonight at our place."

"Oh, man, I'm so sorry. Horrible shame. You lost people, did you?"

Doug didn't respond, but instead downed the shot in a single burning swallow and sipped his chaser. He entered a brief zone of comfort.

Cody refilled his shot glass and looked away. "On the house, friend. Good to see you again."

Doug glanced at his watch. Joan was with her own people and didn't seem to care much to have him around. She wouldn't be missing him any time soon. He could stay here, have a few drinks, and drive straight to the vigil.

For the next two hours, Doug drowned his thoughts in round after round of bourbon and beer, studying the liquor bottles standing in formation behind the bar and smoking one cigarette after another. Between serving teenagers, letting his customers smoke up his bar, and helping Doug rocket past the legal blood alcohol limit, Cody was clearly breaking all the rules tonight.

Doug watched the rowdy bunch for a while, his face sagging and his handlebar mustache dripping with beer. He'd reached an age where he thought anybody under the age of twenty-five looked like a kid. Their energy impressed him. While the world mourned, they were actually celebrating. They'd dodged the bullet. They drank to their health. A girl held up a sprig of mistletoe and invited a lanky boy to lean in for a passionate kiss. The men at the bar glared at them but said nothing.

One of the girls glanced at Doug and smiled shyly before turning to her friends and laughing. Then another glance. She had a clean, pretty face. She barely looked out of high school. She definitely looked like trouble.

He turned back to the bar with a sigh and nursed his beer.

The song on the jukebox, Alice Cooper's "School's Out," faded to the kids' cheers. The men sitting around the bar stared into empty space. The grinding guitar chords of "Bad to the Bone" filled the ensuing vacuum. Doug turned, sipping his beer, to see the girl now standing at the jukebox with her back to him. She wore a brown leather bomber jacket with a big American flag patch stitched onto the back, and a short red plaid skirt that swayed as she swiveled her hips in time with the music.

Doug thought of Joan standing in front of that very same jukebox, all those years ago. The way she moved, she set the room on fire.

Cody leaned on the counter. "They bugging you? Say the word, and I'll toss their asses out on the street."

"No," said Doug. "Let them have some fun."

"Strange days, friend."

Doug nodded and kept on watching the girl.

Before Herod, Doug had a perfect family. He and Joan were losing their youth one birthday at a time, of course, but they were taking a trip through life together, sharing its ups and downs. And he'd never given in to the pull, as some men did, to revise the bad choices of his youth by making new mistakes. Joan had been his rock, and his children his purpose in life.

Taking stock, Doug now had nothing but regret, loss, and less time on this earth to make some new choices. The way he saw it, he had three.

He could live out his days missing the past in bitterness and pain.

He could start fresh with Joan or with somebody new.

Or he could take one of his shotguns and blow his brains out.

He still loved Joan. That was certain. Would she want to start over? She might not want to look ahead. Even if she did, Joan might not want to start over with *him*.

The way she'd looked at him when he left with the kids. Accusing him.

Don't drop him, she'd said.

The anger in her eyes.

No, not anger. Disgust. More specifically, revulsion.

Like he'd killed Nate and Megan himself.

Joan, shouting: *What did you do?*

If she didn't want him, Doug could start over with somebody else, somebody younger. Try to forget the past. Make a new life, with new children if Herod let him.

Of course, there was always the third option.

Start over, or end it all.

"Hellooo?" the girl in the bomber jacket was saying to him. "Earth to man."

Doug squinted at her and stabbed his cigarette into the peanut bowl Cody had given him to use as an ashtray. He emptied his mug in one last swallow and set it down.

Time to go. Joan was expecting him at the vigil a half hour ago.

"Hey, I'm Cindy," she added. She gave him a quick once-over, taking in his suit. Her eyes were large and brown. "Are you a cop?"

"Why? Should I card you?"

"Um, are you like, okay? You just . . . looked so sad sitting here."

Doug lit another cigarette and eyed her.

You have no idea, he wanted to say. *You don't know what you have. You have your youth and you're beautiful, but you're hungry, and that hunger blinds you to what you already have.*

All those raging hormones, making every decision for you. You're always hurting, but you've never been hurt. Not really.

Later on, though, you'll realize youth is truly wasted on the young. Right now, you're pretending you're what, twenty-one? Later on, you'll want to be twenty-one again. Really, no matter what age you are—ten or a hundred—you'll want to be twenty-one.

And, just as when you were a little kid, you'll demand your dignity before you earn it.

That was the essence of what he was thinking. His brain had grown soggy to the point where his actual thoughts were an incoherent jumble.

"How old are you, really?" he said.

Cindy took a long pull on her Bud Light and stared at him.

He could picture her saying, *Who cares? We're all grown-ups now.*

Reality turned fuzzy around the edges. He barely knew what he was saying. His brain was on automatic. She was laughing, her eyes gleaming like candles, drawing him to her light.

He knew he had a duty to his family, but he didn't even have a family anymore.

Doug stood and almost fell over, grabbing the bar for balance. The kids at the tables looked over and howled. The eyes of the other men around the bar shifted to stare. He shouted something like, *Screw you all! I got to piss!* He staggered toward the bathroom and leaned against the urinal. He rested his forehead against random graffiti on the cool wall and drifted.

Reality blurred again. He woke up in one of the stalls, hands gripping the tops of the partitions and tears drying on his cheeks, while Cindy sucked his cock, sloppily but with enthusiasm, until his back arched, and he exploded in her mouth.

The next thing he knew, he was outside and moving toward his truck. He had no idea how he'd ended up here, but hitting the road sounded like a fine idea. He climbed in and sat behind the wheel for several minutes, just breathing and watching snowflakes land on the windshield.

His vision doubled. He slapped his face to clear his head. The front of his shirt was damp and reeked of puke. His fly was open. He lit a cigarette and watched the curling tendrils of smoke. He squinted at his watch. Two hours late now and in no condition to drive.

"Shit." He fumbled with his keys until he got the right one into the ignition. The engine turned over, and cool air hissed through the heating vents. The blast of air gave him a small boost in mental clarity.

Cindy had written her phone number across the back of his left hand. Her last name was Crawford, just like the model. Whatever her age, the girl knew what she was doing.

He drove nice and slow. He rolled down his window when the world began to spin. The earth was turning too fast.

What happened in there? It already seemed like a dream.

He slapped himself again, this time in anger.

"Aw, shit. What did I do now?"

You fucked up, bro.

He licked his hand and tried to wipe off the number.

The parking lot at Union Park was jammed with cars, so he left his truck on the side of the entrance road. The park was filled with people, many of them holding candles that gleamed in the dark. They wandered like restless ghosts, searching for some focal point.

Doug knew where to go. Where he was meant to go.

The skating rink lay dark and empty, a large void ringed by candlelight. Hundreds of mourners had come to place flowers along the edge of the ice. Nate and Megan had died here in his arms. He couldn't protect them. *Somebody's toast is burning*, Nate had said just before the end. A cryptic prophecy Doug could study for years. One of the mourners threw her candle. Another did. Then everybody was doing it. The candles struck the ice like sparks and extinguished.

When the last candle fell, the rink plunged into total darkness.

A horrible keening wail rose up as the mourners gave in to despair.

"It wasn't my fault," Doug shouted amid the screams. "Leave me the hell alone!"

Nobody cared. Doug stood there crying. He didn't bother with the flask this time. No matter how much he drank, he still remembered everything.

Ramona

82 hours after Herod Event

Something about Ross's presence grounded Ramona—made her feel a little less like she was flying apart.

She trudged through the snow, leaning against him. The scent of his aftershave recalled the kiss they'd shared last night after the public health people took away the body of her son. She'd wanted to scream, to fight, but she couldn't. She could only stare blankly while Ross helped her sign the forms. They gave her a receipt. Then Josh was gone.

On impulse, she'd kissed him. They'd kissed for a long time. She'd fallen into it, blanking out her mind.

Ross might have been interested, Ramona reflected, to learn she was considering taking him home after the vigil and screwing him until she forgot her last name. Sex offered hours of blissful forgetting. Maybe she'd even feel something. Now if only she could get him to shut up.

They'd spent the last two days together, just sharing space. He'd shown up at her door first thing in the morning, brewed a pot of coffee, and sat on the couch to read the paper. He didn't talk to her or otherwise place any demands. He didn't say a word about the smell or ask about Josh. He just provided the strength of his presence. She'd come to depend on it. After a while, she began to open up about her regrets. How hard she'd tried as a mother and where she believed she'd failed.

She just wanted him to listen. Once they started talking, however, Ross expressed an interest in fixing her. He looked at life's problems as things to be attacked, at feelings as puzzles that could be solved once every piece found its rightful place. The more she voiced her despair, the more he tried to make it all better. He told her repeatedly that she was being too hard on herself. That she was strong. That she would survive. The confident tone in his voice let her know he thought he was convincing her. He had no clue. There was no making this better. There was no coming back from this.

There was only the hope of forgetting for a little while.

She'd begun to learn little things about him. He'd been engaged once but never married. He was biding his time, waiting for the right woman, and that was okay because he knew what he wanted. He was somewhat straight edge; he didn't drink or smoke and had never even had a joint in his life, his main vice being caffeine. The man was a connoisseur of coffee. As she already knew, he didn't take work very seriously. He exercised every day to stay fit. He liked to golf in the spring. More for the exercise than the sport, he said. He loved the smell of fresh-cut grass.

She didn't care about any of it. This was going all wrong, she knew, and it wouldn't end well. She didn't need a boyfriend. She needed a therapist.

They wandered toward a hill occupied by a crowd of other mourners. The glow of candles along the ridge lent the place a holy atmosphere, making the journey there something of a pilgrimage. It seemed to promise something; Ramona felt drawn to it.

At the top, she found nothing but empty night sky that chilled her even more.

Then the stars came out. Millions of points of light. Ramona imagined they were reflections of the candles on the hill. The souls of the dead children. She tried to decide which one was Josh. He lived up in the sky now.

"Wow," said Ross. "Look at that."

She looked down and saw it. One of the children's burial grounds. The crowd had come here to take in the view of their children being laid to rest, not the stars. It was several miles away, but she could see headlights moving across the fields and hear the distant hum of the big digging machines. The burial ground spanned the horizon. She resented how the sheer size of it trivialized her loss. Made Josh's death seem insignificant.

Josh had been taken there for burial. Now was the perfect time to say good-bye, but she refused. She couldn't let him go. His physical form was one thing. His spirit was another.

A female voice: "Ramona?"

Ramona turned and said, "Joan."

They leaned close enough to exchange body heat. They had a connection they only now perceived and didn't yet understand, taking comfort in sharing space, like survivors of the same plane crash.

Ross cleared his throat and introduced himself. Joan introduced her family.

"I have pictures of Josh I want to give you," she said.

"Thank you. And sorry."

"I'm sorry for your loss too. Josh was a great kid."

"I meant about Josh getting sick. I said some stupid, hurtful things. I'm sorry for that."

"I honestly forgot all about it until now," said Joan. "But thank you."

"He really liked you and your kids. You're a great mom, Joan. I think maybe I resented you a little for that. How you always seemed so comfortable in your own skin being a mother. It was harder for me. I'm sorry I felt that way."

"Being a mom is hard, period," Joan told her. "Nobody understands this. Sometimes even moms forget. Don't beat yourself up—you did just fine by Josh."

They hugged and parted ways. Ramona headed back down the hill with Ross. It had felt good to say those things; honesty, once so rare and precious, had become easy. Her eyes stung as she considered the small piece of wisdom Joan had shared with her.

"Where do you want to go now?" Ross asked her.

Ramona sighed. "I don't care. Let's just keep walking."

"There's a special place I'd like to take you tomorrow, if you're up for it. It's got an incredible—"

"*No.* No plans. Please."

"All right, I guess. I'd still like to come over, though. Can I do that?"

"Let's just be quiet for a while, okay?"

They reached the bottom of the hill and stood under a pathway light. She watched the others wander about in varying states of shock. She saw them not as mourners but survivors. They moved in near silence broken by periodic wails of grief. Many wore photos pinned to their coats, as if declaring they weren't people anymore, but merely placeholders for their missing children.

A bell tolled, loud and crisp. The sound resonated in her brain. She knew what it meant.

The last child in the world is dead. Just as the scientists predicted.

She didn't want to be here.

"Kiss me," she said on impulse.

Ross snorted. "What? I don't know if we should do *that* again."

"I thought that's what you wanted."

"I want to help. I don't want you to think I'm trying to take advantage."

Ramona leaned against him. "Kiss me."

He did. It was a test, and it worked. Her mind blanked out. She wanted more.

Ross smiled. "Wow."

Scattered screams erupted along the top of the hill. At first it was easy to ignore, but the screaming didn't stop. Instead, it multiplied. Screams of horror mixed with hysterical, joyful crying, all of it tinged with a chilling quality, something like insanity.

"What the hell is going on up there?" Ross wondered. "Listen to them."

"The bell tolled," she said bitterly. "It's the end. Herod won."

The vigil offered her nothing. No peace of mind in any case. Only the certainty that all the world's children were now dead, and there was nothing anybody could do about it. No way the parents they'd left behind could move on from the depths of shock.

"Something else is going on," he said. "It's giving me goose bumps. It's like the mall—"

She leaned against him again. He felt warm. This she could believe in.

"Take me home, Ross."

His eyes widened and his arms loosened. "Like I said, I don't want to—"

She nuzzled his throat. "Yes or no, Ross. Say yes."

"Wow," he whispered, and she kissed him again, hard.

"Is that a yes?"

"Oh, yeah. That's a big yes."

"*Mommy*," Josh said.

Ramona turned and stared at her boy in shock.

"Holy shit!" Ross cried, and lunged backward.

"Josh?"

Her voice came out as a tiny whisper. Her lips tingled. Stars sparked in her vision.

Ross shook his head. "It's him."

She fell to her knees. "Josh? Is it really you?"

The boy stared straight ahead, his face slack and his clothes splattered with frozen mud. He didn't blink. Several other children marched past, trailing puffs of quicklime.

"The children," Ross said. "Oh, Christ."

Josh's eyes flickered for the first time, looking over Ramona's shoulder to regard Ross with his unblinking stare.

"*Why were you kissing that man?*"

The shock wore off. Ramona screamed.

David

Hour of Resurrection

The Children's Hospital had been converted into a giant morgue filled with people in scrubs opening bodies, drawing blood, slicing organs, mopping bodily fluids.

David Harris raised his clear plastic face shield, peeled off his gown and gloves, and stretched. It was nearly midnight. He'd done two bodies in ten hours, and he could feel one muscle after another clench, while the burning ache in his leg increased in volume, threatening to become a scream.

He endured it. This was where he belonged. Outside the hospital, the world reeled in shock and tried to find meaning in what had happened. In here, people worked around the clock to help the CDC determine the cause of Herod's and defeat it. If only Nadine could understand that, she might understand him. He wished she were here, fighting at his side.

He gritted his teeth against the pain as he limped away from the table to dry-swallow another Vicodin. A diener—responsible for transporting the bodies and preparing them for autopsy—placed the body David had just finished onto a gurney and wheeled it out of the room.

"Bring me another one, Sam," David called after the muscular Asian-American. "And a bucket."

The recovery beds had been converted into crude autopsy tables. Covered in plastic and tilted to allow gravity to control the flow of bodily fluids into a waste bucket. During a bathroom break after the first body, somebody had stolen his bucket, and now the legs of his scrubs and shoe covers, not to mention the floor, were covered with blood and chunks of tissue.

His mind flashed to Shannon Donegal wailing and hugging her swollen belly in his office. He winced at how he'd handled delivering the news of her baby's fate. He knew too well what she was going through and the hell to which she had to look forward, but the elephant in the room had demanded his attention. Her child couldn't be saved. None of them could. But they had a chance to save billions of future children. Humanity itself.

The process of finding that cure began here.

"Take a break."

He turned and saw Ben Glass. His friend looked terrible. The man hadn't slept or eaten well in days and was overworked to boot.

"One more," said David.

"You've done two back-to-back. Take a break, David. Eat a sandwich. Drink some OJ."

"I'll take a break when you do."

The bodies were decomposing. They all had a brief window to collect fresh samples, and that window was closing.

Sam returned to strip the gore-splattered plastic sheeting from the bed and unroll a new cover for the next body.

Ben rubbed his eyes. "I'm glad you're here, David. I really am."

"This is where we're going to beat Herod's."

"You're doing a great job. You picked up the ABCs in no time."

"It's been a long time since I cut into a cadaver. Medical school."

"If you're interested in a career change, you might think about forensic pathology."

"I'd rather work on the living. But thanks."

"Just remember to take care of yourself. If you feel yourself losing it at any time, call for help, and someone will take over. People more experienced than you have already lost a finger because of fatigue. Okay?"

"Got it. I'll be careful."

Sam brought another body. Undressed, washed, and weighed.

"Looks like you've got another customer," Ben said. "I'd better get back to it myself. CDC wants more X-rays, and I have to beg St. Catherine's for another machine."

"Too bad for the living."

"They'll complain, but that's a privilege of being alive. Good luck here, David."

"It's just you and me now, kid," David told the body, a boy who looked about six years old. He pulled on a fresh gown and two pairs of gloves. He read the chart. "Jonathan Ford. Great name."

Sam placed a plastic bag filled with medical textbooks under the boy's back as a body block to make his chest protrude. "You okay, doc?"

"I'm a pediatrician," David told him. "Old habits die hard. I'm not trying to be creepy."

"No, I like it," said the diener. "Treat them like people, doc. They deserve it." He turned as somebody called his name. "I'll be around if you need me. Just holler."

"Thanks."

Time to get to work. David narrated into a handheld recorder as he inspected the body. Jonathan Ford was Caucasian, male, brown-haired, blue-eyed, six years old, and had a tiny birthmark shaped like the state of New Jersey on his left leg. His legs also had white patches where there was no skin pigment, indicative of vitiligo.

Otherwise, David found no abnormalities. The body was stiff from rigor mortis. The abdomen swollen from gas. Light bruising along the front of his body, which was livor mortis. Jonathan had fallen face-down after he died. Sometime afterward, he'd been turned onto his back. Approximate time of death: three days ago, when Herod's struck.

He scanned the tools on the instrument cart. Bone saw, bread knife, several types of scissors. Hooked hammer, scalpels, skull chisel. Rib cutter, toothed forceps, electric saw.

David selected a large scalpel from the tray. The boy's eyes shined a bright blue even in death. He closed them with his thumbs.

"You don't want to see this, Jon."

Who are you, Jonathan Ford? Who would you have become?

He'd asked these same questions at Paul's grave. He pushed them aside and focused.

What caused you to die?

He stared at the boy's chest. He'd done just three autopsies so far, two of them supervised as part of his training. He found it helped if he visualized the procedure before doing it.

First, he would make an incision from shoulder to shoulder, meeting at the breastbone and plunging down to the pubic bone, creating a Y shape. He would pull the chest flap up and over the boy's face, exposing the rib cage, which he'd cut and remove using the rib cutters. Then he'd detach the organs, arteries, and ligaments. He'd start with the larynx, where the epiglottis, a flap of cartilage behind the tongue and in front of the voice box, constricted to produce laughter.

113

David thought about how Paul used to make him laugh. He'd once read the average adult laughed four times a day. He'd beat that in just an hour with his boy. Over a typical day, he'd set a record for laughing.

He hadn't really laughed since Paul left his life.

Exhaustion was making his mind wander. He wagged his head to clear it.

"After I take care of you, Jon, I'm going to have a nap." He snapped his fingers and tried to focus. "The organs, the organs."

Once he detached the organs, he'd pull out the entire set in a single piece for dissection and study. Individual organs would be weighed. Slices taken with the bread knife. Blood vessels bisected. The stomach opened and examined. It was grisly work. But vital.

In particular, he'd obtain samples of the strange blood from the femoral artery and the right atrium of the heart. In the bodies of the children, some of the blood had congealed, as one would expect. Some of it, however, had become dry, spongy, and pinkish in color. Right now, it was the only abnormality showing up in the initial autopsy results. An important clue. Herod consumed some components of the blood while chemically altering others, leaving behind a moist pink Styrofoam.

After taking these important samples, David would open Jonathan Ford's skull using a Stryker electric saw and the hooked hammer, and remove the brain for study.

The final step was to put Humpty Dumpty back together again piece by piece. He'd end the procedure by sewing the incisions closed with a heavy needle.

A single body took hours of grueling, methodical, detailed work. The task daunted him.

I'd much rather work on the living.

He took a deep breath and prepared to cut. His mind flashed to the cough trick. He used to ask his young patients to cough when he gave them a needle. It often worked to distract them from the sting.

His phone sang the opening bars of the *1812 Overture*. Nadine's ringtone.

"Saved by the bell, Jon."

He set down the scalpel, peeled off his gloves, and retrieved his phone from his bag.

"Yes? Nadine?"

"David!"

He broke out in a nervous sweat. "Nadine! What's wrong? Are you okay?"

"It's incredible!"

"What? I can hardly hear you!"

"I'm at the vigil at the park."

"Okay . . ."

"Shannon Donegal is with me."

"Oh. Did she see her obstetrician?"

"Yes. He confirmed your diagnosis with an ultrasound."

"I'm sorry to hear it. Is she okay? How is she coping?"

"No, it's not bad. I was going to say the diagnosis is wrong. The baby is *alive*."

"That can't be possible. I would trust the ultrasound."

"I felt it kick myself."

"Really," he said. "Are . . . are you sure?"

"Of course I'm sure!" She laughed. "I felt Liam kick. Multiple times. It's a miracle!"

How? Could I have been wrong?

For a moment, the overwhelming sense of doom lifted.

If she was right, he was in the presence of a genuine miracle.

Things were bad. Real bad. But maybe this wasn't the end.

Of the human race. Of him and Nadine as well.

Jonathan Ford's eyes snapped open and turned to gaze at him. The boy's mouth opened.

David dropped the phone and retreated until his back met the wall.

"OH JESUS CHRIST."

The boy rasped, *"You're not my daddy."*

Screams rolled across the recovery ward as Jonathan and about a third of the other children in the room sat up and looked around. The remainder, already cut open, didn't move.

"You're alive," David said.

The boy sucked in a rattling lungful of air and said, *"Home."*

Two of the children hopped down from their beds. The rest followed. They formed a grisly parade toward the exit. David saw a pathologist gripping a girl's wrists and struggling to hold her down, another screaming against the wall, another with his hands in the air as if surrendering. Most stood at their tables in shock, still holding their bloody instruments.

David couldn't believe his eyes. The children certainly looked dead. Their bodies were discolored and bloated with gas. They moved stiffly, dark fluid leaking down their bare legs. But they walked. They *talked.* It defied comprehension.

They're alive and woke up to an environment out of a medieval torture chamber.

"Don't let them go!" David called out.

His words unlocked a transformation among the stunned pathologists. Instead of seeing the children as the dead walking, they saw them as David did—sick children about to wander naked and lost in the freezing night.

Sam shut the doors as the children approached. He blocked it with his body.

The children didn't stop.

"*Move,*" they said.

"You're safe here," Sam told them. "Everything's okay—"

They swarmed against him.

David watched in horror. *Somebody help him!*

They were *climbing* him.

Sam brushed them off. He picked up a tiny naked boy, who kicked his legs and swiped at the man's face with his fingernails, and tossed him away in blind panic. The boy got up immediately and resumed his unblinking advance.

"Somebody help me!" he screamed. "I can't do this myself! *Shit!*"

The children closed in. They latched on to his arms and legs, scratching and biting. The man howled and backed out through the doors.

The children followed, ignoring him now. They flooded the hallway and continued their lurching march toward the exit.

Jonathan Ford turned to give David one last blank stare and then left with the others.

Going home.

Doug

Hour of Resurrection

Doug stumbled among the mourners at the park.

The snow rustled to his left. Several people ran past, moaning like cattle, their eyes wild.

"No, no, *no*, *no*, *no*," a woman wailed. She clutched her head with her gloved hands, as if fearing her brain might explode at any second.

Distant screams pierced the dark.

Doug didn't care. He was screwed. He could take any amount of pain, but not for long, unlike Joan, who couldn't take as much as him but had much greater endurance. His strength had drained out of him over the past few days. He had nothing left.

Everything he'd thought would help him face what had happened had instead undermined him. The loss of his children offered him a million choices, but he wanted none of them. He wanted his family back. The alcohol, which had buoyed him for the past few days, now magnified his grief.

More people ran past with shouts. Panicked faces flashed by.

He was ready to give up. He stood blubbering in the dark, hands at his sides, shoulders quaking.

Somebody ran into him. Doug growled and clenched his fists. The idea of beating somebody with his fists sounded very appealing right now.

"What's your problem, buddy?"

"My kids!" the man yelled back, and ran off into the dark.

More screams. Screams of genuine terror. Something terrible was happening at the edge of the crowd, where the park met the woods. He saw vague shapes seething in the dark near the gazebo.

This is how all the kids died. In a blind panic.

Must be our turn. Old King Herod has come for us all.

"Good," he said.

The idea of dying now didn't bother him. Dying alone did.

"Joanie!" he called.

People collected into a stampede. They flooded out of the dark. Their fear infected him. He felt sick with it. Then the alcohol that had made him sluggish moments ago provided a burst of energy. He shoved into the throng.

"JOANIE!"

He searched the frantic faces for his wife. She'd told him to meet her at their favorite sledding hill. He pulled out his cell phone.

"Doug!"

He put the phone back. "Joanie?"

"Doug, I'm here!"

She ran into his arms. He held on for dear life. "I'm sorry." He felt her warm body against his and remembered how much he loved her. "I'm sorry, I'm sorry."

She struggled against his embrace. "The children, Doug! The kids!"

"I'm sorry. I love you. I just wanted you to know."

Now I'm ready. Do it. Take us all.

"Doug, the children are back!"

He held her at arm's length. "What?"

"The children are *coming back*. I saw them!"

Doug wiped his eyes. "What do you mean?"

Then he saw.

He and Joan stood on a path cutting through the park, illuminated by light poles. Around them, people swirled and ran.

Children streamed through the crowd, walking stiffly with their arms at their sides, like sleepwalkers.

"Holy shit," Doug said.

"It's a miracle," Joan murmured.

The sight filled him with primitive fear. Fear and awe.

The crowd began to thin, leaving clumps of bodies—sobbing parents hugging their children.

Joan pushed Doug away and ran into the dark, calling for Nate and Megan. Doug caught up to her and grabbed her arm.

"Let go of me!"

"Joanie—"

She squirmed in his grip. "I need to find them!"

"They're not here!"

"Where?" Her eyes blazed at him. *"Where are my kids?!"*

"There are two burial grounds. One is close to here; that's where these kids are coming from. They're heading into town through the park."

"Where, Doug?"

"The other site! I'll take us there."

Joan looked around. "Wait, Mom and Dad are—"

"They'll find their own way. Come on!"

They ran through the snow.

The parking lot had snarled with honking cars and shrieking people. The children marched across the beams of the headlights, calling for their mommies and daddies.

"We'll never get out of here," Joan told him as they got into the truck.

Doug started the engine. "Yeah, we will."

He'd parked on the side of the narrow roadway leading into the parking lot, where traffic had created a choke point. He threw the transmission into gear and stepped on the gas. The truck roared onto the snowy field next to the road.

"We're going to get stuck!"

119

"We'll make it," Doug said, praying they would.

A wave of other drivers had followed his lead and was now gaining on him.

They just had to cross the field and navigate the drainage ditch to get onto Stuyvesant Road.

We might make this.

He swerved to avoid a tree. They reached the road. He stomped the gas, hoping they had enough momentum to jump the drainage ditch. The truck lurched across the gap and slammed into the other side. The tires pulled them up onto the road.

A small girl appeared in his headlights. He yanked the wheel just in time.

"Jesus, Doug!" said Joan. "Careful!"

He handed her his pack of Winstons. "Light one for me, will you?"

"Where's this other site?"

"The other side of—*shit*!"

He wrenched the wheel, missing a crowd of children walking hand in hand in the glow of the streetlights. The sight put a shudder through him. Dead people were not supposed to walk. Just what the hell was going on here?

They flew through the downtown commercial district, ignoring the red lights.

"Why is the truck shaking like this?" she asked him.

"Must have hit something in that field," he shouted over the rattle. He didn't feel like explaining the problem with the alignment.

"Well, is it going to get us there? It feels like it's falling apart!"

"Yeah," Doug told her. "We'll get there."

The truck's lighter ejected. Joan lit his cigarette and took a deep drag before passing it over. They drove in silence for several minutes.

"Doug? Is this really happening?"

"Yeah. As far as I can tell."

"Those kids we saw. How did they dig themselves out?"

"They didn't. They weren't buried yet."

"Were Nate and Megan . . . ?"

"No. I know exactly where they—"

"*Watch it!*"

A minivan skidded around the corner ahead as a speeding car plowed into it, sending both spinning into a storefront with a crash of glass. A piece of metal banged off Doug's windshield and cobwebbed it. He leaned on the horn and flew past the wreckage. It didn't even occur to him to stop and help.

He took a quick swig from his flask and cranked the wheel. The truck fishtailed before rocketing onto the highway ramp. A police cruiser caught up to him. Its siren blared as it passed at incredible speed.

"Jesus," said Joan. "Oh, Jesus. It's really happening."

They passed a billboard that read, SPANKY'S PLAY AND STAY 3 MILES, showing a giant photo of laughing kids over which somebody had sprayed RIP in black paint. For Doug, it was an important landmark. The burial ground was just ahead.

He jerked the wheel again. The truck roared onto the dirt road and passed the National Guard checkpoint. They saw taillights ahead, other parents come to find their children.

They topped the rise. The sprawling burial ground, lit up with work lights, spilled into view.

"Oh my God," she said, taking it all in. "I didn't know it was so big."

"There are thousands of kids out there."

He drove the truck onto the frozen fields.

"How are we going to find Nate and Megan?"

"I brought them here. I know where they are."

He stopped in front of a line of body bags laid out along the lip of a trench.

"This is it."

For several moments, they sat in the warm interior of the cab while the truck idled.

He cut the engine. His nerves tingled. He pulled a flashlight out of the glove compartment and gave it to Joan.

The digging machines had ground to a halt across the barren field. Men in hazmat suits ran between the trenches. Tiny figures wandered across the scarred landscape.

Doug left the headlights on as he got out of the truck. Joan knelt in front of the body bags.

The bodies squirmed in the bags like larvae trying to hatch.

"They're in this row here," he said.

"Which ones?"

Doug frowned. He couldn't think. "I'm not sure."

"Let's start from the outside in," Joan told him. "We're going to let all the kids out."

They moved to opposite ends of the row. Doug opened the first bag and recoiled from the stench.

Eyes clicked open on the dead face and regarded him with a flat stare.

"I don't know you," the girl said.

Doug fell on his ass in utter shock. He yelped and crab-walked away from her. The girl sat up and finished unzipping the bag. For the first time, he wondered if they were doing the right thing letting these kids out.

"Thank you, mister." The girl stood and marched stiffly into the dark like a wind-up doll.

This can't be happening. You've gone off the deep end, brother.

"So be it," he said. He moved on to the next bag and unzipped it.

"Daddy?" the little boy said.

"Sorry, kid," Doug said. "You'll see your folks again soon, I promise."

Police cruisers and ambulances roared onto the works. More children wandered past. Doug unzipped a third bag and found another little girl who wasn't his.

"Hurry!" he barked at Joan.

"Dad?"

Next.

"Daddy!"

"Megan?" Doug fell to his knees, taking long shuddering breaths, trying to keep control. He didn't know what he would do if he lost it right now and didn't want to find out. He became aware of his sanity as a separate, fragile thing. "Hey. Hey, princess."

It was his Megan looking up at him from an open bag that reeked of rot and decay. The same face. The same eyes. The same voice. The same little girl, dressed in her Sunday best.

Could it really be her? His daughter was dead.

He saw the jagged pattern on the side of her head from when she'd cut her own hair a week ago.

He leaned away and threw up onto the snow. His eyes flooded with hot tears.

"It can't be," he sobbed. "It's not happening."

Joan yelled, "I found him!"

Then he heard her scream.

"Nate?" he groaned. He heaved again, producing a single ropey strand of foul-smelling fluid.

Megan stood next to him. She touched his shoulder. "I want to go home now, Daddy."

"Oh, God." He wiped his nose on his sleeve. "All right, princess. Come on."

He took off his coat and wrapped it around her. He rubbed her arms.

Nate climbed out of his bag.

"Thank you, Daddy," said Megan.

"Warm you right up," he said without thinking.

He picked her up and brought her to Joan. She felt like a frozen block of wood. Joan was kissing Nate's cold hard face and whispering to him. Doug wanted to laugh; she was using a scolding tone, the tone she used when the boy did something dangerous that worried her.

He set Megan on the ground. "Look who I found, Joanie."

Joanie hugged her daughter with a loud cry.

"Hi, Dad," said Nate.

Doug gaped at him. "Hey, sport."

Nate, exasperated: "What took you guys so long?"

Doug laughed, and Joan joined in. It felt good to laugh. They laughed long and hard.

From insanity or joy, he didn't know or care.

"Yup," said Doug. "That's definitely my boy."

Nate grinned with gray teeth.

Ramona

1 hour after Resurrection

Ramona lay in the back of Ross's car with her arms wrapped tight around Josh's body. He stank like the grave. Holding him was like hugging a large, thawing, rotten steak.

She'd never been happier.

Ross leaned on the horn and tossed his hands in frustration. "This is going to take forever. People are going nuts. There are cars everywhere."

She couldn't see anything except the red glow of brake lights. She pulled her coat tighter over her and Josh to create a private nest.

Ross rolled down the window. Cold air and the blare of sirens flooded the car.

"Put the window back up," she said.

"It smells like something d—" He glanced behind him. "Like something really bad in here."

"He's freezing, Ross. His skin feels like ice. Crank the heat as high as it'll go."

He winced at the stink but did as she asked. Ross was fighting to keep it together, she knew. The world had stopped making sense entirely.

"I don't feel anything," Josh whispered.

"Do you know what happened to you?"

"I woke up in a hole. There were a lot of other kids coming out of sleeping bags. We tried to get out. A boy reached down and grabbed my hand and helped me climb."

He only breathed when he wanted to talk.

Ross slammed the steering wheel. "Come on! Learn how to drive, buddy!"

"It was my fault," Ramona whispered near Josh's ear. "I'm so sorry."

Josh shook his head slowly. "No, Mommy."

She thought of all the regrets she'd voiced to Ross.

Seeing you come out of me, I felt like I'd been born to love you. But it was hard raising you by myself. You have no idea. How could you? It wasn't always just about getting us what we needed. I missed having choices. I wanted more than I had. There was a time when I thought I could have it all. A great career. A man like Ross to love. I gave so much to you. I thought the world owed me something back, and in the dark times, deep down, I thought my life would have been better if you hadn't been born.

"You came back for a reason," she breathed.

A second chance to make things right.

The car built up speed. She listened to the hum of the engine, the smooth roll of the car's tires on the road. She closed her eyes.

"My little miracle," she murmured. Tonight, they were both reborn.

"*I'm hungry*," Josh growled.

Ramona's eyes flashed open. Ross grimaced in the front seat. He glanced at them before returning his eyes to the road with a shake of his head.

"I'll make you something when we get home," she said, studying his pale little face.

The air whistled out of Josh's lungs.

She remembered how, one night, her stepmother had agreed to pick up Josh at day care and watch him for a few hours so Ramona could have dinner with an eye doctor she'd met through a mutual friend. She'd left work excited about the date, gotten into her car, and next thing she knew, she'd driven to the day care center. Her brain had blanked out, and her body had taken over, executing its normal routine.

Body memory, they called it.

Is he real or a copy? A fleeting echo of his former personality? Something of a ghost?

"Are you here to stay, Josh?" she asked.

He didn't answer.

A little louder: "Josh?"

Not all miracles are good. She wondered if this one carried a price.

The car stopped. She sat up. They were in her driveway. Home.

Ross leaped out and walked away from the car.

Ramona opened her door and waited as she normally would, but Josh didn't move. She leaned in and pulled her boy out of the car. His body left an oily black smear on the seat. Dogs barked all over the neighborhood. A car skidded on screeching tires in the distance. Several houses down, a screen door slammed, and a woman screamed. Ross started at the sound.

"Thank you," Ramona told him. "For everything."

"Do you want me to come in? I could put coffee on, and we could try to get our bearings."

She shook her head. He glanced at Josh with obvious relief not to be staying.

"All right," he said. "I'll call you. Soon."

She turned and carried Josh to the door. He felt heavy in her arms. Church bells began to chime across the city. She struggled to hold him in one arm while she rooted in her purse for her keys.

"How about a nice hot bath before I feed you?" she asked him.

The water would both clean and warm him. Ramona took his silence as consent. She carried him upstairs, set him on his bed, and stretched out his limbs. It was hard work. His body appeared to be frozen solid. His skin felt like marble. She wondered how he'd been able to walk at all.

"Mommy will be right back, honey," she said.

He didn't answer. He stared at the ceiling. The muscles in his face were slack. His chest didn't rise and fall. He didn't blink.

She went into the bathroom and turned on the taps. The room filled with warm steam.

Otherwise, the house was quiet.

Maybe he's gone, she thought. She ran into his room and found him lying in the exact same spot. His eyes had shifted to look at her.

"Mommy's going to give you a nice hot bath, little man."

Ramona took his hands and pulled him into a sitting position. She undressed him until he sat naked and pale. His abdomen had swollen and turned green. His back was heavily bruised. He had blisters on his arms and legs. His fingertips were blue.

His body is rotting but something inside him is still alive.

She picked up her son and carried him into the bathroom. It was like carrying a chair. Dead weight. He made no sound as she lowered him into the hot water.

The routine comforted her. This part was familiar. She would give him a bath. No big deal. A typical Tuesday night. She wouldn't scream. She wouldn't run away.

He's still Josh.

She held on to that thought with whatever mental strength she had left.

"Are you in there, Josh?"

No answer.

"Why won't you talk to me?"

Ramona wrung out a sponge and washed his back.

"That's okay, little man. Mommy will wait. I'm just so glad you're home."

As she worked, she sang: "*Hush, little baby, don't say a word . . .*"

She raised one of his arms and sponged it carefully.

"*Mama's gonna buy you a mockingbird . . .*"

Outside, people were cheering. The initial shock had worn off. They were embracing the insanity for the miracle it was, just as Ra

127

mona was. The gift. The children were back. How and why didn't matter right now.

"And if that mockingbird won't sing, Mama's gonna buy you a—"

The water turned black. Ramona coughed. The bath smelled like a rotten stew. She raised the toilet seat and retched over it. She turned on the bathroom fan and returned to the tub.

"I'm going to wash your hair now, so close your eyes."

To her surprise, he did. Josh was still in there. They were communicating.

"You always did hate getting water in your eyes."

Ramona had always figured he would abandon her one day—friends, girls, college, and, ultimately, his own family. She hadn't expected him to die.

And now that she'd gotten him back, she'd never lose him again.

Whatever the price.

FIVE

Doug

8 hours after Resurrection

Doug woke to the worst hangover of his life.

His head ached as if somebody had taken a baseball bat to it during the night. Joan had raised the shade on the window, and the light pierced his eyes like microscopic needles. His tongue felt too big for his mouth. The room spun. He wondered if he was still drunk. It wouldn't have surprised him one bit if he was.

It all came back to him with a jolt.

Nate and Megan had come back from the dead.

"Joanie," he called. He barely recognized his ragged voice.

She didn't answer.

He coughed hard. His mouth tasted like an old ashtray. He took his time standing. He was still wearing his gamey, foul-smelling black suit.

He had to see for himself if they were still here or if it had all been a dream. Hell, he just wanted to *see* them.

He hurried down the stairs. Froze on the bottom step.

Nate and Megan leaned against each other on the La-Z-Boy sofa. Nate wore his favorite pajamas covered with NHL team logos. Megan wore a pink sleeper with a little patch (ballerina shoes) stitched onto

129

the left breast. The daylight coming through the windows wasn't kind to them. They looked like figures carved from wax. Soap, shampoo, and lotion had covered up the stink, but the low-grade smell of ongoing decay tainted the air.

Joan had plugged in the Christmas tree, which filled the room with the parody of cheer.

"Kids?" he rasped.

They didn't answer. Didn't move a muscle, their eyes glassy and unblinking.

"Oh, God." He clamped his hand over his mouth and rushed past them to the bathroom, where he fell to his knees and vomited a single burning trickle of stomach acid. Dry heaves followed.

"That's what you get for drinking," Joan said behind him.

He yanked a handful of toilet paper off the roll and wiped the tears and snot from his face. "What have we done, Joanie?"

"What do you mean?"

He'd been hallucinating last night. What had happened at the park couldn't have happened; therefore, it hadn't. It was one of those events people call mass hysteria. They'd hallucinated, recovered the bodies of their dead children, and brought them home. But they were still dead.

And now they have to go back into the ground.

Then he remembered. They'd taken Nate and Megan home in the truck and carried them inside. Nate said he was starving. Crossing the threshold, he'd said, "Home again, home again, jiggety-jig," and went rock still in Doug's arms.

They'd washed and clothed them and tried to feed them, but the kids had stopped responding. They put them to bed and pressed their eyelids closed. Afterward, they collapsed, exhausted, in their own bed and slept.

No, what had happened last night had been real enough.

He flushed the toilet again, grabbed the edge of the sink, and hauled himself up. When he tried to leave, Joan stood her ground. She held two small cartons of apple juice with straws punched into them.

"Doug, these are our kids."

"They were dead three whole days," he said. "Doesn't that bother you at all?"

Her mouth set in a hard line. "This is a gift. A miracle. The only thing I feel is grateful."

He followed her into the living room and watched her offer the juice to the kids. No takers.

"Have they done anything," he asked, "other than just sit there staring into space?"

"No," Joan admitted.

"So, what are we doing here?"

"I don't know. I'm trying to take things one minute at a time, okay?" Her voice cracked. "What do you want to do? Take them back and bury them again?"

She was right, but that didn't make it any easier being in the same room with them.

"We'll take care of them like we always have," he said. "But to be honest, they scare me a little."

Her expression softened. "Oh, Doug, they're still our kids. You know that, right?"

It was a good question. Were they? If they'd gone into a coma, they'd still be his kids, wouldn't they? Or had a disfiguring accident? Was this that much different?

Of course it is. They're DEAD. They're dead, and we're treating them like living people.

The children's eyes flickered in unison to look at him.

"Jesus," he said with a shudder. "Their eyes are following me."

Joan turned to gape at the children. "They moved?"

The phone rang.

"*Goddamn it!*" Doug roared, venting his stress. He stomped into the kitchen.

Their eyes followed his progress.

"They're moving, Doug! Look! They're watching you!"

He snatched up the phone, nerves jangling. *"What?"*

"What do you mean, 'what'?" Otis shouted back. "You were supposed to be here at six thirty!"

"You want me to pick up trash today? My kids just came back, you prick."

"Language," Joan called from the living room.

"Well, that's lucky for you," said Otis, "because thousands of them haven't had the chance."

"What are you talking about?"

"I'm happy your kids are back. I really am. It's a goddamn miracle. God bless you. But there are still thousands of kids out at the sites. The ones who went home weren't buried yet. The rest are still down there in the ground."

Doug hadn't thought of that. "All right, I'm listening."

"We have to *dig them up*. It's going to be a hell of a lot tougher to get them out than it was putting them in. Hard, delicate work. We've had crews working all night, and they're dropping. We need more people on-site. We need you."

Doug heard frantic music and a giggling cartoon voice in the living room. Joan had put on a DVD. He thought about spending the day with his children. His children with their dead faces.

"My grandkids are still down there, Doug," Otis pleaded.

"I'll be there in less than an hour."

Otis hesitated. Apparently, he'd been unprepared for Doug to agree so readily. "Well, good. God bless you, Doug." He paused again. "Everything okay there?"

"Yeah, just peachy," Doug grated. He hung up.

He returned to the living room. The children's eyes were glued to the flickering images on the TV. Joan stared at them with naked love. She wasn't going to like his leaving right now. He steeled himself for a fight.

"Sorry, babe. I have to go to work."

"Fine," Joan said absently, still watching her kids.

"It's an emergency."

"Great. You should go. Do what you have to do."

"I'm thinking about stopping for a beer on the way home," he tested her.

She didn't answer; she'd stopped listening. Her easy agreement stung. Doug had always figured she would choose the kids over him if push came to shove. He'd always accepted this. He still didn't like it.

Fifteen minutes later, he was driving to the burial ground with a thermos of coffee between his legs and his flask snug in the inner breast pocket of his denim jacket. Church bells tolled in the distance. He dialed around the AM talk radio stations and found a guy who was saying the children's resurrection was a sign of the End Times.

"The final judgment is coming, friends. It's practically here. Now, the question you need to be asking yourself is: Am I right with God?"

Doug turned it off and dry-swallowed some Tylenol. He felt hot and flushed; the guy and his gravelly voice had gotten to him. Just a day ago, he would have welcomed Judgment Day. He'd had a thing or two to tell God when he met Him. But not now.

Doug wasn't a religious man, but he believed in a God who kept score. Taking the children home and playing with them as if they were dolls struck him as an abomination. If his children were truly dead, then they should have stayed dead. It was sad as hell, it was hard, it had broken him and Joan, but it was the natural order.

Those things in his house were not his kids, plain and simple. They were ghosts. A mocking imitation of the children he loved more than himself.

The soldiers waved him through the checkpoint. He thought about the thermos of coffee warming his thighs and decided to have a snort of Jim Beam instead.

The sky had turned even grayer this morning as the temperature dropped and snow began to fall. The big machines growled as they reopened the trenches. Work crews followed in their wake, digging up the children.

Ahead lay the sprawling compound of trailers where the operation was managed, now even bigger with Red Cross tents, ambulances, and school buses filling with children bound for home.

They couldn't get them all. As Doug approached the parking area, he saw dozens of children walking off singly or in groups across the frozen fields. Drawn to the warmth of their homes like moths seeking light.

His skin crawled at the sight. He couldn't shake his sense of foreboding. Fear both primitive and primordial, rooted in millions of years of evolution.

His instincts warned him the long nightmare wasn't over yet. Not by a long shot.

David

10 hours after Resurrection

David stepped aboard the idling school bus with his medical bag, ready to do some good.

The Red Cross had called for volunteers to help care for the children being dug out of the ground at the burial site. He'd come without a second thought.

The children at the hospital had returned from the dead. He'd seen it happen firsthand; it still haunted him. It may have been a miracle to most, but it was a medical mystery to him. In time, the scientific community would need to understand why the children came back as much as why they died in the first place. In the meantime, they needed his care as a pediatrician.

The bus was full. The children stared at some distant horizon, their faces slack and their mouths hanging open. Dead and arranged in this creepy diorama. A gray-haired man in a red ski jacket crouched next to a girl and shined a flashlight into her eyes.

The wall of stench forced him to back off. He waved down a passing paramedic.

"They're all dead in there. Where are the walking ones?"

The woman handed him a surgical mask that reeked of women's perfume. "On the bus. This will help with the stink. See the doctor. I think Dr. Simon's on that bus."

What a mess, David thought.

He put on the mask and breathed through his mouth. He steeled his nerves and climbed back aboard, extending his hand as the gray-haired man approached. "Dr. Simon? I'm Dr. Harris."

The man handed him a clipboard and pointed. "Check vitals on the last five rows on the left and fill out these forms."

"Why? They're dead, aren't they?"

"Oh yeah? How'd they walk here then?"

He remembered how little Jonathan Ford had sat up and hopped off the dissection table. He'd appeared dead as well, as had all the rest at The Children's Hospital. David nodded and approached two girls sitting next to each other.

They were holding hands.

"I'm Dr. Harris," he told them. "I'm a pediatrician. That means I specialize in helping sick boys and girls get better. First, though, I have to figure out why they're sick."

The girls stared straight ahead. If they heard David speak, they showed no sign of it.

He smiled at the one closest to him. "So let's start with you. What's your name?"

No answer.

Unresponsive to verbal stimuli, he scribbled. *Makes no sounds.* His hands shook a little as he wrote, a symptom of too much stress and Vicodin.

(and fear)

He put the pen down and flexed his hand.

"That's okay." He checked the yellow laminated card tied to her wrist. "Sally. I'm going to touch your hand and put a little pressure on your fingernail. Can you tell me if you feel it?"

Any conscious human being would react to the pain.

135

Unresponsive to pain. Makes no movements.

On the Glasgow Coma Scale, these children were in a state of deep unconsciousness. But the Glasgow Coma Scale no longer applied.

"Okay, Sally. Now I want you to look at the light for me."

David produced a pocket flashlight, clicked it on, and shined it in her eyes one at a time.

He sighed, scribbling. *Pupils do not contract in response to bright light.*

He reached into his medical bag and retrieved his stethoscope. He touched the girl's wrist, intending to search for a pulse, and recoiled at the feel of cold, hard flesh.

"You're doing great, Sally." He tried again.

Nothing.

No pulse, he wrote. *No respiration. The skin is cold.*

Outside, the snow reflected the gray sky. He sighed again.

"That's it, Sally. Normally, at the end of an examination, I'd give you a lollipop, but—"

Sally's eyes shifted to regard him with their icy dead stare.

"I'll be damned." David shivered with revulsion as he noted it on the form. He tried to sound natural. "That's great, Sally. Really great."

People thought life was a miracle, but it wasn't. Life was everywhere. The miracle was knowing you were alive. Sentience. Mind. That was the rare, precious gift.

He looked at the dead girl in front of him and knew there was a mind still in there.

His phone rang. He peeled off his gloves and answered it.

"David, I'm glad I caught you," said Ben. "I'm hoping you can help me. Have you had a chance to examine any of the children yet?"

"You're in luck. I'm just finishing up my first examination right now."

"I've been hearing they don't show vital signs. Is there any truth to that?"

"The child I just examined exhibited no heartbeat or respiration nor any response to external stimuli except a movement of the eyes."

136

"What do you mean? There was pupil contraction in response to light?"

"No, not at all. But her eyes turned to look at me when I mentioned I normally give lollipops at the end of patient exams."

"Shit," said Ben.

David noticed more of the children were looking at him. He turned away and said quietly, "What's going on?"

"Listen, once you examine a few more, I need you to bring me the reports right away. As fast as you can get here. Will you do this for me?"

"Of course. But why?"

"CDC thinks the children might be afflicted with some type of disease, a sleeping sickness that *imitates* death but is not real death."

"Something like tetrodotoxin poisoning?"

"Something like it, yeah."

Tetrodotoxin was a toxin found in a number of animal species, parasites, and bacteria. The toxin blocked communication between the central nervous system and other nerve cells in the body. In small doses, it was used to treat migraines and heroin withdrawal. Large doses paralyzed the diaphragm and caused respiratory failure and death.

In certain amounts, however, the toxin left its victims conscious but in a state of near death for days, which led ethnobotanist Wade Davis, author of *The Serpent and the Rainbow*, to theorize tetrodotoxin was a key ingredient in voodoo ritual used to create zombies.

"Ridiculous," said David. "This isn't a simulation of death; it's real death. Their bodies are decomposing. There's no heartbeat, no respiration—"

"But there is some brain activity, right?"

He considered this. Traditional Western medical practice had held that death occurred when your body stopped breathing and pumping blood. Then people invented machines that could breathe and pump blood for you. As a result, the model language in the Uniform Declaration of Death Act, which became accepted in Michigan and other states, legally defined it as "irreversible cessation of circulatory and respiratory functions, or irreversible cessation of all functions of the entire brain, including the brain stem."

If the children had any brain activity, people like Ben Glass could be in a lot of trouble.

"David, I ordered the autopsy and cremation of hundreds of bodies. If the children were alive in any acceptable definition of the word, I could be considered a mass murderer."

David swallowed hard. "I autopsied four children. Am I a murderer too?"

Silence, then: "You might want to lawyer up."

"Jesus," said David. "Surely, people understand the children were dead in every perceivable sense. *Legally* dead. There was no movement of the eyes. No brain function. No circulatory or respiratory function. My conscience is clear, and I hope yours is too. Dead is dead, Ben."

"And yet," said Ben. He sighed. "Listen, my friend. Legally, I think we're in the clear. Probably. It's an unprecedented situation. But imagine you're a parent who's lost a child, and then all the children come back from the dead except yours because some doctor cut him open and cremated his remains. How would you feel? Shit, David. Every death certificate has my name on it. We printed thousands. There are people who want my head on a spike."

The death of the children had deranged everybody, David knew. The mass die-off, the burials, the dead returning, the odd stasis that the children now exhibited between life and death; it was all too much for the human mind to bear.

"What can I do?" he asked his friend.

"I need to know whether the children are, in fact, returning to normal, or whether the resuscitation of brain and motor function was temporary. If they recovered some function, but that function is gone or deteriorating, we are in the clear in every way we want to be."

"It's a hell of a thing to wish," said David.

"I'm not wishing for anything. I just need facts."

"I'll do it. I'll do ten examinations and bring the results right over."

"Thank God you're on my side, David. You're one of the few people who still have their heads screwed on straight in all this shit."

David hung up and called Nadine, who'd given him a ride to the site that morning because his leg hurt too much to drive. He told her he needed a lift to the hospital in about an hour. She was still visiting with Caroline and her daughter Kimberly, and sounded happy.

As he ended the call, he noticed all the children in the back of the bus were now staring at him. He offered them a weak smile.

"Okay, who's next?"

David completed his ten exams, each producing the same results, which he noted dutifully on his forms. This done, he folded the papers and put them in the breast pocket of his coat. He stepped off the bus feeling like a thief.

Nadine had parked her Ford at the edge of the compound. She honked at him and waved. David hurried his pace. He felt eyes burning into his back, certain somebody was going to call him out for stealing critical medical information.

Nadine unlocked the door for him. David sat next to her, sweating.

"What's wrong?" she said.

"Just my imagination, it seems."

The operation here was a mess. Nobody was in charge. He could have stolen the bus and driven it to Detroit, kids and all, and nobody would have noticed.

The children might have. If I stole the bus and tried to drive out of town, I think they'd tear me to pieces.

He remembered Jonathan Ford's harsh whisper: *Home.*

The children swarming against Sam, who stood in their way.

Nadine started the car and drove onto the service road. She looked as tired as he felt. She wore glasses today, her eyes too raw and tired for contacts. Her shoulder-length dark hair, tied up in a bun, had frayed in all directions, and she was so pale she glowed. Frailty was an intrinsic part of her beauty, however. Since Paul died, she'd become a fallen angel. The more broken she appeared, the more attractive she became.

But she was smiling. She looked oddly happy.

"You're in a good mood," he noted.

"I'm having the most wonderful day of my life."

"Good," was all he could think to say. She was happy the children had gone home. David couldn't decide whether the nightmare was over or a new one was beginning.

"The phone was crazy all morning," she said. "Lots of messages. Everyone wants you to examine their children. Standard physicals."

"Good. Let's set up some office hours for tomorrow."

"They don't want to come to the office."

"I don't understand."

Nadine frowned at him. "David, they're ashamed."

"Why? Are the insurance companies refusing to pay?"

"That's not the problem. They just don't want to take their children out of their homes. I scheduled some house calls this afternoon. I'm going to do them myself."

David grunted his approval. "What about Caroline's daughter? Did you have the opportunity to examine her?"

She smiled now. "No vitals, no mobility, but she was conscious."

"Her eyes moved?"

Nadine nodded. "Her eyes didn't just move. She *responded*. It's like her body died, but her soul stayed behind." She glanced at him, unsure how he'd react. "When little Kimmy's eyes moved, I saw the hand of God."

"There's a scientific reason. There always is. We'll figure it out. We just need time."

"The reason doesn't matter, David. Can't you see? The process of death is reversing itself. It's all meant to be."

David frowned, massaging his pulsing leg and holding his tongue. In Nadine's world, everything happened for a reason, unpredictable yet fated. In his, everything had a rational explanation. For most of their marriage, this had worked out well for them. He'd anchored her; she'd helped him dream a little.

Now David no longer felt like Nadine lived in his world. It seemed he lived in hers. Facts had become unreliable. It was a time of miracles. In such a world, one faced constant temptation to hand over the reins of the mind because there was no point in trying to control anything.

"I'm sure you're right," he said.

"Miracles by their very definition don't happen at random. A higher power must intervene. That means a higher power is guiding these events toward a purpose."

"If it is in fact a miracle." He hoped his tone didn't sound too cutting, but his mind raged at the idea.

Why the hell would a higher power kill the children—a miracle—only to bring them back to life—another miracle? What purpose could this possibly serve?

It was insane to even consider it, but these were not rational times. *The real answer lies in science. It must.*

"My poor David," she told him. "Even after I'm proven right, you'll still try to find a rational explanation for it. The children are becoming normal again. I've seen it."

He regarded her with narrowed eyes. She was hiding something. "What did you see?"

"There's a catalyst. Something that brings them back. A loving elixir. I'll tell you if you want, but you won't believe me. You'll have to see it for yourself. I'll take you now."

David frowned. He'd had enough of this. "What is it then, Nadine? Because making them healthy again is going to take more than love, I can tell you that much."

If it took only love, Paul would be here, with him, right now.

Nadine said nothing. He wondered if he'd gone too far. He considered apologizing.

"Here we are," she said.

She slowed the car as they approached The Children's Hospital. A large crowd filled the grounds and visitor's parking. The staff was leaving the building. Some appeared to be demoralized, but most looked relieved to be going home. David spotted Sam, the diener he'd worked with in the autopsy ward.

"Stop the car." He got out and limped through the crowd. "Hey, Sam!"

The man smiled. "Hey, doc. Good to see you."

"You too." David gestured at the crowd flowing around them. "What's going on here?"

"Bomb threat. That's what everybody's saying."

David was about to ask why such a thing could happen, but he already knew why. For some people, The Children's Hospital had become something like Auschwitz.

"But I'm not sure," Sam added. "We were told to evacuate, so I did."

"Where's the medical examiner? Dr. Glass?"

"The cops took him away."

"Was he under arrest?"

"They told us it was for his protection. You know, because of . . ." He didn't need to finish.

David looked around. "So where's the bomb squad?"

Sam followed his gaze. "That's a very good question, doc."

"Something stinks here. It doesn't add up."

Sam laughed. "It doesn't have to."

"What do you mean?"

"The hospital was set up as a morgue because all the kids dropped dead. Well, now they're back. No more dead kids, no more morgue. We're done here. They're going to turn it into a real hospital again."

David shook his head. "We need to continue collecting data on the children. We need to learn how they regained consciousness."

"I wish you luck with that. I really do. As for me, I'm done. If you need me, I'll be drinking a few cold ones and then sleeping for about a week." A shadow fell over his eyes. He rubbed his neck, where a tiny fingernail had left a livid scratch. "Trying to forget what happened."

The children swarming him as he blocked the doors.

"Wait, one more—"

"The kids are back," the man said. "It's over. Good-bye, doc."

David got back into the car and fumed as Nadine drove out of the parking lot.

They'd taken his friend. He had to call Gloria and tell her to get a lawyer.

No more dead kids, no more morgue, Sam had said. *We're done here.*

The rising of the children didn't scare David anymore. But he didn't trust it.

We're being suckered. Herod brought the children back, and it did so for a reason. There's a price. Something terrible is happening, but people don't see it as terrible. Instead, they see their children's faces. They feel love when they should feel . . .

"What's next?" said Nadine.

Fear. They should feel fear.

"Do you need to go back to the burial ground? Or do you want to make a house call with me? I could show you the miracle. You could see it for yourself."

"Neither," David answered. He stared out the window.

Nadine's smiled slipped away. "Where would you like me to take you?"

It's over. Good-bye, doc.

"Home."

Joan

13 hours after Resurrection

Joan hummed to herself as she pulled a package of meat from the freezer and set it on the counter. She wanted to cook something special for tonight. They'd have pot roast, Doug's favorite. A celebration feast, complete with sweet potatoes and salad.

She'd cook enough for everybody, even though the children weren't quite eating.

She just hoped she'd be able to get Doug to eat in the same room with them. The kids weren't exactly great for the appetite, either.

After dinner, they'd get the fireplace going. They'd divide up the presents she'd already wrapped and stored in a safe place in the bedroom closet.

Christmas would come a couple weeks early this year.

If everybody was still here in two weeks, the Coopers would celebrate it again then, too. The past four days had taught Joan not to take anything for granted. Never put anything off. The future was an empty promise. The past hazy and uncertain. The only thing you could count on as reliable and true was the moment you were living in.

Joan peeked around the corner. The children hadn't moved an inch since Doug left. They sat rock still on the couch, their eyes stuck on the TV. For a moment, it didn't matter. Her heart leaped at the sight of them.

And sank again just as fast.

Doug didn't understand. As crazy as the situation was, Joan wasn't. She knew her kids weren't the same. But they were still her kids, and she loved them. Period.

Doug, on the other hand, believed Nate and Megan hadn't quite come back. He thought they were stuck somewhere in between as a cruel twist of fate. Joan couldn't accept that. Joan believed Nate and Megan would continue to get better until they returned completely to normal. Doug saw the bodies and thought he was seeing everything. Joan saw evidence of life in the movement of their eyes. Healing.

They *had* to be getting better. The alternative was too horrifying to consider: trapped, unable to speak or move, in bodies that time slowly turned to dust.

Just the thought of that made her shudder.

Nate and Megan were alive and needed her love and care. End of story. She held on to that happy thought with all her might. Just as it, in turn, held her together.

Last year, Megan had woken up crying with a bad fever. The thermometer read a hundred two. All night, Joan rocked her little girl to sleep in her arms between droppers of liquid Tylenol, warm sponge baths, and waking up Doug to fight over whether they should take her to the hospital. Her heart ached with worry the entire time.

What she felt now was far, far worse.

The phone rang. She ignored it. She didn't want to talk about her kids and how they were doing. She didn't want to be judged because of their condition.

Leave us alone.

The phone stopped ringing. She shivered.

Nate was looking right at her from the living room.

She thought about his strange request for the hundredth time that morning.

Last night, Joan had woken to footsteps creaking on the floorboards outside her room. She sat up in terror. A black shape hovered over her.

Nate, trembling.

"What is it, Nate? Do you need a drink of water?"

Air rattled in his chest, like a tiny motor trying to start.

"Are you all right?"

Froth bubbled at his lips. Next to her, Doug snored.

"*Blood*," Nate wheezed.

"Blood?"

"*Want it.*"

"What for?"

He didn't answer. He'd turned into a statue again. Then she noticed his mouth was still moving, puckering like a fish on land. She brought her ear closer to his face to hear.

bloodbloodbloodbloodbloodblood

He'd stopped once she tucked him into bed. Joan backed out of the room and closed the door. Then lay in bed for hours, trying to figure out what it meant.

Blood, he'd said. He said he *wanted* it.

Why? And for what? It made no sense.

Then came the other questions. Did he mean animal blood? Human

145

blood? She'd swallowed hard before asking herself the ultimate question: *My blood?*

She wasn't about to find and kill some poor animal—the only one that was handy anyway was Major, and there was no way she would hurt him to test a weird theory. Her thawing pot roast was useless as well. Nearly all blood was drained from meat during slaughter. The red meat juice was actually water mixed with myoglobin, a protein that gave it the appearance of blood. No help there.

But she knew just where to get some.

I could just prick my finger a little. Offer it to him, and see what happens.

At this point, she was willing to indulge anything.

But that involved cutting herself intentionally. Seeing her own blood and giving it to her child. She wasn't sure which of these ideas appalled her the most. She'd cut herself more times than she could count during all the meals she'd prepared. Nothing a Band-Aid couldn't cure, and it'd cost her a few days of irritation at most.

This was different. This was deliberate. Just thinking about it made her want to leap out of her skin. She didn't even want to think about what came after that. Giving it to him.

She picked up the steak knife and thumbed its sharp edge. Her eyes shifted from the blade to the soft flesh of her forearm. Cut along the arm and hit a vein or artery, and the blood comes right out—lots of it, in fact—but it can't clot as easily as it would if one sliced across the wrist. Suicide for dummies. She had no intention of doing that.

Just one little cut along her finger.

Maybe she should have answered the phone. Maybe it was one of her friends, and she could ask them if their kids had also asked for blood.

Yeah, that wouldn't be too awkward. She could just picture the conversation.

Hello, Coral? You know how our kids came back from the dead? Well, Nate said he wants blood. I was just wondering if Peter asked for the same thing. Should I give him a cup of it to drink? A transfusion? Blood bath?

Coral would think she was nuts.

You've seen too many horror movies. What is Nate, a vampire?

Joan shook her head and tried to put it out of her mind. Nate had also said he smelled toast burning before he died. It didn't mean anything. She was thinking crazy. She returned to preparing the meal.

Minutes later, she entered the living room holding the knife and stopped.

Her children's eyes had shifted from the TV screen and were boring straight into her.

"Is this what you want?" she said quietly. She showed them the knife. She took a deep breath.

Look at you. You're going to scare them. You're crazy. You've completely lost it, honey.

She turned to go back into the kitchen but stopped again.

If you don't do it, you'll never know.

"Remember when you asked me for something last night?" Joan asked. "I'm going to give it to you. Okay? Should I do that?"

Nothing.

"If you don't want me to do that, you need to tell me right now, okay?"

Again, nothing. Her body felt like a live wire.

She wished Doug were here. *Why me? Why did Nate pick me to ask?*

But she already knew.

Because I'm his mother. It has to be me.

She didn't think men understood how deep the connection mothers had with their children was. If push came to shove, a man would eat his kids to survive because he could always have more of them. A mom was different. If push came to shove, she'd let her kids eat her.

The kids needed a transfusion. A transfusion in a hospital with a matching donor, overseen by licensed medical professionals.

"*Do it,*" she said to herself.

She gasped in pain and shock as the knife's edge parted the skin on her thumb.

The cut rang alarm bells in Joan's brain.

"Ow, ow, *ow!*"

Nothing happened. All that pain, and it didn't even look like she'd pierced the skin. Then a bright red drop of blood bloomed from the wound. The drop became a tiny flood that covered her thumb and dripped onto the carpet.

She held it high with her other hand. Now she worried she'd cut too deep. The initial sting had begun to fade, but her thumb still tingled with angry surprise. The amount of blood was alarming.

"I seriously hope this is what you want."

She was already hating herself. But she knew she was right. Nate was staring at her red thumb. His eyes gleamed. His eyes looked, well, *hungry.*

He didn't want a transfusion.

She opened Nate's mouth and placed her thumb inside.

Drop, drop, drop. Nothing.

"Oh, gross," she whined. "So gross." She turned away and exhaled a loud sigh.

So what happens now? What comes next?

She was starting to feel stupid.

Nothing comes next, you lunatic.

Nate clamped down on her thumb and sucked with incredible force. Joan cried out, torn between the instinct to push him away and another urging her to stay where she was.

She finally pulled her hand away. "Jesus, Nate!" She felt nauseous. Her thumb tingled with the memory of blood draining out of it. "Oh my God. Nate?"

His cheeks blushed a little and his chest rose and fell.

It was working. She couldn't believe it. But a part of her had known it would.

Her eyes brimmed with tears. "Oh, my dear boy. Welcome back."

"Good," Nate murmured. He looked sleepy.

"Anything," she whispered. "Anything for you."

Nate's smile froze into a grimace. His eyes glazed over. The flesh on his face rippled.

"No," Joan moaned. "Wait!"

"*More*," he breathed. "*Pleasssse . . .*"

He sounded like a deflating balloon. His face went slack. His cheeks turned blue. The last of his breath whistled from his lungs.

"Please, Nate. Don't go."

Nothing.

"Wait! Tell me how much more!"

Nothing.

"If I get you more, will you stay longer? Will you stay forever?"

Again, nothing.

More. Pleasssse.

"Okay," she said quietly. It was a promise.

Ramona

14 hours after Resurrection

Little Bear helped Duck find the missing chicks.

Ramona had watched this episode of *Little Bear* at least a dozen times with Josh over the past year. So many times that she'd memorized most of the lines. She'd always found the show charming, but now it just seemed saccharine and haunting. She turned it off, which was Josh's cue to cry and demand more TV.

Instead, he did nothing.

Always nothing.

She sat on the edge of the bed while Josh continued to stare at the black screen as if the cartoon had never stopped.

She grabbed the bottle of saline from his dresser and squeezed a few drops into each of his eyes. She did this because he didn't blink, and she didn't want dust in the air to scratch his corneas and eventually blind him.

"Why don't we play a game together? We could play with your LEGOs."

Saline tears rolled down his cheeks.

Ramona was starting to think she was stuck in some cruel Greek myth. Her grief was so strong that it had recalled her boy from Hades but offended the gods. Now she was doomed to be his mother but remain unable to connect with him. She'd gotten back a facsimile of him. A rotting puppet.

On the heels of this thought came the nagging feeling she'd be burdened by a vegetable forever, one that didn't even breathe, who just lay there and robbed her of life, attention, energy.

The guilt came right after.

How many times did you let him down, Ramona? How many times did you tell him NO because you were too tired? How many hours did you work overtime and leave him in the care of other women? How many times did you put yourself first?

You always wanted things to be perfect. You should have wanted things to be perfect for HIM. You want to make it up to him? Then do it.

She emptied a bag of LEGO bricks onto the bed. "I'll start. You join in when you're ready, okay?" She grabbed a handful of red ones and worked them together. "Guess what this is?"

She glanced at him. His eyes had shifted to stare at the blocky thing in her hand.

"That's right, little man. It's a robot. A giant monster robot. He fires lasers from his eyes. Earth is doomed."

His large eyes shined like carved glass. He looked like a poorly stuffed child. An insane taxidermist's gift to a grieving mother.

"We were fools to believe we could stop it with our paltry weapons," she said in her movie voice. "If only a hero would arise and save the planet from this galactic menace."

Josh should have been shrieking with laughter at this point.

Ramona offered him a weak smile. "Mommy will be right back, okay?"

She hurried to the bathroom, sat on the toilet, and cried her eyes out into a towel.

When she was finished, she stood, blew her nose with a tissue, and dropped it into the toilet.

In the mirror, she saw a haggard version of herself. Dark circles under eyes burning with fear and desperation. She wondered why Ross kept coming back. What he saw in her. Ramona felt as beautiful as dirt.

She stormed back into Josh's bedroom.

"What do you *want*, Josh?"

He was looking right at her. She had his full attention.

She knelt on the carpet next to his bed. "You know how Mommy makes deals with you sometimes and we shake hands on it? Like when I let you watch one *Little Bear* cartoon if you promise not to cry when I say it's time to stop watching? Let's make another deal and shake on it. All you have to do is talk to me. You talk to me, and I'll do something for you. *What do you want?*"

She held his cold hand and tried to smile.

"Make it big, because the sky's the limit, little man. Mommy will give you anything. That's right. Anything at all. You can have chocolate. Gum. Hours of TV. You can stay up as late as you want. You don't have to eat dinner. You can play all the time. I mean it, Josh. *Anything.*"

Her heart leaped as the doorbell chimed. She wanted to scream.

My nerves are fucking SHOT.

It chimed again. Grated like nails on a chalkboard.

She stood and forced a smile.

"Mommy will be right back."

His eyes had widened a little. As if he were afraid. The doorbell chimed again.

Halfway to the door, she hesitated.

Is he afraid of me?

The idea made her realize how afraid she was of *him*.

151

Ramona opened the front door. "Ross, it's not a great time for a—"

It wasn't Ross. A petite woman stood in the doorway.

The woman smiled. "Hi, Ramona. I'm Nadine Harris."

"Yes, of course. Your husband is Josh's doctor. Please come in."

Nadine put her medical bag on the floor and took off her coat. "You have a lovely home."

"Thank you. Pardon the unpleasant smell. It's Josh's condition."

"It's all right," Nadine said. "I'll get used to it in a moment." She looked around. "Is Josh here? Did he come home?"

"Yes. He's in his bedroom. Resting."

"Oh, good. That's good to hear. I'm so pleased for you. I've been making the rounds, visiting our patients. If you'd like, I'd be happy to take a look at him."

Ramona wanted to be left alone. On the other hand, having a medical professional examine Josh sounded good to her. Maybe she'd missed something. Something the nurse could fix.

"I'd like that," she said. "Where's Dr. Harris today? Seeing another patient?"

"He's resting. He spent all morning volunteering at the burial ground."

She didn't have to explain what that meant. Ramona knew thousands of the children were still buried in the cold ground, awaiting rescue.

Nadine added in a brighter tone, "Let's talk about Josh. How is he doing?"

"Not very well." Heat rose to her cheeks. "It's like he's . . . still dead."

"What about his eyes?"

"Yes! His eyes move. They *look* at me. Is that, you know, normal? Is he really in there?" Ramona worried it was mechanical. A reflex. Like Pavlov's dog.

"I think Josh is very much with us. Let's have a look at him."

Ramona led the woman into Josh's room.

"Josh, you remember Mrs. Harris. She's a nurse and wants to take a look at you."

"Look how big you've grown," Nadine cooed. "And handsome!"

She rolled back the covers. Josh lay in his pajamas, arms limp at his sides. She shined a light into his eyes and checked for a heartbeat with her stethoscope. Josh followed her movements with his wide eyes.

"Has he spoken?" Nadine asked. "After he got home, I mean."

Tell her.

"No, he hasn't said a word since we walked in the door."

Tell her! Tell her what he said!

"Nothing at all? Something just a bit out of the ordinary, perhaps?"

Blood.

Last night, Ramona had slept on the floor in Josh's room—an exhausted, dreamless sleep from which she'd woken every half hour. Then he startled her awake with shouting.

"Blood. Blood, blood, BLOOD BLOOD BLOOD—"

By the time she turned on the light, he'd stopped, leaving her wondering if she'd dreamed it. Her heart pounded as if a gun had gone off in the room.

She didn't sleep a wink after that.

Nadine caught Ramona's terrified expression and nodded. She put away her stethoscope and pocket flashlight. "Why don't we talk somewhere private?"

Ramona didn't notice. She was remembering how Josh had bellowed like that in the car, loud as a grown man: *I'M HUNGRY.*

"Ramona?"

She jumped. "Yes? I'm sorry, what did you say?"

"I said maybe we should talk in private."

Ramona made coffee. They sat in the living room. Nadine told her a story about her friend Caroline and her daughter Kimberly who'd returned from the grave and asked for blood. Had said she wanted to drink it, in fact.

She told Ramona how Caroline had begged her to draw her blood.

How she eventually did it. How they opened her mouth and squirted some down her throat.

How Kimberly woke up changed.

David

15 hours after Resurrection

David tried to nap but couldn't sleep, so when Charlie Donegal called and said he'd discovered Shannon eating paper, he agreed to see her right away at his office.

Her obstetrician wasn't seeing patients. The man's two children had come home. The same with her general practitioner. Desperate, Charlie had called David as the option of last resort.

David dressed and washed down a Vicodin with a glass of water.

A nerve in his leg kept spasming. It felt like a little snake had worked its way into the muscle of his leg and was now struggling to get out.

All those months of physiotherapy, all that hard work, and he'd blown it on several days standing on his feet cutting open dead children.

Children who turned out to be not so dead after all.

The first rule of being a doctor is to do no harm.

Maybe today he could do some good. Shannon's problem sounded simple, with a simple diagnosis, but it didn't make any sense.

He found his cane in the coat closet. He hated the damn thing, but he needed the help right now. He didn't want to drive either but forced himself to do it.

Charlie and Shannon met him in front of his office building. She looked pale and withdrawn. Her lips had lost much of their usual healthy color. He led them inside and turned on the lights. Once they were seated in his office, he asked how she was feeling.

"It's like I said on the phone—she's tired all the time," Charlie answered for her. "She's irritable and weak and having dizzy spells."

"My head hurts," she mumbled.

"Headaches too," her father confirmed. "A little short of breath at times. I already told you about her eating paper. I caught her mashing up little pieces of it and shoving them in her mouth like popcorn."

David nodded. Everything added up. But it still made no sense.

"I'd like to examine you, Shannon, if you don't mind."

He pulled himself onto his feet with his cane and led her into his examination room. Charlie handed him Shannon's medical records related to her pregnancy, and he read through them.

David weighed her and discovered she'd lost more than a pound since her last visit to her obstetrician. He checked her pulse and found out her heart rate was elevated.

When he reached for her belly, he hesitated. "May I?"

Shannon nodded. "Jonah's been moving and kicking constantly. I can't sleep more than an hour until he wakes me up again."

"Jonah?" David asked. "Not Liam?"

"I changed my mind about his name."

"Jonah's a great name," he said.

My God.

He'd felt the baby kick. It was remarkable. While the other children struck down by Herod's had wound down into a paralytic state soon after their return, Shannon's was still animated.

"He never stops moving, day and night," she told him.

Charlie steeled himself for bad news. "So what do you think, doc?"

"The baby moving is good," said David. "But Shannon's anemic."

"That's it? Are you sure?"

"I'm as sure as I can be, Mr. Donegal. All her symptoms point to iron deficiency."

Charlie appeared frustrated that he wasn't hearing something worse. "What about the thing with the paper?"

"Another symptom of iron deficiency. What you're seeing is called pica. She may also like to chew on ice or some other things besides paper that aren't food."

The man laughed with relief. "That's right!"

"Our bodies' red blood cells use iron to make hemoglobin," David explained. "That's a protein that carries oxygen to where it's needed throughout the body." He turned to Shannon. "During your pregnancy, your body has been producing more blood—right now, you have fifty percent more than you usually have. Your body has also been using iron to build the placenta. You need about thirty milligrams of it every day. You're not getting enough."

His diagnosis wasn't exactly bulletproof. Anemia made sense only if Shannon were nourishing a baby that was alive in any normal sense. The weight loss added to the mystery. He suspected Shannon had stopped eating altogether, which suggested she was depressed, or she'd lost some blood. Perhaps her body had begun to reject the undead thing inside of her.

Which was all speculative, of course, since nothing about Herod's syndrome was normal. All he could do was treat the symptom. If her condition worsened, he might recommend stronger measures. For now, there was nothing more he could do.

"So what's next, doc?" Charlie asked him. "How do we fix it?"

"Iron supplements and vitamin B-twelve."

Charlie scowled. He wasn't buying it.

"I've been taking my vitamins," Shannon said in protest. "Every day."

"Have you been eating regularly?"

"I've been so tired, but yeah."

"Have you been bleeding at all?"

The question startled her, made her alert. "No. Not at all."

David frowned. There was another possibility, one he considered extremely unlikely, tainted as it was by wishful thinking.

Maybe Nadine is right. Maybe the children are regaining signs of life.

This would suggest Shannon's body was undergoing some sort

of change to support this process. Something that would explain the weight loss and surging demand for iron.

"I'm going to do one more little test," David said. He limped back into his office and returned with the fetal Doppler. "Just to see."

He placed the microphone against her womb.

There it was—the unmistakable *whoosh* of a second heartbeat.

"I don't believe it," he breathed. If only Nadine could hear this.

"What?" said Charlie. "What's happening?"

"I've got a heartbeat. Strong and steady as a horse. The baby is alive. Really alive."

Shannon hugged her swollen belly and smiled. "I knew he was alive. I told you."

The dead had not only come back. At least in this case, they were coming *back to life*.

"But it's incredible!" David laughed. "There was nothing three days ago. Then he kicked. Now his heart is beating. It's nothing short of miraculous."

"That's why I'm naming him Jonah instead of Liam," Shannon said. She gave her belly a gentle pat. "In the Bible, Jonah spent three days in the stomach of a whale like he was dead, and was then reborn. It's funny on two levels."

David laughed as if it were the funniest thing he'd ever heard.

Ramona

15 hours after Resurrection

Ramona stared at the needle. She hated needles.

Nadine pulled on a pair of gloves. "Are you anemic?"

She shook her head. "No."

"When was the last time you menstruated?"

"A little over two weeks ago."

Nadine checked her blood pressure. "One twenty over eighty. Normal."

Ramona swallowed hard. "That's a big needle."

"You'll feel a mild sting as it goes in. The actual procedure won't cause you any pain as long as you relax and keep still. Drink this."

Nadine handed her a glass of water, which she drank slowly.

"Now lie back. Once I start the procedure, it'll be over in about ten minutes. Your body and gravity will do all the work."

"How much are you going to take?"

"Between four fifty and five hundred milliliters. Once it's mixed with the anticoagulants in the bag, it'll end up five hundred, or a unit of whole blood."

"Five *hundred*?"

"Don't worry. It's about a pint."

"A pint," Ramona echoed. She visualized a pint of milk.

"How much do you weigh?"

"One fifteen, I think. It's been a while since I weighed myself."

"You have about eight and a half pints of blood in your body. You'll be keeping nearly ninety percent."

Ramona frowned. It didn't sound very reassuring. *After this, ten percent of me will be gone.* "You sounded really concerned about my iron."

"Hemoglobin, actually. It carries oxygen from the lungs to cells throughout the body. The minimum level is a hundred twenty-five grams per liter. You'll have lost about ten grams when we've finished. If you drop below one ten, it could cause a bit of a problem."

"Like what kind of problem?"

"You could become anemic. You'd feel grouchy and tired, get headaches, and find it difficult to concentrate and think."

"Sounds like a fancy medical term for motherhood," Ramona joked.

Nadine didn't laugh; she was all business. "It's not recommended to give blood more than once every fifty-six days. It takes that long for the average healthy body to regenerate the lost red blood cells. Take too much, and the body starts to shut down."

"But I'm not anemic. So I'm going to be okay."

"You haven't been eating, drinking, or sleeping properly in days. This could feel a bit rough. Ideally, I'd take a drop from your finger and run a hemoglobin test, but I can't do that here. You should understand there are risks. Do you want to keep going?"

Ramona forced down the last of the water and handed the glass back. "Let's get it over with."

Nadine tied an elastic band around her upper arm to form a tourniquet. The vein in the crook of her arm bulged.

"Make a fist. Good. Now let go."

The tourniquet, she explained, increased blood pressure. Opening and closing her fist increased blood flow. She tapped Ramona's vein and swabbed her inner forearm with a prep pad to sterilize it. Then she got the needle ready.

"Wait." Ramona pulled her arm back. "I don't want to do this. This is crazy."

"I told you everything I know and saw with my own eyes. The treatment worked with Kimberly. It worked with another patient I visited before I came here. I'd like to help Josh. I believe I can. But it's your choice. Do you want to stop?"

Ramona's internal timer went off. *I need to check on him.*

Josh didn't need checking. He couldn't hurt himself. Couldn't get lost. Couldn't do anything, in fact, except lie there.

You promised you'd do anything. You promised you'd put him FIRST.

Besides, she couldn't take the constant stress anymore. The stress of not knowing if he was going to wake up again. The stress of not being able to help him. Nadine had told her she could cure Josh. She'd already helped two children become normal again. She'd said that.

But maybe she was lying. Maybe she was giving out false hope.

Maybe this woman is flat-out, bats-in-the-belfry, off-her-rocker nuts.

Which was more likely? It didn't matter.

You want to know what's nuts? This whole situation. The children dying. The children rising from the grave. You still have to try. False or not, it's still hope.

"Ramona? Do you want to stop?"

"No," she whispered.

"I saw the pictures taped to the wall in Josh's room. Does he like to draw?"

"Yes," said Ramona, drawing it out into a hiss as Nadine slid the needle into the vein.

Tricked me. Ouch.

The blood began to flow. Dark, thick whole blood filled the tube and began to pool within the plastic bag on the floor.

Nadine gave the bag a quick shake to mix the incoming blood with the anticoagulants. "Remember we were talking about iron? It's the stuff that makes blood red."

"I don't want to look," Ramona said.

"Blood is beautiful. It's life. It goes around and around inside our bodies, twelve thousand miles a day. Make a fist for me again, slowly. Now open your hand again."

Ramona's lips tingled. "I'm feeling a little sick right now."

"That's normal considering the condition you're in. Just stay calm."

"Normal," she said, as if she'd never heard the word before.

She tried not to think about the blood draining out of her body and into the bag.

"Dizziness is the result of a drop in blood pressure. A little bit of your life is flowing out of you. We're going to put it into Josh and try to cure him. Focus on that."

Nadine made it sound like a routine clinical procedure. Almost normal.

"I hope you're right."

The nurse nodded. "Hope is good."

"Can I ask you a personal question?"

The nurse removed the tourniquet and asked her to make a fist again. "You may."

"Dr. Harris has a picture of a boy on his desk—"

"We lost Paul a year ago."

"He didn't—"

"No one who died of anything other than Herod's has returned."

Ramona opened her eyes and saw Nadine looking out the window, eyes burning with anger. Like a cat ready to pounce and tear much larger prey to pieces.

"I lived alone with all that grief," Nadine said. "No one understood. Not even David. Not really."

"I'm so sorry, Nadine. I shouldn't have brought it up."

"Now everyone understands. Everyone knows my grief, but I still feel like an outsider."

Ramona shook her head. "We're all the same. The only difference is the timing."

"Your boy came back," Nadine said. "Mine didn't."

"I'm sorry," Ramona said quickly. "I didn't mean—"

"Everything happens for a reason. Maybe Paul passed on so I would understand your loss and be able to help you reunite with Josh. Maybe I was meant to do this." She added bitterly, "Like Moses, leading people to the promised land but unable to enter himself."

Nadine withdrew the needle and pressed her finger against the venipuncture site.

"Thank God that's over with," said Ramona. "I feel like crap."

The nurse taped a cotton ball over the wound. "You need to rest for about ten minutes. Here, have this."

She handed Ramona a lollipop. It was orange.

"I want to see Josh."

"You need to rest first. Eat something. Drink some juice. I'll get something for you."

Ramona sat up. A wave of nausea pushed her back down. She tried again, succeeded.

"I need to see Josh. I need to see if the cure works. Please."

"All right." Nadine helped her to her feet. "Now lean on me."

They entered Josh's room. He lay in the exact position he'd been left in. Ramona knelt on the floor while Nadine filled a syringe with blood.

"Josh, I'm going to give you a little medicine."

Josh's eyes flickered to stare at the syringe.

"It's okay, little man," Ramona said.

"Yes, it's a syringe," said Nadine. "But there's no needle, see? So there's no reason to be afraid. Inside is a special medicine. You drink it. See, like your friend here."

She picked up Josh's favorite stuffed animal, Graham the Bear, and mimed feeding it to him. She looked like a mother feeding her baby a bottle.

"Yum, yum," said Nadine. "Do you know the story of Pinocchio?"

"We've read Pinocchio together, haven't we, Josh?" said Ramona. Her voice was shaking now. The suspense was killing her.

I don't give a shit about Pinocchio! Just do it!

"Pinocchio didn't want to just exist," Nadine said. "He wanted to be truly alive. He wanted to be a real boy. This medicine will make you a real boy again. Just like Pinocchio. Would you like that?"

Josh's eyes flashed to meet Ramona's. She saw hunger in them.

Yes, he would like that.

The nurse opened the boy's mouth and inserted the syringe. She pressed the plunger. Fifty milliliters of blood flowed down his throat.

"Down the hatch."

His Adam's apple bobbed.

He's swallowing it.

Ramona had wanted so hard to believe, but now that it was happening, she couldn't.

He gulped the next syringe. The awful sucking sounds made her feel nauseous again. She turned away in fear and revulsion.

"You can look now," said Nadine when she was done.

Ramona turned back hopefully. "Now what?"

"Now we wait."

Nothing happened. Seconds ticked by.

"How long does it—"

Josh's face began to swell.

He screamed. The scream pierced the air, loud and throaty.

She glared at Nadine. "What did you do? *What's happening to him?!*"

The nurse said nothing. She stared at Josh with a manic gleam in her eye. He appeared to deflate. Skin rippled across his face.

"Oh, Josh, I'm sorry!" Ramona cried.

The screaming stopped. Josh sucked in a massive lungful of air and coughed. A dense, noxious stink filled the room. His body twitched. His slack cheeks filled out.

"Oh my God," Ramona said.

Josh sat up, looked around, and fixed his gaze on his mother. His eyes sparkled with life and intelligence. His cheeks burned with health and youth.

He licked his lips and said, "Mommy, can I watch *Little Bear*?"

Doug

17 hours after Resurrection

Digging the children out of their graves was exhausting, backbreaking labor. By the end of the day, Doug was cold, tired, hungry, and fed up. But he didn't want to go home.

Archaeologists had been called in to supervise some of the digging. The rest of the crews, including his own, were simply told to be careful. They didn't need to be told.

Across the site, the pace was ebbing. The initial urgency had petered out. The bodies had stopped moving. When the recovery workers opened the bags, the children didn't sit up and cry for their mommies anymore. Their eyes were open, the sole evidence they'd once woken up, but blank, as if looking inward now instead of out.

As if waiting for something.

The big yellow machines growled across the landscape, reopening its scars. Work crews jumped into the fresh-cut trenches to dig at the mangled earth. When they reached the children, they didn't bother opening the bags anymore. They just pulled them out and loaded them on trucks. Doug had an awful feeling they'd soon have to pick up these same bodies and bring them right back again.

Doug had learned over the past few days that feelings had sharp edges, and he dulled his with another long pull from his flask. His back and shoulders ached, but he didn't care. Quicklime burned in his lungs, but he'd live. Snow continued to fall from the murk above and make a mess of everything; he accepted it.

When he worked, he stopped thinking about the ghosts of his children.

He didn't feel grief right now. The pain of the past four days wasn't there. Something else had replaced it—a nameless fear that came from a deep internal place governed by instincts instead of reason.

At some point, he'd have to go home and face them, but not yet. He just couldn't do it right now. In fact, he could face just about anything other than the mocking imitation of the people he loved more than himself.

Mitch stabbed the ground with his shovel. The men heard the crack of bone.

"Whoops," he said. "Hey, I found another one."

"For Christ's sake, be careful," Tom said.

When Doug had walked onto the site, he'd found Tom, Jack, and

Mitch working in one of the trenches. Although he wasn't looking for company, he'd joined them.

He'd come to regret it. All they did was bicker to pass the time.

"Why bother being polite?" Mitch said. "We all know these kids are toast."

"It's common decency to respect the dead," Tom said.

"Like I care," Mitch replied with a laugh. "They're dead, so what? It's all pointless, college boy."

"We're also responsible, dipshit," said Jack. "Our names are assigned to this group. It's going to end up in the public record. I don't want some screaming mother coming after me because her kid was sent home with a broken leg."

Mitch made a show of gripping his crotch. "If some screaming MILF wants to come at me, I'll be happy to console her."

Doug leaned on his shovel. "Mitch, you're right, it's all pointless."

The kid grinned at Tom. "See? Even Doug—"

"But we live here, and these are our dead. If you hurt one of them again, I'm going to punch your teeth down your throat."

Mitch sneered back at him. He was an expert at trading trash talk and already had a response ready to launch. Then his brain processed the look on Doug's face.

"Yeah, uh, sure thing, boss."

Now it was Jack's turn to laugh, while Mitch scowled.

"How's everything at home?" Tom asked Doug.

"Peachy," he answered.

"I just wanted to say I hope everything's working out for you—you know, with your kids being back and all." The man hesitated, his face flushed, and added, "I'm not sure what the right thing to say is here."

"As little as possible is usually best," Jack muttered.

"I'm hoping everything's okay for you," Tom said. "That's all."

"My kids scare the shit out of me," said Doug. "I'm dad of the year. Okay?"

Tom blanched and went back to work.

Doug's phone rang. He climbed out of the trench and answered it.

Joan's voice: "Come home, Doug."

"Not right now, Joanie. We've got to get these kids out."

"Your own kids need you here."

He shivered as a strong wind blew across the field. "I can't say that I'm ready for that just yet."

"The kids are asking for you."

The old fire burned in his chest. He felt the urge to put it out with a stiff drink. Instead, he said, "That's not funny."

"I'm not joking."

"Don't play with me, Joanie." His heart thumped in his chest. "You're serious? They're really talking? What are they saying?"

"Pick up some milk on the way." A moment later, the call disconnected.

She expected him to come home. No discussion. And God help him if he forgot the milk.

It was a familiar feeling—this was how she had managed him back when she was pregnant with Nate and he was still pounding shots and beers with the other san-men at the Cornerstone Pub.

The message was always loud and clear: *Come home now, or don't bother.*

As he did then, he'd obey now. This time, however, he had an even bigger reason than the fact that he loved Joan.

Just before she'd disconnected, he'd heard Megan laughing in the background.

Which meant she was right—the kids were back. That, or he was losing his mind.

He walked off the site. The other men called to him. He didn't answer.

He was going home.

He walked straight to his truck and drove out of the works. The burial-ground operation kept the access road well plowed, but the public roads were still terrible. Snow fluttered in his headlights. Doug watched it, mesmerized, while he drove at a snail's pace and chain-smoked.

When he passed Cody's Bar, he felt the tug of its gravity.

I could have a quick one. Maybe the girl is in there. He tried to remember her name and laughed. *Cindy Crawford. Just like the model.*

Her number was still scrawled in black marker on the back of his left hand, faded now to a dull smudge. The memory of being with her, equally faded, conjured up mixed feelings of guilt and longing.

He remembered Megan's laugh and drove past the bar.

Love is a powerful thing. So is hope. With love and hope, you can conquer anything. You can even conquer yourself. The worst in yourself. He knew that firsthand. He was a veteran of that kind of war.

He pulled into the parking lot of a 7-Eleven. The lot was full, so he drove his truck onto the sidewalk and parked it there. The store was packed, and the shelves were half-empty. People weren't showing up for work, the world was falling apart, and nobody gave a shit anymore. He grabbed the last gallon of milk and cut in line, his yellow hazmat suit parting the way just as it had at the liquor store. He stocked up on Winstons at the counter, grabbed the jug, and returned to his truck.

Joan had told him to pick up milk because the kids drank it.

He drove on past an endless series of houses, traffic lights, and businesses he recognized, all together, as home. Garbage had been piling up for days on the sidewalks and in the back alleys, another giant mess for him to clean up in time. When he reached his house, he parked in the garage and sat in the dark for a while, smoking and listening to Leo Boon's cover of an old mountain song. *This train don't carry no gamblers, this train. No hypocrites, no midnight ramblers. This train is bound for glory.* Yes, sir.

The idea of the kids magically becoming normal again seemed impossible, even after everything he'd seen. He was pinning his hopes on something that couldn't have happened and therefore simply could not be.

Maybe Joan is losing her mind.

That, or the kids had returned to normal by magic. Which was more likely?

But I heard Megan laugh. I heard it.

Maybe I'm *losing my mind. I heard what I wanted to hear.*

He reminded himself that the kids had come back from the dead. Anything was possible.

But he was too scared to hope.

He hesitated at the garage door. He was breathing hard. He couldn't face it if they were still sitting on the couch like dolls. Something inside him, in fact, might break.

He opened the door to the smell of baking and a pot roast cooking in the kitchen. Joan had the stereo on. He poked his head into the living room, which was empty. The lights wrapping the Christmas tree were on, and presents were laid out under it. Logs blazed in the fireplace. The fire filled the room with warmth and light and the smell of burning wood.

I'm home.

Again, he heard a laugh. He hurried to the kitchen.

Oh, God.

The scene that greeted him was shocking only in how normal it was:

Joan at the stove, her hips swaying to the rhythm of a country music song.

Megan sitting on the counter wearing a little pink apron, making a mess out of Joan's preparations for a cake.

Nate at the kitchen table, looking through his geography schoolbook and wearing his oversized orange Giants hat.

Doug tried to speak. A choking sob came out instead.

Finally, he managed a croak: "Kids?"

They all turned and looked at him.

They're normal.

No, they're not. They're not normal at all.

They're PERFECT.

His hand shot out and gripped the door frame as the world began to spin. "Joanie, are they real?"

Megan screamed: "*Dad-deeeeeee!*" She climbed off the counter and raced toward his legs. He scooped her up in his arms and rained kisses on her warm face.

"Oh, Jesus," he said.

"Stop!" she squealed, and patted his stubble. "Your face is *prickly*."

"Jesus. I can't believe it. It's really you."

"You're not supposed to say *Jesus*, Daddy."

"He can if he's happy," Joan said with a big smile.

Doug couldn't smile, not yet.

"Hey, Dad," said Nate.

"Hey, sport." He extended his other arm to embrace his son.

Now was the time to give in to his joy. Let it light up his face. Instead, he cried. He cried loud and hard. He didn't even try to stop it.

Megan started crying too. So did Nate. They huddled on the floor and cried.

Joan stood at the stove, her hands covering her mouth, saying, "Oh my God."

Moments later, she was bawling.

"It's you," he kept saying. "It's really you."

"Please don't be sad, Daddy," Megan said.

He looked up at Joan through a warm blur of tears and said, "How?"

Joan sniffed, wiped her eyes, and told him a nurse had brought medicine that was reviving the children. Ramona Fox had sent her.

"What kind of medicine?" he asked her.

"Something from the Centers for Disease Control."

Doug had lived with Joan long enough to know when she was full of it. His gaze shifted to the little cotton ball taped over her inner arm, which only raised more questions.

He didn't care. Whatever had happened, he was all for it. His children were back. They were normal again. They were *alive*.

Like the horrible reign of Herod had never come.

"We're going to have pot roast," she said. "And Meggie and I are making a cake for dessert. Why don't you grab a quick shower and get yourself cleaned up?"

A shower was the last thing on his mind. He just wanted to go on hugging his kids until he truly believed they were there. He *did* need to get his bearings, though. That was what Joan was suggesting he do. Step under a hot spray of water and get his head together.

He nodded, weary but happy. His stomach growled at the thought of pot roast. He'd barely eaten in days.

Suddenly, he was starving.

He handed her the jug of milk. "I'll be right back, kids."

"Cool," said Nate.

"You have to take a shower now," Megan commanded. "Stinky!"

He trudged upstairs and peeled off his work clothes.

He groaned with pleasure in the shower. He dozed under the downpour until the hot water started to run out. He gave himself a quick scrub and shave, all the while filled with wonder at what he'd seen. Still not quite believing it.

Afterward, he wiped the steam off the mirror and found a gaunt man looking back at him with hollow, sunken eyes.

But he was smiling.

He wanted a drink but knew he wouldn't have one. He'd never drink again.

They ate their dinner at the kitchen table. Doug wolfed down everything in sight while the kids plowed into their own meals.

"I've never seen them eat like this," Joan said.

Doug helped himself to another couple slices of pot roast, which he drowned in his wife's homemade gravy. A dash of salt made it perfect.

"Can I take Major for a walk after we eat?" Nate said, his cheeks bulging.

"We're staying in tonight," Joan answered.

"I'll take him out for a walk later," said Doug.

"Awww."

Doug studied their faces. "Do you kids remember anything about what happened to you?"

Joan's eyes widened, but she said nothing.

Megan fidgeted. "I don't know."

"I woke up in the dark," Nate said.

Doug and Joan stared at him.

"I remember everybody falling on the ground. Dad was carrying me away from the skating rink. I had a killer headache. Then there was this funny smell, and I went to sleep. I woke up, and everything was dark, and I was in a bag."

"I woke up in the dark too!" cried Megan, wanting in on the attention Nate was now getting.

"I wasn't scared, though," Nate told them. "Even though I really hate feeling trapped. I just knew you were going to get me. After you brought us home, it was like being in a dream. I guess I was pretty sick or something."

"Sick?" said Doug. "Son, you could guess you were *dead*."

"*Doug*," Joan scolded.

"Wow," Nate said. "Was I really?"

"You weren't here, and now you are. You and princess both." Megan laughed as he poked her belly. "A real miracle."

"I wasn't here, and now I am?" Megan raised her hands and wagged her head. "*Whaaaaat?!*"

They all laughed at that. Joan told the kids she had something special planned for the evening.

In the living room, Christmas presents awaited.

"But it's not Christmas yet, is it?" Nate asked.

"Who cares?" she said. "Go get them. And after that, get ready to stay up as late as you want."

Nate howled in triumph. He'd won the lottery and didn't even know he had a ticket. The kids fled the table, pounded into the living room, and tore into the Christmas gifts like animals. Joan chased after them, urging them on. Doug took a final mouthful of pot roast and hurried to catch up.

Megan opened each gift, held it up for all to see, and moved on to the next. She lay on the floor to play with her favorite, a Barbie laptop that taught her words and numbers. Joan settled into the La-Z-Boy and watched her play.

Nate crowed as he unwrapped LEGOs, a Nerf pistol, and a few Hot Wheels cars. Joan had wanted to get him an anatomy model of the human head to encourage any interest he still had in being a doctor one day but couldn't find one. Instead, she'd gotten him a Snap Circuits electronics kit and some books as an education gift.

Then he opened the box containing the ultimate prize—a remote-controlled helicopter. Joan did the Christmas shopping, but Doug had picked that one out special for Nate. He grinned as the boy opened it.

"Wow, this is amazing!" Nate cried.

"It's ready to fly," Doug said. "No assembly required. It's got a gyroscope to keep it steady in the air. With the control, you can make it go up, down, left, right, forward, and back. What do you think?"

Nate held it up and turned the blades. "*Wow.* It's an army helicopter."

"Marines, son. It's a SuperCobra attack helicopter."

"*Wow.* Does it shoot anything?"

"No, it just flies."

"That's okay. Can we fly it now, Dad?"

"Not when it's dark out. It's too big to fly in here; we have to take it outside. We'll do it tomorrow if the weather's okay."

"Promise?"

"You bet, sport."

Nate stood and held up the helicopter. "I'll bet it can go really high and fast too. This is the best Christmas ever!"

Doug and Joan exchanged a smile.

"Oh man, I wish—"

He dropped the helicopter to the floor.

Joan screamed. She leaped out of her chair while Doug froze in horror.

The word *wish* whistled out of the boy's lungs as they deflated.

Megan lay among the wreckage of boxes and wrapping paper. The Barbie laptop invited her to play another game. Her eyes were blank.

When Nate crumpled into Joan's arms, Doug knew his son was dead again.

III

The Long Good-bye

SIX

David

2 days after Resurrection

David awoke to winter sunlight streaming through the window. Nadine was already up, her pillow cool to the touch. He rolled onto his back and put his hands behind his head. The memory of the night before brought a smile to his face.

Dust glittered in the sunbeams. David waved his hand and watched it swirl. *This is all we are. And yet we are so much more than this.*

He plodded into the bathroom and found what he saw in the mirror lacking. *I'm too young to be this out of shape. Time to lay off the potato chips and dust off those dumbbells in the basement.* Last night had given him a reason to care again.

David grinned as he brushed his teeth. And what a night it had been.

Last night, he'd arrived home breathless with the news about Shannon and her baby. Nadine shared her own news; not just Shannon's son, but other children were returning to life. She'd seen it herself. She suspected it was happening everywhere.

Nadine looked radiant. Gone was the weariness and grief of the past year. She looked like the girl he'd married. Like a mother again.

"What was the catalyst?" he asked her. "You said you thought you knew. Were you right?"

Nadine smiled. "It turns out it was love after all."

"Love?"

"Our longing brought them back. Love brought them back to life."

Nadine was an expert in that kind of longing.

"Our collective will?" he said, struggling to understand.

"Sometimes when you really want something you have to give everything. A sacrifice."

She took his hand and led him upstairs. Into their cool, dark bedroom.

They undressed each other quickly, but with gentleness, respecting the act's importance. They hadn't made love in a year. David's entire body tingled. His stomach flipped as his skin brushed against hers. He was nervous. Nervous and more excited than he'd ever been.

They lay on the bed together, kissing and touching. The room filled with the smell of her sex. It struck him they had no protection, and he pulled away.

"Are you sure?" he said.

She put her finger to his lips while her other hand guided him in.

He came quickly, he remembered, but they made love again soon after, taking their time, and again after that. They hadn't enjoyed sex like that in years.

It was a night for starting over.

Something magical had happened to save the children, and some of it had rubbed off on his life. They would put everything behind them and start again. Put the accident in the past once and for all. Let Paul rest. Rebuild the practice, have another child.

It was like waking up from a long, long dream. Life was too precious to waste being miserable. He'd lost a year of his life not wanting to be alive. That would end now. Everything was so clear right now, and he didn't want to ruin it.

The phone rang in the kitchen. David heard Nadine answer it. She spoke fast and quiet. By the time he'd gotten dressed, she'd hung up.

He found her sitting on the couch in the living room, wrapped in his flannel bathrobe. She stared at the television. His stomach fluttered at the sight of her. A full mug of coffee rested untouched on the table next to her.

She shook her head and muttered.

"What's happening?" he said.

She didn't turn around. "The children."

David sat on the couch next to her. A pale woman was being interviewed while a child played in the background.

"He just got up and asked if he could go outside."

"What did you do?" asked the reporter.

"I cried. I hugged him. I thanked Jesus for giving him back."

David noticed the woman's arm had a bulky bandage taped over the wrist. It had a big red spot where blood had soaked through.

That woman dodged a bullet. Must have been in the middle of killing herself in grief when her son returned to life.

He gazed in awe at the small child playing and thought: *This is one of those moments that changes everything. Nothing will ever be the same. Many years from now, on our deathbeds, we'll remember this as if it happened yesterday.*

He turned to look at Nadine, who stared rapt at the TV. They'd been husband and wife for a long time, but he loved her more now than when they'd gotten married. He still found her so beautiful it made his heart ache.

They'd met in college, two premed students commiserating over their mutual hatred of organic chemistry class. They married soon after graduation. Nadine was brilliant, passionate, determined. She would have made a great doctor. Instead, she became a nurse and worked hard at a hospital to put him through medical school. When it was her turn, she decided to have Paul. Then the accident took their son from them. Took everything from her. Changed her from a woman who loved life to one intimate with death.

David's mind had little patience for willing suspension of disbelief. He didn't watch TV or read fiction. If it wasn't real, he had little interest in it. Nadine had encouraged a romantic side of him he'd never known existed. Not romantic as in roses and candlelight, but as in loving something bigger than himself.

When Paul died, that part of him went too.

Last night, it had come back. All of it.

David watched the TV.

"*How do you feel now?*" the reporter asked.

"*I'm so grateful. It's a miracle.*"

"*And do you have any big plans for the day?*"

"*First, we're going to build a snowman in the backyard.*"

"*And after?*"

The woman smiled. "*Anything he wants.*"

David couldn't help but smile too. "It really is a miracle."

He closed his eyes and imagined Nadine sitting right where she was now, her face shining over a baby feeding from her breast. Two small children sat on the floor playing together in the light of the fireplace. His awakened faith was making him think any happiness was possible. It was making him dream. David didn't care about an afterlife. It was too abstract and impossible to know or understand. But life had limitless potential to be good or bad. He wanted all of the good it had to offer. He once again found himself bargaining with a God whose existence he doubted.

Give me this, he prayed.

"It's a lie," Nadine murmured.

David looked at her. "Sorry?"

"It's a lie, David. A show. It's not real."

The phone rang.

"I don't understand."

Nadine turned back to the television while the phone continued its grating ring. "You answer it this time. I can't hear it again."

"That's one of the children right there on TV. He's alive. You were right."

Nadine didn't answer. The phone continued ringing. He finally picked it up. "Hello, this is David Harris."

"This is Doug Cooper," a voice growled.

"Yes, Mr. Cooper." He searched his memory. The Cooper children used to be patients before the accident. "Are you calling about Nate and Megan?"

"They're dead again!"

David's heart skipped a beat. He couldn't imagine the pain of having your children come back, only to die in a freak accident. Whatever had happened had created a reprieve from this death, but not mortality itself. For one of the children to die now was like surviving a fall from the world's tallest building, only to choke on a peanut afterward.

"My God—I'm sorry for your loss. What happened?"

"Your medicine didn't work for shit, that's what happened!"

"What medicine?"

"Are you screwing with me now, after all this?"

"I'm not doing anything, Mr. Cooper."

"You do not want to mess with me, doc."

"Tell me what medicine you're talking about, or I'm hanging up right now."

"The medicine from the CDC. The *medicine*. The *vaccine*."

"There is no treatment from the CDC. I would have heard about it."

The man wasn't listening. David heard the sound of a brief struggle, followed by a woman's breathless voice.

"Dr. Harris? This is Joan Cooper. Sorry to bother you at home. Can I please speak to Nadine? Is she there?"

"Of course." He turned. Nadine was still facing the television but not watching it. Her eyes were vacant, as if looking inward. "It's for you."

She nodded and took the phone from him.

"Hello, Mrs. Cooper, this is Nadine Harris. Tell me what's happening." She listened. "I'm sorry to hear that. It's not just you, I'm afraid. What we did doesn't seem to be holding." She winced. "All right, I'll come. I'll come right now."

Nadine hung up and said, "I have to go."

"What's going on?"

"The children are falling asleep again. I have to see if I can fix it."

David touched the edge of the kitchen counter and leaned on it for support. Nadine disappeared down the hall and into their bedroom.

"What the hell are you talking about?" he called, but she didn't answer. The phone rang again.

"Should I answer it?"

She didn't respond. He picked up the phone. He wanted to hurl it against the wall.

"*Yes*," he said tersely.

"David?"

"Ben, is that you?"

"Thank God I reached you. The police just released me. I need to talk to you. Can you come over? To my house?"

The man sounded terrible, wheezy and weak. It was like getting a call from his ghost.

Nadine hurried out of the bedroom, dressed and ready to leave the house to work.

"I suppose I can," David murmured.

"Please come as soon as you can," Ben said. "It's vitally important."

David watched Nadine put on her coat. "I could do that."

"And, David—David, are you there?"

Nadine glanced at him, her eyes dark and sad, and closed the door. Whatever questions David had, they would have to wait.

"Yes, I'm here."

"I want you to bring your gun."

Ramona

2 days after Resurrection

About two hours. That's how much time Ramona had been given with Josh after watching a pint of her blood disappear down his throat.

They'd watched *Little Bear* and *Caillou*. They played. His appetite was amazing; he ate two peanut butter and jelly sandwiches on gluten-free bread and a bowl of Ben & Jerry's ice cream. He asked for construction paper and pencils, and when Ramona suggested they do something else together instead, he threw a tantrum.

She hadn't minded. Josh had come back, but he was no angel—he was a four-year-old boy who sometimes pounded the floor when he didn't get his way. It was oddly reassuring because it was authentic. If he were just nice, it would have felt fake somehow. Like a trick.

In the end, they'd compromised. They would draw together. Josh drew a picture filled with giant eyes that had swirls instead of irises. It was even more disturbing than the monsters he'd drawn at Joan's. She asked him if that's what he saw while he was asleep these past few days, but he pretended not to hear. When she asked again, he shrugged. He sniffed at the air. His eyes clenched. Then the pencil skidded across the page, and his forehead thudded against the desktop.

No matter how much Ramona begged, Josh wouldn't wake up.

That night, she slept on the floor next to his bed, half expecting him to wake her up again with his morbid shouting. He didn't. She checked his pulse in the morning.

Nothing. Nadine's magical cure had come undone.

Ramona went to the bathroom and peeled the Band-Aid off her inner arm. The puncture site was a little bruised. She caught a whiff of her own funk and stripped off her clothes. Blood loss still made her head foggy; a hot shower would clear it. She caught her reflection in the mirror and started in surprise. She looked like a junkie, drawn and pale and strung out.

But also determined.

She wasn't giving up. Not by a long shot.

There was a chance for Josh, if she fought hard enough. Ramona was a fighter.

The water felt great. Just what she needed. She ran her fingers through her long hair and savored the heat on her scalp.

She'd call Nadine, and the nurse would come and cure her boy. It was that simple. And this time, it would—

Josh roared, *"I'M HUNGRY!"*

She flinched. He hadn't shouted, she knew. It was her imagination. Her mind, and the white noise of the falling water, was playing tricks on her.

"I'M HUNGRY!"

Ramona turned off the water and shivered in the sudden cold.

She began to wonder if she should be afraid.

Nothing.

She turned the shower back on.

"I'M HUNGRY I'M HUNGRY I'M HUNGRY!"

"Stop," she said, and it did.

After the shower, she wrapped herself in her bathrobe and checked on Josh, who lay in bed right where she'd left him.

"You're not being fair," she said. "I'm getting sick of these games. I love you, and you're coming back again. Got it?"

She marched into the kitchen, picked up the phone, and called Joan Cooper.

"Nadine?" said a tired voice.

"No, it's me. Ramona Fox."

"Oh hi, Ramona. How are you?"

She pulled at her hair and enjoyed the mild pain along her scalp. "How are your kids? Are they still moving?"

Joan sighed. "No. They're not doing much of anything anymore. How about—"

"Josh isn't moving either."

"I'm sorry to hear that. The nurse is on her way over. Do you want me to send her on to you when she's done here?"

"Yes, please do that." She tightened her grip on the phone. "I'd like to have a word with her. She lied to me. She said the cure would work. She *promised*."

"But it did work. We got to spend some time with our kids."

"That's not the point—"

"She's just a nurse. She doesn't know what she's doing. She's just trying to help. Have you been watching the news this morning?"

"I've been totally focused on Josh," Ramona answered.

"Other kids are waking up. Lots of them. Some of the moms were wearing bandages. They *cut* themselves, Ramona. We were lucky to have Nadine help us."

Ramona yanked at her hair again. "I'm sick of feeling helpless."

"We can't give up hope. We had Nate and Megan back yesterday. It was a gift. I learned things about them I'd never known."

"Really? Like what?"

"Little things. Nothing important to you, but in my world, they're going down in the history books. They *lived* during that short time. They were *learning*. They were *growing*. They truly came back to life. What happened after was a minor setback, nothing more."

Joan sounded like a woman holding it together by sheer force of will. It was heartbreaking.

"I wish I had your optimism, Joan."

"It's going to be okay. I really believe that."

But she didn't sound okay. She sounded worn out.

I'm stronger than you, thought Ramona with a little thrill. Even now, she couldn't stop comparing herself to the woman. She pulled at her hair.

"So that's it, you think? We just have to give a little more?"

"It worked yesterday. It'll work today."

"How much are you going to give yours?"

"As much as I got. This time, it has to stick."

"I don't suppose you have a little extra medicine to spare for Josh."

"Oh, I'm sorry," said Joan. "I don't think so."

"I'm not asking for much. One or two hundred mils, maybe."

"Nate and Megan need everything that Doug and I have. I'm sorry."

"See? You have a husband. I have no one here. I'm all alone."

"I have twice the number of mouths to feed, don't I?"

"I'm the one who told the nurse to come to your house. You're not being fair."

She heard a gasp at the other end of the line.

"What do you want me to say?" Joan asked.

"I want you to say you'll help me! I need help!"

Joan's voice took on a hard edge. "I have to take care of mine first. That's all I can do. You know that."

The doorbell rang. Ramona hung up on her and hurried to the door. She tied her skimpy red robe tighter around her waist and held it closed over her chest. She felt naked. She'd only partly dried herself; water soaked through the robe and made it cling to her body.

"Who is it?" she shouted.

"It's Ross," was the muffled reply. "Is now a bad time?"

It's always a bad time. He should know that by now.

She opened the door. Ross stood at the entrance hugging several bags and wearing a large grin.

"*You* look nice," he said.

"Oh, God. Come in quick. It's freezing."

The truth was she was glad to see him. She kept telling herself she had no energy or room in her heart for him, but she also knew she couldn't do all this alone. Everybody seemed to have help except her. Joan had Doug. Bethany had Brian. And a small, selfish part of her still wanted to give herself to him and see what happened.

Ross dumped the bags onto the couch. "I saw on the news how the kids are getting better. They're, like, perfectly normal again. I can't believe it. So where is the little guy? Let's go out and celebrate!"

She hugged her ribs. "What's all this stuff?"

"This?" He grinned at the bags. "I stopped at a toy store on the way over here and got a few welcome-back presents for Josh. I hope you don't mind."

She eyed the boxes spilling out of the bags. "You got so much."

"Well, that's the thing. I stopped at the toy store, but it was closed. A crowd of clean-cut, middle-class parents was looting it top to bottom when I showed up. I sort of joined in."

"So you stole some toys for my son."

Ross smiled and shrugged. "Well. Yeah. It's cool?"

"Very cool," she answered. The old Ramona would have been

appalled. Now she didn't care what anybody did. Ross could rob a bank, as long as it benefited her son. She picked up a Spider-Man Learning Laptop and inspected it. "Josh will love this stuff when he wakes up."

"He's sleeping?"

She yanked at her hair. "He's had a bit of a relapse."

Ross blanched at this news. "You mean he's dead? Jesus, God. How? What the hell is going on?"

"His *condition* has returned. The nurse is coming with more medicine."

"Medicine? I didn't know there was a cure. The news said some of the kids were just getting better on their own. They're calling it a miracle."

"There's a cure. Well, more like a treatment." Ramona held out her hand. "Come on. I want to show you something."

He followed her into Josh's bedroom, where her son lay on the bed staring at the ceiling.

"He's definitely, uh, got the same condition," he said. "Damn. I'm so sorry, Ramona."

"Ross, listen to me. I'm going to let you in on a secret about the children."

He crossed his arms while keeping an eye on Josh, as if he expected the boy to leap out of bed and take a bite out of him. "Go ahead."

"The children you saw on the news didn't just return to life. We had to give them something. And what we gave them didn't last. We have to give them some more."

Ross nodded. "You mentioned some type of medicine. The nurse brought it, right?"

"Sort of. This is going to sound really weird to you, but it is what it is, okay?"

He smiled as if to say nothing was too weird for him. "Try me."

You have no idea, she thought, and said, "I'm going to trust you more than I trust most people. I'm going to let you in. Do you understand?"

His smile faded. "Okay."

He sounded guarded. Ramona realized maybe he didn't want that much responsibility so soon. *Now we're going to find out what Ross is made of.* She took a deep breath. "The medicine is blood."

"You're kidding me."

"None of this is anything I feel like joking about."

"All you had to do was give him a transfusion?"

"No. Not exactly."

Ross stared at her blankly. He didn't understand.

She said, "Josh ingested it."

Ross raised his hands and took a step back. "Wait a minute. You're saying he *drank* it?"

"That's right."

"Then he came back to life—just like that."

"Yes."

Ross barked a short, disbelieving laugh. "That's crazy. So he's, like, a vampire."

"Don't be ridiculous, Ross."

But he was right. It was true. Josh was very much like a vampire.

"Ridiculous? This whole thing's ridiculous. It's a nightmare!"

Ramona understood perfectly how he felt. She just didn't feel that way about it herself. She was in too deep. Her boy died, he came back, he asked for blood, and she gave it to him. One thing led to the next. It was that simple. Anything else was just noise.

"It is what it is, okay?" she said.

"I can't believe you actually fed it to him. That you could do that."

Parents trample each other at malls to buy their kids the latest toy, Ross. Cheat and lie to get them accepted into the best schools. Fight with their fists over different parenting techniques.

Do you really think I'd balk at giving him my blood if he needed it to live?

"It's like a transfusion, Ross. Think of it like that if it's too *weird* for you."

Ross sighed and put his arm around her. "I'm sorry, Ramona. I get it. If he were mine, I guess I'd do the same. It's just weird, that's all. It's really weird."

"It's not evil." Her voice cracked. "It's love."

He pulled her to him and hugged her. "It's going to be okay."

Oh, God, yes. That is exactly what I've wanted someone to tell me for days.

She rested her head against his chest. "Will you help me, Ross? I have no one else."

He gave her a reassuring squeeze. "Yeah. Of course I will."

"You really like me, don't you?"

He chuckled. "I would think that should have been obvious by now."

"I have to give blood today, when the nurse comes. What about you?"

"What do you mean?"

"I mean *you*. We can be in this together."

"I still don't—"

"You know what I'm asking."

"You want me to give my blood so Josh can drink it?"

"So you can help cure him. We'll do it together."

She felt his body stiffen against hers. "Sorry, but there's no way I'm doing that."

"Why not?"

"Ask me to do anything else. Please. Ask, and I'll do it. But I'm not doing that."

Ramona pulled away. "I thought you liked me."

"That has nothing to do with whether I'll do it."

She opened her robe. Not enough to whore herself, but just enough to give him a taste. "I thought we could do this together."

"You're going way over the line," Ross said, and stormed out of the room.

"I'm sorry," she called after him. "I'm sorry!"

After closing her robe, she realized Josh was staring at her.

"I'm sorry."

She let it hang in the air, hoping somebody would accept it.

Joan

2 days after Resurrection

Joan despised an untidy house.

She lay on the couch and idly rubbed the inside of her arm while Doug paced the living room like a caged animal. His feet tramped through Christmas toys and wrapping paper. She watched with anxious eyes. She wanted to clean it all up but didn't have the energy.

The kitchen looked even worse. Plates filled the sink. Their unfinished dinner spoiled on the table. Flour and cake batter coated the counter, Megan's work. That's what children did; they made messes. It was her job to clean up after them. On any other day, Joan would have had this place spotless in no time, but today she had no get-up-and-go. The act of giving her blood, and then watching her children return to the darkness in which they slumbered, had taken everything out of her. She felt useless and drained.

She closed her eyes and drifted.

"She'd better come," Doug growled.

His words brought her back. The mess was still there. That, and the horror of being back to square one.

He said, "She'd just better."

Doug always viewed the world as out to get him. The politicians and the bankers. They'd engineered the system to screw people like him and keep them all down. He was no doubt thinking the fat cats were getting all the good medicine, while the little people got a shoddy batch that didn't work.

188

Doug had no idea the bad medicine was his own wife's blood.

She'd believed it was a cure.

I'm sorry, Nate. I'm so sorry, Megan.

It was all her fault. She'd let them down.

The children weren't feeling any pain. At least there was that small comfort. They had no idea what was happening to them or what their mom and dad were going through. Nate said he'd fallen asleep and woken up in the bag, and everything after that was like a dream.

Right now, they were upstairs tucked into their beds.

The nurse was coming and would fix everything again. Maybe the problem was quantity. She hadn't given them enough. Give enough, and they'd be cured for good. It was the only thing she knew to do.

The alternative was to let them stay dead. Which was no alternative at all.

"Are you with me here?" Doug was glaring at her. "It's a bad time to get depressed, babe."

Joan blinked at the sound of his voice. She'd been drifting again.

"I'm not depressed. I'm just really, really tired."

"We need to present a united front. Demand what's right. Be tough."

The air smelled like smoke. He'd lit one of his cigarettes.

"Take that outside. You know better than that."

He either didn't hear her or pretended he hadn't. He puffed away in a rage while he paced. "What we need is the good stuff."

The good stuff.

Nadine had promised she'd come. *It's not just you*, she'd said. The same thing was happening with her other patients. Maybe all the children who'd come back. It wasn't only Joan's blood that wasn't working right. She found a morbid sense of comfort in this.

"She'll be here soon," said Joan. "We'll make it right. They'll be back with us."

"It's a scam, babe. You know that, right? We're on the hook now. She's going to charge us even more money we don't have."

"She's not charging us anything. At least that I know about."

189

Doug stared at her. "She's not?"

"It's a public service or whatever."

He nodded as if to say, *Good*, but he was clearly even more worried now. If it were a scam, that would make sense to him. He'd pay through his ass to get his kids cured. That was how his world worked; it sucked, but it was predictable. And at least he'd eventually get the outcome he wanted.

This was much, much worse.

He's realizing the cure might not work at all. It's out of his control.

Joan wondered how he was going to react when Nadine opened her vein and the bag swelled with blood. She'd thought she would give some blood and the kids would come back, and that would be the happy ending and her secret. He was already afraid of the children. What would he do when he found out they'd become, well, vampires?

She'd have laughed at that word—*vampire*—if she weren't so scared. Doug was a big man and frightening when he got his dander up. It was what gave her the strength to tell him to quit drinking. When he drank, she was a little afraid of him.

Somebody knocked on the door. It jangled her nerves.

"That's the nurse," she said. "You be nice to her. I mean it, Doug."

Her husband marched to the door. "I'll be peaches and cream," he growled.

Nadine entered, took off her coat, and handed it to him to hang up.

Joan sat up on the couch. "Sorry about the mess. We're normally tidier than this."

They were somewhere at the bottom of the middle class, but she'd always been proud of the fact that she kept an orderly home. A doctor's wife like Nadine probably had a big fancy house.

Nadine didn't appear to notice or care. She saw only what she wanted to see and gave it extreme focus. Joan envied her. As for herself, she saw everything.

"Excuse me for not getting up," Joan said.

Nadine nodded and said quietly, "You're tired."

When Doug returned from the coat closet, the nurse introduced herself and extended her hand. He stared at it, shook it warily. Joan felt like laughing. Seeing this slight, poised woman intimidate her big husband struck her as hilarious.

"The children," Nadine prompted.

"They're dead again," said Doug.

"They've had a relapse," Joan said, correcting his language.

The nurse sat on the couch and put her hand on Joan's leg. "Tell me everything."

Joan did. Nadine listened attentively. The bright smile the nurse had worn yesterday was gone, making her look older, more tired. But the intensity in her eyes was still there.

"Right now, you have two options," Nadine told her. "Neither may satisfy you."

"I'm not expecting miracles," Joan said.

"We can give Nate and Megan more medicine or wait and see what happens."

Joan shook her head. "I'm not going to just lie here and do nothing."

"What the hell?" said Doug. "You got medicine, right? Just give it to them!"

Nadine kept her eyes on Joan. "I wouldn't recommend another draw for you again so soon. Your system needs time to recover. I could take a pint at most, but it would leave you feeling much weaker." She turned to Doug. "You may want to consider making this donation."

"What's she talking about, Joanie?"

"I didn't tell him," Joan told Nadine.

"Tell me what?" His face turned red. "Whatever it is, somebody had better tell me right now."

"The medicine I told you about—"

"Right, right."

"It's blood, babe."

"Blood? You mean like a transfusion?"

"Of a sort," Nadine chimed in. "But taken orally."

"Jesus Christ, you mean the kids *drink* it?"

191

"Yes, that's right."

Doug laughed harshly. "Uh-uh. No way."

"Nate asked me for it," Joan told him. "While you were sleeping."

He paced the living room several times. He was trying to puzzle it out. He stopped. "There's no cure from the CDC? You made it up."

"Yes, I made it up," said Joan. "I'm sorry—"

"Or you're making *this* up. How am I supposed to know what's true and what isn't?"

"I'm *sorry*, Doug," Joan said. "I'm sorry I kept it from you. I thought I would only do it once, and it would cure them, and you'd never have to know. I was wrong."

"You want to know what I think? I think you're both fucking nuts."

"Doug—"

"My kids do not drink blood!"

He stomped into the kitchen. To have a drink. Nadine threw Joan an inquisitive look. Joan shook her head. *Wait.*

He came back. "Joanie, please tell me what's going on. The truth. *Please.*"

She said nothing. He turned to go back into the kitchen and stopped. His shoulders sagged. "I thought drinking blood made you sick."

"That's normally true," Nadine answered. "The human digestive system does not like blood, which contains a great deal of iron. The stomach can't handle it. Too much, the stomach rejects it. The children are different. We don't know why. We honestly don't know much at all."

"Then maybe the best thing is to wait. Wait until the scientists figure it out."

Joan cut in. "By the time they do that, it could be too late for Nate and Megan."

"But how do we know—"

"Doug, this is how it is. I need you to be with me on this."

He said nothing for a while. At last, he nodded.

Joan could always count on him to take her side.

He watched with alarm as she rolled up her sleeve. "Joanie?"

"This is how I make them better, Doug."

"The risks are higher than last time," Nadine warned her.

"I don't care. Do it."

"Your husband would be a better donor."

The nurse glanced at Doug, who turned away with a frown.

"You lost your son, right?" Joan asked her.

Nadine frowned. "Yes."

"Then you know I have to do this. You understand."

The nurse opened her bag and took out her phlebotomy kit. She inserted a needle into Joan's hand and plugged a tube into it. The tube snaked to a plastic bag filled with a clear solution.

"What's that?" said Doug.

"It's a saline drip. Do you have a nail or a thumbtack? I need to hang this on the wall."

Doug pulled a framed print off the wall. Nadine hung the bag on the hook.

The saline solution, Nadine told Joan, would replace the blood volume she was about to lose. Replacing the blood volume would help her remaining red blood cells oxygenate her blood. Without it, losing another pint of blood would be a lot tougher on her body.

The solution felt cold as it penetrated her bloodstream. It chilled her up to the elbow. The nurse swabbed her other arm for the bloodletting.

Joan gasped as the needle went in.

Doug watched the blood flow down the tube into the bag on the floor. He chewed his mustache. "Is she going to be okay?"

"She's going to feel a bit rough around the edges," Nadine answered. "Make sure she eats something and gets her rest."

Doug knelt next to her. "You okay, Joanie?"

"I'm cold."

Doug threw another log onto the fire. Then he got her a blanket and wrapped her legs in it.

"For a transfusion to work, doesn't she have to be the same blood type as the kids?" he asked the nurse.

"That's normally the case," said Nadine. "But again, the normal rules don't apply to the children. Medically speaking, we're on new ground here."

Everything speaking, we're on new ground here, thought Joan.

She'd done her homework. She'd fired up the family PC and stared wide-eyed as Google suggested *blood* after she'd typed *how do I get*, based on the popularity of the phrase. She learned there were basically eight blood types, differentiated according to whether the blood had certain antigens. Antigens were substances that reacted against foreign substances in the body, part of the immune system. Some antigens made the system attack transfused blood. Besides A and B antigens, one had to account for Rh factor, which could either be present, marking the blood type as positive, or absent, marking it as negative.

Joan was A positive, which meant she could donate red blood cells to people who were A or AB positive. Doug was type O, the most common type among Caucasians, which marked him as a universal donor; his blood could transfuse anybody's with the same Rh factor. Nate was A and Megan O, but none of that mattered anymore.

The children drank blood and didn't seem to care what type it was.

"The Japanese believe blood type is linked to personality," Nadine was saying. "It's as popular as astrology. People with type A blood are well-meaning, quiet, and responsible, but also antisocial and tense. People with type O are friendly and optimistic but vain, arrogant."

"I think they've got it wrong," said Doug. He took Joan's hand and squeezed it. "Joanie's the social one. She's all those good things you mentioned, in fact."

Joan offered a tired little smile.

Nadine went on, "Asking someone their blood type is common in Japan. There are matchmaking services set up around it. It's grounds for bullying in school. In some Asian countries, Facebook allows you to put your blood type in your profile. It's an interesting idea, isn't it? That who we are resides in the blood?"

Right now, part of Joan was leaving her and entering a plastic bag.

Doug studied her face. "She's not looking too good."

"We're almost done," Nadine told him. "The best thing you can do is feed her some juice and a little food. Something iron rich, such as steak, would be best."

"We got some leftover pot roast. Listen, are you sure this will work?"

"It worked yesterday. It should work today."

"Maybe we should give them more this time. See if that makes it stick."

"You could try that."

"Yes," Joan whispered. "More, Doug."

He looked at her with concern. "Don't talk, babe. You're going to be okay. I promise."

"I'm going to be okay," she said dreamily.

"I love you, Joanie."

Doug was a provider. He knew what to do. He rolled up his sleeve to expose his muscular arm, the veins already bulging.

"I want you to do me next."

David

2 days after Resurrection

David found the orange shoe box where he'd put it at the top of his bedroom closet. He took it down and raised the lid to inspect the gun inside.

The Beretta compact nine-millimeter had a sleek design. He removed the gunlock and hefted it. A confusing mix of comfort and alarm washed over him. He released the magazine to confirm it was empty and checked the firing chamber. The safety was in the safe position. When it switched to the fire position, a little red dot appeared.

Red means dead, he remembered from the firearm safety course he'd taken.

When Paul was born, David had given in to a primitive urge to fortify his home. Global warming, resource depletion, environmental collapse—it was all happening, and nobody was doing anything about it. Having a child had forced him to look around and realize the world was getting worse instead of better. He'd bought the Beretta for home defense and built an emergency food larder in the basement. But Nadine, who hated guns, wouldn't let him near it. He became overwhelmed with the demands of his practice and helping Nadine raise their baby, and the gun sat forgotten in the closet while the cans of food gathered dust in the basement. After Paul died, he didn't care about any of it anymore. His priorities switched from worrying about the future to getting through the day. If the world wanted to end, he was all too happy to end with it.

The gun and its little box of bullets sat on his bed while he dressed. He considered carrying the weapon concealed but dismissed the idea as soon as it popped into his head. There was no need for that. He put the lock back on and returned it to the shoe box along with the illusions it offered. He then picked up the box and brought it to the car.

David still thought it strange that Ben asked him to bring the gun. But he'd known the man for years; Ben wouldn't have asked if it weren't important. He was one of the few people who'd kept their wits when Herod's struck. There was no reason to doubt him now.

He drove slowly, massaging his leg at the stoplights. He didn't need the cane this morning but didn't want to push his luck. There were even fewer drivers out and about today. Lansdowne appeared to have retreated into itself. Life went on behind drawn curtains.

When he arrived at Ben's house, Gloria answered the door with a handful of tissues pressed against her face. She let out a little scream at the sight of him and burst into tears.

"Oh, David. I'm so glad to see you!" She turned and called out, "Ben, it's David!"

He put a hand on her shoulder to steady her. She looked like she needed it. "What's wrong?"

"Ben will tell you everything. He's in the living room."

Ben lay propped up on the couch, wrapped in a blanket with a phone and handgun on his lap. An intravenous tube linked his arm to what appeared to be a saline drip. The man looked terrible. His skin was so pale it glowed. He was sweating. He rubbed his arm as David entered.

"I'm glad you could make it," he wheezed. The room smelled like his sour breath.

"Are you all right? Would you like me to examine you?"

"That's not necessary. I know exactly what's wrong with me."

"Tell him he needs to go to the hospital," Gloria said.

Ben shook his head. "I'm not leaving this house until I'm back on my feet."

Gloria tried to fight off another round of tears, a battle she quickly lost. She excused herself to put coffee on. David sat on the easy chair across from Ben and placed the orange shoe box on the coffee table. He heard Gloria crying in the kitchen.

"I brought my gun like you asked," he said. "I see you have yours."

"That's right."

"Mind telling why I need one? What's going on?"

"You any good with that thing? Can you shoot?"

"I haven't fired it in years, to be honest. Since that time we went to the range together. Remember that?" David leaned forward. "Tell me what happened. I was there when they evacuated The Children's Hospital. I heard the police took you into custody."

"You heard right. What else did you hear?"

"I was told it was for your protection."

"Protection, my ass. I was arrested, David." Ben tried to push himself up farther on the couch but gave up, panting for air. "I spent the day sitting alone in an interrogation room. No one seemed to know what to do with me or even why I was there. I wasn't allowed my phone call."

"I called Gloria when I got home."

"I know, and I appreciate that. She hired a lawyer, who went down to the station. They said I'd been released."

"That's it? You came home?"

"They lied. I was put in a holding cell with a bunch of scumbags. This one big cop, Officer Stellar, had a child who'd been autopsied at the hospital. Oh, he really had it in for me. The asshole actually called me Dr. Mengele, can you believe it? I think he was expecting the others to hurt me. But you know me."

"Yes." David smiled. "You have a way with people."

"They thought I was a general practitioner. Right there, I diagnosed an ulcer and a fungal infection, which bought me some protection. Twice a cop walked past and noticed me in the cell and asked what the hell I was doing there, but nobody let me go. I didn't even get a meal. It was like I didn't exist." He reached for a glass of water on the coffee table and took a sip. "Last night, the good Officer Stellar and two of his friends woke me up and brought me back to the interrogation room. Stellar told me they'd let me go if I did something for them. If I gave a donation."

"They asked for a bribe?"

"They took my blood."

"God, you're anemic! That's what's wrong with you."

"You got it. I told them to let me call my lawyer or put me back in my cell. Next thing I know, I had a gun pressed against my head."

"You're kidding me."

"Honest to God."

"I'm sure they were just trying to scare you."

"It sure as hell worked! I doubt if someone ever put a gun to your head, but I assure you, I was scared out of my mind. A part of me knew they wouldn't dare shoot me in the middle of a police station, but the rest of me was shitting my pants."

"So they took your blood."

"One of them had some phlebotomy training, but not much; he did a sloppy job on the procedure, and now I've got shooting pains up and down my arm, and burning, like it's resting in a vat of hot needles."

"I can't believe it," said David. The procedure had caused mono-neuropathy. The needle had pierced the vein at a bad angle, gone straight through, and damaged a nerve.

"They took three units. After the first, I told them to stop, you can't give more than a unit at a time, and they should give me something to replace the lost volume and prevent hypoperfusion. They asked if it would kill me. I said taking more than three units would probably kill me. So they took three on the nose." Tears streamed down his cheeks and disappeared into his beard. "Do you know how much weight you lose when you give a pint of blood? A pound. 'A pound of flesh, no more, no less.' David, they took twenty-five percent of my blood. A quarter of my life."

He cried out in emotional pain and gasped.

David turned away to give his friend a little dignity. "You're in hemorrhagic shock. Gloria's right. You need to go to the hospital."

"Not a chance. I'm staying right here."

"Did they say what the blood was for?"

"For their children. Officer Stellar called it a payment." He gripped his gun. "I'm calling it a loan."

Something clicked in David's mind.

Doug Cooper's voice: *They're dead again. Your medicine didn't work for shit. The medicine from the CDC. The vaccine.*

Nadine: *Love brought them back to life. A sacrifice.*

"I, uh, think I need to call my wife."

"I'm glad you came, David. I just wanted to warn you."

"Warn me? About what?"

"The police seized our records. Evidence, they said. Your name is on some of the autopsy reports."

David's mouth went dry. "Oh shit."

"Yep. Keep the gun close."

And do what? Point it at a cop? Shoot him?

"I honestly think I'd rather give the blood," David said.

"They might want more than a pound of flesh next time, my friend. People are out of their fucking minds. The suicide rate is still going off the charts, did you know that? Every single one a parent with slashed arms and thighs. Bled out. Always the same. No pills, no cars left running in locked garages. Not a single suicide note. Just arteries slashed with a straight razor. People are not right in the head." Ben dismissed him with a wave of his good arm. "Now go. Go call Nadine. Keep her safe. I'll be all right."

"I'll check in with you again later."

"Fine. I'll be here. I'm not going anywhere."

Ben called after him as he headed toward the door. "One more thing, David. Possibly the most important thing. I got an e-mail from the CDC today. Big news. Someone found Herod itself. Turns out our friend is a parasite. Makes itself right at home in the brain, heart, nervous system, and stomach. Thought you might want to know."

"A parasite," David echoed. *A brand-new life form.*

Even now, there was something exciting about it. His mind raced with questions. Where did it come from? How had it infected everybody? Why did it only kill the children? How had it resurrected them?

Ben said, "So whatever we did to those kids, at least we got that."

The cold air felt like a slap as he left the house. He was still reeling from everything Ben had told him. He stood in the driveway for a while, just breathing. Then he called Nadine.

No answer. He called again. She answered on the fourth ring.

"I'm with a patient," she said.

"I want to know what you're doing. Is there a connection between blood and the children's recovery?"

After a long pause: "Yes."

David felt his day, which had started with magic and a sense of renewal, continue its rapid decay. "Are you transfusing them?"

"In a manner of speaking."

"Where the hell are you?"

"Stay home, darling. Rest."

"No. I'm coming to you. I need to see for myself what you're doing."

"Please don't. I'll tell you everything later. I promise."

"Tell me this. Doug Cooper said the medicine didn't work. You seemed to think that was happening a lot. So those smiling kids on TV are going to return to their morbid state. Is that right?"

"Unless they get more blood."

"Jesus," said David. He wanted to throw up.

Another long pause. "All right. I'll give you the address."

Minutes later, David was driving toward Ramona Fox's house.

He slammed his hand against the steering wheel.

What a fool I was. What an idiot.

He'd believed in the miracle. Everything was going to return to normal. The children. Him and Nadine. The power of love had healed the world's gaping wound. As if by magic.

It was all an illusion, a trick. Herod's trick. It was a clever parasite. It took the children hostage to get what it wanted. And because it was essential to reanimation, there was no destroying it. To kill Herod was to destroy the children themselves.

The sight of children in the playground was so mundane he nearly missed it. He slowed the car.

Real, living children. Playing.

"Oh God," he said. They were beautiful.

He pulled over and studied them through a chain-link fence. Six boys and four girls playing under the watchful eyes of their parents.

There was nothing wrong with them. They looked normal. They laughed; it was children's laughter. They swung across the monkey bars and whooshed down the slide.

Only the adults struck him as strange. They stood at the edge of the play area with anxious smiles. Pale and haggard, they looked more like junkies looking to score than parents. Every so often they glanced at their watches. They didn't talk to each other. They avoided making eye contact, as if they shared an embarrassing secret nobody wanted to acknowledge.

Fear tingled along David's spine. The children filled him with a superstitious awe. He kept expecting them to stop in unison and stare at him, like something out of a horror movie.

Ben's gotten into your head. You're getting paranoid.

Time to get back on the road. The children had returned to life; that was a fact. He needed to get to Ramona Fox's house so he could understand the mechanism.

A rash of gooseflesh broke out along his arms.

The *parents* were all staring at him.

His cell rang. *They're calling me!*

No. Of course they weren't.

Get a grip, doctor. He answered the phone.

"David Harris," he said.

"She's *dead*."

"Who is this?"

"Shannon's dead." Charlie Donegal, crying. "My little girl's dead."

SEVEN

Nate

4 days after Resurrection

Last summer, Mom took him to the community pool. He put on a pair of goggles and swam along the gloomy bottom past prancing feet.

I'm a shark, look out, everybody.

He spun and looked up at the sunlight shimmering through the water. He swam toward it and broke the surface.

Waking up from being dead was a lot like that.

Timeless suspension, followed by a sense of everything moving. *Everything.*

Mom was crying. Dad too. But smiling. They were happy to see him. Nate didn't remember being born, but it must have been like this. Happiness and tears.

And screaming. It hurt to be born.

Fire ants in my brain!

He coughed and coughed.

Air filled his lungs again, but this time, he didn't scream or cough. He sat up in his bed.

He said, "I guess I fell asleep again."

Mom hugged him against her chest. It made him feel awkward, and he wriggled until she got the hint. He said, "I *died* again." He looked at Dad. "I did. Right?"

Dad just nodded.

Nate thought about that for a few moments but came up with nothing.

"Can I play with my Christmas presents now?"

Mom and Dad looked at each other.

"He remembers," said Dad. Mom nodded with a big smile.

"I told you he would. It's the real him. Not a copy."

Nate frowned. He hated when Mom and Dad talked about him as if he weren't there. Their staring made him feel funny. Of course he remembered the presents. Why wouldn't he?

He was the same old Nate. Was there a different Nate out there somewhere?

"Can I go play?" Still a question, but urgent now. They were wasting time here.

"Your father and I were thinking we would all do something together today."

"Okay." He gave them a shrewd look. "Like what?"

"Like maybe go to the park. Are you sure you're feeling okay?"

The park. He liked the sound of that. *Outside.* "I feel great. Really. I'm not sick anymore."

"We should feed him first," said Dad.

"He just ate a big dinner, remember?"

"That was last night."

"Not to him it isn't."

Nate's stomach growled. "I guess I could eat a peanut butter sandwich or something."

"It'll have to be on Ritz crackers," Mom told him. "There's no bread. The store ran out. Is that okay?"

"I guess." Mom *never* asked him if it was okay. She just fed him. Even stuff he hated, his mom made him eat because it was good for him. Mom and Dad acting weird, the jarring jump from opening Christmas presents in the living room to waking up in his bed, even the store running out of something as constant as bread—nothing felt right.

And no school—was it Saturday already? He didn't recall going to school all week.

Then he remembered his dad explaining to him that he and Megan had a disease. He was sick.

His dad's voice: *Sick? Son, you could guess you were DEAD.*

So he'd died again. *Wow.* He knew deep in his bones death was bad, and he didn't want to die, but death wasn't very scary—it was, well, nothing. He had a vague memory of staring at the ceiling, but at the time he didn't know he was staring, didn't know it was a ceiling, and had no sense of time passing. The memory itself was only a flicker occurring just before he woke up.

Death was *weird.*

They left him alone long enough to get dressed. He went to the bathroom to pee and paused to study himself in the mirror. He didn't look sick. He didn't feel sick either. He felt just fine. Ready for anything.

He went downstairs. His Giants hat was in its usual spot on a hook next to the front door. He put it on. The hat made him feel normal again.

Mom put a plate of crackers on the kitchen table and sat with Dad, who was studying a yellow notepad. Dad smelled like cigarettes, a familiar smell, and alcohol, which wasn't as much. Nate threw himself into his chair and stuffed a handful of crackers into his mouth. He chewed fast, washed them down with a gulp of milk, and reached for more.

"Look at him go," said Mom.

"He's a growing boy," Dad told her.

"I grew two inches last year," Nate reminded them, his mouth bulging with food.

Dad tapped the notepad and looked at Mom. "So this is everybody."

"A half pint gives each of them about an hour. So if everybody on the list gives one pint, we'll have twelve hours with both of them."

"It's not a lot. Half a day, total."

"Do you want to add any more names? Are we missing anybody?"

Dad shook his head. "Wait. What about his teachers?"

Nate perked up at this. They were talking about *him*.

"Everybody's going to ask them," Mom said. "We need people we can count on to give. What about Otis?"

"He's got grandkids to look after."

"This might be all we can get. We should try to get it all now and store it. People are selling medicine on Craigslist, calling it 'baby formula.' The prices are crazy."

Dad said nothing. He grabbed a cracker off Nate's plate and chewed it, glaring at nothing like he always did when he and Mom talked about money.

Mom: "If we give them a pint a day, it'll get us to Christmas."

Dad nodded.

Mom: "What are we going to do after that?"

"I'll think of something."

"Ask them all to give another pint? And another?"

"I said I'll think of something! Don't nag me!"

Nate cowered. He hated when they fought in front of him, especially when he was the cause. If he and Megan hadn't gotten sick, they wouldn't be so upset.

"I'll make the calls today once the kids are asleep," said Mom. She cleared Nate's plate. "You still hungry?"

The boy stared at his father's neck, where a vein pulsed.

"Nate? You want more?"

He shook his head.

Dad rose from the table. "I'll wake up Megan."

"Nate's already been up for a while," said Mom. "Give her a little less than half."

"All right." Dad took a bottle out of the refrigerator and trudged upstairs.

"We'll take a nice walk in the park," Mom said to Nate. "Would you like that?"

"Are you and Dad going to die too?"

"Of course not. Why do you say that?"

"Dad has cotton taped over his arm. I know what that means. He had a blood test. And both of you look really white."

Mom hugged him. He hugged her back, his eyes big and watery.

"We're not sick, Nate. We're not going to die."

"But you might."

"One day, we will. We're all on borrowed time. But not for a long, long time. Long after you and Megan have grown up. You'll be a doctor and married with your own kids by then."

Nate nodded. He knew what borrowing was, but how did one borrow time? Were you supposed to give it back? He liked the sound of it, though. He made a mental note to look for chances to say it with a serious look on his face, like a grown-up.

"If I become a doctor, maybe I could heal you, and then you wouldn't die."

"Oh, Nate, you have no idea how happy it makes me to hear you—"

Upstairs, Megan screamed.

Nate wanted to run upstairs and help his sister, but Mom wouldn't let him go, to the point where she had to forcibly hold him back. The more he struggled, the tighter she hugged him, until he couldn't breathe.

"I love you, Nate," Mom whispered in his ear.

"Let me go," he whined.

The screaming stopped.

Dad came back downstairs with Megan.

"Nate!" she howled with glee.

He smiled with relief. "Hi, Megan."

Mom was already handing him his coat to put on. "We don't have a lot of time."

"Wait! Dad! The helicopter! Can we bring it?"

"It's already in the car, sport."

"Excellent! Come on, let's go!"

Mom herded the kids into the Durango while Dad went out back to get Major, who bounded into the backseat and spun in a circle, barking until Nate calmed him down with a hug.

"Good boy, good boy," he said.

The day was looking up. It was cold, but the sun was out. It was a good day for playing. Nate had already forgotten that just minutes ago, he'd been dead.

But his parents argued during the drive, making him tense and edgy. Something about Grandma and Grandpa wanting to spend time with him and Megan if they were going to give medicine. Dad said he didn't like conditions and demands.

Nate didn't like it either. Why would Grandpa withhold medicine from him and Megan? On the other hand, all he wanted in return was to see them. What was the big deal?

His stomach flipped when they pulled into the park. Nate scanned the faces of the few kids running around the playground but didn't see any of his friends.

"I wish Keith was here," he grumbled.

"I'll call his mother, and we'll set something up."

"Okay."

Nate was dying to show Keith the helicopter, even though a part of him was glad his best friend wasn't going to be at the park today, because Keith was also the kind of kid who broke things. He said he was just clumsy, but Nate didn't believe that. Keith also lied sometimes; Nate often couldn't tell if he was telling the truth. When Keith promised something, it didn't mean anything. And whenever Nate believed a lie, he felt stupid, and that wasn't fair.

Keith was one terrific hockey player, though. Possibly the best ever, in Nate's view. He could shoot a puck to the moon.

"I'm going to make a snowman," Megan announced.

"That's a great idea," Nate said with a smile.

She beamed at this and kicked the back of Mom's seat until Mom told her to stop. She said hopefully, "You can help me make it if you want to."

"Dad and I are going to fly my new helicopter."

"But *I* want to fly it."

"You're too little to fly it. You can watch us, though, okay?"

Megan crossed her arms and turned away with a *humph*.

Dad parked the car and let Major out for a run while Mom got Nate and Megan out. By the time Nate ran around to the back of the car, Dad already had the helicopter in his hands, a sleek olive-green SuperCobra. He begged for details about how it worked. Dad said it could go up, down, left, right, forward, and backward. The lithium battery was charged and good for ten minutes of flying. The transmitter required AA batteries; Dad had already put those in. Dad said it used the latest gyroscope technology to keep stable in the air. He said it was controlled using radio waves, so they could fly it outside.

"And check this out," said Dad. "You wanted to know if it fired anything, right?"

He pressed a button, and the helicopter's cannon lit up with a red LED light. The sound of rapid gunfire roared from the toy.

"*Wow*," Nate whispered. He pictured the helicopter doing a low-level strafing run against a horde of zombies. He needed to fly it *now*; the wait was killing him.

Dad showed him how it worked. Nate took the toy and experimented until soon he had the helicopter buzzing through the air, its LED cannon firing, while Mom videotaped him with her digital camera. Megan demanded a turn until Mom carried her crying to the playground, where she shrugged it off and started playing. Major got a workout barking and chasing the chopper. Major was supposed to be on a leash, but Dad said the park rules didn't matter anymore. Nate smiled at his dad, who smiled back.

After ten minutes, the helicopter became sluggish, and Dad said it was time to put it away.

"Oh, *man*," Nate whined. He was just starting to have fun.

"Sorry, sport. We'll do it again next time."

"Promise?"

"You bet."

"Okay." Nate crouched and scratched Major behind the ears. "Dad? Am I going to die again?"

Dad picked up the helicopter and put the controller in the pocket of his denim jacket. He nodded.

"When?"

"Soon."

"Like in ten minutes?"

"Longer than that."

"Twenty minutes?"

"Maybe thirty minutes."

That wasn't very much time at all. Nate couldn't understand how he had to die again so soon. He didn't feel sick at all. He was burning up with energy. He could run and run.

"Why didn't the medicine work last time?"

"We thought we didn't give you enough. We were going to give you a lot more. By the time we were ready to wake you up again, the nurse called and said somebody else tried that, and it didn't work. You'd get more time, but after a while, well, you know."

Nate nodded. He liked when his dad talked to him like he was a grown-up. He had batteries just like the helicopter. They wore out over time. Medicine recharged them.

"Will you get more?" he asked.

"We will."

"And wake me up again?"

"That's right."

"Promise?"

Dad nodded. "You bet."

"I don't want to sleep forever, Dad. I don't want to be dead."

"It's not going to happen."

"I don't even dream. There's just nothing."

"I'm going to take care of it."

Nate believed it. He started running.

"Where are you going?" Dad called after him.

"The playground!"

"We have to put this back in the car first."

"Can you do it, Dad? Please?"

He only had a half hour, and he knew how fast that would go when he was having fun. He wanted to make every second count. He sprinted through the snow until he reached the monkey bars, his lungs working hard to keep up, and swung from one to the next and back again. He fell on the last rung and hit the ground hard but shrugged off the pain. He ran to the slide and went up and down three times as fast as he could. It wasn't as fun doing these things by himself; he looked hopefully at the other kids. They invited him into a game of tag, and he played with them until their moms pulled them away one by one to go home, saying they had to do this before they turned into pumpkins. Soon it was just him again. He ran to the swings. Today, he was going to swing higher than ever. Kick the sky right in the face.

Dad took pictures and short videos of everything. Nate saw him glance at his watch.

Nate closed his eyes and felt the pull of gravity move from his legs to his head each time he pulled back and soared into the air on the swing. He had to pee real bad but ignored it. When he opened his eyes, he saw Mom holding Megan in her arms.

Megan wasn't moving. Mom's mouth smiled at him, but her eyes were sad.

He was running out of time.

It wasn't fair. Next time, he swore, he'd just sit there and do nothing so time would go by really slowly.

Nate watched his sister. She just lay there in Mom's arms. She didn't look like Megan anymore. She looked like a doll somebody made to look like Megan.

He didn't push at the ground with his feet anymore. His momentum slowed.

Is that what I look like when I'm dead? The whole time, I'm lying on the bed like that staring at nothing? Lights out, nobody home?

He winced as a headache bloomed behind his eyes. The world smelled like burning toast.

"No," he said.

I don't want to be a pumpkin.

He leaped from the swing and sprinted across the open field toward the skating rink where he'd died the first time. Major caught up and bounded grinning next to his legs. Mom and Dad yelled at him to come back. Nate ran harder; he wanted to race.

I'm alive, I'm alive, I'm free—

He made it fifty yards before he fell onto the snow.

Darkness. Then not even darkness. Nothing.

He woke up in his bed at home, screaming while his mom hugged him.

Josh

20 days after Resurrection

He wanted to draw a picture of Heaven from memory.

The idea came to him while he sat on Mommy's lap in the rocker. Mommy hugged him and stroked his hair. She'd asked him what he wanted to do today.

Mommy was always hugging him lately and wanting to play with him, but he missed being around other kids, especially when it was really cold or rainy outside. They hated staying inside, but he liked it. He liked playing pretend. Putting on funny glasses. When it was nice outside, it was different. The other kids liked to run and show each other what they could do. Josh often got left out because he couldn't do the same things.

The other kids were never mean to him. They knew he had a *condition*. They always tried to include him, but he couldn't keep up. He got tired so easily. So he created LEGO worlds in which he could do anything. He drew pictures of the things he loved and the things that scared him.

"I want to draw a picture of Heaven," he said.

He'd lost count of how many times he'd gone to sleep, but every time he woke up, he had a clearer vision of it in his head, while everything else in his life continued to blur. Mommy said weeks had gone by since he'd gotten sick, but it didn't feel like weeks to him. His memory was slipping; he found himself forgetting the simplest things. But whenever he closed his eyes, Heaven was there. It was white for the most part. White and filled with ghosts. The ghosts weren't scary at all. They didn't move. They didn't even know he was there.

He felt Mommy's body stiffen and knew he'd said the wrong thing.

"It's not going to be scary," he added.

Mommy didn't like scary drawings. Josh believed she was as terrified of monsters as he was. Monsters weren't real, he knew, but they scared him anyway. That was the secret power monsters had over you. They made you afraid of the unknown. They *were* the unknown. Even if they never attacked, you knew they *might*, and that was how they scared you.

Sometimes Mommy scared him too. She never hurt him, and she never screamed at him in a scary voice like she did over the phone at people who wouldn't give her medicine. But the way she talked and moved all the time—happy on the outside, angry and sad on the inside—made him feel unsafe. He could tell the sadness was real and the happiness put on for his benefit. She would never hurt him, but at the same time, she *might*, and that was scary.

When she screamed at the people on the phone, it made him think of thunder.

"Why do you want to draw Heaven, Josh?"

He shrugged. He couldn't put it into words. He just did.

"Maybe we could draw something nice instead," she told him. "Together."

Maybe meant *for sure*, he knew. Nothing was what it was supposed to be anymore. Mommy never smiled with her eyes. She said everything was fine, but he knew it wasn't. She said everything was going to be okay, but he'd heard her crying in the bathroom.

"Mommy, can I go to Joanie's today?"

Mommy's sigh made him cringe. "Why do you want to go to Joanie's?"

"I want to play with my friends."

The doorbell rang. Mommy's arms tightened. He gasped.

"I'll be right back, little man."

She went to the door and opened it. Slowly, with effort; she walked like Grammy now. Ross walked in and kissed her on the cheek.

Then he noticed Josh. "Hey, look who's up and at 'em."

Josh smiled back. He liked Mommy's new boyfriend. Ross never confused him or made him feel worried by saying one thing while meaning something else. He talked to Josh like he was a grown-up. He didn't look sick, and he was always calm. Mommy was different around him as well. Like she wasn't fighting the world.

"I was just asking Josh what he wanted to do today," said Mommy.

"And what did he say?" Ross asked.

"He wants to go to Joan Cooper's house. He wants to see his friends."

"Hey, that actually sounds like a great idea."

Mommy crossed her arms. "Excuse me?"

"He's a boy. Boys want to be with their friends."

"How do you know what children want?"

He smiled. "I was a boy myself at one time, you know."

"Well, I want to be with my son."

"Of course you do. I get that. But what about what he wants?"

Mommy glared at him. He raised his hands. "Hey, do what you want. It's none of my business."

"It could be." She waited, but Ross said nothing. "Okay, fine. I'll call Joan."

Josh's heart leaped with hope. He hid behind the corner and listened to Mommy make the arrangements over the phone. Everything looked like it was going his way. *Awesome.* He ran to put on his coat and boots.

Mommy found him grinning ear to ear at the front door.

During the drive, Josh fidgeted in his car seat. He couldn't wait to see Nate and Megan and Dillon and Danielle and Joanie again. They liked to play indoor games with him. And Joanie would let him watch TV and draw a picture of Heaven.

"She wanted a pint," Mommy complained to Ross, who was driving. It was snowing outside the car. The windshield wipers ground back and forth.

"I can't believe she expected to get paid."

"She said if she was going to wake her kids up, it was going to be for them to be together as a family, not play with someone else's kids in their house."

Ross shook his head. "I'm with you on this. She should have just said yes or no."

"I don't have a lot left. I'm asking everyone who gave the first time for a second pint. Even half a pint. Only a few said they'd do it. I put an ad on Craigslist."

"They actually run ads from parents offering money for, uh, medicine?"

"The going term on the e-commerce sites is 'baby formula.'"

"I see. Any takers?"

"One so far. The prices are going through the roof."

"I have some money if you need help."

"I don't want your money, Ross."

He said nothing.

"I talked her down to half a pint," she added. "She's going to wake up Megan."

"Good."

"Can't you go any faster? Every second counts."

Blah, blah, blah. It was boring grown-up talk, and Josh tuned them out. He pictured what he would do when he saw Joanie. *Hey, look who's up and at 'em*, he'd say, and saunter past to the living room. Just like that. That'd be so cool. He pictured it again and again. Tickled himself with the thrill.

Ross parked the car. Mommy got out and unbuckled his car seat.

"Look who's up," he mumbled with a vacant grin.

"Thirty minutes, Josh. That's when we'll come get you. No crying at the end, okay?"

"Okay, Mommy."

"Mommy loves you, Josh. Mommy loves you with her whole heart."

"I love you too, Mommy."

She set him down on the snowy road. "Hold my hand."

"Have fun, Josh," Ross said from the front seat.

"I will! Bye!"

Joanie opened the door as they approached the house. Josh broke into a run. Joanie crouched and extended her arms just in time for Josh to slam into her for a hug.

"Hey, look at you," he said. "You're up!"

His face turned scarlet.

"Great to see you, Josh!" said Joanie.

Mommy handed her a jar of Welch's grape jelly. "Here's your medicine."

"Thank you, Ramona. I'm glad you understand. Things are tight here."

"How close are you to the end?"

Joanie winced. "Close."

"What then?"

"I don't know."

They stared at each other. Josh fidgeted.

"Then we do whatever it takes," Mommy said in a quiet voice.

Joanie nodded. "Come on in, Josh. I've got to get this into the fridge. Megan's already up and waiting for you."

He shucked his coat and hat, kicked his boots against the wall, and ran into the living room. Megan lay on the floor playing with a little pink laptop near the Christmas tree, which he remembered from the last time he was here. The room was messy and smelled funny, but he didn't care. It still felt like his second home.

"Look who's up and at 'em!" he cried.

She sat up. "Josh!"

"Where's Nate and Dillon and Danielle?"

"I don't know. Sleeping, I guess."

Joanie entered the room. She walked like Mommy, like just walking was a lot of work.

"What do you guys want to do?"

"I want to play with my laptop," said Megan.

"Meggie, Josh is here to play with you. You should do something together."

"That's okay," said Josh. "Can I please draw?"

"Of course. And thank you for saying please."

Megan jumped to her feet. "Can we *please* have a snack too, *please*?"

"Wow, what good manners. Josh, you're a good influence. All right, come to the kitchen table, and I'll feed you rascals."

Megan cackled at being called a rascal. "Can I bring my Barbie laptop?"

"Sure."

Josh and Megan walked into the kitchen smiling and holding hands. He felt happy and loved. He sat in one of the chairs.

Megan's laptop said in a computer voice: "*Let's play a game.*"

"Okay," she said, and giggled.

Josh laughed along and started drawing with his pencil. Usually, he drew with slashes and large strokes, but he took his time to produce as fine a level of detail as he could manage. He wanted Heaven to be perfect. Just the way he saw it.

Joanie put a plate of Ritz crackers and two small plastic cups filled with juice in front of them. The kids crammed the food into their mouths.

Josh was hungry all the time. He wanted to eat everything. He wanted to eat paper. He wanted to eat Megan.

"What are you drawing?" Joanie asked him, breaking the thought.

Josh shrugged. He felt jittery. If he told her, he might get into trouble.

She gave his work a quick inspection. "It's interesting."

Just like a grown-up, saying one thing and meaning another.

"Rascals," Megan said, and laughed.

Josh reached for his glass of juice and knocked it over.

"Damn it!" Joanie snarled.

He whimpered while Megan looked on with wide eyes.

"I'm sorry I yelled, Josh," Joanie said as she hurried to the sink for a towel. She dropped it onto the table and wiped up the spill. "It's not your fault. Kids spill things. It happens. Joanie is just really, really tired."

He nodded, afraid to call any more attention to himself.

"It's just that juice is really hard to get right now," she muttered. "If you can find it at the store, it's very expensive. Like everything else."

Josh nodded again but otherwise remained frozen. He was convinced all grown-ups were monsters. *They always had been*. They'd hidden it, but the world had changed; now they were showing their true selves.

He stared at her exposed neck while she wiped and studied the path of a vein. He wanted to kiss it.

Joanie threw the towel into the sink and knelt next to him. "Are you okay?"

Megan chimed in: "Are you okay, Josh?"

He nodded. "I'm okay."

"Good." Joanie stood with a grunt, cupped his face, and kissed his forehead. "You're a good boy. You're always welcome in our home."

"You can come over anytime," Megan said. "Right, Mommy?"

"That's right, sweetie."

Josh knew he was running out of time. He wanted to finish his drawing before he had to go home. He closed his eyes and saw Heaven.

The pencil moved across the page, expanding a black lightning bolt. A crack in the world.

"Your mom's here, Josh."

He looked up in wonder. He'd been so absorbed he hadn't heard the knock.

Mommy entered the kitchen with Ross. "Time to go, little man."

"Did you have fun?" Ross asked him.

Josh smiled and nodded. He'd had a lot of fun.

He wanted to cry because he was leaving but held it back. He remembered he'd promised Mommy he wouldn't cry at the end. Mommy expected it, and he wanted to be good.

Mommy said, "What did you draw?"

He said nothing.

"Josh?"

He shrugged, his expression neutral.

Mommy studied the drawing.

It was an intricate pattern of light and shadow. Hundreds of tiny dots dimpled the white page. A black lightning bolt crackled down the middle. And over the top of everything, a light, gentle swirl pulled you in.

"The detail is amazing," Joanie said. She was seeing the finished drawing for the first time. "Very abstract. Boys his age typically don't have that good small-muscle control."

"He's a regular Gustave Doré," said Ross.

"Is that Heaven?" Mommy asked Josh.

He nodded.

The grown-ups gathered around for a closer look. Josh's fears slipped away. They weren't mad. They were fascinated. They *liked* it. It was the kind of drawing Mommy put on the refrigerator door with magnets. The best of the best. Megan leaned, frowning, across the table, trying to figure out what made it good to grown-up eyes.

"Is that what you see when you go to sleep?" asked Ross.

Josh nodded. "See, Mommy? It's not so bad. Heaven's not bad."

Mommy walked away, but he could hear her crying. Josh's joy deflated. He'd made her upset, and he hadn't wanted to do that. He'd wanted the drawing to make her feel good.

His gut had told him not to do it. He should have listened.

Joan stared at the drawing. "Is God there?" Joanie whispered. "Did you see Him?"

Josh shrugged. He didn't want to talk about it anymore.

They went to Ross's car. Mommy rode in the back with him all the way home. She held him close and kissed his head. By the time they got home, he felt warm and safe again in her arms.

They parked in the driveway. Josh wanted to be carried in. Mommy said she wasn't strong enough, so Ross did it.

"Say good night to Ross, Josh," Mommy said.

"Good night." Josh pecked him on the cheek.

Ross smiled. "Good night, Josh. Sweet dreams."

Mommy took him upstairs to his bedroom.

"Look, my LEGO fort came apart!" he cried. "I need to fix it!"

"No stalling, Josh. We only have about ten minutes. If you want me to read you a story, you have to get into bed. We'll skip the teeth brushing this time."

"Okay," he grumbled. It wasn't fair. The sun was still shining. He didn't feel sleepy at all.

He wanted to eat his LEGO fort.

Mommy took out a new pair of pajamas, but he wanted to wear one of his old one-piece sleepers, the brown one with monkeys on it. It barely fit him. He got into bed and snuggled with Graham the Bear.

"Do you want *Curious George*?"

"No, please. I want *Walter the Farting Dog*."

Mommy pulled it from the little bookshelf next to his bed and cracked it open. Walter's farting had gotten him into trouble again. Usually, the Walter stories made him giggle, but he didn't feel like laughing. He felt thoughtful.

"Mommy? Does Megan have the same condition as me?"

"Yes. She does. All the children have it."

"All of them go to sleep?"

"That's right."

He nodded. He liked that everybody was sick just like him.

"And that's why you gave Joanie the medicine. It wasn't really jelly in that jar."

"That's right again."

Josh smiled again. "You're a good mommy. Sharing is good."

Mommy swallowed hard. "Thank you, Josh. I love you."

He snuggled against her. "I love you too, Mommy."

She read him the story, and just before the end, he saw the swirl.

I'm going down the drain again.

"Oh my God," Mommy said.

Josh fought against it, trying to focus. He saw his mother staring at the ceiling over his bed. He felt disembodied, as if he were floating.

"Your drawing," she said.

He followed her gaze to the white, dimpled ceiling with its small crack.

See, Mommy? It's not so bad.

His life drained away into the swirl. He followed the light.

"Heaven," he whispered.

Megan

28 days after Resurrection

She loved hearts. Even more than rainbows. Hearts meant love. Daddy once told her every heart was a kiss. She even used to dream about them, back when she dreamed.

Megan sat on the floor holding a sheet of construction paper. She cut out hearts with her little scissors and Scotch-taped them to homemade greeting cards. Mommy lay on the couch under a blanket and watched with a big smile.

She liked to be busy having fun, especially with Mommy watching. Daddy was at work and Nate was upstairs sleeping, so they were enjoying some special Mommy and Megan time. She wanted it to last forever. She wanted to stay awake and play all night.

Scraps of paper covered the floor. Her stuffies and dollies sat in a circle around a tea party complete with little pink cups and plates. Her Barbie laptop asked her if she wanted to play a game.

She held up a handful of hearts. "Look, Mommy." She stood and handed them over. "Here. You can have these because I love you."

"They're beautiful. Thank you, sweetie."

Megan hugged Mommy's leg and kissed her knee, one, two, three. Mommy praised almost everything she did, and she never got tired of hearing it. Now she wanted to hear Mommy read her a story. She handed her a book of fairy tales. "Can you read this to me, Mommy?"

"Of course I can."

Mommy sat up on the couch. Every little thing made her breathe like Major did after a big run. Megan settled on her lap. She knew Mommy had read the book to her a lot of times but couldn't remember a single story in it now. Every time she woke up, she forgot a little more.

The door to the garage opened. Heavy footsteps sounded in the hall.

Daddy entered the living room and grunted. "What? She's awake."

Megan grinned at him. "Daddeeeeeeeee!"

"I'm sorry," Mommy said. "I needed to see her."

Daddy sat on the easy chair and nodded. "All right."

"I know we only have enough medicine for one more time. I gave her just a little."

"It's okay."

"I needed it. I couldn't take it anymore. I felt like giving up. I just needed to see her again."

"I understand, babe. I really do. I love you."

"Aww," said Megan.

"Don't give up, Joanie."

"We're so close to the end now."

Daddy bent down and kissed Megan on the nose. She giggled. "Daddy!"

"Is Mommy reading you a story, princess?"

"Uh-huh."

"That sounds like a great idea."

"Yes," she said with a nod. "It's a *very* great idea."

"We Coopers don't give up easy, do we?"

"Noooooooo."

"Right now is all there is," said Daddy. "Nothing else matters. Remember that."

Mommy looked at the clock and said, "We only have—"

"I don't want to know."

Daddy stared at Megan with a smile on his face. She glowed at being the center of so much attention and love, without Nate hogging it all. "What about my story?"

"How about we read about Sleeping Beauty again?" Mommy asked her.

"I don't know that one."

"Of course you do. It's one of your favorite stories."

Megan shrugged. She couldn't remember the story, but it sounded good. She nuzzled deeper into Mommy's lap while Mommy read aloud the tale of a beautiful princess cursed by a mean fairy. The princess was going to sleep forever. Only a handsome prince, helped by three good fairies, could break the curse and wake her up with the kiss of true love.

Mommy indulged every *Why?* that Megan could come up with. Daddy took pictures as if they were having a birthday party, not story time.

"Don't, Doug," Mommy said. "I look terrible."

Megan said, "No, you look beautiful, Mommy."

"I'm glad you think so."

"I'm like Sleeping Beauty. Sleeping Beauty is like me, right?"

"That's why I read it to you, sweetie," Mommy told her.

"Because I go to sleep so much."

"That's right."

Megan grinned. "And I'm a rascal."

Mommy made a show of studying the book. "I don't see *that* in the story."

"But that's okay. I love you, so you'll kiss me and wake me up, and we'll get married."

"You've got this all figured out, don't you? You're a pretty smart rascal."

"But what if the prince didn't come and kiss her?" Megan wondered. "What would happen? Would she have to sleep forever and ever?"

Mommy hugged her. Megan bathed in the warmth. "There's no chance of that, honey. He has to kiss her. It's fate."

Daddy choked back a sob. Megan looked at him, wide-eyed, as he lowered the camera and cried. Daddy never cried. He sometimes pretended to bawl to make her laugh. But this wasn't pretend.

"Don't be sad, Daddy."

Daddy wiped his eyes and smiled. "I'm okay. I'm crying because I'm happy I have you."

"Daddy, I love—"

Megan's head tilted to the side as the headache came. The big old stupid headache that came every time she had to go to sleep. Her vision constricted, darker and darker at the edges, until it became a distant point of intense bright light.

Don't give up, Daddy.

She bit down on Mommy's arm, making her scream.

IV

This Is the Way the World Ends

EIGHT

Doug

36 days after Resurrection

Doug contemplated a row of Dumpsters stacked against the rear of a tall white building.

Mercy Hospital produced about three tons of garbage every day, and it all flowed through these Dumpsters. Sharps, body fluids, lab waste, surgical specimens, animal carcasses, common waste.

And blood.

Lots and lots of blood. Enough to keep his kids alive for days. Maybe weeks. It was all there on the other side of this chain-link fence. No protection, no surveillance.

For once, his knowledge of garbage had given him an edge over everybody else.

Or so he'd thought.

In theory, the blood was easy to get. The hospital put the infectious waste into bright red bags. Later, it was burned in the incinerator. Above fourteen hundred degrees, nothing survived. The ash came out germ-free and ready for the landfill.

Until then, the bags piled up in these Dumpsters. Lots of bags.

Over the past five weeks since Herod's changed the world, Doug

227

had learned the rules of the game. The first thing he'd learned: It was rigged against him.

He didn't care anymore if his kids drank blood like vampires. So what. Hell, they could drink cat piss and malt liquor for all he cared, as long as it kept them alive.

The problem was that a pint brought Nate and Megan back for about an hour, and over the past month, he and Joan had exhausted every drop they'd been able to squeeze from family and friends. The well of charity was running dry for everybody. As it did, people grew desperate. Those who had money could buy it. Those who didn't had to get it another way. It wasn't every man for himself, not quite. It was every man for his family.

It wasn't just about wanting to see their children. The kids had an expiration date. If they didn't get blood, they simply rotted until the Herod parasite itself died. Then they'd never wake up again for all the blood in the world. He'd heard enough stories to believe this was true.

So this morning, Doug had called in sick. Otis chewed him out by saying the trash didn't pick itself up, and he had guys either calling in sick or outright missing across the board, but Doug didn't care. If his kids weren't alive, there wasn't much point to working. The garbage could pile up in mountains for all he cared. So he'd pulled on his yellow hazmat suit and driven to the hospital to do some real providing for his family.

Then . . . nothing. All that blood just sitting there, but he hadn't made a move in an hour. Instead, he'd nipped at his flask and plowed through half a pack of Winstons. Pissed off, he wanted to punch something. Put his fist through a wall.

Three tons was a lot of garbage. Most of it was in red bags. He'd have to sift through thousands of pounds of scalpels, needles, and rags soaked with diseased shit and vomit, all to locate vials of blood that might itself carry dangerous diseases.

In theory, the blood was easy to get. In practice, not so much. His brilliant idea had turned out to be not so brilliant after all.

Joan hadn't let him give more than a pint of his own. She said he needed to stay strong and provide. That made him the family reserve tank. He could give another two or three pints. After that, they were done. Time to say good-bye.

Unless he decided to give it all to them. A big guy like him had maybe twelve pints of sweet red syrup in his body. There was always that option.

That, or take it from somebody else.

"It won't work," a voice said behind him.

He wheeled. Three men stood at the edge of the parking lot. Their faces were pale and drawn from blood loss. Fathers like him.

"I work here," Doug said.

"No, you don't," one of the men said. "And your idea won't work."

"We've been watching you watching those Dumpsters half the morning," said a second man. "Wondering if you were onto something."

"Even if you could get at it, you couldn't use it," the first man said.

"HIV," said Doug. "Other diseases."

"That, and they dilute the blood with bleach before they throw it out. If they even throw it out anymore. Somebody's probably selling it."

Doug nodded and lit a cigarette. "It was a stupid idea."

"No, it wasn't. Name's Russell. This is Carl, and this is Howard. You are?"

"Doug."

"You know, Doug, there's another way to get blood if that's what you want."

"No way," said Howard. "He's drunk. I can smell it on him."

"He's also wearing a hazmat suit," Russell answered. "That was smart. I used to work here. A guy in a hazmat suit can go almost anywhere he wants without a hassle. Everybody just assumes he's on official business. Cleaning up some spill."

"I don't know." Howard rubbed the back of his neck. "This is getting out of control."

"Don't chicken out now," Carl said. "I say we let him in for an even share."

"I haven't agreed to shit, if you hadn't noticed," Doug told them.

"If we tell you, and you say no, you can't rat on us. That's the deal."

"I don't care if you tell me or you don't. But I don't rat on people."

"Mercy is a campus," said Russell. "This building is the main hospital." He turned and pointed. "See that smaller building over there?"

Doug spat on the ground. "Yup."

"That's the blood bank."

His stomach flipped. "How much you think is in there?"

"I'm guessing three, maybe four hundred units."

"What's that in pints?"

"About the same."

Doug snorted. "Mother lode."

"The trick is we don't know what kind of protection they've got set up," said Carl. "Normally, they don't guard it. But these days, who knows?"

"That's where you come in," Russell said.

"You want me to do what, exactly?"

"Help us get in. Help us get out."

They were looking for muscle. Doug studied the men, looking for a reason to say no. So far, only Russell inspired any confidence. He was tall, blond, and clean-shaven, and appeared to be the brains of the outfit. Brains in search of brawn. Howard and Carl were medium build, middle-aged, and overweight. A bowling team playing at being criminals. Typical suburban dads who wanted their kids back. Just like Doug.

Nate and Megan scared him when they were dead. He couldn't sleep at night. He pictured them bursting into the room with their grinning dead faces, singing, *Daddy, come play with us.* He wanted them to live. He and Joan had pushed their donors to get as much blood as possible and, as a result, had enjoyed twenty-three hours with their children. Twenty-three beautiful, ordinary hours that had slipped through his fingers, as time does.

The alternative was to let them stay dead. Take them back to the burial ground.

"You got any guns?" he asked the men.

"You know how to shoot?" Russell countered.

"Yup. I got some shotguns at home."

"We're not using guns for this."

Howard dropped his duffel bag and unzipped it. "This is everything." A baseball bat, crowbar, and golf club. He eyed Doug. "Are you willing to do what it takes?"

Doug laughed. "Are you?"

"It doesn't matter if we're brave or cowards," Russell said. "None of us are what we were before. I know each of you will do whatever it takes to protect his kids."

The others nodded.

"Even murder?" said Doug.

"We're hoping it doesn't come to that," Howard told him.

Doug shook his head. *They don't get it.* "If we take all the blood, people won't get transfusions, right? If they don't get transfusions, they'll die, right?"

Howard looked like he wanted to wander off somewhere to puke. "I don't know anything about that."

"I do. That's what will happen. How many will die?"

"Could be a lot," said Russell. He'd obviously considered it. "Especially for the emergency operations, where people show up and need blood fast."

"We don't have to take all of it," Carl offered. "We could just take some."

"This place uses up to six hundred units in a single day," Russell said. "Leaving some might make you feel better, but it won't go near to helping those who need it."

"It doesn't matter," Carl said. "Yeah, there are sick people who need it. Well, you know what? I've got two little ones at home who are sick too, and they'll die without it. Really die. If it's them or my kids who's got to do without, well, it's going to be them."

Russell turned to Howard. "What about you?"

"I'm with you. If sick people come in here needing blood, they can get people to donate it like the rest of us. We have to look after our own." He looked at Doug. "Right?"

Doug nodded. He understood all too well. He thought about Joan crying as he wrapped Nate and Megan in plastic and put them in the garage three nights ago, when the last of their meager blood supply had been used up. After she'd sobbed herself to sleep later that night, Doug had done a terrible thing. His mind reeling with alcoholic despair, he'd gone out to the garage, taken down his sledgehammer, and visited Major's kennel.

He'd killed his dog and strung him up with ropes. Cut his throat and drained the blood.

Only afterward did he realize the horror of what he'd done.

Major had been a constant companion on many a hike and hunting trip. He'd watched over Doug's children when they were babies. He was one of Doug's only real friends in the world. Every time Doug saw the old dog's face in his mind's eye, he'd take another drink to make it stop, like a morbid drinking game. Right up to the end, Major had trusted him.

And it didn't even work. Nate drank some of the blood and choked it back up. Major's sacrifice had been for nothing. Doug had killed his friend for nothing.

Standing in his garage watching the blood—almost black in the fluorescent light—drain into the bucket, Doug had crossed over into a very dark place.

With that came an epiphany. He would do whatever it took to keep Nate and Megan alive. Even if their survival meant other people died.

"Everybody ready?" said Russell.

Doug and the other men nodded. It was a simple plan. After Doug got them past the locked doors, they'd walk straight back and grab the blood. Then they'd exit through Shipping and Receiving. Carl would be waiting outside in the Range Rover.

They marched to the front door. Doug led the way inside. Russell and Howard walked up to the receptionist and said they wanted to donate blood. Doug pointed at the door.

"I'm back from my smoke."

The receptionist looked like she'd given a lot of blood. She barely even glanced at him as she buzzed him in. He entered a bright corridor as the others retreated to chairs in the reception area to fill out medical forms.

He waited. Moments later, a short knock. He opened the door and let them in.

"Administration's on the left," said Russell. "Canteen's on the right. The next area ahead is the donor area. Collections is on the right, Quality Assurance on the left. After that, the lab. That's where they store the blood."

"Let's go, let's go," Doug muttered. He wished he could take one more snort on his flask. His mouth felt dry as cotton.

Howard unzipped the duffel bag and offered them a choice of weapons. Doug took the crowbar. He grunted at the weight of it in his hand. Just a tap on the head with this thing could bring a man to his knees. He wasn't nervous anymore. He felt powerful.

He marched ahead. A grinning man in glasses and a blinding white doctor's coat appeared at the end of the hall as he approached.

"Donors!" he said. "You're a sight for sore eyes. Welcome!"

"We were told to go straight back to the lab," said Russell.

"Who told you that?" The doctor saw the terrible grin on Doug's face. "No. Please. Wait—"

Doug grabbed the front of his shirt and dragged him down the hall. Medical people stepped out of their offices and then dodged out of the way with shrieks and shouts of alarm.

"Please don't do this," the man pleaded.

"Take it easy on him," said Howard.

"Shut up," Doug told both of them.

He shoved the doctor headlong into the laboratory. The four technicians working there looked up like startled deer. Doug showed them the crowbar.

"We're here for a donation," he said.

Russell took charge. "We want whatever blood you have in storage. And then we'll leave. Do this, and nobody will get hurt."

"Don't do this!" said one of the technicians. "People need what little we have left."

"Shut the hell up and cooperate, or I'm going to beat every single one of you with this crowbar until there's nothing left," said Doug.

They looked into his eyes and believed him. Which was good, because he'd meant every word. One of them pointed to the refrigerators.

"It's in there," she said.

Howard crossed the room and opened the refrigerator door. "Problem!"

Doug grabbed the doctor by the back of his neck and shoved him toward the cold storage. He looked inside for himself. The refrigerator was almost empty. "Where is it?" he snarled.

"What do you mean, 'where is it'? The hospital used it!"

Russell said, "I know for a fact this bank always has at least three hundred units on hand."

"Hardly anyone donates anymore because of the children. Thirteen units is all we have left."

"Not enough," said Doug.

"Then leave it," the doctor said. "We can save four people's lives with that blood."

"If I don't take it, my kids die. Understand?"

"And I'm talking about the deaths of four people who could live long, normal lives—"

Doug slapped the back of the man's head. "You want to make it five?"

"No," the doctor said in a quiet voice.

"You want me to take *your* blood?"

The man cringed. "Jesus. No. Fine. Just take what you want and go."

"Leave us alone," a technician said. "We're cooperating with you."

"Now we're communicating," said Doug. He leaned in close to the doctor and added quietly, "You think my kids don't deserve to live, doc? Is that it?"

The doctor bowed his head. "Of course I don't think that."

"Then I ain't got a choice, now, do I?"

"I've got it!" Howard called out. He held up the duffel bag.

"Let's move," Russell told them.

The men ran out the back. Doug followed at his own pace. He felt superhuman. It had all been so easy, taking what he needed. Outside, the cold air dried the sweat on his face. No sirens yet. He climbed into the backseat of the Range Rover and lit a cigarette, flush with excitement.

He took a long draw. After a million smokes, it was the best he'd ever had.

Carl glared at the cigarette. "Hey, do you mind?"

Doug smiled back at him.

"We'd better get going," said Howard. He was shaking from stress.

"Here's your share," Russell said. He handed four pouches of thick red blood to Doug. "You earned it."

Doug exhaled a stream of smoke and studied one of the blood bags. It felt cold in his hands. The label read, Rx ONLY, VOLUNTEER, AB, Rh POSITIVE, RED BLOOD CELLS, ADENINE-SALINE (AS-1) ADDED, FROM 450 mL WHOLE BLOOD, STORE AT 1–6°C.

None of these esoteric terms and numbers meant a thing to him. The only number that mattered was four. Four hours of life for Nate and Megan. A far cry from the hundred pints he thought he'd be getting, but four more than he'd had this morning.

Blood was wealth these days. He felt rich for the first time in his life.

He felt *right*. He'd taken a stand for what was his. He'd finally really *done* something.

"Why does he get the extra one?" said Carl.

"Because we couldn't have done this without him," Russell replied.

"Pleasure doing business with you folks," Doug said.

"Likewise," muttered Howard, who looked anything but pleased.

They drove to Doug's truck. Doug opened the door.

"I'll keep the crowbar, if you don't mind."

"You can have it," Carl said. "Just get the hell out of my car. I think you're crazy."

Doug laughed as he got out. "We should do this again sometime."

"Hang on then," Russell said. He took out a pen and scribbled onto an old receipt from his wallet. He handed it to Doug. "Call me, all right?"

Doug took it and nodded. He'd like that. He'd like that a lot.

Joan

36 days after Resurrection

The world was slowly bleeding to death one pint at a time, but people still needed to brush their teeth and do their laundry and get their shopping done. Joan was no exception. She pushed her cart down the aisle at the supermarket in a mental fog.

Time's passage had a funny way of distorting the past. It had only been about a month, but as far as she was concerned, her children had always been dead. They'd always been dead, and she'd always lived her life in an endless confusing blur imposed by grief and severe blood loss.

Only when she watched home videos did she remember the way things used to be. Only when she dreamed. Only when her children woke up for that precious hour that flew by so fast. That's when Joan, like her kids, returned to life. Only to watch them die again. Every time, it tore a new hole in her chest, and she died with them.

She'd given three pints of blood. Nadine had refused to take any more. She'd replaced Joan's blood volume with saline to ensure good circulation, but Joan's body had to replace the red blood cells themselves, and that would take months. She'd never known how important those little buggers were until she didn't have them. She was irritable and short of breath all the time. She had trouble thinking straight. Her tongue was sore, her nails brittle. She felt close to passing out every time she stood up.

It didn't help that she occasionally cut herself to draw a little more. Always a little more. A teaspoon here, a tablespoon there.

Other women trudged down the aisles, studying what was left on the shelves with blank stares. *We're all zombies now*, Joan thought, though she felt no real kinship with them. A woman was looking at an empty shelf with hollow eyes, as if expecting what she wanted to suddenly materialize. In the time before, one might have mistaken her for a bag lady. But this was her friend Coral. Joan turned away and pretended to be interested in the slim selection of instant coffee.

A month ago, she'd known everybody who lived in her neighborhood, attended her church, or had anything to do with her children's education or social life. All these relationships had deteriorated into nothing. Everybody had retreated into themselves. The only social unit that mattered now was family. Cut off, each to his or her own.

That was human nature. When there was enough to go around, people were all too happy to help others in need. When there wasn't, they kicked each other when they were down.

It was a time for kicking, and she had no wish to be kicked.

Best, in fact, not to be noticed at all.

The deli had no ham, so she bought a half pound of bologna and American cheese and dropped the packages into her cart. The anxious teenager working behind the counter eyed her as if she were a crazy person who might get violent at the slightest provocation. She wondered why she even bothered to continue shopping for the kids, whom Doug had laid out in the garage, wrapped in plastic like leftovers.

She already knew the answer. If she didn't shop for them, she wouldn't shop at all.

The deli sold kosher meat, according to a sign. To make meat kosher, it was soaked in water and covered in salt to extract the blood. Observant Jews ate it that way because God forbade the drinking of blood. Joan had discovered this while reading the Bible for guidance.

What she'd found wasn't very comforting:

And if any native Israelite or foreigner living among you eats or drinks blood in any form, I will turn against that person and cut him off from the community of your people, for the life of the body is in the blood.

It was right there in Leviticus. Instead, God commanded blood be poured over the altar for the atonement of sin. In other words, blood was for sacrifice to God.

The life of the body is in the blood.

"Here you go," said the teenager.

Joan made sure she thanked him.

She maneuvered the cart away from the deli and toward the meat section. She saw some chicken legs and wanted to buy them, but just the idea of having to cook them exhausted her.

A smiling lady walked down the aisle, trailed by a crowd of women. A little girl sat in her cart. The woman called her Jackie. Jackie sang along to "Lucky Star," one of the eighties songs that passed for Muzak in stores these days; her mom laughed.

In the time before, Joan would have smiled. Now she glared with open resentment.

The woman's sleeve was rolled up to reveal a ball of cotton taped over her inner arm. Everybody displayed them these days as a badge of honor. *Look, I gave.* But in her case, it was just fashion. She was a faker. You could see it in her eyes, her face, her body, her clothes.

Her eyes were bright and alert; the whites hadn't turned bluish. Her lips and cheeks were pink from healthy circulation, not from garish makeup. She walked erect and breathed easy and deep; she didn't pant like a dog after a long run. She still cared about her appearance; she'd taken time that morning to style her hair and put on nice clothes.

But the real proof was in the fact that she took her little girl shopping. Nobody wasted precious medicine taking their kids with them to run errands. Blood time was family time.

In short, this woman had never given a drop. She paid others for blood to feed her little girl. And here she was flaunting it like some kind of celebrity.

"Who do you think you are?"

Joan blanched, wondering if she'd spoken her thoughts aloud.

One of the women who'd been following now broke away from the group and stepped in front of the rich woman. Another mother who looked like a bag lady. Reduced to skin and bone, with bluish lips and eyes.

"Hey, I'm talking to you. You've got enough medicine to take your little girl shopping?"

"Excuse me?"

"Even a hundred fifty mils would bring Alice back for a half hour. I haven't seen her in a week."

Jackie's mom frowned. She looked at the other women staring at her and blinked in sudden fear. "I don't have any to spare. I'm sorry."

"Alice's skin is turning green and black. Like marble. Her gut is swelling. The blisters—"

The woman covered Jackie's ears. *"Please."*

"Alice is going to *die* if I don't get more. Do you understand?"

"You look like a really nice person," one of the other women said. "If you have any extra you could give us, we would take anything."

"And I told you I don't have any to give."

"Please, you're a mother too. You have to share."

"I don't have to do anything. I don't even know you."

"You're not better than us!" The skinny woman pointed at the girl. "She's not better than Alice!"

Jackie's mom reached for her purse. "I'm calling the police."

"What else do you have in that bag?"

Alice's mom reached for the purse only to have her hand slapped away. She snarled and swiped at the other woman's face, her hands splayed into claws.

Jackie's mom shoved her. The woman fell back against shelving filled with condiments and toppled to the floor. Bottles of ketchup and mustard bounced and shattered around her. The other women cowered at the violence.

Jackie's mom looked even more terrified. "Jesus. I'm sorry! Are you okay?"

The other woman sat on the floor crying. "Alice . . ."

"I'm sorry you don't have enough medicine. But it's not my problem. Now, please, leave us alone."

She turned to comfort her daughter, who was whimpering in fear. The other women started to drift away, looking deflated. Joan sighed with relief. It was over.

Alice's mom got back onto her feet with ragged wheezes. She held a glass bottle of barbecue sauce. She looked down at it as if trying to decide whether to buy it. Then she threw it.

The glass missile struck Jackie's mom on the side of her face. She staggered, hands groping, and fell as if a rug had been yanked out from under her feet. She sat up in a daze and pressed her hands against her left eye.

"Mommy!"

Joan rushed to the cart to pull out the screaming girl. She couldn't carry the weight. They collapsed in a heap. The girl howled in her ear.

Jackie's mom moaned. "Jackie? Are you okay, baby?"

Alice's mom snatched up another bottle and lurched several paces forward until she stood over the other woman, who was trying to get back onto her feet. She raised the bottle and flung it at the other woman's head almost point-blank. It struck with a sickening thud.

"MOMMY!"

Jackie's mom fell flat on her back to a flurry of screams. She was out cold. Blood oozed from a long, deep cut on her forehead.

Alice's mom fell to her knees and dug into the woman's purse. "Let's see what you've got in here." Two of the other women joined her while the rest fled the scene.

She held up a baby bottle. Tinged dark red, but almost empty. "Not good enough." She ripped the cotton ball off the woman's bare arm, revealing nothing but smooth flesh. Soft, pink, and warm. No punctures, no bruises. "Anybody got a needle?"

The kid from the deli ran into the aisle and skidded to a halt. *"What the hell is this shit?!"*

"Call the cops!" Joan shouted.

"What's wrong with her? What happened?"

"And an ambulance. Go!"

"I want my mommy," the girl whimpered.

Joan hugged her close. "Your mommy's going to be okay. Help's coming. My name's Joanie. I want you to be a big, brave girl for me."

Behind her, the women argued.

"We can use a piece of glass."

"Would a nail file work?"

"You can't just take it from her. What if we kill her?"

"A pint. We'll just take a pint."

"A pint each?"

"Enough talking. I'm doing this with or without you. Are you in or out?"

They were in.

"Come on, we need to do this quick. This is my last hope for Alice."

Joan gathered her breath and began to sing:

Mommy's okay
Mommy's all right
Mommy's just fine

Behind her, the harvesting began.

Joan sang louder until the grisly sounds slipped away.

David

36 days after Resurrection

David checked the young man's blood pressure. Normal. Mitch was a diabetic but had taken his medication the night before. He could give blood.

The lanky teenager sat in David's office with his arm exposed and ready. David expected to answer questions about the side effects of giving blood, but all the kid wanted to know was what it tasted like.

"Like sucking on a penny," said David as he tied an elastic band around the boy's upper arm.

"Really? Why's that?"

"Blood tastes like metal because of iron in the hemoglobin. That's the chemical that makes red blood cells absorb oxygen."

"Cool. Do you think my blood tastes sweeter? You know, with me being a diabetic and everything?"

David asked him to make a fist.

"Don't bother the doctor," said Ramona Fox, who sat next to the teenager. "I'm paying you for a pint, not to be an asshole."

"I'm an asshole free of charge," Mitch said, leering back at her.

"Charming." The woman glared at him with thinly veiled disgust.

"If my blood tastes sweet, it should be worth more, don't you think? There are lots of other moms online who would think so."

They'd dropped the pretense that Mitch was Ramona's cousin doing his part for the family—a lie they'd told because selling blood was illegal. David guessed Ramona had forgotten or had grown too tired and strung out for lies. Likely, she'd found him on some website. The going term on Craigslist was *babysitting*.

He tuned out their bickering as he tapped the teenager's median cubital vein.

He'd trained to become a pediatrician for eleven years. College, then medical school, then three years of residency. Pediatricians didn't make as much money as some other doctors, but as a young man, he'd considered it a noble profession.

When Nadine gave birth to Paul, it became his life's calling. Every day, David treated coughs, broken bones, and the common cold. Anxious parents would call him at all hours of the day and night. He'd woken up every day and gone to bed every night worried about his patients' health.

His patients had all died a month ago, yet he'd never been busier.

He was now a phlebotomist. He felt more like a medieval quack.

Sometimes, he treated one of his old patients. Herod brought the children back exactly as they were, chronic health conditions and all. Kids who were alive only an hour or two a day still managed to sprain their ankles and catch colds.

Most of the time, though, David drew blood.

He swabbed Mitch's vein with a prep pad. The air filled with the crisp, clean smell of alcohol. He waited for it to dry.

I'm your friendly neighborhood drug dealer, and the drug is you.

When word had gotten around that Nadine was making house calls, she began to receive nonstop requests for help. Having a medical professional draw blood with sterile equipment was highly preferable to cutting open veins with straight razors.

At first, David wanted nothing to do with it. The parents were trying to keep their children alive. He understood that. But they couldn't see beyond the next fix. The math was simple. The ninety thousand children in Plymouth County would need about sixteen *million* pints of blood to live about an hour a day for a year. Two million gallons. Fifty thousand barrels, enough to fill three Olympic-sized swimming pools. Every drop of blood in one and a half million adults. There were less than half a million adults in the entire county.

I'm the prison doctor who removes the appendix of a death row inmate, saving his life so he can be executed anyway.

Shannon Donegal had died horribly, fed upon by the child she carried in her womb. She'd died a gray, desiccated husk. Charlie had told him she'd fought against going to the hospital right to the end. She knew little Jonah was too young to survive outside the womb, with or without blood. The same fate awaited all the parents, though in a less direct way. The children were draining them dry one pint at a time, one day at a time.

When he and Nadine went to Paul's grave on New Year's Day to mark the one-year anniversary of his passing, he'd expected a healthy renewal of grief. Instead, she talked about the children. How Paul's death had prepared her to help them. That all they had to do was hang on a little longer until the blood sacrifice was complete, and then the children would stop dying.

David didn't see the hand of God in these events. He saw a greedy parasite with an appetite for blood that would never be satiated. The world couldn't move on until Herod was destroyed, but that meant letting the children go.

Nadine had asked him to help. It was getting to be too much for her. She wanted to set up the office as a blood clinic. Come in, get your blood drawn, and leave with a pint of life in a plastic bag. Desperate parents were slashing themselves. They were dying. They needed professional help. Others were helping. Why not him?

As a doctor, he'd taken the Hippocratic Oath. The original version of it, written way back when people swore to Apollo, included the well-known proverb that a physician should do no harm. David had no idea what that meant anymore. If he refused, parents died. But there were too many mouths to feed. Ben, who was still convalescing at home, kept in touch with the medical examiner's office. He said the number of "suicides" was going up, but so was the homicide rate. An elderly couple was found strung upside down, their throats cut, drained of blood. A woman paralyzed from the waist down had her femoral artery slashed. Several hemophiliacs had been cut and bled out. The police even found a man who'd been hooked up to a dialysis machine in a botched attempt to suck the blood out of him. The official report said the walls had been painted with it. This was where everybody was headed. They were blinded to it, but David could see the future all too clearly. Soon, soccer moms would be slaughtering each other in their living rooms with the TV turned up so the canned laughter would drown out the screams. Walls painted with blood.

I'm Dr. Kevorkian, assisting the suicide of the human race to relieve it from its suffering.

The modern version of the Hippocratic Oath had an even more appropriate admonition against playing God.

Standing on Paul's grave with its little headstone, David still didn't know if Nadine had lost her mind or was simply making a moral choice he didn't agree with. *Do it for Paul*, she'd said. *Do it for me.* In the end, that simple argument won out. He'd seen her only rarely during those weeks of house calls. They'd been distant since Paul's death, but now he was officially losing her. It was a strange feeling to long for your own wife. He agreed to help because he loved her. Just as the parents would do anything for their children, he would do anything for Nadine.

He guessed that made him a junkie as well as a dealer.

"Dr. Harris?"

He glanced at his watch. "Yes, we can proceed."

"Hold it a minute," said Mitch.

Ramona's eyes narrowed. "Now what?"

"I'd like to stretch this out to a pint and a half. Can I do that?"

David sighed. "It's possible. You're young and in good health. It's just not recommended."

"I won't die or anything, will I?"

"That's highly unlikely. But you won't feel well for a while."

"Then I'd like to do it." He winked at Ramona. "That's, what, another hour you could spend with your little boy?"

The woman chewed her lip, clearly torn between greed and suspicion. "And you want what for it?"

Mitch shrugged. "I don't know. I give more, you give more."

"I need a price. I'm not made of money."

He smiled. "Maybe I don't want money anymore."

Oh God, it's come to this. David sat in his chair wearing the white medical jacket that used to actually mean something to people, used to make him feel respected, while he waited like an idiot for them to finish their crude negotiating.

At first, the parents had come. They gave everything they could. Next came friends and family. They gave all that they were willing. Now David drew blood for the most part from undesirables. *Assholes*, as Ramona put it so nicely. The assholes were here for money. And whatever else they could get. Parasites themselves, searching for symbiosis.

David missed working with children. Living children with real problems for whom his skills could make a real difference. He missed doing good.

The coy haggling went on until he decided to tune them out. He thought about Herod.

About how Herod killed its victims.

Everybody was infected. He had it, Nadine had it, everybody did. But it only killed the children. Not a single child was immune. Why? How did it survive in adults? Where did it come from? What had triggered it across the entire globe at almost the same time? And: Could it be cured?

The key to this last mystery resided in the blood.

The heart pumped the blood and kept it circulating through the body's highway system of arteries, veins, and capillaries. The blood itself consisted of blood cells floating in plasma, mostly water plus proteins and other substances. The purpose of blood was to carry oxygen and nutrients to the body's cells and carry away metabolic waste—such as carbon dioxide—to the lungs to be exhaled. Most blood cells, in fact, were red blood cells rich in iron-containing hemoglobin, which carried oxygen. Blood also contained white blood cells, which defended the body against infection and parasites. As Nadine liked to say, blood was life itself.

Herod somehow eluded the body's immune system. The autopsies revealed massive clusters of complex molecules in the blood and concentrated in the brain, nervous system, heart, and stomach lining. At first, scientists theorized a chemical had bonded with the children's hemoglobin. That left less of it to bond with oxygen and resulted in asphyxiation similar to carbon monoxide poisoning. Subsequent research quickly revealed that these objects were dormant but alive—parasitic organisms that ate red blood cells. Their feeding starved the brain of oxygen and caused death by cerebrovascular accident, or stroke, which explained the burning smells, headaches, numbness, and other symptoms.

Since Herod only infected children under the age of puberty, the answer had to be found in their unique physiology. Puberty, however, involved numerous chemical changes in the body. The process began in the central nervous system, one of the areas of the body where Herod resided, and involved the brain's hypothalamus, anterior pituitary and sex organs, and about ten major hormones. Besides that, scores of plasma proteins changed during the transition from child to adult. In short, singling out the specific difference between children and post-pubescent teens that resulted in Herod's being active or not was like trying to find the proverbial needle in a haystack.

The whole mystery was so complex that if David weren't a scientist, he would have been tempted to believe in a supernatural cause if only to satisfy Occam's Razor—the logical law stating that the simplest explanation is usually true. He'd fallen for that idea once. Never again.

In any case, David still believed the children themselves could not be cured. Right now, Herod appeared to be the only thing keeping them alive. To destroy Herod was to destroy the children. Even if a cure existed, it would take too long to manufacture enough doses for all of them. The cure would be for the adults. They had to be cleansed of the parasite. After that, its natural reservoir had to be found and destroyed.

The current generation was doomed, but there was still a chance to save future babies and, with them, the human race.

The problem was, the world might not survive the transition.

"We're ready for you, Dr. Harris," said Ramona.

Mitch grinned. "We sure are."

"One or one and a half pints?"

"One and a half."

David nodded and slid the needle into the boy's vein.

"*Ow.* Damn, doc. A little warning next time."

David's lips curled into a slight smile. The blood flowed through the tube and began to pool in the plastic bag on the floor.

Down the drain, he thought.

Mitch fidgeted. David told him to keep still.

"So how long do I have to sit here?"

"About fifteen minutes."

"Shit, you should put a TV in here."

Ramona pulled a celebrity magazine from her purse. David wondered if it was a new or old one. He doubted new magazines were being printed anymore and couldn't imagine people actually caring about which actress was dating which rock star, or what TV shows were being canceled. Technically, they all were. He leaned back in his chair and closed his eyes, ignoring Mitch's attempts at further conversation.

He wanted to think about Nadine. He thought more about Herod. How it fed.

Vampirism had existed in nature for millions of years. Vampire bats hunted in the dark. They made a small cut with their incisors and lapped blood from the wound. Some bloodsucking leeches used a series of tiny blades to incise the flesh. An anticoagulant was injected to reduce clotting. The mouth, located behind these blades, ingested the blood.

Scientists had even come up with a plausible explanation for the popular concept of human vampirism. The hereditary disease porphyria prevented its victims from breaking down old red blood cells to make new ones, resulting in anemia with very pale and light-sensitive skin, sores, and reddish teeth. Victims were even advised to stay away from garlic, which exacerbated the symptoms.

Real living human vampires didn't exist, however—at least before Herod's syndrome came along. Humans couldn't live on blood for the simple reason human physiology wouldn't allow it. The digestive system in vampire bats had evolved to process blood as food; the stomach lining absorbed it quickly to produce hemoglobin for the body. Some leeches stored up to five times their body mass in blood, which they digested very slowly; their digestive system produced an antibiotic that retarded putrefaction of the blood.

But not humans. Blood contained iron, which irritated the human stomach and digestive system. Anything more than a few teaspoons induced pain and vomiting. The human body also had a hard time getting rid of it. Even if somebody could ingest large amounts of iron without becoming ill, over time, the result would be hemochromatosis, a condition whose symptoms included cirrhosis of the liver, joint pain, and heart disease.

Herod changed that. When the children drank blood, they didn't get sick because they were already dead, and rich concentrations of the parasite in the stomach lining absorbed the blood directly and passed it on to its companions in the heart, brain, and nervous system, each of which performed their own specialized functions.

It was a complex and fascinating path for obtaining food, which is all it was, no matter how diabolical it looked. What was truly diabolical was how it modified the behavior of its hosts, or rather, the behavior of people who cared for the hosts.

Many parasites exerted control over the organisms they infected, and in different ways. Rabies caused the host to become aggressive and produce more saliva, so it could spread by biting. Rats infected with *Toxoplasma gondii* lost their instinctive fear of cat pheromones, which increased their chances of being eaten; the parasite spread through cat droppings. (Some infected humans became more loyal, law-abiding, and neurotic.) The *Spinochordodes tellinii* hairworm forced grasshoppers to jump suicidally into water, which the parasite needed to reproduce. The *Ophiocordyceps unilateralis* fungus turned ants into zombies compelled to climb plants so that its fruiting bodies could explode and spread spores over a large area.

Herod was different in that it influenced the behavior of its host only when it got what it wanted. In doing so, it manipulated others who loved the host to provide it. By taking this path, Herod had almost everybody on its puppet strings. Every day that David continued to draw blood, even he was doing exactly what the parasite wanted him to do.

He checked the time and inspected the bag. He had enough. He disconnected the tube and needle and dropped them into a biological waste bin for sterilization.

"How do you feel, Mitch?" he asked.

"Like shit."

He sealed the bag. "That's normal."

Mitch reached for it. "I'll take that."

He winked at Ramona, who looked like she was about to be sick. David guessed it was dawning on her that she'd gotten what she wanted and was now going to have to pay for it.

David decided to help her get rid of at least one parasite in her life. He eyed Mitch as he pulled off his gloves. "You should avoid any physical activity for at least a few days."

Mitch scowled but said nothing.

David next turned to Ramona and said, "We're out of anticoagulant, so you should take this straight home and put it into your refrigerator as soon as possible. Otherwise, as you probably already know, it will start clotting. Store it between thirty-four and forty degrees Fahrenheit. It should be okay at a typical refrigerator setting."

"Thank you, doctor," said Ramona.

David smiled. He pitied her. She was a beautiful, strong woman weakened by inner frailties. She reminded him a great deal of Nadine. Unfortunately, she was doomed like all the rest.

"I hope I'm not being too personal," she said, "but I understand you and Nadine lost a son. Back before Josh became your patient. I just wanted you to know I'm glad you're a parent like me. You understand. There are two types of people in the world now. People who have kids and people who don't."

"That's not true," he said quietly. "We're all in this together. Everyone's trying to help. But life can't just be about the children."

She snorted. "What should it be about then?"

He had no answer to that.

Mitch did. He stood and grinned at her. He held up the bag and shook it. "Yum, yum."

As always, the young had their own ideas.

NINE

Ramona

36 days after Resurrection

Ramona took her time leading Mitch to her car.

They had unfinished business, but she was in no hurry to pay up. The idea of touching him in a sexual way made her want to vomit. It was too late now to wonder if she was doing the right thing. She'd made a deal. She either had to give him what he wanted or give up the blood. A pint of whole blood was worth twelve hundred dollars, and the price was going up by the hour. He'd easily find another buyer, and they both knew it.

In any case, the world had changed. Old notions of right and wrong meant nothing anymore. There was only what kept Josh alive, which was good, and what didn't, which was evil. By this simple litmus test, giving Mitch whatever he wanted was good as long as he gave her the blood.

They got into the car.

"So how do you want to do this?" he asked her.

The doctor had given her a small chance to delay it. "You're kidding, right? You've lost a lot of blood. You should call me when you're feeling up to it."

Mitch laughed and crossed his arms. "Do you think I'm stupid?"

"The doctor said you need to rest for a few days."

"Your concern is super touching, lady. Seriously. But I feel awesome."

"I have to get the blood home before it congeals."

"It's freezing in this car. It'll keep. Come on, you're wasting time."

"You're not being—"

He frowned. "Now or never, lady. Make up your mind. Yes or no."

There was no way she was taking him home with her or going to his place. She looked at the parking lot. She'd parked near the far edge. Not quite out of sight, but if she did it fast, nobody would see.

She sighed and pulled off her gloves. She couldn't believe she was doing this. "Fine. Take it out."

"Holy shit," he said with another laugh. He unzipped his fly.

If you do this, girl, you will hate yourself forever.

She did it anyway. She took him in her hand and played with it to make him hard.

"You can't even get it up," she said.

"Your hand's cold," he complained.

"This isn't going to work."

"It's going to be awesome. I hear if you come while your brain isn't getting enough air, it's like doing a couple lines of coke. It's supposed to be this incredible rush."

She recoiled in disgust. "Let me just give you the money."

"No way. Warm up your hand."

Let me just get this over with.

She rubbed her hands together and breathed on them. Went back to work.

He reclined in his seat and closed his eyes. "Yeah."

She stroked him until her arm got tired. She was breathing hard from oxygen starvation, which she hoped he took for excitement. The windows fogged up.

Time for the big finish, guy. Let's have it.

She stroked harder. She gave it everything she had, trying to bring him to climax.

"Kiss me," he said.

"That wasn't part of the deal."

"Do it, and you get the blood and go home."

She did, while continuing to pump him fast and hard. He pulled back; she kissed him again, but he turned away, practically spitting her out.

"What the hell?" she asked him.

"Not on the lips. I want you to kiss me *there*."

She winced. "No way."

"Do it, and you get everything."

She hated him now. Hated his sneering face, his long stringy hair, his jeans with the holes in the knees, his long-john shirt, his black leather jacket. Hated the power he wielded over her.

But she did it. Almost gagged before she even went near it.

"Make it last," he whispered. "I want it to last."

She hated him almost as much as she hated herself.

Think about something else. Think about anything else.

She tried to imagine doing it to Ross, but it didn't work. Instead, she pictured hurting Mitch. Killing him. She'd hit him with the car.

"Make it last, and you get your blood. Make it—"

She yanked as hard as she could while she worked him with her mouth, but the rough treatment only excited him. He howled as he came.

"Holy shit." He laughed. "You are so good at giving head."

Ramona pulled away, opened her door, and spit the mess onto the asphalt.

"At least my blood's good enough for you," he said.

"Shut up," she gasped. Then she began retching.

His door opened. She spit one final time and turned back, but he was already gone. The bag containing his blood rested on the front seat.

"I'm still going to kill you," she said. She started the car. She ran her hand across the inside of the windshield to clear their breath from the glass.

Mitch was gone.

She opened her door and threw up instead.

You did it for Josh. You're keeping him alive. You should be proud.

She looked again at the bag of blood on the front seat. The rich, sweet blood of a young diabetic.

You promised you'd do anything to help him. You kept your promise.

Ramona rolled down the windows as she drove to let in the cold air. She squeezed the bag. Mitch's blood rolled between her fingers. Three hours. Three hours of life for Josh.

Once home, she placed the bag in the refrigerator, stripped, and stepped into the shower with a toothbrush, making the water as hot as she could stand it. She felt diseased. Covered in slime.

After stepping out of the shower, she checked the time. Ross was coming for dinner at six. It would be their first time together without Josh since her boy had returned. Just the two of them. It was going to be a real date.

She wanted to cancel, but she needed this. He made her feel human.

Instead, she got busy in the kitchen, whipping dinner into shape in time to spend a few minutes fussing over her appearance.

She stared into her hollow eyes reflected in the mirror as she applied lipstick to cover the bluish pallor of her lips. It only made her look paler. Like dolling up a corpse.

You sucked a kid's dick with these lips today.

She felt an urge to break the mirror. She wanted to break every mirror in the house. She brushed her teeth for the fourth time instead.

The doorbell rang. She hurried to let Ross in.

"I brought a bottle of wine," he said as he entered the house and removed his coat.

"And I feel like getting drunk."

He eyed her. "Everything okay?"

"Nothing I feel like talking about. Dinner's almost ready."

Ross followed her into the kitchen. "Smells good, whatever it is."

"It's nothing special. The supermarkets don't have much in the way of selection these days."

"Tell me about it. I filled up my tank on the way over here. *Seven dollars* a gallon."

Ramona enjoyed the small talk. It almost felt like a real date.

The kitchen timer chimed. She put on a pair of oven mittens and slid the hot pan out. She placed it on the stovetop to cool.

"Macaroni and cheese with chopped bacon and caramelized onions. It's got a few things in it to spice it up. Paprika, some parsley. A little hot pepper sauce."

"It sounds amazing." He popped the cork on the wine bottle and poured two tall glasses for them. He raised one. "Well, cheers."

Their glasses connected, and she drank. It was sweet and cold and fizzed in her brain.

She waved him away. "Go, sit. Everything's on the table. I'll serve."

They ate in silence for a while. Ramona picked at her meal. Every time she looked across the table, she saw Mitch's sneering face. She drank most of the bottle of wine, determined to have some fun, but it only made her feel worse. She opened another bottle and drank most of that too.

"I'm sorry, what did you say?" she asked.

"The company wants to know when you're coming back."

"What are you even still doing there?"

"That new job I had lined up didn't pan out. The company went under. Because, you know . . ." He gestured at the house. The world around him.

"But you were terminated."

Ross frowned. "Yeah, I remember. They brought me back. They want you back too. Bereavement leave only lasted a week. It's like a ghost town. A skeleton crew is running the place. You did too good a job in HR, Ramona. The benefits attracted a lot of workers with families. Now those people are at home with their kids. The company's offering vouchers to people who come back. The vouchers are good for discounts at any of the company's stores. You know how expensive groceries are right now." He looked at her. "So?"

"So what?"

"How about it? Do you want your old job back?"

She poured another glass of wine. "I'm a stay-at-home mom now."

"What about money?"

Ramona laughed. She remembered when she used to care about things like working hard, promotions, raises. None of it mattered anymore. Money would eventually become a problem for her, but not now. She had much bigger fish to fry.

He said something else, but she didn't catch it. She was thinking about a zit on Mitch's forehead. A whitehead near his right eyebrow. At a distance, it had hardly been noticeable, but as she'd leaned forward to kiss him, she'd gotten a good look at it. The mother in her had wanted to reach over and pop it for him. In her memory, the pimple dominated the boy's face. It *was* his face. Something to be stabbed and drained.

Ramona set her fork on her plate. She'd made herself nauseous. It didn't matter; she had no appetite anyway. Ross was telling her how he'd spent most of his twenties living in California as a beach bum chasing the perfect wave. Then his mother had gotten sick, and he'd come back home to take care of her until she died. It had been a real wake-up call for him; it was time for him to grow up and get his act together.

A touching story. It explained much about him, but she couldn't focus on it.

Do you know what a MILF is, Ramona?

Mitch had asked her that on the way to the clinic. She'd pretended not to hear. They'd gone into the clinic, told their lie, and walked out with his blood in a bag. They'd gotten back into her car, and she'd worked his ropey cock with her hand. It was like jerking off a snake. Later she'd put it in her mouth, and it had spit burning gobs of venom against the back of her throat.

Holy shit! You are so good at giving head!

She'd opened her door, leaned out, and coughed his sperm onto the ground. After that she puked up her guts. She'd been forced into it. She'd had no choice, not really. She imagined he'd held a knife to her throat. The two memories merged into one. He had come puke into her mouth, and it had gushed back out.

At least my blood's good enough for you.

Ross finished speaking. She smiled politely, but he didn't seem to notice; he appeared distracted himself now. She drained her glass and poured the last bit of wine into it. The evening was officially a bust.

"I'm sorry I'm so out of it," she said. "I had a crazy day."

Ross nodded as if this obvious piece of information finished some puzzle he was working on in his head. "Right. Of course you did. Like all the rest."

She bristled. "Something wrong with that?"

"To be honest, I was really hoping somehow that tonight would be different. That you could let go of it all for a while. I had to at least try that. I was stupid."

"I don't understand. What did you expect? Josh needs a hundred percent of me. That doesn't stop just because he's sleeping. I'm in the middle of this thing. I'm trying to hold it together."

"Well, there you have it."

"There you have what? You're my *friend*, Ross."

"Right." He exhaled and took another deep breath. "This is kind of hard to say, so I'll just say it." He looked her in the eye. "This is going to be the last time we see each other."

Ramona felt nothing at first. Then she winced at the first stab of regret. Her mouth went dry. "But why? I don't understand."

"The main thing is there's no future in it."

"I told you we're a package deal."

"You did. Yes, you did."

"You knew that. So what's the problem? What did I do?"

Ross frowned. He appeared to be struggling to find the right words. "It's not any one big thing. It's all the little things. It's all of it. Adding up to one big thing."

"I have no idea what you're talking about." She tried to smile. "Come on."

But he meant it. She saw it in his eyes. He wanted to end it.

The truth of this world is people love you, and then they leave.

He said quietly, "It was a hard month."

"Do you think I don't know that?" Ramona snapped. "I'm the one trying to keep Josh alive every fucking day. What the hell, Ross?"

She'd spent the entire month pushing him away, telling herself she didn't need a boyfriend. He didn't have a child, and so he didn't get what had happened, not really. He wasn't in the club. So she'd treated him as an outsider.

But she did need him. She needed him a lot. She was realizing this now, just as he was slipping through her fingers.

And then they leave.

"Yes," Ross said firmly, "it was hard. And it's going to get even harder. For *you*, Ramona. Bringing Josh back an hour a day for the next month is going to take fifteen pints of medicine. Where are you going to get it?"

"Not from you, obviously," she shot back.

"That's not fair, and you know it. If giving blood would keep Josh from dying, I'd do it in a second." He glared at her. "In a *second*. But it wouldn't. It'd bring him back for an hour, maybe two, tops. At first, I couldn't do it because it was . . . horrible. The idea of him drinking my blood was . . . *yeah*, horrible. But now it's because it's just pointless."

"Pointless," she echoed. A second later, she burst into tears. Ross reached out, but she slapped his hand away. They weren't tears of sadness. They were tears of rage. She could barely speak. "You think I could simply let him die? You think dying would be best for him?"

"Ramona, look at you. How much more of this can you take?"

She blinked at him. "What do you mean?"

But she knew.

You sucked a kid's cock with these lips today.

"How much more can *he* take?" Ross said. "He has no real choices. No friends. Just an hour or two terrified this time will be the last time.

It's changing him. Something is. His personality is completely different now. Can't you see that? He's angry all the time. He's actually violent."

Josh *was* getting violent. The fact that Ross was right about that too only made it worse.

"This isn't about Josh or me," Ramona lashed back. "This is about you running away when things get rough."

Like every other goddamn man in her life.

"You don't understand. I really care about you and—"

"And this is how you show it? By running away? You could have had everything. You could have had *me*." Her voice jumped in pitch as she watched him stand. *"So that's it? You're leaving me?"*

Ross closed his eyes. "I just can't do this anymore."

It was too much for him. Of course it was.

"Don't go," she said. Despite her anger, she still wanted him. "Please."

"There's really nothing more to talk about. I'm sorry."

She stood up. She wanted to stop him. Bar the door with her body if necessary. The alcohol and the usual head rush sent her toppling against the table, scattering dishes.

"Jeez, are you okay?" he said.

She stumbled against him and held on. "Please stay. I'll do whatever you want. Anything."

She tried to kiss him. He gripped her arms and held her at arm's length.

"*No*, Ramona. God!"

She cried harder. He looked at her as if she were a stranger. As if she were dirt. Like Mitch had.

"You have no idea what I've done for Josh!" she screamed. "And what I would do. I would do anything. *Anything*. I would give the same to you, but you don't want it!"

"God, listen to yourself!" he shouted back at her. His volume stunned her into silence. He regained his composure by rubbing his face with his hands. "You're slowly killing yourself, and if I stay, I'd end up right there with you. You're out of blood, Ramona. Out of friends, out of money. Anything, huh? What's next? Would you sell your house? Live on the street? Prostitute yourself—"

"*I would never do that!*"

Ross stared at her face. "I can't believe it. Oh my God."

"I said I wouldn't!"

"Whoa. You already have. Haven't you?"

"I didn't do anything!"

He started for the door. "It doesn't matter."

She followed. "Don't you dare look down on me. If you'd given me even a single pint, I wouldn't have done it. It's your fault!"

He shook his head in disgust. "I don't want to hear any more. You're crazy. I have to get out of here right now before I do something I'll regret later."

She grabbed at him again. "No, no, *please*. I'm sorry—"

Her head snapped to the side from the force of the slap. She rubbed her stinging cheek and stared at him in amazement.

He backed away, looking scared. "Oh my God. Oh, fuck. I'm sorry. But just . . . just please stay away from me."

Ramona saw him walk toward the front door. He moved slowly, as if carrying the weight of the world on his shoulders. *Poor Ross. Poor Mitch. They use me and throw me away and feel sorry for themselves.* She followed close behind.

If looks could kill, he would have been dead already.

"I'm not crazy."

He turned, surprised to see her there.

The wine bottle caught him on the side of the head with a hollow thud. He staggered but didn't fall. *Not good enough.*

She swung again and missed. His backhand caught her on the chin and sent her reeling. The world spun as she stumbled against the dining room table.

Ross fell to his knees, cupping his head in his hands. He groaned.

She'd dropped the bottle. It was gone. She went into the kitchen and picked up the cast iron skillet in which she'd fried the bacon and prepared the cheese sauce. It felt heavy in her hand. It was still warm.

Then she returned to the living room. Ross was back on his feet.

"Look," he said in a daze. "This is ridiculous—"

His eyes shifted to the skillet in her hand and flashed with alarm. As she raised her arm, he came at her and shoved her against the wall. Pictures of Josh toppled off their hooks and fell to the floor. The momentum made him stagger. She took another step toward him, and this time he slapped her again. She staggered back with a yelp. For several seconds, they stood with their hands on their knees and tried to regain their senses.

"Please, Ramona," he said. "This is crazy."

"I'm not crazy!"

He looked up as the skillet smashed into his face. The impact vibrated up her arm. He fell back against the wall with a loud crash and slid down onto his rear.

"Stop!" he howled.

His nose looked like a burst tomato. He spit blood and pieces of teeth. He cowered with his arms raised in a pathetic attempt to defend himself. The sleeves of his sports jacket dripped with cheese sauce.

Ramona stared at him and raked air into her lungs in long, shuddering breaths. Her lips tingled. Her entire body felt shot up with Novocaine.

Ross crawled toward freedom. He made it halfway to the front door.

"Oh no you don't," she slurred. "We're still talking."

He raised his hand and tried to wave her away.

"I'M NOT CRAZY!"

The skillet slammed against the back of his head. He went down like a sack of meat. His legs twitched and went still.

She dropped the skillet and pulled at her hair. "Don't you dare look down on me. *FUCKER!*"

Blood pooled around his head and clotted on the carpet. She wondered how she was going to get it out. She remembered reading in a magazine that Native Americans once used blood as a wood stain.

She staggered back to the kitchen looking for Tupperware. Her mind reeled. The place was a mess; she'd never get it cleaned up. She pulled Josh's *Jake and the Never Land Pirates* mug from a cupboard. In a drawer, she picked out a turkey baster but tossed it aside. She grabbed a roll of Bounty paper towels and headed back into the living room.

Ross lay in the same spot where she'd left him.

Ramona fell to her knees next to the body and began sopping up blood, which she wrung out into the mug.

"I didn't mean it," she sobbed. "It was an accident."

Yes, that's all it was.

"I'm sorry, Ross. I didn't want this."

He didn't answer.

You know what they say, her brain taunted her. *Hire slow, fire fast.*

She had to call the police. But if she did, they'd take her away, and nobody would look after Josh. He'd die and never wake up again. No, she couldn't do that. She'd put Ross in the storage room in the basement until she figured out what to do. It was so hard to think properly.

First, she had to get his blood. He would have wanted that.

She tottered back into the kitchen, opened several drawers, and pulled out a pair of scissors and a handful of Glad trash bags. She laid the bags on the floor next to the body. She rolled him onto the bags and went to work. The scissors were good and sharp. She sliced open the jacket, the shirt. Then the cooling flesh underneath. She focused on the major blood pathways in the neck, thighs, and inner arms. Without a working heart to pump blood through them, they weren't very productive. Blood congealed fast. Even so, she ended up with more on herself than where she wanted it.

By the time she finished, she'd recovered about a pint and a half in a collection of mugs covered in Saran plastic wrap. The mugs went straight into the fridge. Coupled with Mitch's blood, she now had three pints. *Six hours.*

Now she had to take care of Ross.

She grabbed his ankles and pulled. By the time she'd maneuvered him to the top of the stairs, her clothes were soaked through with blood and sweat.

She stopped to turn on the basement light and yank more of her hair out.

I'M HUNGRY!

Josh's voice, clear as day. She turned, but he wasn't there.

"Go back to bed!" she called out. "Mommy's busy!"

She pulled the body onto the stairs. His head thumped on the first step. The second.

On the third, his eyes popped open.

She reared back and gripped the banister in time to prevent herself from falling.

The body slid past her feet and shot down the stairs, riding the plastic bags. Ramona watched it thud to a halt near the bottom. For a moment, she'd thought he'd woken up. He hadn't. He was the kind of dead you didn't come back from. His body lay half-naked in a tangle of limbs and rags. His head had turned farther than it was supposed to. One eye looked at her from beyond. The other had closed in a mischievous wink.

Bile surged in her throat. She swallowed acid.

Then she laughed as if it was the funniest thing she'd ever seen. Laughed until she bowed her head onto her knees and let it all out in a long keening wail.

She was still crying as she dragged him into the storage room. The body left a trail of blood and chunks of brain on the carpet. Another mess to clean up.

Ramona grunted as she pulled him the final distance into the dark cool space and laid him to rest among boxes of baby clothes, books, toys, tax returns. She found an old sheet and covered him with it.

She looked down at the body. "I'm so sorry, Ross. At any other time, you would have been the one."

Then she fell to her knees and threw up her entire dinner. Mac and cheese and wine rushed out of her mouth and nose in a geyser.

"It's not you," she gasped, spitting strands of bile. Then vomited again, another liquid torrent. "It's me."

TEN

Joan

40 days after Resurrection

Nate flew at her with a hiss. She caught his wrists, but he was surprisingly strong.

"If you keep this up, you are going to be in so much trouble, young man."

She'd given too much blood. He was stronger than her now. His eyes flashed with this sudden knowledge. He looked up at her and grinned.

"Doug, I need your help! Quick!"

Doug stomped down the hall, gripped Nate's arm, and shoved him into his room. He slammed the door as the boy hurled his body against it. Next door, Megan scrabbled at the wood and screamed to be let out.

"Daddeeeeeeeeee!"

When Doug had brought home four pints of blood, Joan had fallen to her knees and cried. They'd woken the kids four times over four days.

Each time, it was harder to keep them in line.

Today, they were uncontrollable.

The tantrums started when Joan told Nate the ice cream she'd promised during his last wake-up wasn't coming. The stores were out of it; she couldn't find it anywhere. Both kids went absolutely berserk, demanding she find some, and when she said no, they tore the living room apart. Then Nate ripped the throat out of one of Megan's teddy bears with his teeth. Joan watched him eat a handful of the stuffing with a growl that would have been comical if it weren't real.

Joan and Doug had no choice but to force them back into their rooms.

Nate now threw himself against the door, which bounced on its hinges.

"IT'S NOT FAIR!" the boy howled. "I'M HUNGRY!"

He hurled his body against the door again. Again. Again.

"I DON'T LOVE YOU ANYMORE!"

"Daddeeeeeeeeeeeee!"

Doug sat in front of Nate's door with his back against it. Joan did the same with Megan's. They listened to their kids smash everything in their rooms.

Joan glanced at her watch. Forty minutes to go before the kids returned to sleep.

Something cracked against the door behind her.

Megan: "Let me *out*!"

"We'll let you out when you kids learn to behave!" she shouted back.

Nate punched and kicked his door in a frenzy.

"FUCK PISS SHIT! FUCK PISS CUNT! YOU LIKE THAT?"

She looked at Doug with hope that he might have some idea what to do next, but he sat with his eyes closed, as if he'd reached some Zen place where the commotion couldn't bother him. Then she saw the dimple winking on his cheek. She knew it well. He was grinding his teeth in silent rage.

She'd toyed with the thought that maybe they'd gotten a bad batch of blood, but she knew that wasn't the case. The children had been changing for weeks; it was only now getting worse. Each time they woke up, they were missing a little more of themselves.

They were like jigsaw puzzles that lost a few pieces every time they were put together. After a while, it got hard to tell what the complete picture was supposed to be.

Now they were changing into something else. Something new.

"I'M HUNGRY! I'LL CUT MY THROAT AND REALLY DIE THIS TIME! THEN YOU'LL BE SORRY, MOM!"

Joan started to rise. Doug's eyes flashed open. He shook his head. She pressed her fingers into her ears and wept.

"YOU PROMISED! YOU PROMISED, AND YOU'LL BE SORRY!"

It seemed to go on forever. At last, she heard a thump as Nate crumpled to the floor. Another as Megan fell. Then all sounds stopped. The house was quiet.

Doug stood and stared at a spot on the floor with frightening intensity.

Joan slowly returned to her feet and waited for the head rush to pass. She felt compelled to whisper, even though she knew she didn't have to do so. "We should clean—"

Doug reared and punched the wall. A picture toppled from its hook to crash against the floor. He withdrew his fist and eyed the crater it had left behind with something akin to satisfaction.

Joan watched him, too terrified to move or say a word, as he turned and stomped off. She heard his feet pound the stairs.

Only when she heard the TV turn on did she remember to breathe.

She stood still as the shadows around her deepened with the failing light. If she moved, she might disturb her home's fragile equilibrium. Downstairs, Doug watched a daytime rerun of some old sitcom. She listened to commercials for children's toys, suicide hotlines, fast food, antidepressants. Her own bedroom was just a few feet away. Bed sounded like a good idea. A nice long nap, maybe ride the sleep train all the way to tomorrow. Then she'd wake up and undo the wreckage the kids had made, if she had the energy.

She crept downstairs instead. Doug sat expressionless in his favorite chair while the sitcom's laugh track roared on the TV. He sipped at a can of Miller High Life. Three o'clock in the afternoon, and already well on his way to getting drunk as a skunk. Broken toys and plates and cups and pieces of a broken table lamp littered the carpet around him.

She entered the room cautiously and turned off the TV with the remote he'd tossed onto the coffee table. "Doug?"

He stared at the blank TV screen and drank his beer.

"Doug, we need to talk."

"I'm right here, babe. Start talking."

"It's important."

He took another sip from his can. "Okay."

"I think we need to start thinking about letting them go."

He took a final drink and crushed the can in his fist. "I don't. Now we're done talking."

"This isn't about us. Whether we love them or not."

He reached down by the side of the chair and cracked open another beer. "We can handle it."

"I said it's not about us. It's about them."

"We're keeping them alive, ain't we? That's the job."

She sat on the couch. "I think they're dying. I mean, I think their *brains* are dying. I think they're falling apart."

"They were tough today," he conceded. He inspected his hand, patched with a series of Band-Aids, where Megan had bitten him hard enough to draw blood.

"They're not the same anymore. They're changing. It's like they're turning wild."

"Let's not get dramatic. Nate's frustrated. He knows he has to go back to sleep almost as soon as he wakes up, and he doesn't like it. He acts out, and Megan follows his lead."

"It's more than that, and you know it," Joan said. "If you count just the time they're alive, they never sleep, and they eat almost constantly. They barely even know who they are anymore." She paused to collect her thoughts. "Okay. An example. Did you see Nate wearing his Giants hat today?"

"Nope," he said. "He hasn't worn it for a while."

"About a week ago, I asked him why he wasn't wearing it. Know what he said? He said he couldn't remember ever having worn it. His favorite hat. Didn't even know he was in Little League."

Doug chewed his mustache. "Anything else?"

"I was trying to remember the end of one of the Harry Potter books and asked him if he remembered. He didn't remember either. Then I realized he didn't even know who Harry Potter was. Doug, he's read every one of those books."

"Megan . . . can't remember who Major was," Doug said. "She didn't even know we'd had a dog."

"And the anger . . . Doug, that anger they're showing is more than just tantrums. Their personalities are changing. The way they look at us sometimes . . . you know?"

"Yeah." He took a long pull on his beer.

"And the biting . . . I think they're trying to *feed*, Doug."

This revelation surprised even her as she said it, but it made sense.

"They're changing," he said. "Okay, you win. So what do you want to do about it?"

"I don't know! I think . . . I think we need to start thinking about letting them sleep."

"*Sleep*," he said with a wince. "You mean *die*."

She didn't back down. "Yes. Die."

"Just like that, huh?"

"*No*, Doug," she said, pissed off. "*Not* just like that. Nothing about this is *just like that*."

"I don't care if the kids are changing," Doug said. "They can grow gills for all I care. They're my kids, Joanie. Got it? We're in this now. I'll do whatever it takes."

"I *do* get it. They're *my* kids too." She closed her eyes and expelled her anger in a loud sigh. "Doug. Doug, listen to me. There's no more blood anyway. What else can we do?"

"I'll take care of it, babe."

"What's that supposed to mean?"

He turned and looked her directly in the eye for the first time. "It means I'll do whatever it takes."

Joan thought of the women at the supermarket, crouching over their victim like a pack of jackals. Doug had already robbed a blood bank and told her the story of how his four pints could have saved a life. She remembered what he'd done to Major.

"Whatever you do, leave me out of it," she told him. "I think I'm finished."

"Then we're done here," he said with maddening calm. He finished his beer. "Don't worry about a thing, babe. I'll take it from here."

The ties of blood are strong. Others less so.

She'd fought and suffered for her children for over a month, and so had Doug. She'd given up her blood and her health. They'd gone to hell and back.

But right at this moment, their marriage was crushed with the ease of Doug squeezing one of his beer cans.

Doug

40 days after Resurrection

After Joan tramped upstairs for a nap, Doug lit a cigarette and made a phone call.

"Russell?"

"Yeah. Who's this?"

"It's Doug Cooper. You said to call you if, uh, I needed to, uh . . ." He didn't know how to put it.

"Glad you did." Russell gave him an address. "How soon can you get there?"

"Fifteen minutes, maybe twenty."

"You own a gun, right?"

"I own several."

"Good. Bring your favorite," Russell said, and disconnected the call.

Doug hung up with a sense of having done something big. This was what he wanted—to find like-minded people and team up with them to get what they needed.

It sure beat the alternative, which was to walk next door, ring Art Foley's doorbell, and hit the old guy over the head with a claw hammer.

The third option, listening to Joan and letting the kids stay asleep, didn't deserve any consideration. His wife sounded just like her old man, saying the kids were better off dead.

Dead is dead. *Anything* is better than dead.

Every instinct screamed at him to protect them. It was his only real task in life, if one thought about it. Without that, what was he?

Joan had an easier time letting go because she believed the kids would wake up in Heaven. Doug believed in God but thought an after-life of endless happiness sounded too good to be true. Like just another rip-off. If it was that great, why didn't everybody just kill themselves?

There was only one type of life after death he felt certain about. Only one he could count on. One day, he'd die, and all that would be left of him on this earth would be his children. By protecting them, he was safeguarding his one crack at immortality.

Empties spilled onto the floor as he stood, adding to a mess he didn't care about. He walked to the bottom of the stairs. Joan was sleeping. He could hear her rapid, shallow breaths. She'd said she was *done*, and she meant it. His wife was at the end of her rope.

He wasn't. Not by a long shot. He went into the den and unlocked the cabinet where he kept his guns. If Russell wanted firepower, Doug would bring it. He opted for the Mossberg 500, a camouflage-painted, twenty-gauge, pump-action repeater he used to hunt pheasants.

Knowing its purpose, the gun felt right in his hands.

I'll take it from here, he'd said. Damn straight.

He opened a box of shells and loaded the Mossberg. He pocketed the rest. Then he put on his Lovin' Lansdowne cap and jacket and went into the garage to start up his truck.

The address turned out to be a bar called the Shamrock. Twenty minutes later, he walked in and took a seat across from Russell at a dim corner booth.

The man pushed a pint of some dark beer across the table. "You drink, right?"

"Are you kidding?" Doug downed half of it in three long swallows. "Where's the rest of your guys?"

"Chickened out. They're giving up."

"That's them. That ain't me."

"Me neither, I guess."

Doug emptied the glass and sighed. "More for us."

"What did you bring?"

Doug told him about the Mossberg, which he'd left in the truck in its travel case. "Is that what you had in mind?"

"If it goes bang, it is."

Russell had a simple way of looking at things. Doug liked that.

"What did you load it with?" the man asked.

"Three rounds of bird shot. I figure if you want me to point it at people, I should have something that'll be less likely to actually kill somebody."

"I thought you didn't have a problem with taking somebody's life. You were talking pretty big last time I saw you."

Doug bristled. "I don't have a problem doing what needs doing for me and mine."

"Emphasis on *needs*, I suppose," Russell said with a nod, and called out for another round. "I meant no offense. I just like to know who I'm working with."

"What about you? I figured you for ex-military."

"You figured that right."

"You ever take a life?"

"A while back, when I was in Afghanistan. I was hoping I'd never have to do it again. But like you, I'll do what needs doing."

"You really think we'll need the guns?" Doug asked.

"There's only two of us this time. And the hospitals are probably wising up. We could have opposition. We'll go in hard and fast."

He nodded. Russell struck him as the kind of man who'd seen and done a lot in his time, including the dark things one does in war. He was in good hands with this man.

"How many mouths you got to feed back at home?" he asked.

"Three," said Russell. "A pint stretches to about forty minutes. It's never enough."

"I got two at home. A pint gets us an hour. The time does fly."

They sat in silence for a while, each in his own thoughts. Finally, Doug spoke. "Mine have been acting a little funny lately. Yours?"

Russell's face darkened. "You could say that. Rabid is more like it."

"We had to lock ours in their rooms today. They ripped the whole house apart."

"My youngest bit a mouthful out of my wife's leg yesterday afternoon. Ate it right in front of me." The server set two foaming glasses on the table along with the bill. Russell picked up one of the glasses and drank, his mouth set in a hard line. "But they're still my kids."

Doug raised his glass. "That's the way I see it."

They finished their beers in silence, paid up, and walked out into the cold light of day. Doug went to his truck, Russell to his SUV. They traveled about a half hour along Highway 69, heading south toward Addison before catching Route 60 to Magnolia. The truck rattled the entire way. Doug lit a Winston and cranked the heat.

Russell led him to the parking lot of another bar on the outskirts of Magnolia. Doug parked his truck, hopped out with his gear, and climbed into the SUV feeling hopeful.

Neither man spoke for a while as they passed the flask back and forth to build up their courage. Doug decided to float an idea.

"If this doesn't work, maybe we should just find somebody nobody will miss."

"You do talk tough," said Russell. He started his SUV and drove onto the road. "I don't think we're quite there yet."

"Less risk, though. We don't know what's in that hospital. There could be cops."

"You kill a man, you don't get as much as you think. Once the heart stops beating, you need gravity to get it out. And it all starts clotting up fast."

"We could fill the guy up with blood thinners. Coumadin or something."

Russell snorted. "Good luck finding some at a pharmacy. We'd have to use aspirin. In any case, we'd still probably only get a few pints." He glanced at Doug's profile. "Could you do it?"

"If we take blood from the hospital, isn't it the same thing?"

"The end result is the same, I guess. But it's not quite the same as stringing a man up by his feet and cutting his throat over a bucket with a knife, now, is it?"

Doug grimaced. "I already did it to my dog."

Russell blinked in surprise. "I can't believe I never even thought of that. Did it work?"

"Nope," said Doug.

Russell opened his mouth to say something but closed it after catching the pained expression on Doug's face. A sign appeared on the right-hand side of the road: Magnolia Memorial Community Center. Doug wiped his eyes as they pulled onto the grounds.

"It's all one facility," Russell was saying. "They don't have a separate building for the blood bank here like they do back in Lansdowne."

"Looks kind of small," Doug said.

"It's here, and so are we."

He nodded. It was good enough. "What's the plan?"

"We park behind the building and come in through the front showing our guns and moving fast. We go straight through to where they keep the blood, clean it out, and go out the back, where the car will be waiting."

"Do you know where we're going once we're inside?"

"Sure I do. I studied the floor plan. Found it online."

Doug pulled the shotgun out of its traveling case. "Let's do this."

Russell loaded his own gun. "Listen, bud. It sounds simple, but when we get in there, it's going to seem like a blur. Just don't lose your head. Keep your finger off the trigger."

Doug pumped a round into the firing chamber with a metallic racking sound. He followed Russell toward the front of the building with the weapon held low against his leg to make it less visible.

Russell opened the door. Doug strode into the hospital lobby and swept the area with his shotgun. He didn't see any security guards. Russell raised his own shotgun to a flurry of screams.

"Everybody get down on the floor!" Doug shouted.

The waiting area had eight people in it, and none was a threat. Russell was right; it was a blur except for details that leaped out at him. Ashen faces belonging to men and women staggering from blood loss. Cotton balls taped over inner arms.

"Down on the ground!"

Russell hadn't told him about the rush he was now feeling.

The people cowered as he and Russell continued their rapid advance to the reception desk.

"Buzz us in," Russell told one of the nurses.

The woman could only stare at him, her mouth hanging open. She shook her head.

Doug walked up to the nearest patient, a woman lying on the floor in a fetal ball, and pointed the shotgun at her.

"Buzz us in," Russell repeated.

The doors glided open and welcomed them into a bright corridor.

Doug rushed through with his gun raised. People in scrubs and lab coats scrambled out of the way.

They jogged past a row of offices. The hall led to another set of doors. Doug remembered what Russell had told him about the layout. They were already halfway there.

They were going to get blood. Maybe only a few pints, but it would be enough. He'd show Joanie what kind of man he was. A man who saw things through. A man who provided.

He'd surprise her when he got back. He'd wake up Nate and

Megan, and they'd all bring her breakfast in bed. They'd go to the park and let the kids run free.

Russell screamed.

Doug turned and saw the soldier shudder and collapse to the floor. Two security guards were shouting at Doug to drop the gun.

Doug only had time for a single thought.

If I go to jail, Nate and Megan will never come back again.

And for a quick decision.

He swung his shotgun toward them.

Snap.

Wires leaped out of the gun in one of the guards' hands, hooked onto his shirt, and flooded his body with electric current.

It was like getting stabbed in the chest with a jackhammer.

Doug heard laughter. "You thought you'd take *our* blood, bro?"

He saw the swing of the billy club before the world went black.

David

40 days after Resurrection

David watched his wife draw blood from her patient, a young woman gripping her husband's hand.

Nadine noticed him staring and smiled. He smiled back.

They lived together, worked together, but they were still miles apart. All they did was talk and think about the children. About Herod.

But they were together. They were on the same side. He had to admit that in many ways Herod had brought them closer than they'd been since Paul passed on.

Before Paul was born, they used to lie in bed drinking coffee on Sundays. David would read the paper while Nadine did the crossword puzzle. They wouldn't say a word for an hour at a time, but he'd always feel connected to her. When it was cold, she wore her oversized men's pajamas. When it was hot, she wore nothing. Sometimes, he would just sit and watch her lying on her stomach, pencil in hand and her long black hair a tangle on her shoulders and back.

David now felt the same contentment but hoped that, given more time, they could do more than just share space. Nadine believed love had brought the children back from the dead. Was it so much to ask it to save his marriage?

He retreated to his office and started a pot of fresh water boiling on the propane stove. Basic medical resources were no longer available due to huge demand and erratic supply. Bags, anticoagulants, clean needles, saline. They used clear zip-lock bags to collect blood and boiled needles and tubing for reuse.

It would all be over soon. He just hoped he and Nadine would survive it.

The heat from the stove warmed the room. He changed the filter in the coffeemaker and poured in fresh water and coffee. The smell of brewing java filled the air.

The couple stumbled out of the examination room. They hugged Nadine. They were crying. After they'd gone, Nadine entered the office and stared at the stove's blue flame. David poured a cup of coffee and handed it to her.

"Fewer people coming in," he said. "We're getting near the end."

She regarded him. "The end of what, David?"

"The blood supply is collapsing. There isn't enough to keep the children alive."

"Everything is going to be fine," she grated, as if his skepticism were the sole reason her predictions weren't coming to pass. "Something wonderful is going to happen."

"Wonderful?" He stared at her in amazement. "Nadine, you do realize that they're going to eliminate the middleman and start taking it from each other, right?"

"It won't get that—"

"And us," he reflected, "if we're not careful."

She walked into his arms and rested her head against his chest. He forgot his anger.

"I love you, Nadine."

She said, "I'm still trying to decide to whom I'm going to give mine."

"Your blood?"

"Yes. Have you thought about it?"

"I wasn't planning on giving any," he told her. "I don't really see the point."

"Life is the point."

"We've done our part. Haven't we done enough for them?"

"We must give everything. God demands a blood sacrifice. He won't lift the curse until everyone has given every bit they can. If this is the end, now it's our turn."

He stroked her hair. "Do you really believe that?"

"Of course. Otherwise, Paul died for nothing."

If he wanted to keep her, he had to accept that basic premise. In her mind, Paul died so Nadine could do this great work. If the work was futile, if it was all for nothing, then Paul's death was meaningless.

"All right," he said quietly. "I'll give a unit if that's what you want."

"Kimberly. My friend Caroline's daughter. We'll give it to her."

"I'll do it for you. Because you want me to do it."

Nadine pulled away and touched his face. "You still don't believe we're meant to do this."

"No. I wish I did. But I don't. I tried."

"Have faith. All of this is meant to be."

It was a strange feeling to be in love with a crazy person. Wasn't that what one called somebody motivated by delusion?

It's all a big charade, Nadine. The human race is inching toward genocide. Genocide and ultimately suicide. That's the cause we're serving. And if there's a higher power directing all these events, his name is Herod.

But he didn't say that. If he did, he might lose her. Nadine was as invested in continuing the insanity as the parents, and David was invested in her. They were all in this together. To the bitter end, apparently.

Perhaps he was crazy too, by his own definition.

"Meant to be," he echoed. "I hope you're right."

And if she was wrong, it didn't matter. Even if the parents let the children go, the human race was finished anyway if they couldn't destroy Herod. Perhaps killing and dying for love was better than dying of old age, without any hope for the future of the race.

"I'm just glad we're doing this together," he added.

The phone rang in his office.

"You get that," said Nadine. "I need to go out to buy a few things."

"Be careful out there, okay?"

She offered him a weak smile and patted his cheek. "I'll be all right, darling."

David stepped into his office and picked up the phone on his desk. "David Harris."

"David, it's Ben."

He sat in his chair. "How are you?"

"The great thing about being out of breath all the time is you don't have to do small talk."

"Given your condition, it's hardly small talk. I also happen to care."

"My CDC contact told me Herod is changing. Or rather its victims are. Interested?"

"I'm listening," said David.

"Herod reanimates the body and reboots the mind, which draws upon information stored in body tissues to re-create the individual . . ."

David already knew this background. Everything that made people who they were—emotions, moods, memories, personality—lived in body chemicals stored in cells, the smallest unit of the body. Ultimately, there was no "mind over matter" because mind *was* matter. Memories, for example, were stored in certain cells in the hippocampus region of the brain.

These chemicals survived death until final decomposition, which provided Herod the raw materials it needed. The parasite revived the mind, which in turn drew upon the stored body chemicals that made a person who and what they were.

At first, it was feared that Herod was modifying the children's behavior, a notion later disproven. Herod was software, not information.

Ben told him that was now changing.

"Every time the children die, the integrity of these stored body chemicals is eroding a little more," he explained. "Wiping the information stored in them."

"So they're—"

"Losing their memory, right. And not only that. Their personalities are disintegrating."

David sighed at this depressing news. "I suppose it makes sense. Every time they die, they stroke out, and strokes cause neurological damage."

"But unlike a normal stroke, the damage is selective. Herod is very clever. Motor, speech, and ocular function, and most of the higher brain functions, remain unimpaired."

"How is that clever? What's the endgame? Two billion children becoming what, mindless? Or will they finally permanently die? How does Herod benefit from that?"

"The children retain their minds. But here's the rub, David. As their humanity fades, Herod's programming takes over and supplies the body's identity."

David took a moment to consider the horrifying implication. He could scarcely get his head around it. *This is one of those moments*, he thought. They were piling up.

He rubbed his eyes. "Shit. Tell me you're making this up."

"I wish I were," Ben told him. "And worse, the process appears to be accelerating."

Herod wasn't a person. It was pure hunger. The children were not only infected with bloodsucking parasites. They were *becoming* bloodsucking parasites. Monsters.

Around the world, two billion vampires were being born one resurrection at a time.

"What's CDC going to do?"

"Well, that's a whole other—wait a minute."

"Ben?"

"Hang on."

David heard Gloria's voice in the background. They were shouting at each other.

"Sorry, I have to, uh, go. The police are here."

Ben sounded terrified. Like a child caught doing something bad and awaiting his punishment.

"Ben—"

"Good luck, David."

The call disconnected. David stared at the receiver in disbelief.

It's nothing. They just want to ask him some questions.

He thought about Ben lying on his couch with his handgun, waiting for the police to burst through the door. He stood but sat down again just as fast, rooted with fear.

What can I do about it?

If he did nothing, it would haunt him forever. He had to do something, anything

Ben's house is twenty minutes away. Whatever's happening will be over by the time I get there.

David leaped out of his chair and raced to his car, ignoring the pain in his leg.

As he drove to the Glass house, he hoped he was still living in the America he knew. He slowed the car to a crawl as the house came into view. A police van sat in the driveway. Two police officers carried a human-shaped black bag down the front steps.

"Oh, God," he moaned, and pulled over. He limped toward a cop dressed in bulky black riot armor.

The cop put his hand on the grip of his service weapon. "Sir, stop where you are."

David raised his hands. "I want to see Dr. Glass."

"Dr. Glass is deceased."

He paled. "His wife?"

"Mrs. Glass is also deceased."

"How can they be dead? I was just on the phone with him!"

"Oh really?" The cop scowled. "Did you know he had a weapon and planned to use it against us?"

"Of course not!" David shouted at him.

"I'm going to have to ask you to calm down, sir."

"What's your name? I want your badge number."

The cop frowned. "And you are, sir?"

"David Harris."

"Well, now I'm going to have to place you under arrest, Mr. Harris."

"For what?"

"For being at the wrong place at the wrong time."

David took a step back. "I'm not going anywhere with you."

The cop drew his baton from his belt, stepped forward, and jabbed it hard into David's stomach.

The pain was incredible. He couldn't breathe.

He woke up facedown in the snow. He cried out as his hands were yanked behind his back and cuffed together.

Nadine—

"Sorry it has to be this way, sir."

"I take it back," David groaned. "I won't tell anyone anything."

"I know you won't, sir."

"Don't do this! I'll make a donation!"

The cop hauled him to his feet and dragged him to the van. "I know you will."

The other cops stepped aside as they approached.

"Help me," David begged.

"What's the deal?" one of them said.

The cop tightened his grip on David's arm. "We're taking him with us."

They shrugged and opened the doors.

A group of men sat on benches inside, hands cuffed behind their backs, their heads covered in black hoods. Their clothes were ragged and filthy. They stank like alcohol and vomit.

At their feet lay two shiny black body bags containing the bodies of his friends.

"To answer your question, Mr. Harris, I'm Officer Stellar."

David screamed for help as the cop slipped the hood over his head.

Doug

40 days after Resurrection

Doug awoke in a doctor's office, his head swimming.

Something's wrong.

The room was tiny. It was *shaking*.

He lay on a very narrow bed, his face a stiff mask of pain. His jacket was gone, and his sleeve had been rolled up to expose his arm. A piece of tape held an IV tube in place over his vein. His tongue probed broken teeth and tasted blood. He swallowed it.

I got hit by a car, he thought, but couldn't remember any of it.

He tried to sit up. Restraining straps held him down.

"Dude, be cool, be cool," a voice said. "I'm Ted. I'm here to help you."

A long-haired teenager with a wispy mustache smiled down at him from a bench next to the bed. He wore a dark-blue uniform and glasses with yellow-tinted lenses.

"Are my kids okay?" Doug croaked.

"You were by yourself when we picked you up. I mean, it was just you and the other guy."

Doug winced as he remembered their botched robbery. "Russell?"

The kid shrugged. "I guess. I didn't get his name."

"Where am I?"

Ted laughed, as if it should have been obvious. "You're in my rocking ambulance."

"What happened?"

The paramedic appeared to find this question amusing. "My guess is somebody fucked you up pretty good."

Doug remembered the blurred swing of the billy club. The pain. Blacking out.

"Where's Russell?"

"Your friend's in another ambulance. Anyway, you're okay now. Are you still hurting?"

"Is he awake?" yelled the driver from the front of the vehicle. "What the hell?"

"I got this!" Ted shouted back. He rolled his eyes at Doug. "My partner. He thinks he's my mom. Don't worry about him. I'm here to help you. We're the good guys, brother."

"It hurts," Doug gasped. "Everywhere."

The kid laughed. "My face hurts just looking at yours. I'll fix you up." He prepared a syringe. "This'll get you high. Knock you right on your ass."

"I have to get home."

"Not in your condition, dude. Trust me."

Doug's head swam. He turned his head and retched as the wave of nausea passed.

"Hey, don't puke in here, okay?"

"Where?" Doug swallowed. "Where are you taking me then?"

To jail, he answered himself. *They're taking us straight to jail. My kids won't have anybody to provide for them, and they'll die.*

"We're taking you to the hospital. Where else would we take you?"

"Why isn't that man sedated?" the driver shouted. "He's still awake!"

"Because we don't have a lot of this shit left, *Jason*. I'm trying to *conserve*, okay?"

"Well, put him down!"

"What do you mean?" said Doug. "I was just *at* the hospital."

He tried to sit up again, but the straps held him. He looked down at his IV.

The tube was red.

Ted smiled. "Dude, just be cool, okay?"

Their eyes met. Understanding passed between them.

"Oops," said Ted.

The needle lunged. Doug caught the paramedic's wrist and held it.

The kid chuckled. "It's just something for the pain. Don't freak out."

Doug grunted, surprised at his lack of strength. Black seeped into the edges of his vision.

I'm going to pass out. The needle will go in, and I'll never wake up.

The paramedic's face twisted into a hateful grimace. "Just be *cool*."

Doug pushed back with everything he had. Sweat stung his eyes. The pressure only increased. He couldn't hold it.

He let go instead. Twisted the kid's wrist as he did.

The needle pricked the kid's thigh. Doug pushed it in and thumbed the plunger down.

"Shit," groaned Ted. He fell back against the wall. He blinked. "Wow."

Doug freed himself and pulled the tube out of his vein with a spurt of blood. Legs splayed and eyes closed, Ted sat drooling. Doug reared back and punched the kid's face with everything he had. The nose flattened under his fist. Blood poured out of it.

The driver looked back at him with murder in his eyes.

"Stop the ambulance," Doug said. "I'm getting off."

"Screw you, pal. You're dead."

"Stop, or I'll hit him again. I'll stick this needle in his eye. I'll blind him."

The driver swore and pulled over. Doug took off Ted's jacket, pulled it on, and pocketed his flask and two bags of blood he found on the floor.

Both of these bags, he knew, belonged to him.

He opened the doors and jumped down from the back of the ambulance. The driver was still shouting at him. Doug walked away at a brisk pace, pain lancing through his head and face at each step. He swayed and almost fell; his head felt like it weighed a ton.

The empty stretch of road bordered open fields white with virgin snow. Beyond the closest field sprawled a residential community over which a water tower loomed. On the other side, a forest. Billboards advertised a legal firm and a matchmaking website.

The driver left the ambulance. Doug turned and clenched his fists. The man closed the rear doors and got back into his rig. Doug jogged several steps in the opposite direction before doubling over to catch his breath.

The ambulance roared. He looked up in time to see it bearing down, lights flashing.

Doug threw himself into the ditch as the vehicle flew past with a shriek of its siren. Doug covered his head with his hands as gravel and snow splattered him.

The ambulance disappeared into the distance.

Doug stood and brushed snow off his clothes. The paramedics were gone, but he wasn't out of danger. He had to get off the road. He had to find someplace warm before night fell and he got lost. He scanned the darkening horizon, looking for landmarks.

There it was—the hospital, its crown barely visible over the distant woods. The sons of bitches must have been driving around it in circles while they'd bled him. Looking at the sun, Doug figured north, and from there, the rough location of the bar where he'd left his truck.

The path would take him across the empty field, through the middle of the residential neighborhood, and over the treed hill beyond.

He trudged through the knee-deep snow, stopping often to rest. Sparks floated in his field of vision. Now he knew how Joan had felt these past few weeks. That constant feeling of being suffocated. *Asphyxiation*, it was called. He kept giggling at himself but didn't know why. The joke always seemed just out of reach.

The day's light was failing fast as he neared the houses. The people who lived here appeared to have either given up or gone away. No lights shone in the windows. Curtains were drawn. The streets hadn't been plowed, and it looked as if nobody had shoveled their driveways and sidewalks in a long time. The snow lay piled in drifts shaped by the howling wind.

Doug felt exposed here; he knew he was in a dangerous position. He remembered some advice he'd heard just before a trip to Detroit: *If you ever feel unsafe in a neighborhood you don't know, walk like you own the place.* Good advice, but he didn't have the energy. On his last legs, frozen to the bone, he wasn't going to fool anybody by sticking his chest out. Everything about the way he looked broadcast that he was an easy mark.

He couldn't keep going. He had to stop. He'd walk up to one of the houses, knock on the door, and throw himself at the mercy of whoever lived there. The houses all looked the same; one was as good as the next. Cold and fatigue had him shaking uncontrollably as he staggered up the steps of the nearest porch. The front door was open. Snow had drifted across the entrance and dusted the carpet inside. He looked behind him and saw no tracks other than his own.

The streetlights switched on. Otherwise, the place was a ghost town.

The absence of people suited him just fine. He walked inside and forced the door closed. He moved to flip the light switch but stopped himself. Best not to draw attention. There might be people living somewhere in the neighborhood, but lying low like him.

The first step was to explore the house to make sure he was secure. He entered the living room, navigating by the light of the streetlights outside. Someone had been here before him and trashed the place. The mess reminded him of what Nate and Megan had done to his own house. The couch had been stabbed and gutted. Broken toys lay scattered on the floor. Crude smiley faces and stick figures were carved into the wooden coffee table. Childish, crayoned graffiti covered the bottom half of the walls.

The rest of the house was in similar shape but empty. He thought about turning on the heat but didn't. The house was cold as a refrigerator, and he wanted to preserve the blood he carried. He draped blankets over his shoulders instead. A search of the kitchen turned up little. He topped off his cursory meal with a snort from his flask and a cigarette.

He pushed aside one of the curtains and took a long look outside. The other houses stood dark and empty. Nothing moved.

Creepy, he thought, but didn't feel creeped. He was too numbed by exhaustion. His face throbbed with pain. Upstairs, he built a nest of blankets in the walk-in closet, closed the door, and fell asleep the moment his head touched the pillow.

During the night, he woke to a piercing scream but went back to sleep, certain he'd dreamed it.

David

40 days after Resurrection

Shoved onto a stool. Handcuffs removed. Hood ripped from his head. He blinked at the light and massaged his aching wrists.

A grimacing pig stared down at him. He cowered at the sight.

The pig was a mask. The police officer cracked his knuckles.

"I'm Officer Smiley," the cop said.

The man backed away until he reached a chalkboard on which was scrawled, BLOOD = PAROLE. David spared a glance at his surroundings and saw little desks piled in the corners. Crude drawings and giant snowflakes cut from color construction paper on the walls. Posters of the alphabet, numbers, and common animals and foods.

"What are you going to do to me?"

He already knew. The van had been filled with angry men who

smelled like cheap booze and old vomit. Muttering in the dark. One wouldn't stop yelling about his rights until the others kicked him into silence.

They'd made two stops before coming here. At each stop, somebody new was shoved into the van.

The police were rounding up the homeless.

The cop held up a baton with two prongs protruding from its end. "Guess what this is."

David swallowed hard and said, "It's a cattle prod."

"Smart man! Some guys who come in here—you know what I do? I give them a taste of it right away to let them know what it's like. But I won't do that with you. I can tell you're going to cooperate. You're going to cooperate, aren't you?"

David stared at the prod. "Yes. I'm going to cooperate."

"You want to get out of here, right? No problemo. We want something from you first."

"My blood."

"Bingo! Cooperate, and everybody gets what they want. First, you will completely disrobe, including any jewelry. You will put on the hospital gown in the cardboard box behind you. You will put all other items into the box. Is that understood?"

"I think so." A hundred questions clamored in his mind, but he knew better than to ask.

The pig mask shifted. Beneath its bulging rubber cheeks and brutish snout, David could tell the cop was grinning at him. "Then start cooperating!"

David put on the paper gown, which made him feel naked and humiliated. His entire identity was going into the box. After that, he'd be nobody. Just another inmate. A number.

"Listen, this is all a big mistake," he said.

"Remember what I said about cooperating?"

"I'm a doctor."

"Yeah?" The officer pounded the door behind him with his fist. "I'm Columbo."

The door opened, and another pig-faced cop entered, twirling a cattle prod.

"I'm Officer Smiley," said the second cop. Different man, same fake name. "Come with me, sir."

David knew he had no choice. He meekly followed the cop into the hallway, where giant cutouts of children, brightly painted with smiling faces, adorned the walls.

The hall led to the gym.

The doors opened, revealing the blood farm.

David saw dozens of cots arranged in rows, each filled with a moaning man under a blanket. Their gray, emaciated faces pointed at the ceiling. Their arms were linked to IV bags on poles. Wide-screen televisions displayed a recorded football game with the sound off. Muzak played at a low volume over the public address system, sounding tinny and distant.

A second cop sat at a desk with a reading light, monitoring the room, while another pig-faced man in a blood-splattered lab coat roamed the aisles between the cots, spot-checking IV bags and blood pressure. A few heads turned to regard the new arrival.

"I don't belong here," David said in a small voice.

"Of course you do."

"But I didn't do anything wrong."

The cop chuckled. "Then why are you here?"

"I'm a doctor. Look in my wallet. You'll see—"

The cattle prod crackled at the back of his neck. It was like getting hit by a sledgehammer. David fell howling to his knees. More heads turned to fix their blank stares on him. The cop at the desk stood and watched.

David felt himself hauled to his feet and dragged to one of the beds, where the pig-faced man in the lab coat strapped him down with restraints. A cold bedpan was shoved between his legs and a thin blanket tossed over him.

"I'm Dr. Smiley," said the man in the lab coat. He dragged a stool next to the bed and sat. "Try to relax."

David sobbed in a terrified daze. "What are you doing to me?"

"Nothing dire, buddy. I'm setting up your drip. Stay still, or you could get hurt."

The man inserted a catheter into one of the veins in David's hand. Then he plugged an intravenous infusion line into the catheter's connecting hub. David watched to make sure the man didn't blow the vein.

The doctor produced a clipboard and crossed his legs. "And how are we feeling today?"

"I'm scared."

The doctor thumbed his pen. "I'm sorry to hear that. I'm sure you'll feel better in just a moment. I'm going to ask you a few questions about your health. Please answer honestly. Do you have any medical problems?"

"No."

"Had any medical treatments in the past year?"

"No."

"Had sex with anyone who has HIV/AIDS?"

"Yes." It was worth a try to lie. Maybe they couldn't take his blood.

The doctor put his pen away. "Good. That's enough for the interview."

"What happens now?"

The doctor tied a tourniquet around David's arm. "Make a fist for me."

"But I'm not eligible."

"We're still going to collect it. And we'll be testing it. Even if you have HIV, we'll find a recipient. You weren't lying to get out of it, were you?"

David said nothing. The doctor sighed and took out his clipboard again. He asked David whether he had a tattoo or took drugs using needles.

After recording the answers, he took David's blood.

By then, David was no longer afraid. He began to mellow. He felt like watching TV.

"I'm feeling much better now," he said dreamily.

"Of course you are," the doctor told him. "This is a happy place."

They put something in that bag with the saline. Something good.

"You're competent with a needle," he said. "I was watching."

The doctor checked his watch. "Thank you."

"I was afraid I'd end up with mononeuropathy."

Dr. Smiley stared at him. "How do you know that word? Are you an intravenous drug user?"

"No."

"Tell me the truth. Did you lie on the questionnaire again?"

"I'm a doctor like you. A pediatrician."

"And how does a pediatrician end up on the street? You must have a very sad story."

"I have a practice. A house."

"You're lying again."

"Call my wife. I'll give you the number. I'll give you the address of my practice."

The man leaned closer and lowered his voice. "Seriously . . . what are you doing here?"

"I was kidnapped."

"They don't do that."

Before David could say anything further, the man got up and walked toward the end of the row of beds. The overweight cop behind the desk glanced at him and then returned to his book.

David's mind drifted. The TV called his attention.

"What did you do?"

David turned his head. The doctor leaned over him. His eyes gleamed through the holes in the mask.

"Kidnapped."

"This isn't right. Somebody made a mistake. It started with criminals. Blood for parole. Now they're bringing in the homeless. They're not supposed to bring anyone else. They drew the line at the homeless."

David forced himself to concentrate on the man's words. "Does anybody ever get released?"

"A lot already have. They were on death's doorstep from blood loss. The cops bought them bus tickets and shipped them off to Detroit to make them someone else's problem. I doubt they survived the trip."

"Why do you work for these people?"

The man turned away. "I'm a father."

They're paying him in blood.

David closed his eyes and floated. He heard the men breathing and moaning around him, filling the room with their sour breath.

"So that's it? I'm going to die here?"

The idea still terrified him, but he felt detached from his own terror, as if he were afraid not for himself but for his favorite character in a movie.

"They don't murder people here," the man said.

Oh, that's where you're wrong, doctor. Murder is exactly what they do here. But not outright, though. Not yet. They're still working their way to that. One little rationalization at a time. For now, they just bleed men until they can't survive on their own.

David was struck by a vision of the room transformed into a slaughterhouse. A place where pigs slaughtered men. An assembly line with screaming people hung upside down from hooks. The pigs cut their throats one by one and drained the blood into troughs.

"What's like an assembly line?"

Had he been talking? He opened his eyes and looked around. The overweight cop looked down at him with his leering mask.

"I don't belong here," David whispered.

"Why do you say that? I heard you talking to the doctor here."

"He doesn't know what he's saying," said Dr. Smiley.

David said, "I'm a pediatrician. A doctor."

"We're giving you your fix," the cop told him. "Just relax. It's good shit. Just give it a chance."

"I don't want any drugs. I don't live on the street. For the past three weeks, I've been drawing blood for men like you to give your kids. At my practice on Wilshire."

The cop's head tilted. "What's your name?"

"David. David Harris."

"Easy to remember. Nice to meet you, David. I'm Officer Smiley."

The cop walked away with heavy footsteps.

"Please call my wife," David called after him. "Her name's Nadine. Please tell her I'm alive."

The doctor shook his head. "You shouldn't have done that. You seriously fucked up, buddy. You just did the worst thing you can do in here. You got noticed."

The doctor's words failed to interest him. David stared at the images on the nearest TV, but even that slipped away. He closed his eyes and found the dark most interesting of all.

Doug

41 days after Resurrection

A shivering monster stared at Doug from the mirror.

The security guard's billy club had torn a nice, big gash in his forehead, now held together by a bulky bandage made out of napkins and tape. The entire right side of his face had swelled and discolored around it, turning into one giant bruise. He needed stitches. A lot of them. The gash had already begun healing badly and would leave one hell of a scar to remind him how stupid he'd been to walk into a hospital pointing a gun at people. He'd been lucky to get out of that situation with his life and freedom.

He tongued broken teeth. He sure didn't feel very lucky.

The monster in the mirror was crying.

I screwed it all up. Joanie's right. It's over. We're finished.

The monster frowned. Shook its head.

It would never be finished.

He'd slept a long time; it was morning. As much as Doug wanted to crawl back into his nest of blankets, it was time to go home. The house looked even worse in the light of day, but it provided. He scavenged another meager meal, some warm clothes, and a broom handle he intended to use as a walking stick. His blood had kept well overnight. Very little clotting. He walked out the front door happy he would arrive home with at least this small victory in his favor.

He hesitated on the porch, wondering about Russell. He hoped the man was okay but had a strong feeling he wasn't. He pushed it out of his mind. The world was a dangerous place now; the familiar had quickly become unfamiliar. If he wanted to make it home, he needed to stay sharp. Russell was Russell's problem, whatever Doug's feelings about the man.

The sky was gray but bright, making his eyes water as they adjusted to the glare. A gust of wind struck him. Snow and ice peppered his face. He walked down the road, taking time to inspect each house he passed. Covered in snow, they appeared derelict. Dark and still, curtains drawn. This was once a nice place to live. Now it was a ghost town.

Why then do I feel like I'm being watched?

He tried to pick up his pace, staggering through the snow until the first spots appeared in his vision. He told himself not to push too hard. He'd lost a lot of blood in a short amount of time and still had a long way to go before he got home.

The street ended in a cul-de-sac at the base of the treed hill he'd have to cross. The first stage of the journey was over; he'd reached the edge of the residential community. He paused to take in the wreckage of a Christmas tree, trailing tinsel and branches that lay strewn across the front lawn of one of the houses. Several sets of footprints led from the front door to the tree and back. The tree had been flattened, its ornaments crushed, the snow around it packed.

Somebody had taken this tree out here and stomped on it for a good long while. Doug marveled at the amount of energy that had gone into this pointless act of violence. The tree confirmed what his instincts already told him: He wasn't alone.

Turning to inspect his own footprints, he realized that, if somebody wanted to find him, he'd blazed an easy trail to follow. His eyes followed his tracks back where he'd come from, and he saw two children standing on the road about a hundred yards back.

Sure enough, he'd been found.

Doug squinted at them. They were eight- or nine-year-old boys wearing identical blue coats. At this distance, they looked so alike they could have been twins. A blond-haired girl dressed in a pink snowsuit skipped out of a nearby house and joined them.

One waved, and he waved back, nerves tingling. He kept an eye out for the parents. The way Doug figured it, the people who cared for these kids quite possibly had systematically cleared out the entire community. Whoever they were, they obviously had no reservations about doing what needed doing. He had to get out of there fast before they did it to him.

The children started walking then, following in his steps.

Doug passed the house with its mangled tree and paused at the bottom of the hill. The forest ahead stretched to the top of the rise. It'd be hell to climb but necessary; on the other side was home.

He stopped after a short distance and looked behind him. He glimpsed color through the trees. A blue coat, a red hat. The children sang as they followed his tracks.

Where are the parents?

A classic trap. The children create a distraction; then the parents take him. He scanned the woods, looking for signs of ambush, but saw nothing. The only sound was the snow rustling as the children worked their way up the hill.

He started moving again.

A boy's falsetto voice: "Hey, mister!"

He ignored it.

"Hey, mister! Hey, you up there!"

Doug leaned against a tree and sucked oxygen in gasps. His heart drummed against his ribs. His legs trembled.

"Our friend got hurt. Can you help us?"

"Go away," he growled, resuming his upward march.

"Come *on*! He's hurt really bad!"

He saved his breath. He was almost at the top.

"Aw! Please! All the grown-ups *left*. We're all *alone*."

None of it made any sense, until it did.

Megan biting down on Joan's arm. Joan's face as she howled in pain.

Megan's bloody teeth after he pulled her off laughing.

"Hey, mister!"

He groaned with the effort of trying to move faster. The sound sent the children into peals of playful laughter. Reaching the hilltop and standing on the rise, he found the bar right where he thought it was, its parking lot almost full even though it was barely lunchtime.

He'd never make it.

Behind him, the children were rapidly closing in. Branches thrashed and cracked. Doug gripped the broomstick in his hands, his only protection.

They were just kids.

But kids drank blood these days, and he barely had enough energy to stand.

"I know what you want," he said.

He reached into the pocket of his EMT jacket, where he'd put one of the blood bags. His hand came away wet.

"Fuck," he sobbed.

The bag hadn't closed properly. Most of its contents had leaked out. Blood dripped from his fingers onto the snow.

The kids stopped. Grew quiet. Sniffed the air.

He saw a flash of steel. A knife.

They *growled*.

He pulled out the other bag. It was full. He threw it toward the children and ran down the hill as fast as his oxygen-starved body would allow.

At the bottom, he spun, ready to fight, but saw only trees.

If he'd had the energy or breath, he would have laughed. He'd never thought he would ever have to run in terror from a bunch of kids his son's age.

297

Two pints of blood, gone just like that. He'd just lost two hours with his children. Two hours of *life*. *Memories.* It was like winning the lottery and losing the ticket.

The road was empty. He crossed over, followed it for another two hundred yards, and shuffled into the bar parking lot, still angry at himself.

At least I'm alive, he thought.

His luck held. His truck was right where he'd left it, thank God.

A man's voice: "Hey, buddy!"

Doug turned as three men walked up to him. "I didn't do anything," he croaked. He felt for the keys in his pocket.

They glanced at each other. "Didn't say you did," one answered.

"I was just leaving."

"Jesus, Lloyd," said another. "Look at his face. Somebody messed him up good."

Doug backed away. "I'm okay."

"Buddy, you need some help."

He gripped the broomstick. "Stay away from me."

"Take it easy. You're a dad, right?"

Doug said nothing.

"I could tell. So are we. We're all in this together, right? All in the same boat? What's your name?"

Doug didn't answer.

"You from around here? You're not from around here, are you?"

He threw the stick at the men and lurched to his truck on stiff legs. He climbed in and slammed the door.

A bearded face appeared at his window. "What's wrong with you? We're just trying to help!"

He fumbled with his keys. The engine turned over but wouldn't start.

Jesus, Mary, and God—

The truck roared to life. Doug revved the engine and threw the transmission into gear.

A fist thudded against the window next to his face. "Why won't you let us help?"

The men ringed him with their hungry eyes.

Lloyd stepped in front of the truck with a smile. "You're not thinking straight, buddy." His smile widened. "We're going to help you."

Doug smiled back.

The truck bolted forward. The bumper thumped into the man's body, the momentum trapping him against the radiator. The man clawed, screaming, at the hood. The truck built speed.

He slammed on the brakes. Lloyd flew away and crashed against the windshield of a parked car.

Doug cranked the wheel and sped across the parking lot. The truck roared onto the road in a cloud of exhaust.

He watched his rearview until the bar dropped out of sight. He was shaking. His head throbbed. He'd just seriously hurt a man. Maybe even killed him.

"You didn't give me any choice," he said.

The road behind him remained empty all the way back to Highway 69, where he began to breathe a little easier. He laughed, but it was forced and didn't last long.

Safe. For now, at least.

I'm alive. I'm alive.

Fuck you all. I'm alive.

David

41 days after Resurrection

David felt like he was floating. Somebody wheezed next to him. He turned his head and looked at the man wasting away in the bed next to his. The man's face was the color of ash. He stared at the nearest TV with a blank smile.

In less than a week, David knew, he would look just like him.

Dr. Smiley had already taken a pint from him last night and was working on another this morning, replacing the volume with saline solution. Gravity brought saline, basic nutrition, and a barbiturate into his body from one bag, and took blood out of his body with another.

The steady introduction of saline into his body replaced the lost blood plasma volume and ensured adequate circulation. Dr. Smiley was heating the saline before giving it to the prisoners to reduce risk of hypothermia.

The average person could safely donate a pint of whole blood every fifty-six days. Platelets could be taken every two weeks. Plasma every forty-eight hours. If a man remained very still, half or even more of his blood could be drawn if the lost volume were replaced. People had been known to survive with blood containing just a third of its original amount of hemoglobin. They survived, but only barely, turned into drained husks.

David knew he'd be bled until he died or was near death. There was no real parole. It was a convenient lie the cops told to the inmates and themselves. Eventually, his systems would crash, and the cops would put him on a bus for Detroit with a smile on his face. He'd curl up in a ball on one of the seats and die.

He heard the steady hiss of breath beneath the grating Muzak. Dozens of men were being farmed, all of them criminals or homeless. Many had nobody who missed them in the outside world. None had connections with people who could get them out. They were considered easy to dehumanize. One could justify doing all sorts of evil things to them. After all, it wasn't like the cops were draining and murdering soccer moms. Or doctors.

David wondered what Nadine was doing now. Pulling blood from some asshole's arm, most likely. The great cause would go on even after he was dead. Had Dr. Smiley called her as David asked? Had she called the police? Were there any cops who weren't in on this and could help her find him? Even now, against all reason, he clung to hope of rescue.

It pained him to think that she'd carry on in her hopeless mission alone. It was more than just delusion that brought her to work every day; she had a good heart. It was one of the reasons he'd married her and one of the things that had made her such a wonderful mother. He wished he were there to protect her from what was coming. If the police were farming people for blood, things were even worse than he thought.

Missing her, he cried.

He had one last chance to help himself. Soon it would be too late. They were keeping him drugged, and every day they took a little more blood. He would grow steadily weaker and more disoriented. If he was ever going to escape from this place, he had to try soon.

Dr. Smiley was making his rounds. David watched the doctor with the bloody lab coat perform his duties with meticulous precision. Unmasked orderlies—hard men with prison tattoos, likely recruits from the jails—walked the aisles, changing bedpans. The overweight cop who'd taken an interest in David yesterday had returned and now sat at his desk with the reading light on, the snout of his mask buried in a magazine.

His main hope was the doctor. He'd appeal to the man as a fellow physician. Remind him of the Hippocratic Oath. Moved by this plea, Dr. Smiley would undo his restraints. When the cop behind the desk left the room for a toilet break, David would sneak out and go home.

The drug helped him believe this was possible. He fantasized it several times, and each time, it appeared even more possible.

He turned his head. The cop had lowered his magazine and was staring at him. David turned away to feign interest in the nearest TV.

He watched it, too afraid to move, until the images blurred.

"David."

Nadine?

"Nadine!" he cried.

"Be quiet," Dr. Smiley hissed.

The pig face leered down at him. He turned. The cop had left his station and wasn't in the room.

Now was his chance.

"My name is David. Tell me your first name. Please."

The doctor hesitated. "It's Jeremy."

"I don't belong in here, Jeremy."

"I know."

"So get me out."

Jeremy patted his shoulder. "Don't make this difficult."

"Help me. Please."

"We only have a minute before he comes back. I just wanted to make sure you're comfortable—"

"You know I don't belong in here."

"I'm sorry, David. I really am—"

"Loosen one of these straps. Free my arms. I'll do the rest."

The doctor turned toward one of the exits. "He's going to be back soon."

David reached and gripped the man's wrist. "Help me, Jeremy."

"You know I can't do that."

David stared at him. "You mean you won't."

If he escaped, the cops might blame it on Jeremy, who would stop being a business partner and instead be treated like one of the criminals. Just as bad, if David escaped, he might bring other police here to bust up the operation, and Jeremy would lose the source of blood he needed to feed his own children.

The doctor peeled David's hand from his wrist. "I *can't*."

"You're a coward."

"It's not my fault."

"I'm going to die if you don't help me."

Jeremy clapped his hands over his ears. "Stop saying that!"

"I'm begging you!"

"Stop it!"

The doctor bolted. David cried at the ceiling. "Call my wife! Tell her I love her!"

A soft moan passed like a wave through the other prisoners.

He heard heavy footsteps. The big cop plodded toward him. Weapons and gear jingled on his belt.

The cop stopped at David's bed and looked down at him.

"I'm Officer Smiley. Remember me?"

David groaned in fear. "I'm cooperating."

A grim orderly appeared on either side of the bed.

"Get him on his feet," the cop ordered.

The men nodded and went to work removing David's tubes and restraints.

"What are you doing?" David said. "Please don't do this."

The cop unhooked the cattle prod from his belt. "I think we need to have a private chat, Dr. Harris."

"I'll behave," David said. "I'll do whatever you want."

"Bring him to Room Five A."

The orderlies hauled David to his feet and pulled him toward the exit.

Jeremy was right. I should never have told the cop my name. He made a call to his cop buddies, who recognized my name from the autopsy reports.

They were going to kill him for it. A bullet in the head. A flash of light, and then oblivion.

He couldn't resist them; he could barely stand without the men supporting him.

Instead, he pissed down his leg.

"Jesus," one of the orderlies said, while the other snickered.

They marched him down the corridor and into one of the classrooms. The orderlies released him there and returned to the gym as Officer Smiley pushed him toward the middle of the room. David fell to his knees and cowered in the dark.

Retreating into his mind, he saw Nadine lying in a hospital bed, beaming a radiant smile at him as she held their infant son in her arms. At the time, David had just finished his residency and was starting his practice. He wasn't sure he could handle helping Nadine care for a child. He wasn't sure he'd be a good father at all. The second he laid eyes on Paul, though, he fell deeply in love. He realized, from that moment on, he would do anything for his son. He understood these cops more than they ever might have guessed.

The lights switched on.

The room was empty except for a cardboard box.

"Please don't do this," he begged.

"Get dressed," said the cop. "Put your clothes on."

"I don't understand."

"I'm taking you home, Dr. Harris."

"Home?" David didn't believe it.

"I checked up on you. You don't belong here. Your clothes are in the box."

"Home," said David, thinking of Nadine. He began to cry.

"You're going to forget all about this." The cop slapped him lightly on the face. "Listen up." Again. "This is important. If you call the police and try to report what we're doing here, just remember, *we are the police*. We'll answer the phone, take down your complaint, and then come back and get you. We'll come and get you and every person in your entire family. Then there'll be no pardon from the governor. Follow me?"

The threat had been very clearly spelled out for him. "I won't say anything."

"Just so we understand each other. I'm taking a serious risk here. You say a word, and you'll be back, I guarantee it. And I'll be in the bed next to you."

Officer Smiley dropped a black hood over his head.

Ramona

42 days after Resurrection

Ramona inspected her naked body in the mirror.

She'd always been thin, but her collarbones and ribs were pronounced now. Blood loss and a subsistence diet over the past few weeks had done wonders for trimming those extra pounds that always plagued her. She thought somebody should name a diet after it.

Her eyes paused over the bruises where Ross had hit her. Already the discoloration was fading, but she hated the sight of them. She'd been right to end things with him. In the end, he'd been just another man who couldn't handle the idea of sharing responsibility for raising her son. Who couldn't accept that Josh required 100 percent of her.

She picked up her glass of wine and gulped half of it. "Men are pigs," she muttered.

She heard a crash downstairs. Howling. She sighed.

"I didn't mean you, Josh."

Ramona leaned forward and put a little more eyeliner on while her mouth hung open. Just a few touches here and there; she believed a little makeup went a long way to call attention to a woman's features. It also did wonders for covering up blue lips and fingernails.

She put away her makeup bag. "There," she said.

Then she practiced smiling.

Ross had taught her an important lesson. She no longer cared what people thought of her. All the people who'd judged her or compelled her to judge herself. They didn't exist anymore in her world. Nothing mattered except keeping Josh fed.

She found it liberating. There was purity in such targeted clarity.

The doorbell rang. Her guest had arrived. She finished her wine and smiled again. It looked almost real. Then disappeared just as fast, leaving a hard red line.

"Coming," she called.

She walked into the kitchen, put on an apron, and checked the oven. Then she walked to the front door and opened it.

An overweight man stood in the doorway. Her eyes prowled his girth while his shifted nervously before settling on her chest.

"I'm George."

"Hi, George," she said. She remembered to smile. "I'm Ramona."

He fidgeted and smiled back. "You look even hotter than your picture on the site."

"Aren't you charming?" she said. "Come in."

He took off his coat and sniffed the air. "What's that I smell?"

"Macaroni and cheese with chopped bacon and caramelized onions," Ramona told him. She put her hand on her hip and turned a little so he could see she wore nothing under the apron. "Why don't we eat a little something before we get down to business?"

George chortled at his good fortune. He followed her into the kitchen.

The way to a man's heart is through his stomach.

To get into a man's stomach, Ramona knew, a knife would do nicely.

In the kitchen, she had a lot of knives.

ELEVEN

Joan

44 days after Resurrection

Joan and Doug sat in their dark living room watching the news while their children lay wrapped in plastic in the garage, awaiting resurrection.

The TV showed the shaky image of a squad of soldiers standing against the wall of an old red brick building. The first in line leaned past the corner and fired a few rounds at some distant target. The camera panned to reveal a row of dilapidated homes, one of them on fire and pumping smoke.

The caption read: FIREFIGHT IN DETROIT.

In cities like Detroit, National Guard units had moved into the poorest neighborhoods to destroy the blood trade, which had caused thousands of deaths and disappearances.

Joan couldn't believe what she was seeing. The U.S. Army fighting street gangs on American soil in a massive operation involving thousands of troops.

The firepower on display was impressive, but the whole thing struck her as pointless. As if they would accomplish anything when the violence was happening everywhere.

On the TV, soldiers ran past a burning car.

The caption: ARMY CRACKS DOWN ON BLOOD TRADE.

Doug sipped his beer and snorted. "They're not cracking down on it. They're putting it under new management. Leeches. They're all a bunch of goddamn leeches, babe."

"Please don't use that word," Joan said. "I don't like that word."

Doug sipped his beer, radiating fear and resentment like a furnace.

Four days ago, he'd left the house without even a good-bye and returned the next afternoon wheezing with a broken, lacerated face and a paramedic's bloody jacket. He wouldn't talk about what had happened. He refused to go to the hospital for stitches; the very idea terrified him. He'd obviously tried to get blood and failed. In fact, from the looks of him, he'd lost some. Whatever happened, it was horrible, and it had damaged him inside as well as out.

She'd poured hydrogen peroxide on his wound and taped it shut. There was no point in lecturing or delivering an ultimatum. Instead, she'd taken a soft approach. She told him to go back to work. Get back on a schedule. Pick up the trash that had piled up everywhere. Earn a paycheck. Stop carrying the world on his shoulders. The children would be here when he got home. They weren't going anywhere.

When he left for work that first morning, she decided to practice what she preached by throwing herself into her household chores. For the first time in over a month, the house was clean and didn't smell of rot and decay. Later, Doug came home angry and reeking of booze, but at least he hadn't gone off and done anything crazy again. He could read the writing on the wall. Unless he was willing to go out and murder somebody, he wasn't getting any more blood for the children.

It was a harsh truth: *no more blood*. It was the end.

Joan was willing to kill for her kids—she really was—but only in defense. The idea of murdering an innocent human being—some woman out for a morning jog—horrified her as much as the prospect of letting her children go. Besides that, the children just weren't themselves anymore. Their bodies were the same, but their minds were turning to mush. They were turning into monsters whose sole aim was to feed. *It's over.* She wanted Doug to process this truth just as she had. The Coopers didn't give up easily, that was true, but sometimes they had no choice.

For her, the hard work had already begun as she'd started to work up the courage and mental strength to say good-bye. Being a mother was all she'd ever wanted, but she couldn't do this anymore. She was tired of fighting God. She was worn out. She would accept the extra time she'd been given with her children over the past weeks for what it was, a gift, and let them go. After that, she had no idea what she would do next. She'd have a lot of choices and a ton of baggage. Maybe life would be worth living, maybe not.

The caption: DHHS PRESS CONFERENCE NEXT.

Joan turned from the television and studied Doug's hideous profile. *We're all broken people now*, she thought. *He just happens to look it.* She still loved him—boozing, violent temper and all. Whatever happened, she wanted to stay with him. He was a good man.

And he'd tried. He really had.

"It's going to be okay, Doug."

"I haven't seen Otis since I came back," he said. "He's gone. Most of the guys are gone. I have to work my route by myself, driving and hauling."

"It's good that you're there. I'm proud of you."

"I found two bodies in the garbage just today. One was rolled up in a carpet. The other was hacked into small pieces and stuffed into trash bags. Drained of blood."

"Oh God, Doug," she said, horrified.

"Usually, people come out to yell at me for not hauling away their old bathroom sink. Do you want to know what they do now? They invite me in for coffee with a big old smile."

Joan could tell he admired them. The people who would do anything.

"You always think the world's out to get you," she said. "For once, I think you're right. We can't trust anybody right now except each other. Not anybody."

Doug nodded. "It's all coming to an end."

"I'll be with you no matter what. We'll be together."

The images of destruction on the TV flickered across his face. "You're all I got left, Joanie."

"It's going to be okay, Doug. I really believe that. We can do this."

Neither of them spoke for a while. She took one of his beers, cracked it open, and took a sip. It tasted good. On the TV, a soldier fired his rifle. The camera lurched, and Joan caught a glimpse of the enemy.

The men firing back wore the same military uniforms.

The image cut to the scene of a press conference in Washington, DC.

David

44 days after Resurrection

Standing at a podium flanked by men and women in suits and lab coats, the Secretary of Health and Human Services began his press conference.

The caption read: BLOOD CRISIS.

David didn't want to watch. He lay on the couch, clutching at Nadine while she rocked him and stroked his hair. He'd escaped the blood farm, but his mind remained trapped within the nightmare. Every time he closed his eyes, he saw it all. The massive room that smelled like vomit, shit, and death. The gray, emaciated men in their beds. The cops with their cattle prods. The masked doctor in his white lab coat splattered with the blood of his victims.

He'd never felt so alone in his life. So helpless and degraded. At that moment, he'd been as good as dead, cut off from everything and everybody he knew and loved. Doomed to die, alone and unloved, without hope.

Pure, naked terror.

He'd escaped, but not really. A part of him was still back at the farm.

David ground his teeth and shivered.

As a doctor, he treated his patients for their diseases using the four cornerstones of diagnostic medicine: anatomy, physiology, pathology, psychology. He understood emotional trauma and its symptoms all too well. *Diagnosis: You're fucked up, doctor.*

Ever since the cop had brought him home, he'd popped his remaining supply of Vicodin while wandering the house checking the locks, handgun shoved into the pocket of his bathrobe.

Ben had been right to be paranoid. He'd been right all along. Herod's syndrome had afflicted the parents worse than the children. Herod had the entire world dancing to its crazy tune. All David had accomplished by drawing their blood was to prolong their suicide, not prevent it. Meanwhile, the children were being reborn as monsters.

David was done helping people. It was time to focus on survival. As soon as he was able, he'd board up the windows, reinforce the door, and turn the house into a fortress.

On the TV, the secretary said the government had a solution to the Blood Crisis.

The pig-faced cop cracked his knuckles. "I'm Officer Smiley."

"It's going to be all right, David," Nadine said. He was shaking.

He hugged her tighter. "You'll stay with me?"

"Of course, I'll stay. Tell me what happened to you."

He couldn't. He hated even thinking about it. And it was all he could think about.

Besides, if he told her, he'd have to do something about it. Right now, scores of men were being bled to death back at the farm. He wanted to help them. She might want to do the same. But if they tried, they'd both die.

Physician, help thyself.

"Just stay with me," he said. "Don't go out. Not yet."

"I'll stay."

"Really stay. Don't go out at all for anything."

He felt her body stiffen. What he'd just asked was very difficult for her to give. Maybe even impossible. She wanted to continue helping the children.

She said, "I'll stay with you, David."

He sighed with relief, content that she really loved him.

"We have to get ready. They're going to come for us."

"Who is?"

"The parents," he told her. "The children."

"It's all going to work out." She didn't sound as sure as she once had.

He closed his eyes and tightened his grip on the gun in his pocket.

Red means dead, he thought. He repeated the phrase as a mantra, trying to keep the dark thoughts at bay. He began to doze again.

Nadine woke him. On the TV, the Secretary of Health and Human Services proudly declared the blood crisis would soon end.

The government, the man announced, had developed a hemerythrin-based human blood substitute that kept the children alive.

Doug

44 days after Resurrection

He sat on a box filled with deposit bottles and cans in the garage. He smoked. He drank. He stared at his dead children wrapped in plastic.

It's not fair, thought Doug. *But it's typical.*

The government had just announced a blood substitute. The world was no doubt rejoicing. The only problem was it wouldn't go into production for at least a month—too late for his kids. Their bodies would fall apart long before then. Herod worked miracles but had its limits. After too long, he knew, even blood wasn't enough to put Humpty Dumpty back together.

Doug didn't see how anybody would be able to make it that long. The rich could, of course. The millionaires could easily pay for enough blood to keep their kids alive a month. It was a simple thing for those who had money. Even now, the rich took care of their own, and screw everybody else.

He'd been smacked around by the rich all his life. By them and the government, the big corporations and banks. He wore his scars and humiliations like badges of honor. No matter what happened to him, he always got up and found a way to stand tall for what was his. He'd been smacked down, pushed around, and even crushed, but never defeated.

Until now.

Getting beat was a horrible feeling. He spent his days stewing in his hate but didn't know whom to hate.

He no longer hated Herod. Herod was now his ally.

Herod could bring his children back again. He just had to give it blood.

Joan still insisted the right thing to do was let the kids go to God. Even if the blood substitute came today and they could keep the kids alive forever, all they'd gain would be reanimated corpses running wild. Their kids would still be gone. The Nate and Megan they'd raised and loved were dead forever either way.

Doug's instincts, however, told him to keep fighting. He saw National Guard troops shooting at each other on TV, and it had excited him. He didn't know how they'd ended up fighting each other. He didn't care. They were fighting over blood. That much he knew. Again, he had that feeling other people knew something he didn't, had courage he lacked. For millions, it wasn't going to be over until it was over. They would fight for their kids until the end.

He wanted to join them and win it all or go down fighting. He'd been tested and failed; he wished he could be given another chance. Even now, with his weakness, constant pain, and dizzy spells, he felt a strong urge to knock on Art Foley's front door and bop the old guy on the head. He was finding it hard to accept the prospect of the long, hard middle road—letting his kids disappear into the past and facing his long, bleak future.

A future cleaning up the mess while the world went to hell. He saw mountains of garbage in his mind's eye, surrounded by clouds of flies and scavenger birds. Drained corpses rolled up in carpets. Bodies chopped up in Glad plastic bags.

Doug stepped on what was left of his cigarette. He looked at the claw hammer on the shelf. Then he went back into the house.

He found Joan sitting in the darkened living room. She was smiling at the playback screen on the family digital camera.

"What are you doing?" he said.

"I'm saying good-bye."

"What about the blood substitute?"

She said nothing.

"If we could hang on a little more, you know, we could save our kids."

Her laughter startled him. "Look at you two with that helicopter."

He decided to leave her alone. She'd gone to a happy place. God knew that was a rare thing these days. He opened the refrigerator and pulled out another Miller High Life.

The phone emitted its grating ring. Doug cracked open the beer and picked it up.

"Yeah," he said.

"Doug? Doug Cooper?"

He took a gulp and stifled a belch. "Yup."

"It's Tom. Remember me? Tom Rafferty. We worked together at the—"

"Burial ground. How'd you get this number?"

"You're listed."

"Right, right. What do you need?"

314

He recalled Tom being the sentimental type. And now, because he'd been stupid enough to answer the phone, he would have to listen to the man drone on and on about how sorry he was for Doug. If he heard the words *blood crisis* even once, he would tear the phone out of the wall.

"Actually, I was wondering what you need."

Here it comes. Get ready for it.

"We don't need anything. We're just peachy over here, Tom."

"What about—you know?" His voice dropped almost to a whisper. "Blood?"

"I said we're good here. Was there anything else on your mind, Tom?"

"Oh." The man sounded disappointed. "I was just wondering if you needed help."

Doug gripped the phone tighter. "What are you saying, exactly?"

"My girlfriend and I have been lying low for the past few weeks. Staying out of the city at her family's cabin. You were right about the burial ground, Doug. What I saw at that place stayed with me. I couldn't get the sight of those dead kids out of my mind."

"That's terrible," said Doug, feigning interest.

"So we decided to get out of town for a while. We knew the kids had come back, and everything looked like it was going great. Now we hear about this blood crisis thing. It's just incredible. Your kids too, right? I mean, they need . . . ?"

"Blood. Yup."

"I heard about the blood substitute, but a month sounds like a long time."

Doug's hopes were flagging. He decided to cut to the chase. "You asked if we needed blood over here. You said you could help. Do you know where we can get any or not?"

"My girlfriend and I talked about giving some blood. We each picked someone. I chose you. I'd like to give you two pints of my blood. That is, if you want it. Would that help?"

Doug closed his eyes. *It's meant to be.* "It surely would."

"Good. Then I'll do it."

"Why me?" he asked, his voice cracking.

"I worked with you at the burial ground."

"That's it? No strings attached?"

"I don't want your money, Doug. I don't want any—"

"Then why? Why would you help me?"

"I saw the pain you went through. I can't get it out of my mind."

Doug didn't know what to say. It was the greatest kindness anybody had ever showed him in his life. He swallowed hard to get rid of the lump in his throat. "God bless you, Tom. Your call came just in the nick of time. You're a good man. I won't forget this."

We could ration out those two pints to keep our kids going another week. Enough to prevent them from rotting too far. After that, we'd only have three more weeks to go.

At that point, maybe he'd be ready to visit Art Foley after all.

Three weeks, three bodies. His kids could live out their lives. If as monsters, then so be it. It struck him as a small price to pay.

It's meant to be, he thought again with fresh hope.

"How do you want to do this?" Tom said.

"Let me get everything set up, and I'll call you back."

He wrote down the man's number, thanked him, and hung up.

Joan laughed on the couch. She'd put the digital camera away and had cracked open one of their old photo albums. Doug walked behind her and glanced at the spread on her lap. The photos showed a screaming baby swaddled in a blanket.

Nate had entered the world just as he'd lived it. Fast and furious.

He returned to the kitchen, picked up the phone in his sweating hand, and hesitated. It was eight o'clock at night. The doctor and his wife wouldn't be working now. He paged through the phone book until he found their number.

The doctor answered on the fourth ring.

"Who is this?"

"Dr. Harris, this is Doug Cooper."

"Doug, what are you doing?" Joan called from the living room.

"Yes, I remember you. And how are—"

"We've just hit on some terrific luck here, doc. The most amazing thing just happened. A friend agreed to donate two whole pints of medicine to our kids."

After a long pause, the doctor said, "I'm very happy for you."

"I'm sorry to bother you on your personal time and all, but I wanted to see if I could make an appointment as soon as possible to get this done."

Joan appeared frowning in the doorway. "Doug, we need to talk about this."

He turned away from her. "It's been a while since we woke them up last, doc. We need to do it tonight if we could. Tomorrow at the latest."

"I'm sorry, Mr. Cooper," said the doctor, "but our office has been closed permanently."

Doug's heart sank in his chest. "What do you mean?"

"I mean Nadine and I aren't drawing blood anymore. We're done with it."

"But you . . . you can't be done with it."

"All of this has gone too far. It's over for us."

"It's not over. I'll tell *you* when it's over."

"Okay then. I'm hanging up now, Mr. Cooper."

"What about my kids?"

"Your children are dead. I'm sorry."

The doctor disconnected the call. Doug gripped the phone, his chest burning with rage.

"What happened?" asked Joan.

Doug was tired of getting pushed around. He tore the page out of the phone book and stomped off toward the garage.

Joan called after him. "What are you doing?"

"Providing," he answered.

He was going to straighten that doctor's ass out in person.

Nate and Megan needed this blood. If they didn't get it, they'd die forever. And if the doctor refused to help, he in effect would be killing Doug's kids.

Not me.

"Doug, no!" she pleaded. Her voice rose to a scream. *"Don't do this!"*

He slammed the door behind him and got into his old truck.

Finally, Doug's hatred had a face.

Ramona

44 days after Resurrection

Ramona sat on her living room couch, a cup of tea going cold on her end table and an address book open on her lap, calling everybody she knew.

"Hello, Denise? How are you?"

"I'm sorry. Who's this?"

"It's Ramona Fox. How have you been?"

"I'm just fine, thanks."

"Has the high school reopened yet?"

"No. Not yet. Um. I'm sorry. Did you need something?"

"Well, I know it's late notice and everything, but I was wondering if you could come tomorrow evening, say around six, and watch Josh for an hour?"

A long pause. "I'm sorry, but I really can't, Ms. Fox."

"It won't take more than an hour. I'll pay you—how does fifty sound?"

A boy's voice: "This is Randy, Denise's boyfriend. Don't ever call here again."

"I'm just calling about some babysitting."

"No, you're not. We know what you're trying to do. If you ever call here again, I'm going to come over there and kill you."

Denise howled in the background as he hung up: "And feed you to your kid!"

Ramona pulled at her hair. The pain felt good. She plucked out a single strand and dropped it to the floor.

Josh pounded on the basement door. *"I'M HUNGRY!"*

"Mommy's working on that, little man."

The boy stomped back downstairs into the basement.

The last time she had a guest, Josh had helped after she'd killed the man. He lapped up every drop of blood from the floor and sucked the body until there was nothing left but a gray, emaciated corpse with skin the consistency of putty.

He's learning how to feed himself, she'd thought with not a little pride.

The phone rang in her hand. She checked the caller ID and accepted the call.

"Bethany?"

"Long time, no see! How are you?"

"Great!" said Ramona. She put on a smile to make her voice sound right. "Everybody's great. What about you? How are you holding up?"

"Fantastic. Well, we're a little short of medicine for Trent, but who isn't these days?"

"I know. I know. I hear you."

"I've been talking to some other moms. This blood substitute thing has everybody thinking maybe we could get through this crisis. We were thinking about pooling our resources."

"How so?"

"Get organized. Strength in numbers. Share and share alike. What do you think?"

Ramona pictured a room full of arguing women. "Oh, that's not for me. I'll have to pass."

"What do you mean?" Bethany lowered her voice. "You're not letting Josh go, are you?"

"No, I've got an angle."

"What kind of angle?"

Ramona glanced at her watch. She had to get to her next call. *The* call. "Sorry, I have to run. Josh needs me."

"Oh, my goodness! I didn't know I was intruding on family time. You shouldn't have answered the phone. Before you go, though, could you share what your particular angle is?"

"I can't. Sorry."

"Come on! It's *me*, Ramona."

"I really have to go."

"Seriously, Ramona. We're *friends*. Why can't you tell me?"

Josh slapped his hands against the basement door. *"I'M HUN-GRY!"*

Ramona pulled at her hair and forced a grin. Saying the right things, smiling at the right places, controlling her voice—it was hard work. But she was getting better at it.

"Okay, Bethany, I'll tell you about it."

"Would you? You'd be a real lifesaver!"

"But I can't actually *tell* you. I have to show you. I'll be up for a bit. Why not come over tonight?"

Bethany hesitated. "Um. Well, we're—we've got—"

"I'd really love to see you again. It's been too long."

Bethany said nothing. The silence stretched.

Ramona said, "Hello?"

"God," Bethany said quietly. "I just can't believe it."

"Believe what?"

"What happened to you?"

"Nothing," Ramona said, her voice hard now. She waited. "Hello? Bethany, are you there?"

"Just stay away from me."

Ramona's smile stretched until it hurt. "What's wrong?"

She sighed. Her friend had hung up.

Friend, she thought with distaste. Friends were a luxury she could no longer afford.

Now she could make the call she'd been saving for just the right night. Mitch.

Mitch, the little punk who'd debased her. Mitch, with his black leather jacket and sneering face and ugly zit—

The phone rang in her hand again. "What now?" She answered after checking the caller ID. "Hello, Joan, how are you?"

The woman sounded panicked. "I'm glad I caught you. I didn't know who else to call."

Ramona glanced at the basement door. "Everything all right?"

"Doug found somebody to give us some medicine, but Dr. Harris won't take it for us. He shut down his practice."

"Did he? I didn't know that. Anyway, I'd love to help, but I don't see how."

"Doug's on his way over to the doctor's house to talk to him. He's been drinking, and I'm scared it could get a little rough. Your house is on the way, so I was wondering if you might come along. I think if you were there, Doug wouldn't do anything crazy."

"Really," said Ramona. It was a ridiculous request.

"I really don't think he'd do anything if you were there."

"That's comforting."

After a long pause, Joan sighed and said, "I'm sorry I called. It was a stupid thing to ask you to take a risk for me."

Ramona forced a smile. "I'd love to help you!"

Mitch would have to wait.

"Oh, thank God."

"For a pint of medicine."

"We don't have any medicine!"

"You said you had a friend who was donating."

Joan's voice turned hard. "If he donates, you can have it all."

"I'll be ready. Honk when you get here."

Ramona hung up and went to the basement door. She put her ear against it and listened.

She heard fingernails gently scratching at the wood. She recoiled at the sound.

321

"Josh," she whispered. "My little man."

Even after everything, he could still terrify her.

Joan

44 days after Resurrection

Joan slowed her Dodge Durango just enough for Ramona to open the door and drop into the passenger seat. Then she took off.

"Thank you for coming," Joan said.

"No problem. I was glad to get out of the house. Mind telling me what's going on?"

Joan did. She told her everything. Ramona took it all in without a word.

"We were settled," Joan finished. "We were going to let the kids go. I just don't know what Doug thinks he's accomplishing."

"It sounds to me like he's fighting for his family," Ramona said.

Joan wondered about that. While it was true Doug never went around looking for a fight, he certainly didn't mind an excuse to get into one. "Getting drunk and losing control is not fighting for your family. He's fighting for himself."

Ramona shrugged. "You're talking about method. The result is the same."

Joan narrowed her eyes at that. She glanced at Ramona. Why wasn't she backing her up? "He can pick a fight with somebody else. That doctor and his wife helped us more than I could ever put into words. I won't have Doug going over there and beating up the guy for it."

"I'm going to tell you something personal that is a little painful to say, so listen carefully," Ramona said. "Before Herod's syndrome, I failed Josh. I failed him so many times."

Joan hated this kind of talk. "No, you didn't—"

"You don't know me, Joan," Ramona said, almost shouting, then resumed at her normal volume. "You really don't. I'm not like you. I'm a single mom, and even if I weren't, I still wouldn't be like you. Even if I didn't have the job."

"There's nothing special about me. You're—"

"*Listen*," Ramona said, shutting her up. "This is not like before, where we lied to ourselves and other people all the time. We're past all that now, don't you think?"

Joan stared at the road and nodded.

"There were so many times I was too tired to play with him. Too distracted by work to really listen. Too irritated by his tantrums and sickliness to be *present*. Understand? But not now. I look back sometimes, and I can't believe what used to matter to me. The things I used as excuses to get away. Not now. This is a different time. A purer time. I've never known such clarity. The only thing that matters is blood." She added, inspired, "The blood that binds."

Joan shook her head. "No," she whispered.

"You don't see it. Doug sees it. Many other people do too. More every day. It's almost impossible to get blood now. People have their backs up against the wall. There's a war coming. What's the word? *Fratricide*. Things are about to get even simpler."

Joan gripped the wheel. "It's not going to be like that. We're not savages."

"It takes time for things to break down. But they will. They already are. For most people who have children, there's only one choice left. Let their children die, or kill for them."

Joan thought about what she'd seen on the TV. American soldiers shooting at each other. "What about you, with all this tough talk? Are you going to fight in this war?"

Ramona said, "Who says I'm not already?"

Joan realized she didn't really know the person in the car with her.

"So let's all kill each other," she said bitterly. "What about me? Would you kill me? I asked you for help tonight because I thought we were friends."

"Friends," Ramona said, as if she'd never heard the word before. She didn't say anything more for a while. "We have a bond, Joan. We bonded after the children died."

"I feel—"

"But I didn't push you out of my body. I didn't make you from nothing. I didn't give you years of my life. We're not the same blood. Do you think anything can compare with that?"

"I see you've thought it all through," Joan said.

Ramona turned to look at her. Her eyes gleamed in the dark. "What else is there to think about?"

"But it's crazy. All of it. It's crazy."

"*Crazy*," said Ramona. She clearly hated the word. "It's not *crazy*, Joan. It's survival."

They drove the rest of the way in silence.

Doug

44 days after Resurrection

Doug pulled up to the curb and killed the engine. He sat in the dark for a while, watching the Harris home. He was a little surprised by the digs. He'd expected to find the doctor and his cute little wife living in a big fancy mansion instead of this modest Tudor house.

He flicked his smoke out the window and lit another. Leo Boon sang: *Look away from the cross to that glittering crown.* Yes, sir. Yes, sir, indeed. He turned it off and took a long snort on his flask, closing his eyes as he swallowed, breathing through the burn. From the seat next to him, he picked up the cold black crowbar—the weapon that had brought him luck during his first blood heist—and hefted it.

Empties spilled out of the truck with a clatter as he opened the door. It was time to have a little talk with the good doctor, man to man. He thrust the crowbar in his belt behind his back. He emptied his flask with a final pull and tossed it into the truck. Then he approached the front door of the house along the neatly shoveled walk.

He'd scrapped the idea of going in there with a plan. The idea of throwing the dice excited him. His face was killing him. He was tired of the constant pain. He wanted to lose control and let the winner take all. Doug was prepared to gamble everything he had, but that was nothing to a man like him, a man who no longer had anything to lose.

He rang the doorbell. A shape moved in the window. The porch light turned on.

"Open up, doc," he said quietly, displaying calm before the storm.

David

44 days after Resurrection

David turned on the porch light and stepped back, the reassuring weight of his gun in the pocket of his bathrobe. His heart galloped in his chest; his breath came in shallow gasps. Cotton-mouthed, he peered out of one of the curtained windows framing the door.

"Mr. Cooper, is that you?"

"Yeah, it's me."

"What happened to you? Are you all right?"

"I got mugged a few days back. For my blood. I got a great, big cut on my head."

"I'm sorry to hear that. If you drop by the office tomorrow, I could take a look at it for you."

"I didn't come here for that. I came here to talk to you about my kids."

David checked the lock. He placed his hands against the door and leaned against it. "I'm afraid I've said everything I have to on that subject."

"Five minutes, doc. It's important."

"Go home, Mr. Cooper."

He almost added, *Or I'll call the police!* It only reminded him how isolated he was. This was how Ben felt, he knew, just before he died. Like his back was pushed against the wall so hard he couldn't breathe.

Before he could stop himself, he slammed his palms against the door with a loud thump. "Go home, I said!"

The police had terrorized him for days. Now this overbearing giant had showed up at his house trying to bully him. David was tired of being pushed.

Nothing happened. He waited with his head pressed against the door. He heard nothing. He glanced at Nadine, who stared at him from the couch, her hands covering her mouth. She shook her head. *Don't open the door.*

David shrugged. "I guess he left."

He staggered back as the decorative window on the left shattered, spraying glass across the hardwood. Moments later, a hand reached in and groped for the lock. David stared at it in dumb shock. The inconceivable was happening. His home was actually being invaded.

The hand found the lock, which turned with a click.

The door opened, and Doug Cooper stepped into David's house, reeking of alcohol and gripping a crowbar.

Doug

44 days after Resurrection

The doctor reeled away from him, looking pathetic in his bathrobe and slippers and old T-shirt. Without his tie and lab coat, he was just a tired, middle-aged man. The nurse sat on the couch wearing oversized men's pajamas. She gaped up at him with doe eyes.

Doug closed the door behind him. His boots crunched on broken glass. He felt a little silly after briefly inspecting the damage he'd done, but it was too late to turn back now. He was already committed. The dice were still in the air.

"I'm sorry to bust your window, doc. But you weren't listening to me. I need you to listen."

The doctor and his wife just stared at him. Doug hadn't expected that. He felt even sillier.

"Here's how it is," he explained. "You take blood from my friend. Two pints. Then I'll be out of your hair for good. You'll never see me again."

"Mr. Cooper," David rasped. "You're the one who's not listening."

Doug scowled. "What the fuck did you just say to me?"

The doctor licked his dry lips. "We helped you. We helped you, and this is how you repay us. By breaking into our home like a common criminal!"

"You do my friend, and we're good. I'll call him right now."

"We've done enough. All we want now is to be left alone!"

Doug shook his head. "You heard the news. A substitute is on the way. We hang on a few more weeks, and we could have our kids back forever. They'll grow up. Maybe our son will even be a fancy doctor like you."

"Whatever they've got, they said it's not going to be ready for a month," the doctor told him. "Then they have to start production. There are *millions* of children. It could be months, even years, before you see a drop of it. It's a lie, Mr. Cooper. A lie to give you false hope."

Doug blinked. The doctor was making sense.

But none of it mattered.

327

"Don't care," he said. "We want our two pints. It's the only chance we've got. Our kids are about to pass on. They need the medicine. It has to be done soon. Tonight."

"And how are your kids, Mr. Cooper? What are they like now? Are they changing?"

He tightened his grip on the crowbar and snarled, "Don't you talk shit about my kids."

The doctor was going to say what Joan said. They were changing. They were monsters. They weren't worth saving. Doug could take it from his wife but not this man.

Behind him, the door opened wider, and in walked Joan with Ramona Fox.

"Doug!" she said. "Doug, no more of this! You did enough here. Come home with me!"

"It's too late for that, Joanie."

It truly was. When he turned back, the doctor was pointing a gun at his face.

David

44 days after Resurrection

David felt new confidence holding the gun. One of the first things he'd learned during his firearm course was never point a gun at a human being unless you were willing to shoot him dead. He was okay with that right now. Either way, he'd already taken back some control of his life by simply exercising the choice.

Nadine stared at the gun. "I'll help you, Mr. Cooper. I'll draw your friend's blood."

"No, you won't," David told her, his eyes locked on Doug Cooper's.

"But the *children*—"

"Are *dead*!" David said. "They're gone!"

"No," Nadine said with a shake of her head. "That's not true."

"The children are becoming vampires. Isn't that right, Mr. Cooper?"

"They've gone wild," said Joan. "Tell him, Doug. They barely even know us anymore."

"I know them," said Doug.

"Doug, listen to me," his wife said, persisting. "This is crazy, what you're doing here. Crazy and pointless. He's right. We don't need the blood. Come home to me, babe. I need you home."

"Stay out of this, Joanie." The big man took a step closer. "Let's try that listening again, doc. Because what I'm going to say is pretty important. Here's how it is. Either you take my friend's blood, or I'm going to take yours. Right fucking now."

"All for a few hours with children who don't even know you anymore," David said. He kept the gun leveled at the man's chest. "Is that worth a man's life, Mr. Cooper?"

"I think we're on a first-name basis now, doc. And yes, it is. Even yours."

David remembered to flick off the safety. *Red means dead.* "Then the real parasite is you."

Nadine sobbed. "David, *please*—"

I can't shoot, David thought. He took a step back and wiped sweat from his forehead. The gun trembled in his hand. Doug matched him by taking another step closer.

If I give in, this man will own me, and so will Herod.

"*Doug, stop this right now!*" Joan screamed.

A wave of calm washed over David. *He actually wants me to do it.*

"This doesn't have to happen," he said. "You can still walk out of here with your life."

Doug inspected the crowbar in his hand and looked David in the eye. "This is my last chance."

I just wanted to help people.

David squeezed the trigger.

The roar filled the room, making them all jump. David opened his eyes. Through an acrid puff of smoke, he saw Doug pat his chest, looking for a wound, while Joan Cooper screamed.

He lowered the gun and gaped in disbelief. Had he missed from just five feet away?

Doug turned. "Joanie, are you okay?" He laughed. "Holy shit, doc, you scared the living shit—"

David stepped forward to close the distance and squeezed the trigger again. The gun kicked in his hand with an electrifying bang and flash of light.

The first slug punched a red smoking hole in Doug Cooper's chest. The second shattered his skull, spraying blood and bone onto the man's screaming wife.

Doug grinned as his body crumpled to the floor, his brains spilling onto David's Persian rug. With humor or relief, they'd never know.

Ramona

44 days after Resurrection

Rich red blood pooled thickly around Doug Cooper's shattered head, Joan was screaming to wake the dead, and all Ramona could think was, *It's going to waste.*

This wasn't crazy. This was survival.

The difference lay in one's priorities.

Yes, a man had been murdered in front of her, and that was upsetting.

If she indulged the horror she felt looking at his corpse, however, she couldn't save Josh. Rather than get upset, she brushed those feelings aside and focused on how much blood she could harvest from Doug's body.

If only she could get at it.

The doctor raised his gun with his shaky hand and shouted at her to leave. At his feet, Nadine pointlessly checked Doug's vital signs; the man was obviously dead. Joan, splattered with Doug's blood and bits of brain, wouldn't stop screaming.

They needed to harvest the body fast. The blood was already clotting.

"Out!" the doctor was shouting. Nadine scooped up Doug's crowbar and stood at her husband's side, quaking in her slippers.

Ramona looked at her. "We need the blood. *Josh* needs it."

Nadine said, "David—"

"No," said David.

"But—"

"I told them to get out, and they're getting out. They can take the body with them."

"We'll never get it home in time," Ramona said. "We need tools to collect the blood. Right, Joan? You have nothing in your car we could use to harvest it."

Joan had stopped screaming. She breathed in short little hiccups and stared down at the body.

The doctor stepped closer with the gun aimed at Ramona's face. "I don't care what you people do. You're not my problem. I just want you the fuck out of my house before I shoot all of—"

He dropped to the floor with an explosive grunt.

Nadine stood over him. The crowbar looked large and heavy in her hands. Her husband writhed next to Doug on the Persian rug. He grimaced at the pain in his leg while he pointed the gun at his wife.

"Why?" he cried.

"The children," she said. She brought the crowbar down against his forearm.

He screamed and rolled. He pointed the gun, still held in his good hand, at her again. He didn't shoot. He couldn't, or wouldn't.

331

"Please don't do this," he begged.

She hit him again. "I'm sorry, David." He lay groaning in a fetal ball. "I'm so sorry."

Ramona had already gone into the kitchen and found what she needed to collect the blood. She was an expert at this by now. Time was critical; she moved quickly and harvested her first pint with ease.

"Stop it!" Joan screamed at them.

Ramona paused long enough to glimpse Joan standing with her fists clenched. Then she returned to work. "You promised me a pint, and I intend to collect. You should be helping me. This blood could keep our kids alive for hours."

"Stop defiling his body!"

She sighed. There were too many distractions here. She needed to simplify things. She picked up the gun from the floor. "Sorry, Joan," she said. "This is survival."

Joan was already running for the door.

The gun recoiled with a powerful boom. She leveled it for a second shot, but Joan Cooper was gone.

Her ride had just left, but no matter.

She turned toward Nadine and David and thought, *I'm rich*.

Joan

44 days after Resurrection

Joan unclipped the handle of her purse and tied it below her knee as a tourniquet. She pressed handfuls of snow against the jagged holes in her leg to staunch the flow of blood.

Aw, fuck. The pain was incredible. Blinding, heart-stopping pain.

The bullet had ripped through her calf as she ran out the door. She'd stumbled off the porch into the bushes, certain Ramona was one step behind her with the gun. She fled into the dark next to the house until her leg gave out beneath her, and she fell hard.

She cried out as a gunshot boomed in the house, accompanied by a flash of light in the window over her head.

BANG.

BANG.

BANG.

Then nothing except the ringing in her ears.

Joan wept for the doctor and his wife. For Doug, most of all.

A pale little face appeared in one of the dark windows of the house next door. Joan looked back in horror as two more appeared. The children pressed their tiny hands against the glass. They stared at her leg with gleaming eyes.

Oh God, no.

She needed to get out of here fast.

Joan gritted her teeth and got back onto her feet, using the wall for support. Then she began hopping one step at a time toward her car.

She heard crunching and slurping noises behind and craned her neck.

The neighbors' children had left their house and were following her blood trail, shoveling handfuls of red snow into their mouths.

They were gaining on her.

She hopped again. And again. Then spared another glance.

The children were even closer. They were on all fours now, biting at the snow.

Joan hopped again. This time, her good leg gave out from exhaustion and dumped her onto the ground. She began to crawl. Teeth clicked behind her.

She reached the car with a cry of relief. She climbed inside and sat gasping behind the wheel. In her mind's eye, she saw the side of Doug's head explode in tiny red fragments. She couldn't believe he was dead.

"Oh, Doug," she sobbed. "Oh, my poor man."

She screamed as the children slapped their hands against the windows. They pressed their faces against the glass, nostrils flaring. They could smell her. Their breath fogged the windows.

"Go away," Joan hissed. "Leave me alone!"

She started the SUV and backed out of the driveway.

A dark shape appeared in the living room window and waved as she drove off.

Her body knew the way home. The road appeared to move, not her. By the time she recognized her house, she felt as if she were floating. She hopped toward the front door until she fell hard and writhed on the ground in piercing agony. Again, she crawled.

Again, she made it.

Joan dragged herself into the kitchen and sat on the floor with her back against a set of drawers. The pain in her leg had dulled to a steady, throbbing ache. A massive headache bloomed behind her eyes. Every muscle in her body felt stiff and disjointed. The house stood dark and empty. This was home, yet without her family, it didn't feel like it. It was just a big empty space without Doug and Nate and Megan to fill it up. She shook off these thoughts. If she wanted to live, she had to get help. Her leg was still bleeding. She wrapped her leg in dish towels and held them tight.

Her phone was in the pocket of her jeans. She took it out and stared at it. If she called the paramedics, they'd bleed her to death. She couldn't trust the police. She couldn't trust any of her friends. She decided to call the only people she could still trust.

Her mother's voice: "Yes?"

"Oh, Mom." She covered her face with her hand and sobbed. "Thank God."

"What's wrong?"

"It's so good to hear your voice, Mom."

"Did something happen, Joanie?"

"I need help. Doug's *dead*. He's dead, and I'm hurt bad."

Mom gasped. "Where are you?"

"I'm home."

Mom asked her a question, but Joan didn't pay attention. She'd heard a familiar creak.

The door to the garage had opened. Somebody was in the house.

"Joanie? Joanie, are you there? Please!"

She heard the patter of little feet in the dark living room.

"Stay there. We're coming to get you!"

Joan whispered, "I love you, Mom."

"Joanie? Joanie? Oh my God, Joanie—"

She dropped the phone on the floor as Nate and Megan entered the kitchen. They looked ghastly in the bright light. Gray-faced and stiff, they walked in short, jerky steps. She watched them come with a mix of love and dread.

They were on their feet. Without blood.

Just as they had that first night they'd come back.

It was another miracle. Maybe this was the end. The final change Nadine had promised.

The children stopped. They stared at her with dull, unblinking expressions.

Joan held out her arms to hug them. She'd lost the only man she'd ever truly loved, but she wasn't alone. She still had her children. Her sweet, beautiful, perfect children.

Nate fell to his knees and hugged his mother. He felt cold. Joan closed her eyes. *I'm so happy to see you again.*

Most people didn't understand how strongly mothers felt toward their children from the moment they were born. That this screaming thing in your arms was your entire reason for being. That you would do anything to make it happy. That you would fight, kill, die.

Who could understand the devotion, the constant pain, the sleepless nights, the endless worry? Love given freely, without conditions?

It's not crazy, she thought. *It's survival.* Ramona was right about that at least.

Joan's leg twitched and began to sting.

She opened her eyes and gasped. Megan was sucking at her wound. Her face ballooned like a feeding tick.

Nate growled and pushed her away. Megan rolled onto the floor, her teeth clicking.

It was his turn to feed.

Joan watched her boy suck her blood. Her heart raced. Her vision flared with colorful stars. Death felt close.

That's enough. She reached out her hand to push him away.

And stroked his hair instead.

"My beautiful boy . . ."

You were right, Doug. They're still ours.

Darkness swirled at the edges of her vision. It didn't hurt anymore.

Eat, Nate.

Grow up big and strong.

One day, you're going to be a—

Midnight

Herod

They slept during the day.

At night, they came out to feed.

The gunshots ended. The Boy heard a scream. Screaming used to scare him. Now screams meant food. And getting more food was all that mattered. Survival.

He led his pack toward the sound. The little tribe of children tramped down the middle of the road swinging their weapons. Hockey sticks, rolling pins, knives. The streetlights showed them the way.

The houses flanking the street stood dark and still. The foodpeople locked them up good and tight at night. For a time, the pack had enjoyed a routine. They'd break into a house, feed, and build a nest. Then sleep in a pile until the sun fell and the hunger woke them.

As food became scarce, however, the hazards grew.

Back in the beginning, many of the grown-ups had given themselves to the children, just as the Boy's own mother had.

Those early days of easy pickings had long passed.

Now the foodpeople killed the children on sight. The grown-ups hunted during the day, but the night belonged to the children.

In the beginning, their little tribe had consisted only of the Boy and Sister. Over time, he'd accepted new members to add to his strength. The others helped him overpower the bigger grown-ups, and in return, he kept them fed. The pack was always losing members and recruiting new ones. Right now, it numbered eight.

The screams stopped, but no matter; they'd found the house. A dying woman with long red hair lay on the living room floor, surrounded by children writhing against one another as each sought the best place to feed. They'd torn off her clothes and latched on to every inch of exposed skin with their mouths. She'd fought back. The dead bodies of children littered the room, and she still gripped a gun in her hand.

The pack was too late; these children had already sucked her dry.

The Boy whistled. The pack attacked the others with their weapons. The children weren't alive in a human sense, but they could be killed. The little skulls broke open one by one, exposing the insides to air and light and death. This done, the pack burrowed their faces deep into the swollen bellies to drink the sour-tasting, half-digested food.

After he fed, the Boy picked the gun from the woman's hand. He held it high to display its power while his pack hooted with red-stained grins.

In the basement, the Boy and Sister discovered a small boy sniffing and clawing at a locked door. They knew the boy from the time before and let him join the pack. Together, they forced the door open. It was full of corpses, but none worth eating. The Boy pulled a black leather jacket off one of the bodies. He thought he looked pretty cool in it.

The others piled blankets and cushions in the middle of the living room floor. The Boy wanted them all to get out of here. This was a bad place. They were fed and sleepy and didn't want to leave, but he kicked at them until they returned, growling, to their feet. This done, he led them back out into the cold night.

Scores of children waited for them in the warm glow of the streetlights.

The others had been looking for him a long time. He and his pack were the only children he knew of who fed upon their own kind. To-night, they would make him and his friends pay. There would be no discussion, no trial. They were going to tear him to shreds.

The Boy grinned. They had to catch him first.

Catch me if you can!

He raised the gun and fired, the shot echoing over their heads, and ran with his pack at his heels. The howls of pursuit filled the air. His black leather jacket made him harder to see in the dark. Well fed, he ran faster than the rest. They scrambled through backyards and into the parking lot of a small office building. Beyond that, he led them into a park, still holding Sister's hand. He needed to keep her safe. They'd disappear into the trees, go somewhere new, start over. The world was so big and full of choices.

Bright light burned into his eyes. He staggered to a halt.

Spotlights.

As his eyes adjusted, he saw grown-ups on two wooden towers connected by a chain-link fence topped with barbed wire. Beyond, houses. A fortified community. He'd seen them before.

Muzzle flashes burst in the dark. Gunfire roared.

The Boy's tribe fell twitching into the snow around him. He froze, struck by an ancient memory of standing on a stage with other children, singing in front of a room full of grown-ups while his mom and dad watched. At the end, the grown-ups applauded and took pictures with their little cameras, which flashed and popped.

His mom and dad had loved him.

The Boy raced to the fence, flung his body against it, and held on. Sister followed. The other children forgot the feud. Dazzled by the prospect of a killing feast as rich as those of the old days, they surged at the fence.

The Boy shrugged off his leather jacket and draped it over the barbed wire. He waited for Sister to catch up.

She was laughing when the bullets sheared her off the fence.

The scent of so much warm food distracted him from his grief. The hunger overpowered everything.

He swung over the top and hit the ground hard, feeling little pain in his dead limbs. As he scrambled to his feet, he saw a teenage girl with a rifle sprinting toward safety. He raised his gun and fired until it emptied. The girl was down. He chased after to feed upon the arterial spray.

Behind, the other children swarmed over the wire, leaving a field of dead behind them. The grown-ups retreated, firing their guns. A howl went up. The children flooded the streets, hacking at anything that moved. They pried the boards off the windows and crawled into the houses. The gunfire intensified. So did the screaming.

The Boy drank deep from his kill.

He cried while he fed. Not from sadness, but from joy.

A new world was just beginning, and it belonged to him.

ACKNOWLEDGMENTS

Special thanks to Doree Anne, Peter Clines, Randy Heller, and Timothy Johnson for their valuable editing support and encouragement. I'm also thankful to Agnieszka Halas for providing some useful information about the effects of blood loss on the human body.